CHIMERAS

A thriller by E.E. Giorgi

*To Jack
enjoy!
EEgiorgi*

Cover art © Christopher Germano, all rights reserved. DNA image created by DeviantArt artist PublicCenzor. Photoshop chemistry brushes by DeviantArt artist Finner. Stock image © captblack76.

CHIMERAS

Copyright © 2014 by E.E. Giorgi

All rights reserved. No part of this publication may be reproduced, stored in a retrieval system, or transmitted by any means – electronic, mechanical, photographic (photocopying), recording, or otherwise – without prior permission in writing from the author.

Printed in the United States of America
Print Edition
ISBN: 978-0-9960451-0-0

*To my father,
who introduced me
to epigenetics.*

ACKNOWLEDGMENTS

It takes one brave author to turn ideas into printed pages. But it takes a lot of people to make those printed pages come to life.

I'm mostly indebted to my patient, smart, and supportive beta-readers: Cristina Rinaudo, Cindy Amrhein, Christi Lane, Karen and Alex Alaniz, Rowan Greene, Nancy Matuszak, Jack L. Pyke, and Kathy Hamm. Many thanks also to firefighter Michael Galassi, for tips on how to get out of fires (which hopefully I'll never get to use!), and to district attorney Mark Pryor who answered all my legal questions. I owe the accuracy of the autopsy scenes to D.P. Lyle and Peter Cummings, fellow writers and medical examiners/forensic pathologists. A lot of feedback that made this book much better came from literary agent Tris Coburn, my current awesome agent Nicole Resciniti, and Random House executive editor Anne Groell. To all these people go my heartfelt thanks.

No, I'm not forgetting you, Tim. I'm saving you for the best part.

You see, Track Presius would be issuing parking tickets on skid row right now if it weren't for the one and only, retired LAPD officer and story-teller Timothy Bowen. Not only did Tim introduce me to the LAPD *modus operandi* and lingo; not only did he double-check my plot and police procedural; Tim patiently answered every question I had and added his own stories and anecdotes, bits of which gave life to—well, yes, you've guessed it—Detective Satish Cooper. It is also thanks to Tim that I was able to tour the LAPD headquarters, both the old Parker Center and the new one (although the new one is not mentioned in the book because the story takes place in 2008, one year prior to the opening of the new headquarters). If you want a taste of Tim's hilarious stories I highly recommend reading his memoir (ASIN: B005TAGE4W or check the link on my webpage). But remember: don't read it in public places unless you don't mind people staring wide-eyed at you as you burst out in laughter.

Finally, these acknowledgments would not be complete without mentioning my supportive family. My parents always knew I was restless, though I'm not sure they ever anticipated to what extent. *Grazie babbo e mamma*! My husband is my harshest reader and I love him to pieces for that. And to my kiddos I ask for forgiveness as for years they've been wondering what mom was doing tied to her laptop until the wee hours of the night. I love them to pieces, too.

CHIMERAS

With the exception of Robert Klark Graham,
who was indeed the founder of the "Nobel sperm" bank
(http://en.wikipedia.org/wiki/Robert_Klark_Graham),
all other characters and events appearing
in this work are fictitious.
Any resemblance to real persons, living or dead,
is purely coincidental.

PROLOGUE

It was one of those hot summer afternoons, with air made of cobwebs and a glare as sharp as pencils.

"Something's wrong today," I said.

"It's L.A.," my partner replied. "Something's always wrong in L.A."

A few hours later Johnny Carmelo was dead, his brains skewered by the whistling path of one of my bullets. He collapsed on the pavement, a red trickle of blood weeping down his face.

They told me they weren't going to clear me back to duty until the investigation was over. I left the next day. I drove up to the Sierras, camped in my truck, and hunted at night.

There are days I long to disappear in the wild, go back to the predator life I was meant to have. Kill the prey or be killed: it's in my genes.

E.E. Giorgi

A chimera, that's what I am. And this is my story.

CHAPTER 1

Friday, August 22, 2008

Yellow smears of wildfires marred the horizon toward the mountains, tainting the air like a bitter aftertaste. Downtown hovered through its usual smokiness, and traffic along the One-Ten was a steady hiccup.

"Damned lunch hour," I muttered.

My partner looked out the window. "Speaking of which. I think I'm smellin' Tommy's chili. How 'bout you, Track?"

I rapped the steering wheel. "I smell car exhaust from traffic. I smell chutney and tamarind from that orange stuff you always have for breakfast. I smell shoe polish even though I've no idea why you'd wanna polish your shoes on a day like this. And I still smell the fucking dog piss from the blue hair that flagged us at Hollenbeck Park."

Satish scrunched his forehead. "That was last year!"

"The blue hair? Course it was last year. I keep dumping bottles of shampoo and deodorizer on the back seat and I still smell the dog piss."

He laughed, shook his head sideways. "You and your sensitive nose."

The AC rattled. Red brake lights winked in front of us.

"Damned lunch hour," I repeated.

Satish checked his watch. "Almost there, shouldn't take too long. We ask our questions, show the guy the license plate number, see what he's got to say. Same old, same old. In thirty minutes we'll be biting into our juicy hamburgers at Tommy's."

"Traffic permitting," I replied.

We hiccupped down the One-Ten, the sleek towers of the business district looming over us with the familiarity of an old lover. Passed the bridge under Fourth, I steered to the right and tore onto the Wilshire exit ramp. I made a left on Lucas and entered a secondary road sandwiched between scrubby apartment buildings that smelled of rusty gutters and beer.

Tucked between Koreatown and Echo Park, Westlake was home to a young population of Latinos, Filipinos, and illegal immigrants whose career paths included street dealing, prostitution, and smuggling false documents. The few times I'd been loaned to this part of town as a street copper, I ended up working overtime and skipping lunch.

"Gotta love this neighborhood."

Satish snickered. "Back in my street days, me and my partner, we'd cruise up to MacArthur Park, pick up winos and drop them off in the sheriff's section just for fun. Hey, pull over. It's right here. Mac's Auto Shop—that's the place."

Red brick building, the name of the shop painted in blue over three garage doors, a Smog Check banner, an old

Beemer on one of the lifts, and the rest of the vehicles scattered around like forgotten words. I switched to reverse and turned into the lot.

"Name's Johnny Carmelo, age twenty-two," Satish said. "Clean sheet, he just recently moved into town. And it's *sambar*." He opened the door and scrambled out of the car.

I got out on the other side and locked the Charger. "What is *sambar*?"

Satish loosened the knot of his tie while surveying the place. "The orange stuff I always have for breakfast."

"What about the shoe polish?"

He laughed, rolled up the sleeves of his shirt. A harsh sun glinted off the pavement and pearled his forehead with sweat. "Why is it, Track, that I can never hide anything from you?"

"Not if it's got a smell, you can't."

The place had an overcast shade of charcoal. Gasoline and car oil mingled with the smells of sweat, urine, and instant noodles. The clonking of the hydraulic lift clashed with the loud rock music coming from the stereo of a white Chevy.

Satish banged on the roof of the car. "Anybody home?"

A grease monkey with gray eyes and unshaved cheeks emerged from behind the open hood of an old Mercedes. He lifted his chin, sized us over, and drawled an unsentimental "Can I help you?" while wiping his hands with a ragged cloth. He looked like the kind of guy who would've shouldered through the swinging doors of a saloon and fired four rounds at the bar.

"We're looking for Mr. Carmelo." Satish flashed his badge, his body slouched into the casual stance of a routine chat over a stolen car.

Mechanic Joe frowned at the LAPD tins, then craned his head toward the back of the shop. "Johnny!" he called, shoving the cloth in one of his pockets.

I caught a swift movement behind a VW camper covered in derogatory bumper stickers. The squeaky hinge of a back door set my adrenaline off.

"He's making a break!" I yelled.

I ran to the car, Satish bolted to the back of the building to give chase on foot.

"I just hired the guy. I swear. I know nothing about the man." Mechanic Joe's apologetic yapping trailed off.

A clean sheet and a dirty conscience. Or maybe just a crackhead high on dope.

I whipped the Charger around the block and entered a construction zone littered with metal bins, wooden pallets, and steel construction pipes piled up along the right lane. Carmelo jumped into the street and delved into oncoming vehicles. Satish huffed behind him. Startled, the driver in front of me hit the brakes, sending his car over a row of traffic cones.

Carmelo knocked over a plastic barricade, leaped over the pipes, and then pushed them into the street in a cacophony of clangs. I stomped on the accelerator, yanked the wheel left, and slammed on the brakes. The Charger spun to the side and flung against the rolling pipes. I groped for the door handle and yanked it open while radioing a code three to request backup. I got out of the car and broke into a run.

By now I was pissed. My shirt was drenched in sweat. I cursed at the asshole for making me run in this heat, and at the LAPD etiquette for imposing formal attire and dress shoes.

Carmelo vanished in the shadow of an underpass, Satish followed. By the time I got there, I spotted Carmelo do a one-eighty around the corner and pull three-quarters of his trigger.

"Satish!" I yelled, one second too late.

As soon as there was enough cop to shoot, Carmelo fired.

Satish jerked backward and keeled over.

The next bullet grazed my ear. I held my Glock on target and fired four rounds. The gun recoiled in my hand. Carmelo curled into a question mark and flopped to the sidewalk. One by one, the spent shells dropped to the ground, yet I kept shooting, intoxicated by the smell of blood and the rattling of fire, as if every new bullet sinking into his body had the power to rewind time.

To fix my own failings.

Revenge hardly mends anything. The son of a bitch you want to crush does not exist. The son of a bitch is your own self.

The muted clicks of the trigger startled me, my fingers so tightly wrapped around the grip it hurt to slide them out of position. I holstered the Glock and inspected the body. Blood sprawled across his chest and drenched his dirty overalls. The scent was warm and inebriating.

Careful, now. I prodded his left hand with the tip of my shoe. *No watch.* I moved my eyes quickly, searching. No rings on his fingers, no laces on his shoes. I had to find something, anything. I slipped a hand into his pocket, felt something hard, grasped it, and slid it into my jacket.

The wailing sirens of backup broke a surreal silence. I scrambled by Satish's side and slid two fingers along his neck until I found the faint trace of a pulse.

"Code three, officer down," I barked into the radio. "My partner's down, get me a fucking RA unit *now!*"

Man down, one of our own. My partner. I let my partner get shot.

CHAPTER 2

The acrid smell of wildfires and dry soil, the blinding sky, the scent of orange trees and her sun-kissed skin, a flower randomly tossed in the air, a promise, *See you next summer*, and then silence, long winter days waiting, bicycling along the arroyo back when you could still bicycle in L.A., the setting sun flashing on and off between palm trees…

Her eyes.

Waiting at the window, a cottonwood branch tapping against the glass, *tap, tap, tap*, time slugging by, she didn't keep the promise, she never came back, Mom turning the TV off, *Don't watch the news tonight, honey, not tonight.*

Not tonight.

Her eyes, pleading.

CHIMERAS

I couldn't save her pleading eyes.

Saturday, August 23

"Ulysses."

I jerked backward and flew a hand to my holster, the light around me too bright and too sudden. Dr. Watanabe didn't move a muscle, his narrow eyes scrutinizing me as if they'd never seen me before. I exhaled, bent over, and rasped my unshaved cheeks.

How long was I out?

"Sorry. I uh—I didn't catch much sleep last night."

He gave me a quick pat on the shoulder. "My fault," he said. "I kept you waiting for too long. Come on, let's go talk in the office."

I shuffled up the stairs behind him, the images from the nightmare I just had spinning in my head. *No, not a dream. A memory.*

"You said on the phone it was self-defense."

"The first bullet was," I replied.

Watanabe's office was tidy yet crowded, with too much furniture, too much light, too many books, and too little of anything else. A shaft of afternoon sun poked through the curtains and framed a cone of dust motes. I could smell everything in the room, and it bugged me like loud static in a bad reception.

Watanabe motioned to the chair. I walked to the window and stood there.

"The sprinkler in your garden must be broken again," I said. "Were you able to fix it this time? Is that why your wife brought you *sake* after making you teriyaki beef with rice noodles for lunch—your favorite, I seem to remember."

Watanabe sat behind his desk, laced his fingers across

his lap and smiled, placidly. "I get the *sake*," he said. "I brought the mug here in the office, and I'm sure your refined sense of smell can still detect the alcohol even though I drank it over an hour ago. How did you guess the rest?"

I leaned against the windowsill. "There's a tiny residue of your lunch on the right cuff of your shirt. And I smell wet grass from the soles of your shoes. Given that it hasn't rained in over three months, it had to be your sprinkler, and the only reason why you'd want to walk around your sprinkler while it's off is to check that it's working."

Watanabe was used to my ways, old tricks I pulled to procrastinate talking about me instead. "What did you do yesterday, after you fired?"

I'd lost count of how many times I'd been asked the same question over the last twenty-four hours. I turned to the window and pretended to stare outside. My eyes glazed over, and what I saw instead was Carmelo's blood on the pavement, the zipper of a body bag closing over his face. I saw the FID officers taking my gun and asking about the shooting. "What did you do after you fired?" I didn't tell them. I didn't tell the shrink either. For two hours he picked my brains, as protocol mandated after a deadly shootout.

"Ulysses?" The pen he was holding gave out a few soft taps. "What did you do after killing the suspect?"

Ulysses.

The rest of the world called me Track, as in tracking dog, because of my nose. I got it back when I was in Gang and Narcotics—I could find a buried body faster than the K9 unit. Only Watanabe still used my birth name.

"You should ask what I *didn't* do."

I heard him smile. "What did you *not* do?"

"I didn't feel for Satish's pulse. I *should've* felt for Satish's pulse right after he'd been shot. Instead..." I pursed my lips.

"Instead?"

"You know what I did instead."

"You collected your prize."

The pen resumed tapping. I undid the top button of my shirt. "The air's stiff in here."

Watanabe weighed his words over long pauses. "You said Satish is out of the woods."

I nodded. "They had to open him up and fish the bullet out of his lungs. So far things look good. If there are no complications, he should be out of the ICU in a couple of days."

"What about you?"

What about me? "The LT told me I can take a desk job until the BSS—the Behavioral Science Services shrink clears me back to duty." I snorted. The hell I was going to take a desk job. "Of course, there's the issue of all the rounds I flew. And you know what happens every time the FID officers nose into my package again…"

I inhaled, smells of old and new clashing together across the bookshelves. My very own oracle of Delphi, this small doctor who held the key to my DNA, stared at me through folds of sagging skin.

"You don't believe me," I said.

The slightest furrow crossed his forehead. "Of course I do."

"I don't mean about yesterday. I mean—the other stuff. What I told you happened when I was a kid." I snorted, shook my head. "You think I'm crazy."

"No," he replied, as empathic as a nail in the wall. "I think you're extraordinary."

Extraordinary. Right. I flopped into the armchair he'd offered earlier and clutched the armrests. I remembered the first time I sat in this chair, six months earlier. I'd clutched the armrests with the same fierceness but for a different reason. I was nervous. I'd spent a lifetime repressing my instincts, pretending I could mold them into normality. I came to see Doctor Watanabe the day after my mother's funeral. The little I disclosed on our first meeting was enough to fascinate him.

"You have a very sharp eyesight," he said, "both frontal and peripheral. I bet you can see perfectly well at dusk. Your vomeronasal organ is highly developed and very sensitive to pheromones. Though your vision is enhanced, you see mostly through your sense of smell. It adds a fourth dimension to your sensorial landscape."

"You've had other patients like me?" I asked.

"No. But before getting into human genetics, I studied zoology."

The comment wasn't flattering.

He seemed to know so much about me and yet the one thing I cared about, to this very day, he still wouldn't disclose.

Why?

Why was I a monster, with monster traits, monster senses, and monster instincts?

Watanabe bent over, opened a drawer, and produced a brown envelope. "The MRI images you brought the other day."

I leaned back in the chair. "What about them?"

"You said you were a healthy kid growing up. Nothing worth mentioning, aside the usual flu or mumps? No hospital scare?"

"Doc. I had *one* scare and it was in the woods, not in a hospital."

"I'm not talking about that. I'm talking about your medical history. You haven't provided me with any."

I slammed a hand against the armrest. "That's because I don't have any, Doc. The only relevant thing in my life—"

"In that case I would like permission to look for myself."

I blinked. "Look for what?"

"Your medical records." He pulled a white piece of paper out of the brown envelope. "I need your signature. I'm requesting your permission to access medical archives from the 'seventies and search all documents under your name."

I took the piece of paper he slid across the desk and signed it.

I wasn't in the mood for short talk. I got up and walked to the door.

"I'm taking some time off, Doc," I said. "Until they clear me back to duty."

He nodded, clicked the pen some more. "Do you know what a Chimera is?"

I had a hand poised for the doorknob. I shoved it back in my pocket instead. "A monster," I replied. "Part lion, part goat, and part snake." At Watanabe's smile, I added, "Is that what I am? A Chimera?"

He shook his head, smoothly rolling the pen between his fingers. "Not a genetic one, no. But you have me thinking, Ulysses. Those traits you have—" He waved a hand, as if traits were culpable things. "We all have ancestral genes—genes we used for hunting back when we were predators—but they're no longer expressed. However, a serious shock or trauma, especially early on in life, can cause genes that normally wouldn't be expressed to suddenly turn on."

I stood by the door, hands shoved in my pockets. Confused. "So, you do believe me, Doc?"

He put down the pen and laced his fingers across his lap. "Those brain scans—" His eyes strayed to the brown envelope on his desk. "I need to find out more about you."

I bobbed my head, probably a little too enthusiastically to look spontaneous. "Right. You go do that, Doc. I'll see you back in six weeks. Tell your wife to have some *sake* for me too, next time."

This time I did turn the doorknob and left.

CHAPTER 3

Tuesday, October 7

The night casts a black shroud over the mountains. Soft sounds bud out like blossoms: the rustling of the trees, a rodent running away in a bush, a woodrat scuttling along a boulder and diving into a crack beneath a rock.

A handful of gravel tumbling down the incline.

She taps her nails against the steering wheel and squints through the windshield. Eyes glow in the distance. They bob and grow larger: the headlights she's been waiting for. She flicks her own lights then turns the engine off. On the other side of the road, the vehicle pulls to the curb and waits.

The air is brisk, she notices, getting out of the car. Her high heels make a few pebbles skitter off the rough edge of the asphalt. The vehicle waiting by the curb is not the one she had expected.

The headlights flicker impatiently. She sighs, opens the passenger's door, and slides inside.

"What happened to your car?"

Rhesus leans forward and brushes the back of his hand along her neck, his hand cold on her skin. "Contingencies," *he says.*

The car lurches, muffled cries come from the back. That kind of contingencies, *she thinks. Her eyes harden.* "Why do you always make things so difficult?" *She opens her purse and produces a gun, black metal against the stark white of her hands.* "For you, my love," *she purrs, her gaze soft again.*

Rhesus stares at the pistol. He wavers, for no more than a second, then snags the weapon and storms out of the car. She drops her head against the headrest, closes her eyes, and smiles. As the trunk pops, a long groan spills out. Then silence. Get on with it. *The bang. And then another, and another, while she idly examines her nails.* Enough. *As though he heard her, Rhesus slams the trunk shut and returns inside the car. He is sweating heavily, dizzy from the rush. Intoxicated. His face is sprayed with blood and gunpowder, as are his clothes. The reek of a new initiation, the aspersion of a blasphemous baptism. She is pleased.* Is she proud of him? Or is it the realization of the power she has on him that's making her smile?

"The gun," *she says, extending an open palm.*

The grip is slippery with sweat. She drops the weapon back into her purse, then lays a hand on his chest. His breathing is still uneven. Her voice is mellow, comforting, as she whispers in his ear, "You did good," *and then nibbles his earlobe. He beams, his pulse once again quickening. Adrenaline careens through his body, making his heart pump faster, fiercer.*

"Are we doing it here?" *he asks, as her hand slides into his waistband.*

"Yes," *she replies, warm breath lingering on wet lips.* "I want privacy tonight."

CHAPTER 4

Thursday, October 9

"So. The shoe polish."

"What about it?"

"You never figured that one out, did you, Track?"

"You knew it was your day to go to hell, so you figured you'd better go with clean shoes."

Satish laughed, I chortled. It was good to have him back at the Glass House.

Thinner, and a little whiter at the temples, he didn't look too healthy, but he didn't look too sick either—just happily hanging in between. Not bad for somebody whose right lung had been pierced through and through by a full metal jacket only six weeks earlier.

Detective Satish Cooper and I had been partners since

I'd joined RHD, the Robbery Homicide Division of the LAPD, five years earlier. The first day on the job together we stood six hours under the sun plucking fibers off a stiff a wino had found sprawled across his cardboard home at the back of a Walmart. The wino wanted his home back, the Field Unit wanted a pay raise, the removal crew wanted a whole body and this one only came in half, and the lieutenant wanted to know who the hell the stiff was. Bodies don't come with tags, and this one looked particularly lonely and forlorn. At the end of the long day, Satish shook his head sideways and said, "I don't drink and I don't smoke and after a day like this all I wanna do is sit down and eat. What do you think of Angus steak and a glass of Merlot?"

"I thought you said you didn't drink."

He rocked on his heels and smiled. "Did I? Well, then, I must've meant water."

Over the five years we'd been together, I'd never seen him boss around, patronize, or raise his voice — save the half a dozen "assholes" he'd spit out from time to time, but a cop who never says asshole is like a Bloody Mary without vodka.

We saluted the officers on duty at the front desk and walked past the metal detector to the elevators at the back.

"Such a waste," Satish complained. He looked down at his feet. "Had to buy a new pair of shoes. The other ones got soaked in blood."

I clicked my tongue. "Should've used blood-repellant shoe polish."

The elevator chimed, the doors slid open. Satish stepped inside, then turned to hold the doors for me. I stared at the crammed elevator car and didn't move.

Right behind Satish, a lady pulled the straps of her purse up her shoulder and glared. A uniformed officer crossed his arms, the radio hanging by his belt barking a four-fifteen code. His partner sneered. All there, waiting for me. The idea didn't excite me, yet I had no choice but step inside and pitch in my own contribution of morning breath washed down with coffee and body perspiration concealed with dissonant brands of deodorant. To my nose, it was the equivalent of listening to Mahler played by strings out of tune.

The doors closed and the elevator chimed its way up.

Once on the third floor, the elevator gave a jolt, and the light flicked. The doors let out a tired groan and opened. We all filed out without taking notice. Completed fifty years earlier, Parker Center, or the Glass House, as we called it, would've never passed a safety inspection. The LAPD police administration building was old and outdated; the walls stunk, the floors whined, the elevators creaked. It had the familiar smell of things too old to forget. In the five years spent at the homicide table, I'd gotten used to the decay—the cracks in the walls, the battered look of the desks and cabinets, the stains on the peeling linoleum floors. It had become one of our favorite jokes, to die under a pile of rubble from one of the last non-seismic-compliant buildings in the city, after all the years spent risking our lives in the streets.

The squad room hadn't changed much during my six-week leave. Dusty Venetian blinds teetered against the same chafed window trims, and the same stale draft seeped inside, lulled by the droning of the Santa Ana freeway. The musty tang of the walls mingled with the usual smells of aftershave, sweat, mildew from old plumbing leaks, burnt coffee grounds, a hurried breakfast wolfed down in front of a terminal.

"What are you up to today?" Satish asked.

My eyes strayed to the lieutenant's office. "Gotta say hi

to the boss and tell him I'm back. You?" I glanced over the reports strewn across his workspace. "Still tied up to the desk?"

He slumped in his chair and shrugged a shoulder. "You mean handcuffed. Doc's supposed to clear me next week. Until then, I'm running background checks for the homicide table." That was just about what "light duty" meant in cop jargon. He tipped his head backwards. "In fact, I'm the one who ran the lady on your desk."

I blinked. Only my usual chaos reigned on my desk. "What lady?"

I rapped the glass pane of the lieutenant's office, opened the door, and poked my head in. "I'm back," I said.

Lieutenant Al Gomez was on the phone. Late fifties, bald forehead, protruding eyes, and bulging upper lip, the Lieu had the dazed look of a toad. Unfortunately, no princess had ever kissed him, only an ex-wife of whom he talked very little and never in a pleasant way. As soon as he saw my face poking through the door, he wrapped a webbed hand on the phone. "Huxley file, on your desk. Give it a couple of days. If nothing happens, file a cold case. Yeah, I'm here," he barked into the mouthpiece.

A couple of days. A missing persons. *What the hell?*

I didn't leave. Gomez ignored me, his voice trailing off into a litany of complaints over lack of funds, unacceptable working conditions and understaffing, until his glare fell back on me. "I'll call you back," he mumbled and hung up. He rubbed the archipelago of pink moles on his wide forehead. "Look. Captain Hu called. They're slammed at the DSV division and could use some help."

He stared, I stared back.

He rolled his eyes and sighed. "It's not a setback, Track."

"A missing persons?" I said.

A fuse at the back of my head buzzed. Getting into RHD, the LAPD Robbery and Homicide Division, had been the dream of my life. We handle high-profile crimes, like the Brown-Goldman double murder, or the Grim Sleeper serial killings. We're the cream of the crop. The competition to get in is fierce and for a guy like me with zero connections and a controversial acquittal at age seventeen the chances were close to zero. I made detective four years after entering the LAPD academy and was promoted into Narcotics three years later. For four years, I cleared all cases I was assigned and made it to RHD in 2003. At the time, I was the youngest detective on the team. And now the lieutenant tells me a missing persons is not a setback?

Gomez exhaled a ruthless whiff of halitosis. It made the fuse at the back of my head buzz louder. "Do you know how many rounds we tallied on Carmelo's body?"

The fuse blew. "The son of a bitch opened fire on my partner. My only fault is that I let it happen. I should've protected my partner."

I looked over my shoulder. Half of the homicide table stared back at me. I stepped inside Gomez's small office and slammed the door behind me. The blinds—a whimsical illusion of privacy granted only to the higher ranks—rattled against the doorframe. "BSS cleared me," I snarled. "It was a clean shooting."

"In his report Washburn strongly *recommends* a second session. And with your package—"

"I've been cleared for every fucking OIS on my package." I was fuming. Each time I squeezed the trigger, the Behavioral Science people went through my file—or package, as us coppers call it—with a fine tooth comb and sent me to spend quality time with their shrink, Dr. Adam Washburn. I hated the man. He had the sadistic habit of fixing me through long stretches of silence while pinching the skin below his lower lip, probing for more: a tiny detail, or maybe a little vice of mine I thought I'd be excused from mentioning.

I'm not stupid, Doc. I know what to hide from you.

Gomez looked like one of those stress-relief gadgets whose eyes bulge out when squeezed. "The Danny Mendoza case," he said, very carefully.

I squashed my voice down to a hiss. "That was a long time ago."

His features curled into a grimace. "We all make mistakes, Track. We bury them—some of us quite literally—and then move on. Somehow, your package seems unable to do that. It keeps popping up, and I'm getting quite sick of it. Huxley's missing persons report is on your desk. Clear it, and then we can talk again." He swiveled back to the phone, lifted the mouthpiece, and dialed.

I left his office and shuffled back to my desk. The piles of blue file folders, unread mail, and overdue reports contrasted with Satish's bare desk—even when stuck to light duty he managed to be way neater than me. I opened the first drawer, grabbed a paper clip, bent one end, and stuck it in my mouth.

It helps me think.

The missing persons folder sat lopsided across my nameplate, ULYSSES M. PRESIUS. I know. Thank goodness everybody calls me Track.

Jennifer Huxley had been reported missing by her mother two days earlier. An enlargement of her driver's license had been clipped to the first page of the report. Small, black eyes and a round face buried in a mop of dark curls. An anonymous face—although anybody looks anonymous to me without a smell, and photos only smell of paper and of the resins and polyesters they're coated with.

Five-foot-eight, one-twenty-five pounds. A graduate from UCSD—got an MS in molecular biology—she worked for a pharmaceutical company in La Jolla for two years, then moved to L.A. county where she landed a job as lab technician at the Esperanza Medical Center in Westwood.

A Ziploc materialized on my desk with a loud flop. Luke propped his ass on the only clear corner of my working surface and smirked the way some people do when they have nothing better to do. "Your usual piece of evidence, Track. Arrived as soon as Gomez assigned the case to you."

Luke was still new in our office, transferred only a couple of months earlier. The rookie thought he was entitled to give me the ain't-you-weird treatment. I plucked one corner of the clear bag he'd flopped in front of me, lifted it up, and stared at it. It contained a maize-yellow T-shirt. "It's not washed, is it?" I asked.

"Straight from her dirty laundry basket," Luke replied. He looked amused. "Would you have preferred a bra instead?"

Unprovoked, I stared back and sized him up. "You had eggs and sausage for breakfast, Luke. Washed it down with a double shot latte, hazelnut syrup. The sausage wasn't your favorite kind, does a number on your stomach. You should try Italian, next time, a little kinder on halitosis."

The lame smile faded from his face. He raised a hand to his mouth. "Do I—?"

I dropped the Ziploc and twisted one of my paperclips. "No, no," I reassured him. "Your breath doesn't stink too bad. It's just me. You brushed good after breakfast. Colgate, right?" He nodded, his jaw dropping like the door of a glove compartment. "It's the aftershave that bugs me, Luke. Aqua Fria. Man, I hate that brand. It's damn cheap, you know?"

Luke sprung back to his feet. His mouth moved, as if about to say something, then closed again. I watched the tall drink of water shuffle away from my desk and shook my head. He didn't find me any less weird than before, but he wasn't likely to come bug me again any time soon either.

I opened the plastic bag he'd left and took a sniff inside. I inhaled the feminine smell that came with the T-shirt. I worked my way through deodorant and artificial fragrances, the nerves inside my nostrils alerted, scanning the human scent hidden within. This Huxley woman was either vegetarian or ate very little meat. She exercised regularly. If she had a boyfriend, she hadn't seen him the day she wore the T-shirt. Enough for one sniff. I closed the Ziploc, got up and left.

CHAPTER 5

Thursday, October 9

Established in 1969, the Robbery and Homicide Division saw its beginnings with the Manson Family investigation. The LAPD needed a special squad dedicated to the most debated and controversial cases—murders, robberies, rapes and serial killings that made it to the national headlines. Exceptional detectives were drafted uniquely for this unit, men notoriously sleek and engaging, able to schmooze with witnesses and suspects alike. Finding clues is only the beginning. Most cases are cracked sitting down face to face with your suspects. We're the sleekest of predators. We coax, cajole, embrace our suspects with a safety net of trust until they make a false move and slip.

I was promoted to RHD on August 9, 2003, a blistering hot day. The lieutenant eyed me at my desk and summoned me to his office. I marched to his door with my chest puffed up, looking forward to my first case. Instead, I was sent home and forbidden to come back without dress shoes and tie.

"We're elite, we dress like elite," he told me.

It didn't take too long for the other detectives to dub me the black sheep in the group. Unspoken, the Mendoza case, for which I was acquitted at age seventeen, weighed over me like a sword of Damocles. Only one of the older detectives openly mentioned it to me. He took me aside one day, squeezed my shoulder and said, "You were just a kid. And that's what freaked everybody out. But to me—to me, you'll always be a hero."

He never spoke of it again, nor did anybody else at the Homicide table.

They all had their practical jokes and affable mannerisms, while I talked little and minded my business. They relied on luminol and polygraphs, whereas I had my sense of smell. Through chemicals released by the pituitary glands, I can detect fear, elation, deception. Human emotions are scents to me.

My first assignment was a five-year-old case that had baffled a team of four detectives, mostly retired by the time I got to it. I cleared it in three months, partnered with Satish, and nobody ever questioned again my MO—my *modus operandi*. They tell me I have a gift. I shrug and reply it's in my genes. Nobody asks for an explanation, nor do I ever offer one.

Leaving the murky skyline of downtown, I took the One-Oh-One northbound and merged into the uniform flow of the Southern Californian traffic. Shiny Mercedes, BMWs, and Porsches whipped by, flashes of wealth nurtured by blown up credits and a sense of entitlement. I passed a truck loaded with Toyotas, right as a sports Beemer materialized in my blind spot. Hair splayed by the wind, the cocky driver flattened the accelerator, then cut me to right-pass the slow poke clogging the fast lane.

Welcome back to L.A., I muttered to myself, as my mind lingered on the uncontaminated sheet of blue sky hanging over the Sierra Nevada. Up on the mountains, the fugitive line of the horizon is so wide you can watch the contour of a storm develop, mature, and dissipate in the distance. With a thud, the wheels of my Dodge Challenger entered a stretch of rugged cement, the vibration adding a new frequency to the roar of traffic embedded in my ears.

Silence is an unknown ghost to the Californian commuter.

Huxley lived in a North Hollywood residential neighborhood made of postage-stamp yards with manicured lawns, dogs on leashes and their byproducts tucked away in stinky blue baggies, and I-mind-my-own-business neighbors who turned away as soon as they glimpsed me. A large magnolia tree shaded the condo's white and gray façade—a double row of windows alternating to boxy balconies. The flaky paint had been concealed with crawling ivies, and the cracks in the stucco had been sloppily caulked. A lower middle class building with cheap management, I concluded. I parked my vehicle in the street and walked around the corner to door number three, careful not to step on the rolls of newspapers strewn by the doorstep. I donned latex gloves and protective booties, and unlocked the door with the key Jennifer's mother had left us when she filed the missing persons.

Inside, Huxley's place was tidy and compulsively clean. The first thing I smelled—in every room—were detergents, antibacterial sprays, and a fruit basket of artificial fragrances. The walls, impeccably white, were decorated with impersonal pictures of flowers and landscapes, save for a small frame hanging by the console in the foyer. "Lord, make me an instrument of your peace," it read. Next to it, a birdhouse-shaped key holder held a lonely mailbox key.

Nothing in the apartment was out of place, not even the usual mug on the coffee table or a hairbrush next to the bathroom sink, and nothing pointed to the woman having packed or prepared for an imminent departure. Among the items in her fridge were a wilted head of lettuce and half a gallon of milk gone sour. Everything was perfect. Her bed sheets were clean—no boyfriend detected there, no pills or condoms anywhere else in the bedroom. Her laundry basket contained two items—three, if you counted the T-shirt now in my possession—and the thin layer of dust on her shelves confirmed the few days since her disappearance.

The answering machine was flashing with a fairly innocuous message, "Hey, it's Kev. (Pause) Any chance we could talk?"—which the caller ID attributed to a Kevin Rutherford. No car keys to be seen anywhere, no vehicle sitting in the garage either. The absence of a wallet, cell phone or purse indicated that she had intentionally left home. If she had been abducted, it was not from her house.

I sighed and walked back to the living room, the phrase "cold case" making its way through my lazy neurons. A closed laptop lay on the desk, next to a CD column with about a hundred disks organized alphabetically by artist's name. I brushed a gloved hand along the back of the couch, and the fabric released the scent of an odor-eating spray.

I was ready to call it quits, when I detected something else. Something vague, a few days old, though still lingering in the air. I kneeled by the cushions and sniffed. Masculine smell, a hint of tobacco, faint, yet enough to make me think cigar, not cigarette, wine drinker, not heavily though. And a distinctive cologne, European brand, not cheap. The guy sat on this couch, maybe shared a glass with the hostess. If I could still detect the smell, the encounter had to be pretty recent. Maybe the night before Huxley disappeared. It wasn't much, but it was something.

On my way out I accidentally stepped on one of the newspapers on the walkway. I picked it up, and as the thin layer of plastic crinkled in my hand, something dawned on me. Two rolls, two papers, one dated Wednesday October 8, and the other one Thursday October 9, today. Jennifer Huxley had returned home the night of October 6 and never showed up for work the next day.

A mailman's van whirred by the post of condo mailboxes across the street. A rusty swing set groaned from a yard. Two driveways down, a plastic playhouse created a splash of color in the middle of a green lawn. The rest of the street, a few blocks from the bustling parts of town, seemed dormant: the windows held silent, the shutters were closed, and the doors still. A neighborhood of working families with school-age children. The only exception, an old rocking chair whining against the planks of the porch across the street, the face of the man sitting on it buried in a newspaper. I reached for my tin and walked over to the white picket fence outgrown by untamed rose bushes.

"Sir," I called from the sidewalk. The daily headlines rustled—the pages scrunched by long, bony fingers—and then lowered, revealing deep, blue eyes completely free of lashes. A fine web of purple capillaries lined the sides of a gaunt face with sandy cheeks. He folded the paper on his lap and without silencing the rhythmic whine of his chair, pointed his index finger at me.

"I don't need *that* to know you're a cop, young man."

I shrugged and slid the badge back in my pocket. "Do you get the paper every day, sir?" I asked, motioning to the pages he had just folded on his lap.

"Every day for the past seventeen years," he lisped.

"What time do you get the paper around here?"

"This?" he said, flopping a hand on his lap and making the pages creak. "You could set your watch on it, ya know? Five-o-seven at this door, five-o-six at the building you just visited."

"Are you sure? Exactly the same every morning?"

He gave me a full grin this time. Shiny gums on one side, golden crown on the other, next to the last two yellowish molars he had left. "Yes, sir. 'Cause you see, ol' Harold—house number five-six-six—he hates the paperboy. Bangs the thing at his door and wakes him up. The guy can't sleep until three in the mornin'. And then the paper comes and he's up again. Some kinda issue right here." The man tapped his temple. "Those brain cells, he ain't lubricated well enough, ya know?" He slapped both hands on the knees and guffawed. "Me, I'm up by four forty-five and wanna read my paper right away. And then I read it again. Makes me smarter. These brain cells of mine, they ain't going nowhere."

He leaned back in his rocking chair and winked. I grinned and reciprocated the gesture. Because thanks to Mr. Number Five-six-zero who loved to keep his brain cells in good shape, I'd just learned when Jennifer Huxley had left her home on October 7: sometime between five-o-five and seven-thirty, when her mother initiated the first of numerous calls left unanswered.

As soon as I stepped out of my vehicle, a wave of hot air enveloped me. "It may be fall, but it won't feel like fall," the radio warned, announcing a high in the lower nineties and dry Santa Ana conditions. I sighed, found relief under the shade of a large oak, and studied the place. In the distance, the heart and lungs of metropolitan L.A. reminded me of their omnipresence in the roar of highway traffic, and the occasional dinging of a railroad crossing. Yet in front of me sprawled an oasis of green. The rustling of the trees muffled the city buzz, and the fragrance of the rose garden mellowed the lingering odor of gas exhaust. A private clinic and cancer research center, the Esperanza Medical Center gave the casual stroller the illusion of visiting a botanical garden. It's a beauty meant to conceal the ugliness of the disease lurking behind the modern architecture and the glass façades. A mirage in the desert, an attempt to pamper the heart when a cure for the body doesn't always exist.

The guard at the entrance booth handed me a map of the campus on which he circled in bright red the location of the genetics building. "I can get you a driver on a cart, Detective."

Despite the heat, I declined the offer. Willows and cottonwoods shaded the campus, and the stroll would give me the chance to ponder over Huxley's file, the growing number of Officer-Involved Shooting reports filed under my name, and where the hell I was at that point in my life.

Another Ulysses searching for his way home.

"Lerville Research Institute," I read next to the main entrance of a gray building. There was no front desk in the lobby, so I walked straight to the first lab on the right, took a peek through the glass panes in the double doors, then entered brandishing my badge. The two ladies in the room—one bent over an optical microscope, and the other frowning at a computer screen—looked like they'd never seen a cop before.

"Jennifer Huxley, you said?" the woman by the microscope asked, the lapels of her white coat freshly sprayed with coffee spatters. "Do you recognize the name,

Sam?"

"Might be the Jen in Cox's group," the other replied. "Those people all have their offices upstairs."

"Mind showing me the way?"

The woman sent a furtive glimpse to her colleague before proffering, "Sure," in a *lovely* British accent. She led me out the door and up a flight of stairs. Plump, late-twenties, with the facial expression of a ten-year-old, Samantha Green smelled of rose deodorant and sugar glaze, the sticky kind you find on donuts.

"I take it you didn't know Jennifer personally?" I asked.

"Oh, we'd say hi and all, of course." *Of cou'se.* "But there's five different research groups in this building alone, lots of people coming and going," she explained, skipping the r's and indulging me in the soporiferous cadence of the Oxfordshire accent.

The hallway upstairs was dark, the walls lined with metal cabinets. The last door on the right bore Huxley's nametag. Samantha pointed to it and then stared at me with large blue eyes begging for gossip. "Has something happened to her?"

"No idea. When was last time you saw her, do you remember?"

Samantha shrugged. "I wouldn't recall... Definitely not yesterday or the day before, because I'd remember... She seems sort of quiet and always keeps to herself. Are you guys looking for her? But she wouldn't vanish like that, would she? I mean—she seems such a nice person and all... You know, we're all *lab rats*, but Jen beats us all. Never seen her outside or at the cafeteria. Just here, sitting at her desk or in the genetics lab. Sometimes I wonder if she's got a life at all."

In the five minutes I spent with her, Samantha managed to ask a dozen questions for every query of mine she left unanswered. I finally dismissed her with a curt thank you—her face hung with the disappointed look of a child who's just been denied candy—and worked my way around the office: small, crammed by two long desks, each one with a computer, a chair, a file cabinet standing by the door, and no space to move your legs around. It smelled musty, of old, molding wood. Despite the claustrophobic environment, Huxley's workspace was just as neat and tidy as her home. Her pens and pencils were all in a jar, grouped in three different compartments; her papers were stacked in color-coded folders on one corner of the desk, and her paperclips stored away in the drawer and sorted by size. *What a freak.*

I sat on the swivel chair and touched the mouse of the computer. The screen flicked to life and asked for username and password. I picked up the folder at the top of the pile on the desk, labeled "Leukemia Study," and opened it. There were several sets of stapled papers, the first of which looked like a drafted manuscript, with penciled corrections in two different calligraphies. "Incidence of leukemia in children under twelve in LA County, a preliminary study," the title read. A list of authors followed: Huxley was the first one, and the last one was a J.A. Cox, MD, PhD, listed as corresponding author. I attempted some educational reading while flipping through the pages, but typically got lost after the third word in each sentence. As I closed the folder and placed it back where it belonged, a bright pink sticky note fell out. Handwritten in capital letters, it read, "GN WHITE, AGE 8, CHROMO."

I puzzled over the note, didn't understand it, and the fact that I couldn't understand it made it interesting enough to copy the information on my notepad. Satisfied, I got back on my feet.

The Watson and Crick Laboratory for Genetic Studies was located at the very end of the building's west wing. This was where Huxley spent most of her days, according to Samantha Green. A pale light seeped through the frosted glass of two high windows and shimmered against rows of glassware of all sizes and shapes. Stacks of boxes filled the shelves between the windows, some pried open and their contents exposed: latex gloves, pipettes and pipette holders, tweezers, glass tubes, sheets of packed swabs. The air was acidic, thick with reeks of alcohol, antiseptic liquids, gels, biological solutions—all combined in one acrid odor. Pungent in an unpleasant way. A large fridge hummed at the back, a piece of paper taped to its door warning it did not contain food.

Like the stink wasn't enough of a warning already.

More signs decorated the cabinets hanging all around the walls, some pleading for their contents to be returned at the end of the day, others boring me with an endless list of vials and lot numbers stored within. Beneath the cabinets, a variety of instruments cluttered the scratched Formica countertops: optical microscopes, centrifuges, precision scales—all familiar but one. A sleek copy machine, I would've guessed, although it lacked a lid and had only few subtle buttons on the front.

"Isn't she a beauty?" a voice behind me said. It came with a whiff of caffeine, a badly digested lunch, and fabric that reeked of chemical reagents—a lab technician.

"Yeah," I agreed without having a clue to what exactly we were talking about. "What the hell is it?"

"An Illumina Beadstation," the man replied, his voice betraying disappointment in my question. I bobbed my head and humbly submitted my ignorance to his judgment.

"What does it do?"

"SNP genotyping."

It must have been my lucky day: I kept running into the most useful people. I slid the badge out of my pocket and flashed it in front of the man's nose. "I'm looking for Jennifer Huxley," I said. "I'm told she usually works here."

Fabian Payanukis had ghostly white complexion, a precociously hunched back, and long eyelashes hidden behind thick lenses. His outdated sweater smelled feminine, too flowery to be the scent of a girlfriend, a mother rather, the kind who calls three times a week and sends friendly reminders in the mail, lovingly tucked in pink, perfumed stationary. We each pulled a stool and sat at the corner of the working bench, in front of a compact centrifuge whose two dials kept eyeing me sternly.

"Jennifer and I work together on the leukemia study," he told me, grabbing an abandoned pipette bulb and pressing it between his index finger and thumb. His fingernails were polished and struck me as too long for a guy. "It's kind of strange she hasn't showed up for three days in a row," he said in a low voice. "Maybe she had a family emergency?"

"Tell me about this leukemia study you guys work on."

"The project is funded by an NIH grant. The recipient is Dr. Cox, my boss. The purpose of the study is to find possible genetic predispositions with the disease. We call them genetic markers: mutations along the genome that can predict the onset of leukemia. Genetic markers for breast cancer have already been published. Women who carry these mutations have a higher risk of developing breast cancer." While he talked, Payanukis blinked often and rarely made eye contact. His voice was as flat as an ironing board—perfect for Sunday morning readings on public radio.

"The Illumina we have in our lab is a million dollar baby," Payanukis's voice surfaced over my digressions. "It's the state of the art for DNA sequencing."

An Asian guy with spiky hair stepped into the lab,

acknowledged our presence with a brisk nod, and then sat by an optical microscope at the other end of the room, the sour smell of the fish-based lunch he'd just consumed trailing behind him.

"What's Jennifer's role in all this?"

"She prepares the samples to be genotyped and feeds them into the machine," Payanukis replied. "Sounds simple, but the whole process is fairly complicated and takes hours of work."

I had no doubt. "How many hours a day does she spend here at the lab?"

"It depends. Lately she's been at her desk a lot, writing a manuscript. She's always out of here by five, though."

I winced. Not quite the picture Samantha Green had depicted. "Are you sure?"

Payanukis nodded. "We usually leave together. I work on a second project, at another lab on campus. I walk her to the parking lot every night." He looked down while proffering the last bit. Beads of perspiration appeared over his brows. *He fancies her.*

"And you've never seen her come back here afterwards?"

He paused for a moment and then pointed a bony index finger at me. "You know, come to think of it, once I forgot my notes, so I came back around half past six and found her here."

I imagined him walking by Jennifer's side at the end of the day, living off her small smiles and polite nods, while her mind wandered elsewhere, racing ahead to the moment when she'd bid him goodbye, drive around the block, and then sneak back to the lab. Unseen, and away from spying eyes.

"What was she doing?"

"She was sitting at the computer station, the one

connected to the Illumina, probably reading some output."

"Did she look tired, as if sleep deprived?"

Payanukis shrugged. "I would say yes. But then again, we all do when there's a deadline approaching."

I got off the stool and adjusted the holster on my waistband. "So, where do I find Dr. Cox?"

CHAPTER 6

Thursday, October 9

Julia Cox shouldered out of the double doors without bothering to hold them open for the man behind her. "Julia! Wait!" the man called. "There's always Science—"

Cox marched away with her nose stuck up in the air as if she were wading in high, stinky waters. The hems of her white coat billowed, and the stethoscope around her neck tapped against her chest pocket. The man stood by the door, waiting, a shade of weariness clouding his face. The outer corners of his brows came down a notch.

Two women in green scrubs walked by, their heads focused on patient charts and medication trays, yet their eyes covertly staring at Cox's *prima donna* scene. Sunk in her black swivel chair, a receptionist with a five-inch tall hairdo yawned and flipped through the pages of her magazine. Hanging from the ceiling, a muted TV broadcasted the animated face of a reporter, the numbers of the Dow Jones running in a banner at the bottom of the frame. The blue light of the screen washed down on the reception desk, next to a sign warning patients to have their insurance cards ready.

Julia Cox took a few more steps, then froze in the middle of the lobby, one hand poised in midair as if caught by an afterthought. She spun on her feet and walked back to her colleague.

"Science?" she snarled, arms crossed and head cocked to the side. "Science has a cut-off of two thousand words—it's hardly enough to present the data, let alone discuss our conclusions. Plus, the resubmission will take another four weeks, which will give Jim's group plenty of time to publish their results and scoop us." The pretension of her posture jacked up her height a couple of inches. A woman of intensity, I noted, the kind you *don't* want to share your bed with. Her colleague opened his mouth as if about to object to something, his frown stuck somewhere in between concern and perplexity.

"No. You listen to me, Dave," Cox interjected, raising a finger and pressing it against his breastbone. "You know as well as I do who the second reviewer is. He's been sitting on our manuscript for weeks, giving Jim plenty of time to clean up his data and submit after we did. Of course he was going to reject us, he—"

"Julia, you're reading too much into this stuff."

"Oh yeah?"

"Dr. Cox?" She startled at the sound of my voice, as if suddenly realizing she'd been entertaining a work conversation in a public place. "I'm sorry to interrupt," I lied, flashing my badge.

The man by the door straightened and blurted, "Oh, no interruption at all. We were just about done."

I grinned, not missing the relief in his voice. Cox frowned, dazzled by the sight of my tin. "Dave!" she called, though the man had already vanished behind the double doors. A disoriented look on her face, she brought a hand to her stethoscope and turned back to me. "What's this about?" The tone of her voice betrayed a shrill of annoyance.

"I'm told you're missing a member of your research team," I replied, sliding the badge wallet back into my pocket.

She looked at me in a daze. "Missing? I thought she—" She bit her lip and didn't finish the sentence. "Is this about Jennifer?"

I confirmed it was about Jennifer. She ran a hand through her hair and gave one last glance at the closed doors. They held still and shut, her colleague by now probably two buildings away and still running.

"Let's go talk outside, if you don't mind," she murmured. As she strode by the reception desk, she brushed a hand along the mahogany countertop, and, without looking at anybody in particular, said, "Taking five."

"Yes, Doctor," the receptionist with the tall hair replied, her voice echoed by the squeaks of her swivel chair. I glanced at the towering hairdo, my hands itching to catch it were it to fall off any instant.

The pneumatic doors hissed open and the afternoon breeze yawned in my face. I slid my jacket off and inhaled. Despite the heat, the warm air lulled my senses, washing away the hospital tangs of medicine and antiseptic. An ambulance idled in front of the loading dock entrance, its lights throbbing for no apparent reason. Two EMTs shared a smoke on the sidewalk and casually discussed the previous night's soccer game.

"Let's sit at one of the cafeteria's tables," Cox said, pointing to the green bistro tables scattered in front of the building across the street. We sat in the shade of a large willow tree, its scented boughs drawing wavering patterns of light on the ground.

"You seem young to be a detective," she commented, taking off her lab coat and flopping it at the back of the chair.

"Job didn't come with an age requirement," I replied, realizing she'd been assessing me as much as I'd been her. I was thirty-eight and still looked younger than most dicks in my squad. Not an advantage when rank and seniority are often mistaken for the same thing.

She wearily flopped on the chair, raised her hands to her head, and collected her frizzy hair into a small bun. It sat precariously at the side of her neck and nodded along with each movement of her head. An outdoor sports lover, I noticed from the golden hue of her tan and the nice curve of her biceps. Her breath smelled of Arabic coffee, her scrub Tee of old bloodstains resilient to the harshest detergents, and her hands and arms—lightly peppered by freckles—of antibacterial soap. So far she had not spoken a word about Jennifer. Not a hint of surprise at her disappearance, not a trace of worry. If she was concerned, she was good at hiding it.

Once she was done fixing up her hair, she leaned back, crossed her arms and stared at me, a silent "So?" hanging from her cozy lips.

"When was the last time you saw Jennifer?" I asked.

"This past Monday, here at work. Who called the police?" she shot right back at me, her voice defiant.

"Her mother found it worrisome she couldn't get a hold of her daughter for three days in a row. You don't seem to share her concern."

She sighed, as if the whole conversation were a nuisance to her. "It's not weird, you know," she replied, her index finger tracing the relief design on the table.

"What isn't?"

She reached for the stethoscope hanging from her neck, either to check it was still there, or maybe just out of habit. I do the same with my gun holster. "That she would suddenly not show up to work. She looked stressed, these past weeks. Always working late. This field is highly competitive, Detective. Especially for a woman. Some make it, others don't."

I raised a brow. "Some just vanish in thin air?"

She rested her brown eyes on me and flashed a bitter smile. "No. It would be a first. But some do burn out. *That* I've seen before."

"Is Jennifer the kind prone to burnout?"

Her eyes slipped away. I sensed a change in her perspiration, her pituitary glands releasing a spike in adrenaline. "I don't know her that well," she said. "Personally, I mean. She's extremely good at her job. I don't have to spoon-feed her or breathe down her neck to get her to do her job. Whether or not she has personal issues, though, I wouldn't know."

"You said she looked stressed lately."

"She'd call me late at night, sometimes. From the lab."

"About work?"

She nodded. "I hope nothing bad happened to her. I really need her on this project."

My mouth twitched to a smile. "Wherever she is, Jennifer must be thinking exactly the same thing."

Cox received my sardonic comment with a blank stare. I pictured her in the examination room, interviewing patients with the detachment of a sphinx revealing her oracle.

"What did Jennifer talk about the last time she called?"

"It was work related. She mentioned additional data she was about to obtain." Cox passed a hand through her hair and pursed her lips. I cleared my throat, stared at her, and waited. The woman didn't yield.

"I'd like to know more, Doctor," I finally prodded.

She exhaled and swung one foot back and forth underneath the table. Her movement had been so brusque her hair bun came loose and disarrayed curls flopped around her neck. "I have patients to attend to, Detective. What we discussed on the phone pertains to the leukemia study we've been working on—I don't see how these technicalities can help you find her. I bet she just had a breakdown and fled to some hot place with a white beach and a five-star hotel." Her voice spiked with a sudden harshness, an alertness I didn't fail to miss. I rapped my fingers on the table, unwilling to hide my exasperation. Cops get snowed by hookers, pimps, lawyers, bankers, and all sort of thugs. At the bottom of every investigation there's a good dose of joggling different shades of true and false until a fragment of consistency emerges through the chaos. The delusion of a truth, one of many.

"You must be treating your employees really well, Dr. Cox, for them to be able to afford a white beach and a five star hotel." I ignored her glare and prodded, "Would you mind elaborating on the additional data Jennifer wanted to discuss with you?"

Cox sighed. "She just told me she was going to get additional data relevant to our study, but wouldn't be more specific on the origin of it, so I told her no way."

"Why?"

"More data means more plates on the Illumina, which cost a lot of money, Detective. Once I get a grant, I'm responsible for how and when the money gets spent. I can't pocket the funds and then use it at my technician's whim."

"Was it the first time she made such request?"

"At some point she requested looking at different regions in the genome for a subset of patients."

"And I suppose you nixed that idea as well?"

Cox sat upright and addressed me with a murderous glare. "It's *my* study, Detective. I don't have to justify what I do and how I do it. You have no idea how hard I have to fight to get money from the NIH. The competition is fierce. Despite all the big talk about equality you hear, the plain truth is that the scientific world is still men's territory. Women have to work twice as hard to get the same credibility. One has to spend sleepless hours writing grants, preparing talks, and making sure people understand the relevance of what it is you're trying to prove. My patients die in the most horrible ways and nobody seems to give a shit."

I held her glare throughout the rant. I believed her. I also believed I had to do my job, which implied finding out what Huxley was up to before vanishing in thin air. And whether by any chance she might have hampered the project her friendly boss had worked so hard to get funded.

"What about *your* data? Do they all come from patients of yours?"

"Mine and my colleagues' here at the clinic. The families that agree to participate."

I pulled the notepad out of my pocket and flopped it on the table, pointing to the name and age I'd copied earlier from the sticky note found in Huxley's papers. "Do you recognize this name as one of the patients in your study?"

Cox glimpsed at the note and then stared back at me. "I wouldn't know, Detective. All patients' personal information is protected under the HIPAA privacy act. The data we collect is labeled under a patient ID code, not a name."

I frowned. "What about the people who collect the data? They must keep record of the actual names."

"Yes, but they cannot share."

They meaning her and her fellow physicians. For some reason, I had a hard time picturing a clinician placing her stethoscope on the patient's chest, and cheerfully pleading, "Now give me a big breath, LS543," or whatever ID the child had been given. I sighed and rapped my fingers on the table. The breeze rose and momentarily alleviated the afternoon heat. Not my annoyance, though. "Dr. Cox, this name was on a note on Huxley's desk, in a folder labeled 'Leukemia Study.'"

"Huxley is not supposed to know the names of our patients either. If she did, she broke the HIPAA agreement and could lose her job."

"Can you think of any reason why she could've obtained the information?"

"Other than insanity? No."

A man and a woman dressed in surgical scrubs came out of the coffee shop and sat at a table nearby. The woman dug a finger into the gooey frosting of her muffin and brought it to her mouth. I tried not to think of where those same fingers might have been twenty minutes earlier. A lady briskly zigzagged between the tables, angrily tapping her heels on the cement until she disappeared inside the shop.

I stared at the names I'd scribbled on my notepad. "What about the word 'chromo,'" I asked. "Does it ring a bell?"

"I can't think of anything. Maybe she wanted to write chromosome?"

Right. And play hangman while she was at it. "What if I *really* wanted to know if this eight-year-old child was at some point under your care, Dr. Cox?"

For the first time throughout our conversation, her lips stretched into a smile. Her eyes sparkled, as if enjoying the fact that here I was, a law enforcement officer with nothing to enforce on her. "You'd have to get a warrant, Detective."

The R's rolled off their tongues like balls on a pool table. A fan swooshed on the ceiling, the cold meat slicer hummed behind the counter. The place was narrow and the shelves crammed with jars and boxes bearing unfamiliar names and smells—a curiosity to me, a home away from home to the other regulars. Exotic scents lingered in the air—garlic, paprika, marinated olives and cumin. The cadence of the background voices lulled my senses. I thought of the two hours spent at Parker Center trying to educate myself on leukemia. Google walked me through symptoms, possible causes, impossible cures, incidence, and a bunch of non-profit organizations asking for my credit card number. A quick search in the white pages under GN White yielded about a hundred hits in the metropolitan L.A. alone. Two hours very well spent indeed.

"How about some pastrami with your *gharsi*, Detective?"

"Not tonight, Areg," I replied, taking the white bag he handed me across the counter. He exchanged a few more rolling R's with his wife—a fake blonde with blood-red nails and full breasts with an attitude—and then added, "The *kadaif*'s on me, Detective. Those punks never bothered us again," he added in a lower, conspiratorial tone.

"You call me if they come back." I smiled a thank you, paid cash just to watch the blood-red nails flip through the exact change of three dollars and fifty cents, and then walked out, the foreigner feeling following me down the streets of Citrus Grove, a Glendale neighborhood buzzing with Armenian shops. From there to my home in Chevy Chase was a five-minute drive, which I covered at a painfully slow speed. I drove watching the setting sun turn the hills gold and red and wondering how long until the jacaranda trees covered up in purple again.

"Crappy day," I said to myself, unlocking the door. "Crappy, crappy, day." I said to Will as he ran to the door and slimed me, my face, and my legs with wet dog kisses. I slid the gun out of the holster, tossed the whole paraphernalia of gun holster, handcuffs, spare magazines and cell phone on the couch, and then rolled on the floor and played rough with my boy.

From the windowsill, The King—yes, *The* King, the only cat in the neighborhood whose name was composed of two words, he deserved them both—looked down on us and regarded us with the detachment of his feline superiority.

My half shepherd half Labrador mutt smelled of *toyon* and spruce trees.

"The hell you been, huh?" I teased him, roughing him up around the neck. "Hunting again? That's my boy!"

Will yapped.

"You hungry? Me too."

I set the Armenian take-out on the kitchen counter, went to the pantry and reached for a bottle of Sangiovese. The drawers disappointed me with the lack of a bottle opener.

"Helluva crappy day." I scuttled around the house trying to remember where I could've left the damned thing. The bedroom was unlikely, though my own entropy has often baffled me in the most creative ways. I brushed my fingers between the couch cushions and laid hands on a flattened box of condoms instead. On the bookshelf, behind the Bill Evans Trio Village Vanguard set, I found an old edition of a Pirandello play I'd forgotten I owned. I rummaged through the piles of Game and Fish magazines, the glass recycling bin in case I'd tossed the opener with the beer bottles, and the shelves of ramen noodles and tomato cans in the pantry. Until my eyes fell on something totally different: a glass jar, half-full with old keys and paperclips, a shiny object buried underneath.

Will yapped, I ignored him.

I grasped the container, plucked out all sorts of keys—old lockers, mailboxes I no longer owned, big keys, small keys, rusty keys—and groped for the little silver box sitting at the very bottom. I took it out slowly, as if made of paper instead of old, tarnished silver, brought it to my nose, sniffed it, and then opened it. A stern face glazed past me, her lips pursed, refusing to yield the smile the photographer had probably in vain prodded from her. *Damn it.* Of all things I could've plucked off Carmelo's body after emptying my Glock on him, it had to be his deceased mother's photograph. I thought of my own mother, whose photos I no longer had.

There's an invisible bond linking a predator to his prey. Even the ones he didn't choose himself.

It's been six weeks already. I snapped the box closed and dropped it in my pocket. *Time to put it away with the others.*

Will looked at me with steak eyes.

"No steak, tonight, buddy. Armenian is all we get."

I pulled down two cans of pet food and emptied them in the guys' bowls.

The King hopped on the countertop and watched me.

"Fancy Armenian tonight, your majesty?"

He gave me a snobbish mew of criticism and licked his paws.

"Sorry," I said, unwrapping the *gharsi* and *lamjoun* and transferring it all into a plate. "That's all I have tonight, bud."

His amber eyes rested on my plate and disapproved of my dinner. He ate his can food, and when he was done, he trotted back to the living room and conquered my couch with the entitlement of somebody who's claiming what belonged to him all along.

Will licked his bowl all the way across the kitchen.

I warmed up my dinner, turned the TV on, and settled to eat on the recliner by the couch, a can of coke the miser replacement of the Sangiovese I wasn't going to have tonight.

CHAPTER 7

Saturday, October 11

The intercom buzzes and the woman shifts excitedly. A few bubbles spray on the glass of wine she is holding. "It's her, finally!" she says, putting the glass down.

Her husband drops lower into the tub, making the water gargle. "This late?"

"She couldn't make it earlier," she replies, springing to her feet. For a second she stands naked in front of him, rivulets of water dripping down her body, bending around her curves, and insinuating in secluded crevices. The husband admires and, despite the familiarity of it, still finds the sight enjoyable. It's not offered for too long, though. She hastily steps out of the tub and runs to answer the intercom.

"Careful not to slip," he calls, reaching for his glass of wine.

Sunday, October 12

The first rays of dawn stain the sky over the Tate University campus. The air is nippy and the lawns humid, fragrant with the dew accumulated in the wee hours of the day.

The cobblestone walkways are deserted, except for the occasional student who has spent the night at the library preparing for a test, or the graduate assistant who instead devotes his nocturnal hours to a never-ending lab experiment. The door to the Kellogg Laboratory opens, and the wheels of a bicycle whirl out on the portico. In front of the library, the fountain rushes to life after a few minutes of inactivity. The jets of water reach their peak and then slowly die out again.

"Excuse me, sir," the cyclist says to the man lying at the foot of a bench. How come security hasn't spotted this one? *he wonders.* He must have rolled off the bench after falling asleep. *The man doesn't move, and the cyclist has no choice but get off his bike and walk around him. As he turns to take one more look, something catches his attention. The cyclist props his bike against a pillar, turns around, and crouches over what he now realizes is not a sleeping man. It's a body drenched in blood.*

CHAPTER 8

Sunday, October 12

The low morning sun brushed the foothills with gold. Blown by the breeze, a handful of sand swirled up in the air. The steel swingers gave the faintest nod. I scanned the one-hundred-yard line and fixed my eyes on the second to last plate. The light wind at muzzle was going to add to the fun.

I positioned the frame on the V-through of my handgun rest, held the revolver—a five-inch S&W M327—on target, and squeezed the trigger, flying three rounds down the range. Earplugs and headset muffled the roar of gunfire. The blast sent a shock wave up to my arm and shoulder. Dust came down from the rafters. My target swung and clanged.

Wait. I couldn't hear it clang.

Clang. Clang.

I pulled off the earmuffs and plugs and turned. Officer Kimberly Nelson stood behind my bench, clanging a key ring against the metal pillar. Pretty, in her mid-thirties, and smiling. I may have dated her once. Or twice.

"Did you forget to set the buzzer on your cell phone, Track?"

I adjusted the shooting glasses on my nose. "I didn't pull cover this weekend."

Her smile didn't fade a notch. "That's what *you* think. Gomez told me to show you this." She handed me what looked like a photocopied picture of the back of a car. I took it from her and brought it to my nose. It smelled of the cheap quality ink used in fax machines. Gone through a few hands before Nelson—Gomez, a couple of others I didn't recognize. The car was a Ford Focus, an older model, and the plate number was clearly readable despite the low quality of the image. And awfully familiar. I read the date and time at the top of the page: it had been faxed from the West L.A. station forty minutes earlier.

"What does Gomez want me to do with this?" I asked.

Nelson cocked her head and motioned me to go talk inside.

The range master shouted the "all clear." I holstered the revolver, picked up my range bag, and followed her. I'd left my duty weapon—a Glock 17—at home, but I wasn't wearing a tie either, so the hell with regulations.

Officer Kimberly Nelson smelled of cheap perfume and bubble gum. "We shouldn't go this long without seeing each other, Track," she purred once in the lounge. She had one of those rich and juicy voices you could put on playback and sleep right through it. By contrast, her talk was as sharp as a paper cut and as stinging as a double shot of whiskey.

"You could've called me last night, and we would've

made it a date," I replied. "Where was the pic taken?"

"At a crime scene, picked up by a surveillance video. The responding team ran the plate number through the NCIC and found the record to be active."

The NCIC, or National Crime Information Center, is the FBI database for stolen property, criminal records and missing persons—the first place where a law enforcement officer checks a plate number, a weapon, or a suspect.

"A crime scene?" I prodded, as we exited through the front office.

"Double murder, husband and wife, whacked in the head in their home in Beverly Hills. The guy was a big fish at this genetic company—" She turned the fax over and read through her handwritten notes. "Chromo Inc., it's down in Century City. Anyways, Gomez said you've been investigating the vehicle's owner."

I stood outside the range office, gunfire blasting in the background, and froze. *Huxley's note.* GN WHITE, AGE 8, CHROMO.

Huxley vanishes, and one week later her car turns up at a murder scene, the victim linked to the name Chromo.

My missing persons just got upgraded to double murder.

"Was the case transferred over to us?"

Nelson nodded a little too enthusiastically. "Yup. Ready to go check it out?"

"With you?"

Pretty or not, the rookie's best police work so far had been writing speeding tickets.

Her lower lip curled into a pout. Without a word, she turned away and started down toward the parking lot. I shouldered my bag and followed.

"Gomez wanted me to remind you your partner's on light duty and RHD is down on manpower," Nelson sang. The sky was clear and the light bright. I kept my glasses on.

"Nice of him to remember."

A black and white cruiser was parked on the west end of the lot, but Nelson spun to the left, walked straight to my Dodge, and clutched the door handle to the passenger's seat. It didn't yield. "Track," she said, glaring.

Car keys jingling in my hand, I said, "Spit the bubble gum out before you step into my vehicle."

She stared at me half smiling. "Why?"

"It stinks."

Her lower lip curled again. She spat the bright yellow blob into her fingers, crouched down, and stuck it in a groove in the front tire.

Sleek little thing.

"Track, have you ever wondered why you're still single?" she said as we wound down Tujunga Canyon Road.

"Who says I am?"

Nelson let out a snort, which sounded more like a mew in her voice. "Look at you. You're handsome, even charming on a good day, and yet you keep being such an asshole with women."

I grinned. "I'm for equality, Nelson. I'm an asshole to everybody."

"You know, I could give you a few tips."

I shot her a sideways glance. There she was, slouched in my vehicle with her perfectly ironed uniform buttoned all the way up to the neck, soaked in some artificial fragrance she got half price at Macy's during one of their end-of-the-season clearance events.

"Tips? In exchange for what?"

"You know I'm pricey, huh?" she replied, her voice as gold as honey. She leaned closer, brushed a finger along my shoulder while purring a little sexy roar, then slumped back on her seat and laughed. Cute, had it not been for the stinky bubble gum breath.

"Ah, you're funny, Track. No, all I need is a word with Gomez so I can stay at the Homicide table after the freeze. Right now I'm on a six-month loan," she added, switching off the mellow in her voice.

"So I'm funny, huh? Because suddenly your heartfelt compliments—handsome and charming—assume a completely new meaning."

"Oh, come on, Track."

"Fine. You gotta work for it, though. Asshole Track wants to know about the crime scene."

Nelson unrolled the sheet of specs she had brought along. "Double homicide. Vics are husband and wife, whacked in the head in their home at 12300 Cielo Drive, Beverly Hills, some time after ten p.m. last night—the pics you saw was taken at ten seventeen p.m."

"The Benedict Canyon neighborhood," I considered. Etched at the foot of the Santa Monica Mountains, between Coldwater and Franklyn Canyons, Benedict Canyon is one of the high-end neighborhoods of Beverly Hills. Surrounded by sycamores, majestic oaks, and palm trees, single-family homes rise above the pollution of downtown and enjoy crisp mountain views and clear skies. An expensive privilege in Los Angeles County.

"Who found them?"

"A neighbor called nine-one-one at five twenty-three this morning. He was awakened by loud growling and found the vics' yellow Labrador roaming and yapping in his backyard. Can you imagine? The poor thing."

"Yeah, that early in the morning I'd be pissed too."

Nelson's forehead rippled. "Jeez, Track. I meant the Labrador. He must've been so scared!" Female cops. You can have ten victims in a room, yet if there's a dog, they'll run for the pet first. "The neighbor phoned the vics. Nobody picked up, so he walked the pup home. He got suspicious when nobody answered the gate either—that's when he dialed nine-one-one. The responding officers found husband and wife dead in the master bathroom: Robert Tarantino, age fifty-five, chemical engineer and executive vice president at Chromo Inc., and Tamara Tarantino, age forty-eight, housewife."

"How many shots? Does it say in the log?"

"One each, both to the head."

"And the neighbor was awakened by the dog's growling but not by two shots in the middle of the night?"

Nelson shrugged. "People mind their own business. The dog had trespassed his property."

"Hmm. We'll have to talk to this guy. This Chromo Inc., what does it do?"

"Let's see, what did they give me here... 'The company specializes in genetic sequencing, gene expression, and gene therapy'—whatever that means, I'm reading from the log." She let the papers flop on her lap and stared at the road. "The lieutenant said you've been investigating the owner of the car turned up on the cc camera. Do you think your missing lady did it?"

A workaholic woman who every evening lets a geek walk her to her car so she can pretend she's going home when in fact she's sneaking back to work? One day she vanishes and her car turns up at a double murder scene. "Nelson, this woman is as dead as the two bodies they just found." And with that, I plunged the vehicle into the Two-Ten and effortlessly swerved into the carpool lane, feeling the ecstasy of a Sunday-morning-deserted freeway.

Tall hedges splashed with magenta bougainvillea blossoms circled the property, their height a claim of privacy and a statement of wealth. In L.A., poverty is for everybody to see, yet affluence is hidden away and left to the imagination. By the wrought iron gate, a uniformed officer from the West L.A. station checked our badges and radioed the responding team about our arrival.

"Who's in charge in there?" I asked, as he returned the tins.

"Detectives Spencer and Donoghue," he replied, lifting the yellow tape. "Go ahead, Detective. They're waiting for you."

I bet they are, I thought, recognizing the names.

Red and white oleanders bordered the driveway. It wound uphill through the lush green of a manicured lawn, until, surrounded by cypresses, a Tuscan style villa in light pink stucco loomed into view against a stark blue sky. Speckled with sage bushes and chaparral evergreen shrubs, the rust-colored hills of the California scrubland painted the background. Both the ambulance and the SID—the Scientific Investigation Division—field unit van were already on the premises, carelessly parked at the top of the driveway. I pulled in next to two patrol cruisers, got out of the car, and stared at the façade of the house. A long pergola propped over Corinthian pillars encircled the ground level and extended into a portico above the main entrance. Twin lions flanked the stairs to the door, both frozen into a stern glare—some pseudo-artist's idea of house guardians.

Interesting mix of architectural elements.

I walked around my Dodge, opened the trunk, and took in the familiarity of my own chaos: cardboard boxes filled with tools, flashlights, spare batteries, a blanket, paper towels, evidence bags, a box of extra magazines. And a bag of beef jerky, because you never know.

"Aspiring Detective Nelson." I tossed her a bundle of latex gloves and protective booties. "Let's start from the basics."

Badges clipped on, we walked past the usual streams of yellow tape and made our way to the entrance. A gaunt figure was pacing up and down the pergola, his head lost in a cloud of tobacco mist.

"Hey, Track!" He waved an oversized hand at me, curly billows of smoke jetting out of his nose. Dr. Thomas Ellis, L.A. county medical examiner: ashen face, aquiline nose, and long cheekbones jutting below gray, hollow eyes. He was skinny everywhere but on his stomach, which was as round as a cantaloupe and sat on his lanky frame like an Afro wig sat on Asian face. His wardrobe consisted exclusively of gray suits, which nicely matched the grayish tint of his complexion, and his body odor was a unique blend of nicotine, formaldehyde, hypochlorite and dead flesh.

I introduced Nelson and scrunched my nose in disgust. "What the hell is that, Doc? You've changed brand of smoke?"

"You noticed, huh? My wife talked me into this lighter stuff." He looked at the half-smoked cigarette between his index and middle finger, the heel of his fingernails rimmed in nicotine yellow. "Man, it sucks."

From a second-hand smoker's point of view, I couldn't have agreed more. "Of all people, I thought you'd be the first one to stay away from tobacco."

He shrugged. "What can you do? Human nature is weak. I'll see you up there in a sec," he added, taking another drag. "I'll let you settle yourself, first."

I caught on the comment and snorted. A little too often crimes in the Hollywood area turn into high-profile cases. The divisional detectives arrive on the scene and get their asses moving locating witnesses, calling the paramedics, identifying the victims. When some high-ranking boss calls and tells them to get out of the way because the case got transferred downtown, the news is not always welcomed with enthusiasm. Facts turn into innuendos, and findings are shared only under highly privileged conditions, in a more or less implicit battle for territory.

The main entrance to the house had been left ajar. As I pushed it open, I noticed an injured camera perched atop the door and miserably gaping at me. Gunfire, I realized, counting two bullet holes. The device had been tagged and numbered, which meant the SID guys had already logged the piece of evidence. Nelson and I donned our protective gear — the latex adhering to my hands like a suffocating sheath — and got to work.

Inside, the villa was a continuation of mismatched styles: the cotto floors, partly covered by Persian rugs in the living room, gave way to cream-colored carpet in the office. The kitchen had Spanish tiles, pueblo-style niches in the walls, and Italian appliances. A German grand piano dominated the ballroom, surrounded by walls decorated with African masks and Japanese watercolors. Bits of interrupted life recurred everywhere — a half glass of water on the kitchen counter, an open musical score on the piano, a bunch of keys casually tossed on a console, a magazine flopped upside down on the couch. They clashed with the different hues of fingerprint dust dutifully brushed on all light switches and doorknobs, and the loose crime tape rattling against the windows.

I inhaled old and new scents, smells that belonged, and ones that didn't: I smelled blood, sifting down from the open loft, together with the first hints of decay and methane coming from the dead bodies. It mingled with a trace of male sweat and nicotine, and the metal of guns rubbing against leather holsters.

I smelled testosterone. Loads of it.

Nelson paced quietly behind me, her eyes straying wherever mine went. Voices barked upstairs. She stared at me. "So. Do we wait here, or do we go introduce ourselves?"

I didn't need to answer. A face emerged from across the banister of the loft and looked down at us. "Oh, look. It's Presius. Changeover time. Beer for us, double stiff for you. And you're welcome, by the way."

"Glad to take it off your hands, Spencer," I replied.

"Yeah, right."

"Be good, Don. Let's do this civilly, shall we?" a second voice interjected, slightly higher in pitch and diplomacy.

Nelson stiffened and mouthed, *What the – ?*

They took their time as they came down the circular stairs: tasteful civilian clothes, the straps of their shoulder rig holsters visible from underneath their black jackets, their white shirts rimmed by halos of sweat and the stench of nicotine. Spencer stared at me defiantly, a strip of forehead stuck between a low hairline and a pair of bushy eyebrows. Tufts of black hair sprouted out of his wide nostrils like spider legs. He stood in front of me in a wide-legged stance, his face inches away from mine, and his clean-shaven chin scalloping down to his neck.

"Sorry, pal," he mocked in falsetto. "We didn't get you a murder weapon, this time."

"It was hardly a bonus, last time."

A robbery gone wrong in Beverly Glen, two years earlier. Spencer and his partner found the smoking nine-millimeter as Satish and I were en route, and by the time we got to the scene they claimed the case was theirs. Too damn good to let go. The battle for turf escalated, forcing Gomez to step in with a few phone calls to the Hollywood brass in order to grease the way. We got the case, and Spencer never forgot.

"Let it go, Don," Spencer's partner said, almost quietly. "We're all following orders, here." Leaner than his partner, with an angular jaw line and a buzz haircut that badly camouflaged the thinness of his hair, he squeezed Spencer's shoulder while flashing me a somehow conciliatory smile.

Spencer wasn't done, though. "I just hate it when some people get it easier than others," he spat, his breath a mix of black coffee, smoke, and useless Listerine strips. "It's not fair, ya know?"

"I didn't hear you caught the perp already," I replied.

Spencer narrowed his eyes in a slit of defiance. "You like free rides, huh? Is that how you got into RHD? Kissing ass?"

You like free rides...

His sneer blurred, my surroundings went out of focus. I was seventeen, in the fucking cell they'd put me for the night, and it was cold, so freaking cold I couldn't keep my teeth from rattling. Blood dripped down my nose, but it was nobody's concern. The correction officer barked to my face, his breath laden with alcohol and nicotine: *You like free rides, kiddo? Well, I got news for ya. You either take your fuckin' pill to sleep like a baby, or I'll putcha to sleep like a baby.* He hit me again with his studded belt and slammed the heel of his boot into my shins.

It was a flash, and then the cell vanished. Not the rage, though.

"Come on, Don. Let's go."

Spencer's voice resurfaced. "Yeah, let's go. This is no longer our dump."

I watched them turn away from me, blood pulsing in my head. I pounced on him from behind, snatched the back of his jacket, and slammed him against the wall. The glass chandelier clinked, a couple of photo frames on the piano fell. Nelson flew a hand to the pepper spray. Spencer staggered, and before he could get back at me, I clutched the collar of his shirt and pinned him to the wall. "The only reason they call you dick is because you're a *real* dick," I spat through clenched teeth. "Now get your ass off *my* crime scene."

"Whoa, whoa!" His buddy waved his open palms up in the air. "Let's cut it out, guys, ok? We're cool, right, Don?"

Spencer was seething. "Get your hands off me."

I gave him a little taste of my own breath and snarled to his face, nice and slow, "Out of my way," before letting go of him. He smoothened down his shirt and readjusted the straps of his holster, his short forehead glistening with a film of sweat.

"C'mon, Don. The show's over."

Nelson drew in a sharp breath. "Great job, Track. They probably interviewed a dozen witnesses already and found evidence they'll never disclose."

"They've been here only a couple of hours. We'll get the field interview records from the responding officers," I replied, distracted by a new presence I suddenly sensed, farther away, watching. I turned to the stairs.

"I uh—" The woman blushed, a round, Asian face with porcelain cheeks. "Carolyn Ling, SID evidence logger," she quickly blurted out. She'd watched the whole scene, I could tell from the way her fingers nervously fiddled with a black strand of hair that had escaped her paper cap. "We're ready for the walkthrough upstairs."

Suddenly the whole Spencer exchange looked frivolous and damned stupid. Here we were again, hard-wired cops butting heads over what? Dead bodies. Like vultures circling over somebody else's prey.

CHAPTER 9

Sunday, October 12

A pair of man's trousers lay crumpled at the foot of the bed. A purple shirt was sprawled across aquamarine blankets, and a skirt had landed atop the nightstand lamp. Skin-colored pantyhose snaked on the carpet, a black bra drew a slanted smile across one of the pillow shams. The trail of garments continued toward the bathroom, where some time earlier the air had smelled of body lotions, naked skin, and bath fragrances from the tub. I imagined husband and wife running up the stairs: he grabs her ass, and she squirms, laughing though, playing the usual game of chasing and teasing, prodding and slipping away, only to come back and prod again. They get to the bedroom giggling and touching; she unbuttons his shirt, he unfastens her bra. The water in the tub is running. Billows of steam waft up and fill the air, the fragrance of bath oils mingling with their anticipation.

It was all gone now, choked by the sweet stench of death. Behind marble vanities with brass faucets, a wall-to-wall mirror reflected the bodies. Tamara Tarantino's blood had coagulated into a dark-maroon clot around her prone head. Her husband was still in the tub, soaked waist down in maroon water. A round hole gaped from the middle of his forehead.

The shattered remains of a bottle of wine were scattered on the floor, a half glass still intact on the edge of the tub, while a second one had rolled off and cracked. Circular halos of dried-up foam traced a path across the marble tiles, from the bathtub to the door and then back to Tamara Tarantino's feet.

My mind plunged backwards in time. Both naked, husband and wife slip into the tub. She goes in first, while he fills the two glasses of wine. He joins her in the water, his thighs touching hers, prompting more smooching and more giggles. Until the idyll is suddenly broken and the wife gets out. Why? She hops out of the tub in a hurry, water runs down her naked body and forms a pool on the floor. She doesn't bother to get a towel, leaving a wake of soapy drips on the floor. She heads back to the bedroom, and when she comes back she's wearing a bathrobe. Maybe he said something to upset her. Maybe they got into a fight and she decided the fun was over.

By my side, Nelson stiffened. "I'll uh—I'll go see if there's anything interesting back in the bedroom." She whirled on her feet, walked past the two crime scene investigators who'd escorted us upstairs, and vanished.

"So, where's Matt Gallo?" I asked, my eyes glued to the milky way of blood spatters decorating the wall behind the tub. Matt was the CSI who'd worked most of our crime scenes in the past. I'd expected to see him there, just as I expected Satish to walk in any minute and bore me with all the technicalities and nuisances of crime scene SOPs.

"Assigned to a different case," the woman behind me replied. "I'm in charge on this one." A few more seconds of silence followed. "Diane Kyle, DNA specialist," she finally said, stretching out her hand.

"Presius," I replied. Our gloved hands squeaked as they touched, sealing our acquaintance like the clinking of champagne glasses. On a crime scene, human contact is filtered through an antiseptic layer that wraps the body and a bubble of detachment that cushions the brain.

Carolyn Ling handed me pen and clipboard. I signed the log and saw that Spencer and Donoghue had arrived at the scene at seven fifty a.m., confirmed the victims were deceased, and made the usual calls to the paramedics and the SID Field Unit. Several West L.A. officers were still canvassing the neighborhood trying to locate possible witnesses. The closest relatives amounted to an elderly sister and the victims' daughter—a senior at Columbia University—who'd been notified and was currently flying back home.

"Fill me in," I told Diane, returning the homicide log. And she did fill me in, not with words, though. Because until then I hadn't really seen her. Garbed in the clunky SID coveralls, her scent had remained hidden away from me. As soon as we walked out of the bathroom, she removed the protective cap, and the olfactory landscape around me abruptly changed.

Diane's auburn locks fell across her forehead and neck, bathing me in strangely familiar scents—delicate and melodic like the harmonies of a Bill Evans solo. I smelled the pearls of sweat along her hairline and the root of her hair, the detergent on the collar of her shirt and the skin enclosed within. Her scent felt engaging to my nostrils, soothing and foreign at the same time. And she had a man. *Him* I smelled when she leaned closer and asked, "Can I call you Track? I heard that's what everybody calls you."

For a moment I drowned in a sensory storm during which all I could think of was, *And who the hell are you?*

She stepped back, the bubble she'd enveloped me in popped, and the usual homicide tangs resurfaced: decaying tissue, coagulated blood, *livor mortis*, a surviving hint of burnt gunpowder.

Carolyn collected Nelson's signature as well, then clutched the clipboard to her chest, and asked, "Shall I go get Peter?"

"Please," Diane replied. "Peter's our photographer," she explained. She gathered the notes she'd left on a chair in the bedroom and handed me a transparent plastic folder with a white sheet of paper inside. "This was by the woman's body."

One corner blotched in blood, it read, "I am the Lord your God, do not have any other gods before me," all typed in caps. *From the Bible, First Commandment*, I considered. The prayer framed in Huxley's foyer immediately came to mind. Was it just a decoration or a statement? And what about the note I was holding: was it a signature or a way to lead us off track? Unusual choice of victims, if this truly was the course of action of a religious lunatic.

I slid a finger along the edge of the folder and brought it to my nose. "Smells foul," I said.

Diane winced, as if finding the statement outrageous. "Everything on a crime scene smells foul."

No. Not everything.

"No bloody fingerprints, I suppose?" I asked, holding the folder up against the window.

"Not to the naked eye. We'll need to fume it at the lab for regular prints."

Nelson moved over to canvass the walk-in closet and let

out a whistle. "You've got to see the shoes this woman had!"

I ignored Nelson's remark and checked the small writing desk by the window. A few personal items were scattered on its surface. One by one, I picked them up and brought them to my nose: a man's watch, a wedding ring, a cell phone, a box of Montecristo cigars. All drenched with a definitely masculine smell, expensive aftershave, distinctive deodorant fragrance. A vaguely familiar combination.

From the closet, Nelson let out another one of her high-pitched trills. "Twenty pairs of high heel pumps and still counting."

I scowled. "You're looking for evidence, Nelson."

She stepped out of the closet holding one of the high heels. "Seriously? You could stab to death with one of these."

"Too bad our vics were shot to death, not stabbed. Keep looking."

She gave me the "Track, you're an asshole" look and turned away.

"We didn't find much," Diane admitted, staring blankly at me as I brought every object to my nose, sniffed it, and placed it back. "No forced entry, no indication the house was searched. We photographed a few depressed areas on the carpet, clearly distinct from the vics' bare foot prints. A man's shoe, size ten to eleven, which puts him between six and six-eight feet in height."

"A man," I repeated. "Did you use the lifter?"

Her brow twitched. "Nothing unusual turned up, not even a speck of dirt."

"You didn't even get a partial?"

"We tried several spots with the electro dust lifter and all fibers that came up were from the carpet." She squinted, a hint of nervousness hanging from her lower lip. "We recovered a slug. It exited the second victim and entered the wall across. No spent shells, though."

Mulling over the dustless shoe print, I opened one of the desk drawers, even though I knew Nelson had already canvassed them, and tossed around its contents. I found a daily planner and felt a tinge of annoyance. "Nelson!" I called, at which both women in the room winced. I tossed her the planner, which she caught in midair. *Good reflexes.* "Don't overlook things like this, okay?"

She stared at it. "What do you want me to do?"

"Find out what our vics did yesterday. Any name in there, see if there's a corresponding number on the cell phone and call them." I passed her the mobile as well, and then motioned to Diane to resume her briefing. She stared at me in a momentary daze, then quickly averted her eyes. Between what happened downstairs and my erratic sniffing around the bodies, by now I was sure I'd made the hell of a first impression.

"It must've been quick," she said. "I'm guessing five to ten minutes max from when he entered the home and when he left. No sign of a struggle; plenty of jewelry and valuables scattered around the house in plain sight and left untouched."

"No forced entry," I pondered. "How did he get in?" And as soon as I formulated the question I knew the answer. I walked around the California king bed and let my nose follow the invisible traces Tamara Tarantino's wet feet had left on the carpet. The intercom button by the bedside had a smudge of dried bath foam along the edge. *She got out of the tub to let the killer into the house.*

I turned to show it to Diane, but she already picked up on my train of thoughts. "It wasn't an intruder who did this. It was somebody they knew."

"Somebody so close she didn't mind letting them in while her husband was still soaking in the bathtub." A *religious lunatic who knew them well.* I made a mental note to double-check the victims' affiliations, if any.

Diane nodded. "Whoever wanted them dead knew how to get them at a vulnerable time."

The medical examiner's voice boomed from the bedroom. "Can I get those stiffs off your hands now?"

"All yours, Dr. Ellis," I replied.

Followed by the summoned photographer—a small man with narrow shoulders, a few, wispy hairs sticking out at the sides of an egg-shaped head, and a prominent overbite partially concealed by a whimsical mustache—the M.E. strode to the bathroom, then froze at the door. His hollow eyes bulged out of their sockets as he took in the sight of the two bodies in the room. The dismay quickly vaporized from his face. "Wow. Do you ever get it in a tub, Track?"

I shrugged. "Something like this I believe you only get once, Doc."

I glimpsed a coy smile escape Diane's lips. It made up for the smirk sprawled on Ellis's lipless mouth. He squeezed my shoulder, kneeled by Tamara Tarantino, and flopped his bag on the floor. "Very funny, Track. I meant the fun part, not the bullet. Jeez. My tub's too small."

Peter the photographer stood behind the coroner with his lens poised. "And my wife's too large," he said, tittering at his own joke.

Ellis rolled the body on her back. Tamara's face was a mask of dried blood. Ellis wiped the clots off her face, and then examined the shot wound. The bullet had drilled a hole across her right temple. "Hmm. Somebody wanted her dead, that's for sure. You pop somebody in the head like that, you don't give them the time to blink."

Tamara hadn't blinked. Her eyes—two glassy wells of black—were sprung open. Despite the smears of blood and the rigor mortis, her face looked much younger than her actual forty-eight years of age.

"The husband got the same treatment. What's your guess on the TOD?"

"With the usual disclaimer, Track: nothing confirmed until the autopsy report. And we're talking dry stiff right here. The soaked stiff is a whole different matter, but hopefully we can assume they were killed at the same time."

"I don't think he would've entertained his wife's killer in the tub while waiting for his turn." In fact, the picture was clear: husband goes down first, one round straight to the forehead. Wife turns to watch him get whacked and gets the second round to the temple. Wise killer: always do the man first. Good shooter, too.

Ellis palpated the body's face, neck, and shoulders. "Dilated pupils. Jaw and neck pretty rigid. Upper torso just starting to set." He brandished a pair of tweezers, stuck them into the woman's nostrils, and fished out a lump of what looked like rice grains.

"Unhatched *diptera* eggs," Ellis explained, storing the precious find in a small jar.

Smile, I thought, as the photographer's flash went off.

Ellis proceeded to spread open the bathrobe and exposed the victim's chest, blemished by purple patches of *livor mortis*. He made a one-inch-long incision below the ribcage, then carefully inserted a long thermometer probe, which he maneuvered until the tip touched the liver.

"Hmm. Internal body temperature of eighty-point-eight. Assuming the room's temperature is at the usual seventy-two, say her body temperature decreased one-point-five degrees per hour starting from ninety-eight-point-six — what do you get?"

"She died almost twelve hours ago." I looked at the watch. It was eleven-forty, so around the same time the night before.

"Thank you, Track," Ellis said. "I hate to do that kind of math off the top of my head."

I sat on the living room couch, opened the laptop, and pressed play. The quality of the video was grainy, with the borders obscured, and the halo of a streetlight drawing a visual cone in the middle. The perp had destroyed the CC camera at the door but overlooked the one by the property gate. I watched it, started over, and watched it again. Tarantino's car appeared on the screen at ten seventeen p.m., waited for the gate to open, and then careened out of view. Thirty-eight minutes later, Huxley's car pulled into the frame. Positioned behind it, the camera gave me a make and model (2003 Ford Focus, green), but not a face on the driver. A hand appeared from the window and pressed the intercom, the wind the only witness of that conversation. The light above the gate started flashing, and the entrance slowly opened. I rewound, froze the frame, and zoomed in. Something glistened on the hand. *Could be a ring.* A small watch on the wrist, round, feminine. Was it really Huxley behind the wheel? Couldn't tell from this shot. The only other certainty the camera granted me: by eleven thirteen the perp was out, and both husband and wife were dead, according to the M.E.'s preliminary findings. I closed the laptop.

Nelson sat on an upholstered armchair across from me, a cell phone glued to her ear as she interviewed one of the Tarantinos' friends whose number she'd found in the planner. Two men from the coroner's office carried the first body down the stairs. The blue shroud jolted and waggled, until it was flopped on a stretcher at the bottom of the stairs and wheeled away.

"This one didn't know anything about it," Nelson

concluded, terminating the call. She slouched back in the chair and stared vacantly at the daily planner on her lap. The two pages covering the week of October 5 were scribbled with tiny notes in black ink: one-line reminders, a name, a book title to check out at the library, plenty of doodles and exclamation points. A single entry in a slanted handwriting filled the line under Saturday, October 11: "Horowitz BDay Party," it read. No phone number was listed under Horowitz, not in the planner, not in the mobile.

"We could search in the database under Horowitz and DOB October 11," Nelson offered.

"Birthday parties are not always timely." I got up and paced around the living room. Nelson sighed and dialed another number. A cold fireplace sported several picture frames on its mantel: two men in fishing gear embracing one another and proudly showing a two-foot long salmon; a freckled girl with a braced smile posing in a cheerleader uniform; a teenager too unhappy about the huge pimple on her forehead to smile at the camera.

"Hello, this is Officer Kimberly Nelson from the LAPD."

Glass doors to the back yard framed the blue outline of the Santa Monica Mountains. I stepped closer, pulled away the sheer curtains and stared outside. Or such were my intentions.

I sensed a lingering presence, feminine, one hand clasping the curtain. Did she look into the darkness outside? What drew her here—fear maybe? Or doubt? I inhaled. Feminine scents are elusive. Women don't always stick to one fragrance like most men do, and their secretions change from day to day with their hormones. I can get a global picture of a feminine smell, but if I want to break it apart, get into the components of it, one woman alone is a maze of scents.

I let my hand slide down the curtain, perusing its folds

and billows, searching.

"Nelson."

"Shit! They hung up on me."

"Nelson!"

"What?"

"Go get Diane."

The afternoon glare made me squint. I reached for my sunglasses, inhaling. The air was crisp and alive. *Clean murder*, I thought. *The killer comes, fires, leaves. Not much to start off: a doubtful note and a plate number, the vehicle missing, together with its owner.*

I leaned against the portico railing and checked my phone. It was three fifteen. The field unit guys were packing up their tools and loading the van. In the distance, the Mediterranean colors of the Californian scrubland weaved with the profile of the hills. Trimmed shrubs of oleanders bobbed in the breeze, their elongated leaves drooping and whispering. A row of garden lights followed the edge of the lawn. A flock of birds-of-paradise flowers guarded the east wall of the house.

The black sedan parked next to the Field Unit van blinked, and its door locks popped up. In his dark suit and gray tie, the deputy district attorney ambled out of the house, swinging his tattered briefcase in one hand. "Still here, Track?" he said, dispensing a broad smile. No crime scene could ever affect Mr. Udall's ethereal serenity, no matter how gory the details. His jaws were stuck together in a dolphin smirk, which came with the complimentary small eyes—eerily split by thick bifocals—and matching underbite. Worked miracles in the courtroom. He stopped at the bottom of the patio stairs, slid a hand in his pants pocket, and said, "October seems to be the month of murders. Must be a Halloween thing. The rest of my day is packed with meetings, but if you get those warrants to me tonight, I should be able to review and sign them by tomorrow morning. How does that sound?"

"Sounds terrific, Mr. Udall."

He nodded, his drooping cheeks dangling happily along. "Have a good one, Track." He walked to his car, plopped his briefcase in the back seat, and waved. I watched him drive off jingling my car keys, except I was distracted, jingled too hard, and dropped the bunch. As I crouched to retrieve it, my nostrils detected a trace, faintly teetering with the breeze.

The porch was planked in stained redwood and railed with wrought iron rods. The pillars flanking the front steps and supporting the portico were in stucco laid over wood, with plastered Greek motifs at the top and bottom, and ivy plants crawling around them. I brushed my fingers in the fine groove between the stucco base and the wood floor and found a clump of blue fibers stuck beneath a splinter. I pulled it out and brought it to my nose. I smelled plastic, dirt, wood stain, and blood.

Nelson's overused fragrance tickled me from behind. "What'd you find?"

"More evidence." I stood up, reached for an evidence bag in my pocket, and sealed the fibers inside. I handed it to her and said, "Tell Diane there's blood on it. I wanna know what the fibers are made of and whose blood this is."

Nelson crossed her arms and gave me one of her "u-uh" looks. "You buyin' on Friday?" she mewed.

I grinned. "Nope. Chuck's turn. I rang the gong the most on the long shots last week." Cops' favorite hobby: betting booze and coffee at the shooting range.

She raised a thin, skeptical brow and then snatched the evidence bag. "As long as somebody's buyin'," she sang, her voice trailing down the porch stairs.

CHAPTER 10

Sunday, October 12

"My brother is an atheist," Martha Tarantino—Robert's sister—told me, as we sat on opposite sides of a metal desk at the West L.A. police station. She spoke softly, her sentences trailing off, one finger poised in mid-air as if trying to grasp a fleeting thought. "Now, Tammy... I think *she* goes to church." Her eyes wandered to the ceiling, where the silent blades of a fan sliced the light from an open window, the reflection pulsing on the opposite wall. The dullness of a hot Sunday afternoon draped us with hushed conversations and the rhythmical thrumming of a copier at the end the hallway. Over the interview Martha talked of her brother and sister-in-law stubbornly clinging to the present tense, while her knotty hands clenched a crumpled

Kleenex.

"Cordelia will inherit everything, won't she?" she asked at some point, her voice and movements abated by who knows what cocktail of sedatives her thoughtful physician had blessed her with. Cordelia was the Tarantinos' only daughter, currently en route from New York. Nelson had already arranged a meeting with her for the following morning.

After Martha Tarantino left, I studied the field interview cards compiled by the responding officers at the crime scene. The neighbor who initiated the nine-one-one call had found the victims' Labrador roaming in his backyard. He'd rescued the dog as it looked scared, cold, and disheveled. Benedict Canyon, especially the part nestled on the Santa Monica Mountains, is home to bears, coyotes and cougars, and abandoned pets often fall prey of wildlife. After several attempts to contact the Tarantinos, the neighbor worried something might have happened to them while walking their dog the night before.

Of all other neighbors questioned by the responding officers, only one claimed to have heard two shots within the time interval framed by the CC camera. When asked what she did afterwards, the lady shrugged and said she went to bed. Next to a penciled double question mark, the interviewing officer noted, "Witness thought the noise had come from TV downstairs."

I left the West L.A. police station musing over the religious note found by Tamara Tarantino's body, its possible meaning, or lack thereof. Robert Tarantino didn't believe in God, but Huxley did. He was the executive of a big genetic corporation, she worked in a genetic lab. He was dead, she had vanished and her car had turned up at the murder scene.

The squad room on the third floor of Parker Center was

deserted, save for a scent still lingering in the air. I stepped inside and sniffed. Three people were in the vicinity. One was Lieutenant Gomez, but the other two I didn't recognize. I peeked at the LT's door, glimpsed movement through the glass panel, then slumped behind my desk.

A lazy sun poked through the Venetian blinds and drew jagged lines of light and shade on the walls. I spent the rest of the afternoon sucking on a paperclip while writing the warrants and organizing my notes, crime scene floor plans, and logs for the murder book—the blue binder where we record the chronology of every investigation. I flipped through blood spatters, *livor mortis*, spent shells. Not much gore to stare at: no bruises, no cuts, no signs of a struggle. The shooter came, killed, and left. Somebody the victims knew well, a piece of the puzzle that didn't fit in the hate crime picture. Then why leave the religious signature? And what about Huxley's car? The plate number had been dispatched to all patrols in the city.

Don't jump to conclusions.

I closed the binder, wrote "Find missing body" on my notepad, and then drew a box around it. My pen ran out of ink. I swore and started tossing around the jumble of papers, folders, books, a small toolbox I once brought in to fix the washer of my swivel chair—a new seat an expenditure our under-budgeted department couldn't possibly afford—desperately looking for the most obvious thing anybody should have on a desk: a writing tool. Instead, my eyes fell on the Ziploc containing Huxley's yellow T-shirt.

The recollection of an already encountered olfactory trail flashed before me: laundry detergent, air freshener, man cologne, woman perfume. The scratchy odor of the Montecristo cigars I'd spotted on Tarantino's desk imprinted on Huxley's couch.

They knew each other. He sat on her couch, shared a glass of wine, perhaps even her bed. Was it an extramarital affair that cost Robert Tarantino his life? What if Huxley was a jealous lover? She believed the man's heart all for herself and found he regularly had fun with his wife, too. Crimes of passion leave plenty of evidence behind though, not a clean scene like the one at the Tarantino home. And it had been Tamara Tarantino who'd let the killer in.

The door to the lieutenant's office opened and two men filed out. Cops, no doubt, the faces vaguely familiar. Valley Bureau was as far as my memory could go.

One of the two grinned. "Detective Presius!" His memory went farther than mine. He strode to my desk and came to shake my hand. Short, with icy blue eyes, a lower body considerably smaller than the upper one, and more hair than he seemed able to handle.

"Kirk Donoghan," he reminded me, at which I gave a meaningful bob of the head. "And my partner, Jade Krecks."

Kirk and Jade. It sounded just as nice as Starsky and Hutch.

"Detectives Donoghan and Krecks, from the North Hollywood station, just brought in a big fish," Gomez explained, emerging from behind the looming figure of Kirk's partner. "Jeremy T. White."

A respectful silence followed.

I have no problem breaking respectful silences. "Who the hell is Jeremy White?"

Kirk broke into a rattling laughter. "You can't be serious, Presius. *The Mantra Trilogy, Ride to Death, Samantha Young* — Jerry White directed some of the best movies in the biz."

"I don't suppose that's why you guys brought him in, is it?"

I was starting to hate the rattling laughter. The partner replied this time. "We brought him in because he shot a Tate

University professor this morning, ditched his gun—a Sig Sauer P-220—twenty feet away, and then went home and got drunk."

My turn to laugh. "Right. And you found the gun, ran the registration number, got a name and address, and picked him up. I bet now you're gonna tell me this celeb's so dumb he even 'fessed up."

Kirk and tall partner exchanged glances. The partner shrugged, though it looked more like his long neck sunk in his shoulders rather than the other way around. "Yeah... That's—er—correct."

"Look." Kirk no longer found the whole exchange funny. "We have a witness, a student who was at the Tate library at five a.m.: he heard two shots and then a car screeching away. He didn't get a make but swears it was a black sports car. So we grab a couple of blue suits and go to White's mansion. There's a black convertible Mercedes parked in the driveway. I take a peek inside and spot maroon blotches near the gas pedal, there, in plain sight—enough to get a phone warrant. We knock at White's door, and he starts laughing and saying he's been waiting for us all along, that the bastard slept with his wife and deserved to die. Our criminologists are shaking down his modest nine-thousand-square-foot home as we speak. Last I heard they lifted gunpowder residue from the steering wheel of his car. And there's the blood, waiting to be matched to the victim's. White being a big shot and all, we booked him one of your best rooms downstairs." He grinned.

I jacked up an eyebrow. "The big celeb claims the professor slept with his wife?"

Jeez, I'm in the wrong business.

Gomez rubbed his mottled forehead. "He wasn't just *any* professor, Track. He was a Nobel laureate, and quite famous, too."

Even better. All I could come up with were crinkled faces, bald, egg-shaped heads, and thick glasses. Mrs. Movie Director must've had some refined tastes.

Kirk's partner straightened up and recited: "Vic was pronounced DOA at 0653 hours on the premises of the Tate University Campus—building 302—and later identified as Michael J. Conrad, faculty professor and 1989 recipient of the Nobel Prize in Chemistry. Whacked with one to the head and one to the chest."

Kirk made a big show of checking his watch. "Well, I s'pose the lawyer will be here any minute now. And we better go turn in our overtime slips." He flashed one last smile, and his right hand—uninvited to do so—came clapping my back. "We nailed a career case today. That's what I call a slam-dunk. Pleasure to see you, Presius." He stretched out his hand again, then beckoned his partner to the door. Gomez left last with a slight bob of the head.

I closed the murder book on my desk and stared out the window. Downtown had turned into a geometrical maze of glimmering lights, the lives of over three million people humming in the background. My thoughts drifted off. I plucked the jacket from the back of my chair, slid it on, and then froze. Jerry *White*. How common a name is it? Still.

"Hold the elevator!" I yelled on my way out of the squad room.

I saw the ghost of a man through the two-way mirror. Unshaven, wearing a sport tank and shorts, Jerry White bent over the table and buried his face in large hands. I studied him. He had well-proportioned arms, lean and muscular. His fingers laced in graying, longish locks. A dark stubble shaded his jaw, and a tiny earring shone from his right lobe. Despite his unkempt looks, White looked nothing like our usual guests down in Felony, the Jail Division on the first floor of Parker Center. He wasn't covered in obscene tattoos, he didn't glare with spiteful defiance, he didn't rabidly deny any connection to the crime he was being accused of.

"So, he lawyered up, huh?"

Gomez snorted. "What'd you expect?"

It was just the two of us waiting for the lawyer, and a bored watch sergeant flipping through some magazine behind his desk. Starsky and Hutch from North Hollywood whose names I'd already forgotten had been happy to hand the hot potato over to us, as is standard procedure with VIP cases. We stared blankly at the two-sided mirror, our glum faces reflecting off the glass.

I said, "Guess he didn't appreciate the splendor of our facilities. So, what do we know about his vic?"

Gomez rubbed his forehead so hard it turned plum red. "The Nazi professor."

"The who?"

"Michael J. Conrad. A few years ago somebody spray-painted the word NAZI below his office window. Tate played it down as a prank, but our professor had a stigma. It all started when he publicly announced at the Nobel Prize Award ceremony that he was going to donate to Graham's sperm bank."

I frowned. "A sperm bank? For the freaks who think of cum as an investment?"

Gomez sniggered. "I guess you could say so. They called it 'Repository for Germinal Choice.' Robert Klark Graham, an eyeglass business suit, founded it in 1980. The guy had loads of money and a handful of ideas: collect semen from Nobel laureates and 'create' smarter people."

"You're friggin' kiddin' me," the watch sergeant muttered. Gomez ignored him, and the rustling of magazine pages resumed.

"Conrad started giving lectures on the so-called 'selective breeding.' Somebody dubbed it scientific racism: with the excuse of creating a better humanity, he believed only 'genetically advantaged' people should be allowed to have children."

"Genetically advantaged?"

"Brainy people. Nerds."

"And what did he propose to do, castrate the dumbasses? We'd be out of a job!"

"The whole thing blew up. The idea of collecting, quote, high IQ sperm, end quote, made people very edgy. Tate University had to distance itself from Conrad's statements."

I pondered. "And White claims he killed the Nazi professor because he slept with his wife?"

"Ex-wife," Gomez corrected. "They divorced five years ago."

I almost laughed. "Please."

"You wait until the news is out. TV crews are already swarming around White's property like horseflies. This guy's got enough money and persona to make another O.J."

My thoughts were somewhere else. White. Jerry *White*.

"I'd like a word with him."

Gomez's forehead rippled. "He's not talking. He zipped after they patted him down. His lawyer's currently en route from Malibu."

"Then I'll ask for an autograph. I'll give him a Sharpie and have him sign his Sig Sauer."

Gomez sighed. "We went that route, you know? We praised his movies, tried to get him to relax a little and talk about his work. He's tanked a good dose of alcohol, though, and by now he's starting to feel the hangover."

Our reflections in the window laced over White's hunched shoulders.

I placed a hand on the doorknob. "Let me give it a try."

"Track—"

"I'll be the one talking."

Interview rooms are small, uncomfortable, and lit by cold halogens. When the bulbs are at the end of their life and start flickering, nobody bothers replacing them until they're dead. The hypnotic pulse adds to the abrasiveness of the place. You step inside and immediately feel the urge to leave. The walls reek of human sweat and stale air, the kind that makes you unbutton the collar of your shirt, or loosen the knot of your tie.

Every time I step into one of these rooms I remember how it feels to be on the other side.

Once a killer, always a killer.

I chased the memory away and closed the door behind me. White barely raised his head and then dropped it again.

"Hello, Mr. White," I said and introduced myself. I let my hand hang for a few moments, then pulled a chair, and sat in front of him. White didn't move a muscle. I inhaled and tried to read his scent. Old sweat, plastered all over his skin. No gunpowder—he must've showered once he got home. I could still sense remnants of soap and shampoo, now covered by alcohol, a snort of cocaine, and the various odors he'd collected on his way here: police car interiors, the latex gloves that had patted him down, the stale coffee somebody had offered him over the long wait in the interview room.

His skin exuded a bitter smell, not the pungent odor of fear or the sour taste of deception. This guy was lonely and forlorn. What the hell happened to his life?

"How's your child, Mr. White?" I asked. I could've checked before dropping the question. But with the lawyer on his way, I didn't have the time. The ball was rolling and the pins were lined up. He raised his head and glared. His body odor spiked in adrenaline, his receptors sending new signals to the brain, quickly switching from apathy to rage.

"Gaya's dead," he spat.

GN White, I thought, age 8. The mysterious note I'd found on Huxley's desk.

Strike. "My deepest sympathy," I offered, sincerely.

White dropped his chin on the heel of his hands. "You don't give a shit."

Second frame up, ball rolling again. "Did they take good care of her at the Esperanza?"

This time White shot his head up and stared at me for a long time before answering. He had strong eyes, sharp, a first hint of expression lines at the corners. His lips slanted in a sad grimace. He let his arms fall to his sides and sank back in the chair. "What do you think, Detective? They didn't save her life, did they?"

Strike number two. I bobbed my head in sympathy. "I'm truly sorry. I'm sure Dr. Cox and her team tried everything they could."

White flashed a bitter smile. His blue eyes rested on me for a full minute, trying to read me. *You're a fool,* they said, his wound still open. "She didn't save my child, the bitch. All those big doctors care about is their fucking career. They can all go to hell."

And on my third strike, the door opened and the lawyer stepped in, holding his hand up as if to catch in midair any other question that might've escaped my mouth.

There, Dr. Cox. To you and your fucking HIPAA. I now knew who GN White was.

A dome of yellow streetlights projected onto the night sky and embraced a checkerboard of blinking windows. The daily voices of downtown had snoozed down to a mellow drone: the humming of the climate systems gushing out white billows of vapor; the mumbled roar of the Santa Ana freeway; the distant whooshing of a helicopter circling over Echo Park.

I left Parker Center and merged into the One-Oh-One, swallowed by a headless snake of taillights. The hiccupping trail of vehicles was lethargic. I clenched my fists around the steering wheel and seethed. One hour later I landed at the gym, my legs thrashing on the elliptical trainer, resistance and incline set to maximum. I couldn't concentrate, and after fifteen minutes I stepped down and moved to the treadmill. I pounded my legs angrily, thriving on the rhythmic whooshes bouncing off the belt. I closed my eyes and focused on the sounds: feet, heart, lungs, all pulsing at the same rhythm, numbing my thoughts.

It didn't last too long—I was too distracted. I couldn't block the smells of sweat or the squeaking of iPod ear buds around me. Tamara Tarantino's bloodied face kept haunting me.

I pounded harder on the treadmill and kept my eyes on the woman in front of me. I never saw her face, only her perfect body, tight, with proportioned muscles she rhythmically flexed and relaxed. Her taut buttocks swayed up and down as she jogged, their hypnotic movement drawing my eyes like a pendulum. I stared and slowly forgot the dead bodies. I stared, and my thoughts shifted. To *her*, Diane Kyle. She had glared at me with the skepticism of a scientist when I told her the shooter had not entered the house alone. A woman had been there too the night before, waiting downstairs by the French doors. I thought of how Diane's scent, finally freed from the constraint of the forensic coveralls, had aroused my nostrils, tickled and intrigued them on our way out of the house.

Twenty minutes later, I stepped off the treadmill and returned to the locker rooms. I showered, dressed, grabbed my cell phone and dialed.

Hortensia picked up immediately. "I missed you."

Her liquid voice gargled in my ears.

CHAPTER 11

Monday, October 13

The light was too bright. I groaned, rolled over, and sunk my face in the pillow. The ring went off one more time. A sleepy "Hello?" A pause. A drawled "No." Silence, again. *Where the hell am I?* Rugged cotton brushed my face. I inhaled: turpentine, oil paints, charcoal, chalk, and paper. The salty scent of seashells. Catharsis.

I called Hortensia last night.

My brain slowly slid out of lethargy. I flinched. Brightly colored faces stared at me—blue, red, and gold. Black panthers with human eyes and lipless smiles; a tiger whose long body intertwined with that of a turquoise woman languidly seated on a purple sofa; toucans with vibrant feathers, a dolphin diving in a bright green sea. Naked bodies with cone-shaped breasts, large, dopey eyes, and fleshy lips.

I turned the other side and faced Hortensia's pale shoulders, the soft bulges of her spine drawing a sinuous line all the way down to the small of her back. I wrapped my fingers around the nape of her neck, her red hair fanning over the white pillows. "Hort," I mumbled.

"Hmm."

"What time is it?"

"Dunno. Can't read the time on your phone."

I shot up. "You answered *my* phone?" She turned—the hem of the sheets printed on her right cheek—and stared at me aloof, her parted lips an invitation to be devoured all over again.

"You wouldn't answer the damn thing," she scolded, rubbing her eyes. No point in asking why she didn't pass me the phone. Whatever does not concern her, Hortensia does by inertia. When she even bothers.

I reached over to grab the mobile on the nightstand and snapped it open, surfing through the list of calls. *Diane Kyle*, the display informed me. *Damn it.* If sex is a catharsis, love is a catastrophe. I tossed the phone on the pillow and got out of bed, meandering through the stacks of painted canvases piled against the walls.

"Don't step on my paintings!" she growled, pulling the sheets over.

"It'd help if you kept them all in one place!"

I'd met Hortensia years earlier at the opening of one of her exhibitions in Santa Monica. She stood in the middle of the gallery like a Greek goddess, her pearly white face a full moon crowned by red hair. All around her, vividly colored women lay abandoned in their men's arms, watched over by wild animals with disturbingly human eyes. Over cocktails and hors d'oeuvres, she asked me if I'd pose for one of her paintings. I was a street copper at the time, and though flattered, I told her I only posed in uniform. Art has never been my forte, yet that night we both drew and painted, our naked skins the canvas and our lips and fingers the paintbrushes.

Occasional lovers, Hortensia and I never were soul mates. It's one of the constants in my life: skim through relationships like a surfer in rough seas, drifting from one buoy to the next while contemplating my solitude. It fits Hortensia's personality as well, and neither of us ever complained.

"I finished your painting," she told me as I stepped out of the shower.

"*My* painting?"

She padded to the kitchen and a minute later I smelled ground coffee. "The one I dedicated to you," she said. "Check it out, it's the one on the easel. Still thinking about a title."

I walked over to the easel and stared at the painting while towel-drying my hair. A bright red woman with large emerald eyes lay on her side among lush green leaves, an ecstatic look about her face, her nipples and navel dappled with black stars. A cougar hovered from behind, its muzzle wedged between her left shoulder and neck.

"What's the cougar doing?"

"Tasting her."

"Wha—Hort, is this supposed to represent *me*?"

She chuckled, her laughter like water rushing down a creek. "You're a predator, aren't you?"

In the kitchen the coffee pot started gargling its brewing song. I slid on my pants, buttoned my shirt and tucked it into my waistband. The whole time, I kept my eyes glued on the bright red lady with emerald eyes, her smile oblivious to the beast about to banquet on her. *A predator.* I found myself wondering, What does *she* taste like? Diane Kyle. Not in the way Hortensia meant. In a very different way. I closed my eyes, saw Diane's neckline, and felt the urge to brush the tip of my tongue along her skin. Skim it down, sink in the secluded notch at the base of her throat, inhale her scent, and then lick my way up. To her lips. What would she taste like, I wondered.

You are a predator. Aren't you?

I returned Diane's call on my way to work. She informed me she had gathered a task force of experts from Trace, Photography, and Firearms, and she'd have some preliminary results for me the following day. Given how slow the scientific division had been in the past, I poured my enthusiasm over the news. My next call was from Satish, who whined about aches and soreness for a good five minutes and then told me the doc had just given him a slap on the back and the all-clear to return to full duty. He was eager to get started on the Tarantino double murder, except I had different plans.

"There's Jerry White's bail hearing at ten. I can't go, but I thought you might—"

"Track," he interjected. "You know how we roll in the LAPD. Experience before beauty. The bullet took a chunk of my lung, not the twelve years I got on you."

I rolled my eyes. "And that's why *you* should be talking to Gomez. Let me make a goddamn decision for once, 'kay? I want the White case."

Silence.

"Did you just say *Jerry* White?"

"That's what I said."

I heard the sound of synapses crackling through his

brain. "At ten in court. Will keep you posted." And with that, he hung up.

Once at Parker Center, I met briefly with Cordelia, the Tarantinos' daughter, a shaky twenty-year-old with brittle blonde hair and round, watery eyes. Through repressed sobs, the girl divulged the hardship of her first two years at Columbia, and how this tragedy was surely going to affect her grades. At least she had Tracy left—the yellow Labrador—and not all family was lost. Despite conducting the interview in one of the cubicles at the back of the squad room, when I saw her back to the elevator lobby I read it on the other detectives' faces that her shrieks had been widely appreciated by the whole homicide table.

A detective from Homicide II shook his head and mumbled, "If there's an afterlife, those two poor souls of her parents must be heart-warmed to see how concerned their daughter is that we catch their killer."

His partner nudged him. "Don't be too negative, Roy. The kiddo didn't even ask how much she inherited."

I snorted. "Course not. She saved that question for her accountant."

I found a note from Nelson on my desk. It read: "Guess where the Tarantinos were the night they got murdered? Dan Horowitz's mansion." A string of five exclamation points followed.

Famous showman, singer and entertainer, occasionally improvised producer and even screenwriter, Dan H. Horowitz was one of those rich people who could afford to do anything, including publishing books. He owned a mansion in Bel Air where he hosted chums and foes alike so he could show off his two Ferraris, fine wines in his cellar, and an artificially rejuvenated wife. Last Saturday night the official excuse to dance and have fun was his daughter's sixth birthday. Together with half of Hollywood, the list of partygoers included a good portion of L.A.'s lawyers and plastic surgeons, who, altogether, represented the showbiz's warranty for a golden retirement. The reason escaped me, but it appeared that the Chromo CEO and executives had been among the privileged invitees as well.

I thought of what Diane had said: *Whoever wanted them dead, knew how to get them at a vulnerable time.* A party at the Horowitz residence could have easily reached over one hundred people. If the Tarantinos had been smooching all night, anybody could've guessed what their plans for the rest of the night were.

I spent the rest of the morning hunched over one of our terminals. On Jerry White's Wikipedia page I found a link to the daughter's obituary: Gaya Nicole White, October 19, 1999—January 3, 2008. She died at age eight, after a nine-month-long ordeal of chemotherapy and hospital stays. A battle lost to leukemia.

Former Mrs. White, British-born actress Hannah Kelson, married Jerry White in 1986. Rumors that the couple was expecting a child made their appearance in the tabloids in 1993, but it wasn't until 1999 that the family actually expanded. I looked at the pictures posted on the web: a beautiful little girl, blonde, with large blue eyes. The disease was diagnosed in March 2007, and by then the cancer was already at an advanced stage. From the beginning there was little hope to save Gaya.

Whether or not he was a murderer, and whatever his motive, just staring at the child's blue eyes put White under a completely new light. A lot of things didn't quite add up, though: his wife and he had been divorced for five years now, and according to the various press releases, the separation had been consensual. No hard feelings on either side. I searched under the words "Kelson," "Conrad," and "affair," but nothing came up, not even in the pettiest tabloids.

On the other hand, I found a wealth of information under Michael J. Conrad: there were countless articles on his eugenics statements backing up Graham's sperm bank. After receiving the Nobel prize in 1989, the biochemistry professor became an advocate for selective breeding, giving talks and "raising awareness," if one could call it so. None of this was mentioned on the Tate University website. Instead, the institution praised Conrad's academic achievements, lauding the research that led to the Nobel recognition, the discovery of some important biochemical reaction—nothing to do with genetics. His passion for the DNA code and the possible ways of manipulating it dawned on him a few years later. He wrote editorials on how the human race was bound to see a decline in intelligence and only selective breeding could counteract it. Such statements fomented hatred and indignation among the public. People accused him of echoing Hitler and the Nazis. In 1996, at the peak of the debate, Tate University issued several statements in which the institution distanced itself from Conrad's views. That same year, Conrad left Tate for two semesters. "Personal leave," the university website claimed.

I mused over White and his ex-wife. Whether or not there had been a relationship between Conrad and Hannah Kelson, why would it incite a murderous rage *now*, after the divorce had long been settled? What was it to White, if his ex-wife slept with a sixty-three-year old professor? The director was likely under a lot of stress from the loss of his child. It had been over six months already, though. And the typical pattern in these scenarios saw the violence reverberate in the family. It would have been more predictable if White had shot his ex-wife instead. The more I thought about it, the less sense it made.

Detective Roy and his chatty partner walked past my

computer station and out of the room, packs of cigarettes bulging from their pockets. Nicotine and caffeine, the only drugs one could legally abuse on the job. I followed their scents as they trailed out of the room, took a turn around the corner, swirled down the west wing, and drifted into the elevator lobby, soon replaced by a whiff of cheap aftershave. An annoyed look hanging from his pimpled face, Luke trotted into the squad room and slammed a piece of paper in Gomez's inbox.

"Gomez is at White's bail hearing, Luke," I said. "What'd you leave him?"

He stopped and shot me a deep scowl. "The key to solve Conrad's murder. Our line hasn't been this hot in months. Forty-six tips—psychics, tarot readers, devout students who talked to the deceased's soul—and twelve anonymous confessions in the past twenty-four hours alone, all twelve claiming the victim was a racist and the world will be better off without him. Now if you'll excuse me, I think I hear the phone ringing again."

I mulled a few minutes longer, tapping a pen on my notebook. *The hearing should be over by now.* I reached the phone and dialed Satish's number.

"What do you think of deputy district attorney Mark Auerbach, Track?" he asked. There was half a teaspoon of sour in his cocoa butter voice. From the vociferous background I guessed he'd just stepped out of the D.A.'s office.

I pondered the question. "His eyes are set too deep and too far apart in his forehead to convey intelligence," I replied. "He's an asshole." A large head grown atop a thick bush of rusty-gray beard, Mr. Auerbach loved to boss cops around and made it a point to always find a flaw in the cases we presented. If he didn't have a one hundred percent certainty he was going to win the case, he didn't bother.

"People are like wine, Track. Some age to be a Barolo, and some end up vinegar. Just watch what's in your salad."

"I hate salad. I'm a shameless carnivore."

A sound between a snort and a grunt came out of his throat. "Auerbach dismissed the search warrants to White's house and vehicles, slammed the new hire who signed them, and told Gomez that without any compelling evidence linking White to Conrad we have no case." Satish heaved a sigh. As he walked out of the court, the loud conversations in the background were replaced by the growl of street traffic. "So, basically, we're on a quest for motive."

"We?"

The sour vanished from his voice. "I spoke to Gomez, Track. You wanted the case, and we got the case."

"Excellent!"

Huxley, Tarantino, Conrad, and White: I didn't know how or why, but something told me they were like dominoes lined one after the next. The first fell and the rest followed.

"My client is an award winning member of the Director Guild of America," Satish said, mocking White's lawyer. "And that asshole of Auerbach drank it all."

Traffic was steady on the One-Oh-One northbound. Most vehicles at this time of the day were coming into town, not getting out of it.

"You know what this reminds me, Track?"

"What does it remind you?"

"Of mangoes."

"Mangoes?"

"Yes, sir. Sweet, ripe mangoes."

"Mangoes," I repeated.

"See, my old man wasn't very fond of those. *They smell*

like a woman's breast, and one don't eat a woman's breast, he'd say. Ma was from the western coast of India. Every July through late August, she'd get the mango frenzy. She'd buy boxes of them, fill up the car, bring them home, and line them up on the back porch. She'd use the green ones to make chutney. With the ripe ones she'd make mango *lassi* and *mambazha kaalan*. The rest she sliced and let dry in the sun. We called it the mango season.

"One of those frenzied mango days, it was just Pa and me at home. *Don't forget to bring the hapoos inside if the weather gets nasty*, Ma said on her way out. She used to call them *hapoos*. *It's July, baby*, my old man replied. *It's July*.

"So I sit on the doorstep to the backdoor and watch. I let my toy car climb up and down the stairs. The wind picks up. A few leaves from the old elm tree in the backyard blow in my face. *Vroom, vroom*, I go. Gray clouds appear in the sky and rush forward. My engine keeps roaring. *Vroom, vroom*. The clouds billow, whirl, and accumulate. They turn black. The trees by the fence whine. My engine stops. The sky is a shroud of black. *It's gonna rain, Pa*, I say. *It's July, pumpkin*, he replies. He rocks on his chair and reads the paper. A drop as big as a bumblebee falls on my nose. Another one on my knee. And then another, and another. Some drops aren't really drops, they're rocks, and they start speckling the backyard. They bounce on the grass, hit the fence, smash the ripe *hapoos*.

"*It's hailing, Pa*, I yell. *It's July, pumpkin*, he replies. I look up at the sky and think, *They're missiles*. I drop the car and pretend our yard is under bombardment. *Wheeeeew boom*." Satish sucked in his lower lip and whistled, his closed fist mimicking the trajectory of the missiles hailing down the sky.

I chuckled. "And then your father got another bombardment when your mother returned?" I took the

Vineland exit and proceeded north. The first fraternity and sorority houses appeared on the right, empty beer cans sprawled all over the overgrown lawns.

"Ma was mad. The *hapoos* were lookin' no good! You wanna know what she did with the smashed *hapoos*? She worked day and night for three days and made *moramba*. Jars and jars of *moramba*, all lined up against the walls in the kitchen." His hand swept an arch in the air, brushing the imaginary stacks of jars. "They lasted the whole year. She invented new dishes to use all the *moramba* she'd made: she'd put it on sticky rice for breakfast; she'd use it to marinate the chicken for lunch; she'd simmer the spinach in it for dinner. And my old man ate it all. Not once did he complain. *It was July*, he'd say through each meal. And ate it all."

I parked on Camarillo, got out of the car and locked it. Satish stepped on the sidewalk, shoved a hand in his pocket, and ambled toward the campus entrance.

"Wait," I protested. "What's the moral of the story?"

He frowned. "The moral?"

"Yeah. You said what happened in court today reminded you of mangoes."

"The moral," he said, shaking his head sideways. "Always looking for a moral. People make choices in life. Sometimes they make the right ones, some other times they screw up and make the wrong ones. That day my old man decided it was July and the weather was gonna be fine. He made a choice. But then, he held his chin up and paid the consequences: he ate *moramba* for twelve months. I mean the man grew up on fried pork, roasted corncobs and sweet potatoes. And he hated mangoes. Take this celeb, Jerry White. A spoiled son of a bitch. Blows up, takes his gun, kills a man. And then calls his lawyer to come and fish him out of the shit. You better keep your balance, if you choose to shit in the field. That's what my old man used to say. And if you fall, get up and wipe your ass."

A clique of garrulous young ladies passed us, as cheerful and colorful as a flock of lovebirds. In high heels and low waists, they padded along the red brick sidewalk, love handles wobbling, and a generous cleavage spilling out of their skimpy tops. The air around them was saturated with gossip, giggles, and pheromones.

"Man," I said. "Fifteen years ago I would've found the spectacle attractive."

"Ah, you're aging, Track. To them, it still is attractive." Satish pointed to the pimpled lad who, distracted by the Three Graces ahead of us, almost ran over a fire hydrant with his bicycle. We had a meeting with Professor Anthony Troy, former student and colleague of Michael Conrad, at the university café near the School of Engineering. The place was buzzing with life: skinny students in baggy T-shirts rattled by on bicycles; freshmen flip-flopped from one building to the other while complaining about midterms; a colorful Indian family proudly escorted their nervous son to his doctoral defense. All around me, I recognized the smells of my college years: hot dogs, barbeque sauce, Irish beer, joints, overuse of cheap deodorant, sweaty bed sheets, and condoms. Girls, lots of them, most forgotten, save a first name, a pair of breasts and a set of lips still lingering in my memory—whether or not they had belonged to the same gal though, I couldn't recall.

Professor Troy sat at a table outside the café, absorbed in his reading. The spot was beautiful, shaded by magnolia trees and surrounded by historic buildings that exuded stories of intellect, academic achievement, and plain geeky-ness.

"I hear you already have a suspect," Troy said, as we shook hands.

"The case is far from closed, Professor," Satish replied, bitterly. Even with the kind of evidence we had, without a motive, our grounds were shaky.

We dragged a couple of chairs over and sat at his table.

Troy bobbed his head, his green eyes clouded with grief. "Michael Conrad will be greatly missed." He ran a hand through his wispy comb-over, then rested it on his protruding stomach. "The scientific community lost a great mind. I can't tell you how deeply this event touches me." His voice broke. He dropped his chin and stared intently at the gourd sitting in front of him.

"You drink *maté*," Satish noted.

Troy smiled. "An old addiction of mine."

"How well did you know Conrad, Professor Troy?"

"I met him in 1975, when I came here as a graduate student and he was a young professor. Always been brilliant: he became professor at age twenty-nine. He was my advisor through 1981. I left Tate after I graduated, but I'd still see him maybe two or three times a year at conferences and meetings."

"Did you keep working together?"

"No, not really. We resumed when I came back to Tate, in 1991. We published something like thirty papers together since then."

"On genetics?" I asked.

Troy shook his head. "No, actually genetics wasn't Michael's field—nor mine, as a matter of fact—even though he was often mistaken for a geneticist because of his opinions. Some people revered him as an expert in the field, people who found his positions convenient for their own purposes."

"What's your field, then?"

He gave out a shrill, nasal laugh like the whinny of a horse. "I'm a jack-of-all-trades, Detective. I know a little bit of everything, which often translates into knowing nothing at all. That's the true spirit of science, though, isn't it?"

"I wouldn't know, Professor," I said.

"Who would find Conrad's opinions convenient rather than controversial?" Satish asked.

Troy wrapped his fingers around the gourd. "After he received the Nobel Prize in 1989 and publicly announced he had donated to Graham's sperm bank, Michael became the target of many biotech corporations. They all wanted him: it was good publicity to have him on their side. Here's a famous, intelligent man, who not only backs up selective breeding—he actually advocates a scientific way of perfecting our genes. Michael started doing his own research in the field around that time. He had the money and people willing to provide him with the means."

I perched my chin in the L between my thumb and index finger and smiled placidly. The man could've talked for hours and I would've listened for hours. He had a nice intonation to his voice and a well-rehearsed rhythm, which accommodated calibrated pauses and sensible punctuation. I pictured him in front of a blackboard filled with diagrams and formulae, while intently captivating the curious minds of the first two rows of devoted students. Farther back, hidden by unruly hair and torn jeans, the other rows busied themselves text-messaging, finishing the homework for the next class, downloading podcasts, and catching up on hours of missed sleep.

Satish leaned forward on his elbows and laced his hands together. "Who was willing to provide Conrad the means?"

"Michael could afford being picky. Small, big, rich and poor—they all wanted him. In the end, he chose a fairly unknown company later to become famous: Exgene Solutions."

I frowned. "I've never heard of it."

Troy smiled. "No, Detective. As I said, it was small at the time. Two years later it merged with Novine, and the new corporation was re-named Chromo."

Ha. Chromo and Conrad. Conrad and Chromo. The name Chromo ends on a sticky note together with Gaya White's name. The person who wrote the note vanishes. White kills Conrad the morning after a Chromo executive is assassinated with his wife. The perfect riddle: you know there has to be a connection and yet you're missing the clues to find it.

"What did the company offer Conrad?"

"Access to a genetics lab, for one thing. Paid consultations. He gave public lectures on Chromo's behalf, advertising the corporation's services. At some point, he got so busy he took a sabbatical from Tate University. He said he didn't have time to teach. I suspect it was retaliation because Tate didn't back him up in his public opinions. In the end, though, Michael was not made for the private sector. He missed his students. He came back to Tate one year later and, in 1999, when Graham's sperm bank closed, he announced he was leaving Chromo for good."

"Was it the end of the genetics euphoria?"

"He kept defending his ideas. But he definitely retired from the public eye."

"And you said he never published anything in genetics? What kind of research was he conducting in those labs then?"

Troy shrugged, an airy expression painted on his face. "He was playing with ideas, mostly. But for Chromo, it was all publicity."

"What about Conrad's personal life?" Satish asked. "He was married briefly from 1977 to 1981 and never re-married. Do you know if he was ever in any important relationship after that?"

Troy brought the straw of the gourd to his lips and sipped thoughtfully for a few moments. "You know, he was very private about his personal life," he said. "And very intense on the job. I can see how he wouldn't leave much room for anything else."

Satish raised a brow. "He human, ain't he? Suppose a beautiful woman approached him—"

"A beautiful woman, Detective? Have you seen pictures of Michael? And the way he acted and spoke... He was quite a self-centered man."

"Suppose it did happen, though," I insisted, backing up Satish. "Somebody who maybe wasn't as charmed by his physical appearance as by his ideas. You said it yourself: he was in the public eye for a while, plenty of chances to make new acquaintances. Wasn't the sperm bank supposed to attract interested ladies in the fertile years of their lives?" Which meant, ovulating women who embraced Conrad's ideas, possibly with a dysfunctional husband or no partner at all.

Troy frowned. "You know, come to think of it... There was a name, but it was only a name, mind you, which came up in a few conversations a few years ago. I think it was the summer of 2004... But it sounded like a platonic thing..."

"Whatever it was. Do you remember the name?"

"Hannah. If there was a last name, he never mentioned it."

Satish and I exchanged a glance full of unspoken meaning. Could've been a coincidence, but Hannah was indeed former Mrs. White's first name.

CHAPTER 12

Tuesday, October 14

Rhesus's car gives a jolt. Another fucking hole, *he thinks, the ruts in the road making the wheels skid. The sky is black, dawn procrastinating its appearance. Hidden in the brush, swallows break into a contentious litany of tweets and chirps. Rhesus sinks back in the driver's seat, one hand on the steering wheel and the other on the gearshift. The air is humid, he notices, as it careens through the open windows. It doesn't conceal the odor permeating his clothes.*

The road comes to an end. Wispy tamarisk shrubs scribble fringes of black in the feeble light. Rhesus parks and gets out of the car. He feels a thrill of anticipation as he walks to the back and pops the trunk. The stench is so strong it makes him falter. His eyes burn, his throat itches with the urge to vomit. It's only a moment, though.

Control.

Rhesus thrives on control.

Under the lights of the trunk, his prey lies defeated in front of him. Imperfect, he realizes, staring at the ill aimed shot in the shoulder. Nothing like his second job. He outdid himself there — he got it all, the excitement of the kill, the blast of the shot, the inebriating scent of blood and gunpowder. And then the anger at her for prompting him to leave quickly, no time to stay, admire his masterpiece, and collect his prize.

His nostrils are now immune to the reek of death, his eyes adjusted to the sight. Under the light, a golden cross glimmers on a chain around her neck. Rhesus stretches his hand but then changes his mind.

No. Too flashy. Something else. Something less conspicuous.

A quick movement through the prey's hair makes him wince. A moth flutters on her forehead, crosses her eyelids, then creeps down to her ear. That's when he sees it. Perfect, he thinks. He bends over the body and snaps off one earring.

A theater of shadows, the sky slowly lights up. The swallows' garrulous chirps ebb off. Rhesus wipes his sweaty face with the sleeve of his shirt.

Damned fucking job, she made me do. It's okay. It's over. It's my prize.

Rhesus walks down the road, his boots crunching the gravel. The reds die into yellows and whites, and a grainy veil of haze sets over the valley.

You did good, *Rhesus thinks.* You did damn good.

CHAPTER 13

Tuesday, October 14

The Santa Ana winds that had swept through Southern California for the week had finally subsided. Temperatures dropped, and the moisture seeping inland from the ocean cloaked Los Angeles in a blanket of fog. We were eastbound on the Ten, the overcast sky mottled with skinny palm treetops. Telephone and electrical wires hung in the haze like lone spider threads. This part of the freeway was just cement, billboards, and wired fences—a few eucalyptuses thrown in the mix to distract the eye from the gray.

Behind the wheel, heedless to traffic, weather, and any other earthly concern, Satish whistled to the tune of *What a Wonderful World*. I rapped my knuckles against the car window and grunted. Satish ignored me.

"Sat," I muttered. Again, he ignored me. "Hell, Sat, will you cut it out?" I bristled.

He hung his face in a callow grimace, shook his head sideways, and quit whistling. A few seconds later he was drumming the tune on the steering wheel. What put him in such a good mood escaped me.

We'd spent the first half of the morning at the coroner's office, where a medical assistant had pulled the Tarantinos' dead bodies out of the refrigerated vault so their daughter could see them one last time. The morgue's chills were still biting into my bones, and Satish's good mood irritated me.

Wonderful world my ass.

The day had started with all major headlines dishing out on the LAPD for *unreasonably* booking Hollywood genius Jerry White. The atmosphere at Parker Center was jittery, and the LAPD brass edgy. Our captain had muttered a few sympathetic words in the squad room, before disappearing in the safe haven of his office. The commander in chief had nixed any comment to the press. The veterans in our squad—the few detectives who'd survived the wave of transfers and *encouraged* retirements following the O.J. case in 1995—expressed their ominous presages with the dark joke: "Get ready for another major housecleaning. You guys better polish those resumes."

In spite all this, Satish hummed his favorite song and I seethed. We took the North Eastern exit ramp and landed in the Cal State L.A. campus.

Inaugurated in May 2007, the Hertzberg-Davis Forensic Science Center fostered the new headquarters of the Scientific Division. It was a boxy, red and gray building, with rows of blue windows and a crest of metal eaves that hung along the southern edge of the roof like a long, misplaced aileron. Everything inside was polished, sleek, and had the artificial and expensive smell of new. The building thrived with noises: heels clacking on shiny black tiles, fingers tapping on keyboards, laughter reverberating down the hallway. A pale disk of sunshine peeked through the haze and bathed the offices. It wasn't Mount Olympus, yet here, three miles away from the morgue, it felt like we'd finally resurfaced from Hades.

"Where did you find the fingernail fragment again, Track?" Diane asked as our steps resonated through the corridors.

"It was stuck on the curtain by the French doors in the living room. Tell me our suspect had the bad habit of biting her nails." Saliva on the nail fragment meant traces of DNA.

She laughed, her smile sweeping away the last crumbs of gloom. "No, it wasn't the case." She unlocked the doors to one of the conference rooms and ushered us inside. "Besides, it wasn't anywhere close to the crime scene. Anybody could have left it."

"Did you analyze the fragment just the same?" I remembered the face she'd made at the crime scene when I told her the fingernail stub belonged to a woman who'd been there the night of the shooting. I could still read disbelief in her eyes.

"I did," she confirmed. "But first, let me tell you what we got from the other labs."

Diane was wearing a lab coat today, which typically reeks of chemical reagents and chloride. Not on her, though. Anything smelled good on her, the air around her hoisting the tiny particles emanated by her skin, cradling them all the way to my nostrils. We sat around a large, oval table that still retained the traces of aftershave, coffee, and deodorant of its previous occupants. Diane arranged several photos on the center of the laminated surface, including three transparent evidence bags containing respectively the fingernail stub, the clump of blue fibers I'd found on front porch, and the bloody note with the first commandment.

"We'll have to wait for the fingerprint results. Latent Print is understaffed and backed-up." She sat at the edge of the chair and bent closer to pick up a folder labeled "Trace Unit." Her white neckline flashed before my eyes, and a whiff of her hair tickled my nostrils. Tinged with a hint of nervousness her scent was baffling and delicious at the same time.

I reluctantly leaned back to let her retrieve the folder.

"I had the guys at Trace look over the fibers you found on the porch outside, Track. You were right about the blood: it matched Tamara Tarantino's type. I sent it to serology for DNA to make sure."

"Good call. What are the fibers made of?"

She opened the folder and showed me a printed report on the physical, optical, and chemical analyses run on the piece.

"High-density polyethylene film," I read.

"The fibers are about one tenth of a human hair in diameter," Diane explained. "They're not woven but flash-spun together." She tapped her pen. "It's Tyvek."

My hands flattened on the table. "Tyvek?"

Satish snorted. "Well, that explains the blood."

Diane's voice switched to defensive. "We've done everything by SOP, and our coveralls are tear-free."

"All our Tyvek coveralls are white," I said. "Those fibers had to come from shoe covers."

"Shoe covers? Are you thinking our guys or the perp?" Satish frowned.

"Why not the perp? It would explain why the dust lifter didn't pick up anything."

"A perp so mindful as to slip on shoe covers before shooting? That would be a first."

"Coveralls and shoe covers are not the only things made

out of Tyvek," Diane objected. "It's used to make house wrap, car covers, medical packaging, and protective clothing for surgeons, mechanics, and painters."

Satish folded his arms across his chest and tapped an index against his elbow. "Did the Tarantinos have any work done on their house lately?"

"We'll have to look into that," I agreed. "Same question for their vehicles. I spotted a couple in the garage and one in the driveway."

"How many hours' worth of recording do we have from the camera at the gate?"

"It goes a few days back. I already requested Electronics to provide freeze-frames of all cars coming and going."

Diane waited quietly as Satish and I considered several hypotheses and jotted down notes—additional people to interview and possible strategies to use—before moving on to the blood spatter analyses. From the traces found on the scene, she nailed the shooter's position at a thirty-degree angle from the bathroom door.

"And yet the guy didn't leave any prints on the door frame?" I asked.

"This guy ain't no stupid," Satish muttered. "He gloved up and left no trace."

"Except for the note," Diane reminded us.

"Which was left by his lady accomplice," I declared. Yes, I do enjoy a bit of theater whenever I get the chance. At my audience's bewildered glare I added, "Together with the fingernail fragment down in the living room."

Diane tilted her head. "How can you be so sure it belonged to a woman, Track?"

Smells and their elusiveness. Can you put a signature on a scent? Can you stamp it with a date and time? And yet I knew without doubt. It wasn't just a fingernail stub—it was a fragrance left on the curtains and materialized into an image in my head: a woman, callously looking out the glass doors, waiting. Was she Atropos, ready to cut the thread of life? Or was she Clotho instead, holding the spindle and pulling the thread farther?

I grinned, unfazed by Diane's skepticism. "I be right about the lady, ain't I?"

Satish shook his head and pinched the bridge of his nose. "Help us God if he's not."

I felt Diane's tension ease. A smile escaped her lips. "He probably is, Satish," she replied, reaching for a new photo to show us.

"Probably?" I protested.

Perhaps amused by the playful tone our conversation had taken, Diane's shoulders relaxed, and the tension I'd sensed earlier evaporated like a sprinkle in high deserts.

"I found traces of cyanoacrilate and acrylic resins on the fragment," she said, flipping a couple of photos in front of us. "I placed it between two glass slides and stuck it under a microscope. And this is what I saw."

She tapped the picture, a black and white enlargement of what looked like a stack of misshapen phyllo dough layers.

"When do we get to the part where you say I was right?"

Diane flashed me a broad, conspiratorial smile. "After you hear how clever *I* was."

I hate to get sentimental, but that sly smile of hers left a dent in my cool.

"Ah, you've got competition, Track. Please enlighten us," Satish said.

"Cyanoacrilate is a fast-acting glue," Diane explained. "At first I thought of an electrician, as it can be used to assemble small electronics. It can also be employed in hospitals to substitute sutures. The presence of acrylic baffled me, though. Until I thought of the perfect combination of both: nail glue and artificial nails, which are made of acrylic."

"Ha. A woman, then. However, Tamara Tarantino or the cleaning lady could've left the fragment," Satish interjected, playing devil's advocate.

"No," Diane replied. "Neither woman suffered from biotin deficiency."

"What the hell is that?"

"A vitamin. Biotin deficiency causes nails to grow in a pointy fashion and to be brittle and thin. As a consequence, they break off very easily. It's exactly what I saw when I put this nail fragment under the microscope."

I drummed my fingers on the table. "Malnutrition?"

Diane shook her head, the swaying tips of her hair sending delicious wafts to my nostrils. "I doubt it. Biotin is commonly found in most foods. You would have to be on a pathological diet not to be getting enough from food, in which case it would be a whole range of vitamins and nutrients one would be missing."

"Any other hypothesis, then?"

It was Diane's turn to throw in her very own *coup de théâtre*. "Only one," she said, her eyes sparkling with intrigue. "Anticonvulsants. Our lady is epileptic."

CHAPTER 14

Tuesday, October 14

"Ding, ding, ding! Signed warrants for Detective Presius!" Luke scuttled across the squad room waving the papers above his head. He flopped them on my desk and stood right there, a sheepish grin plastered on his face.

"What?" I growled.

He frowned. "Gee, Track. What an asshole. I don't mean a thank you, but at least a sign of appreciation for my new aftershave!"

"Oh," I said, snapping closed the murder book I'd just updated with the new photos and reports from Diane. "This one's okay. It's the bad ones I notice. Are the lines still hot?"

"Course they're hot," he griped. "Now that White's name's out, calls come in two groups. Those who claim the director's a saint, and those who grieve the loss of the professor. In the meantime, journalists are harassing the press relation department." He trotted out of the squad room shaking his head and muttering between his teeth, "I hate celebrities."

I gestured to Satish to come over. "Call Electronics," I told him as I reviewed the warrants Luke had just dropped off. "We need their gurus to come seize Tarantino's computer."

He nodded, reaching for his mobile. "The neighbors don't recall any work done on the house in the past three months," he informed me. "Did you get phone subpoenas as well?"

I got up, adjusted my belt and holster, and slid on my jacket. "Yup. I'll leave them with Nelson. She can take care of that part."

"I'll meet you at Chromo, then," Satish said, sauntering away while thumbing the Electronics extension.

I had Nelson sit at my desk and lectured her on how to get the Tarantinos' phone logs and what to look for: any business number she found, she was to call them back and learn what kind of services they provided. We were after house updates—walls, exterior stucco, insulation—and car jobs. She listened carefully, then looked up at me with large fawn eyes and said, "I have a question, Track."

"Shoot."

"When I'm done with my gum, can I stick it under your desk?"

I threw a paperclip at her. On the way down to the first floor my cell phone rang and Diane's number flashed on the display. "You're going to Chromo without me?"

I stiffened, taken aback by her bluntness. "We figured we'd need Electronics—"

"What about Prints? Did you forget I'm the scientific

lead on this investigation? Come pick me up at Cal State. I'll gather my stuff and meet you at the parking lot."

I hung up wondering whether to let a deliciously smelling lady boss me around like that. *Hell, yes.* I flipped the phone closed and grinned. Like an idiot, I grinned.

The campus of Chromo Inc. was located in Century City, a half-hour drive that was going to take us twice as long, courtesy of afternoon traffic. Sluggish, the radio defined the current status of the Ten. They say Eskimos have about fifty words to characterize snow and ice. Californians have just as many to describe congested traffic conditions.

Bathed in Diane's ambrosial scent, I couldn't care less. We spent the time going over Chromo's specs and Tarantino's job overview. Diane listed the company's services like my grandmother would've gone through the beads of a rosary: gene expression profiling, gene therapy, genetic engineering, DNA and RNA sequencing. From Nelson's searches I'd learned Robert Tarantino got his B.S. from Penn State in 1975, and his Ph.D. in chemistry from Tate University in 1980, the same institution that six years earlier had hired the rising genius of Michael Conrad. The connection didn't end there: when Exgene Solutions hired Conrad in 1996, Tarantino was already a promising engineer with the company.

"You think the Tarantino murders and Conrad's are linked?" Diane asked.

"Worth looking into."

Past the sign announcing the Four-Oh-Five junction in three quarters of a mile, I hit the brakes and entered the bumper-to-bumper zone the radio had warned us about.

"Damn it. We should've gotten off on Overland."

"I'll never get used to this," Diane said. "Where I grew

up it's either the train or cattle crossing the street ruining the commute."

"What do they call bumper-to-bumper traffic there, round-to-chuck?"

"Aw, Track!"

We both laughed and put an end to the strictly work conversation. We spent the rest of the drive challenging one another on who remembered the most idioms Southern Californian radio stations use to describe traffic conditions. And when we exhausted all the ones we could recall, we invented new ones.

Shaped like a sail, the façade of the Chromo building was made of sleek blue metal and tinted glass panels. Its contour embraced an open court paved in red bricks. Brass plates engraved with milestone in the history of genetics drew a path to the main entrance. Water jets splashed along the edges of a circular water fountain, while at its center, in a copper-colored mesh, stood the artistic rendition of two gigantic X chromosomes, one the mirroring image of the other. Stripped of all its sensuality, it was the bare essential of femininity.

As we climbed out of the car, a funky song from the '80s chimed, muffled at first, until Diane, frantically fumbling in her bag, produced her loud mobile. In the frenzy to get the call, she lost the grip on the phone and sent it flying between my feet. I crouched, picked it up, and mentally noted the number on the display before handing it to her.

It's called occupational hazard.

"It's Jim," she mumbled, pressing the phone to her ear. I heard her mellow "Hey, hon," as I trudged toward the main entrance without bothering to check whether she followed inside or lagged behind to take the call privately. Pretending not to be bothered by the existence of Diane's boyfriend, I entered the Chromo building.

The high vaulted lobby smelled of new construction, synthetic fibers from the overly vacuumed carpet, paint, wood cleaner, and a cornucopia of perfumes and aftershaves. The glass effigy of a DNA double helix loomed in the middle of the hall, a twisted ladder that crossed the space from floor to ceiling. Sunrays from tall windowpanes shimmered along the beads bridging the two coils, their shadows drawing rainbows on the opposite walls.

Chromo knew how to make an impression on its visitors.

"Second floor, room two-forty-nine," the receptionist told me. "Your colleagues are there already." Watery eyes enlarged by thick, convex lenses gazed at me with maternal love. "This is such a tragedy," she added softly, shaking her head. Her white, static locks smelled of hairspray, the folds of her neck of talcum powder. Juliet Hennessy, I read on the nameplate on the reception desk.

Two pens lined next to a sign-in clipboard, a bowl full of sugar-free candy, hand-sanitizer, a floor map: Juliet Hennessy thrived on details, the kind of person who plucks a hair off your shirt when she spots one and tells you when you are due for a new haircut; who notices every new hairdo and pair of shoes stepping through the main entrance to her reign, and doesn't mind letting you know what she thinks of them.

I reached to my pocket and held out an enlargement of Jennifer Huxley's driver's license photo. "Do you remember ever seeing this woman here, Ms. Hennessy?" I asked. "Maybe looking for Dr. Tarantino?"

She adjusted the glasses on her nose and brought the picture so close to her face a film of condensation appeared on the glossy surface. "This woman? No." She shook her head and handed back the photo.

"Are you absolutely sure?"

Her eyes sparkled. "With all the people coming and going, Detective? Of course I could be wrong. But if the lady ever was here, I can tell you the one person who will know for sure."

Ms. Hennessy directed me to Human Resources, a maze of cubicles with nametags on the second floor.

"Nah, never seen her," I was told at the public relation desk. A tattooed hand with black nails returned Huxley's photo.

"Does the name Jennifer Huxley ring a bell? Did she ever call?"

"Huxley, you said?" a shrill voice asked.

"Yes. Do you recognize the name?" I prodded. A tiny woman with hair too black for her age approached the counter. Her purple frill top was as tacky as a joke on a candy wrap. She took the picture and studied it religiously, while her ringed fingers fiddled with a gaudy collection of beads around her sagging neckline. She nodded and tapped on Huxley's forehead. "Yes, I'm sure it was her. She came a few weeks ago and asked to meet with Dr. Tarantino."

Bingo! "Did she say why she wanted to see him?"

"Uh-uh. Without a reason I couldn't arrange a meeting. I tried to convince her to talk to one of our managers first. Our executives are very busy people, you know?" The woman looked sadly at the picture. "She insisted she had to talk to Dr. Tarantino. That's why I remember her."

"What did you tell her?"

"I made her fill a written request and told her I'd get back in touch once I had the chance to speak with Dr. Tarantino."

I beamed. "Tell me you still have the form."

An offended frown curled her forehead. "Of course I do,

Detective. I never throw away anything!"

I stared at her desk and saw what she meant. The anti-Huxley workplace, a monumental collection of recyclable garbage: knickknacks of all shapes and colors, from the happy man in a hula skirt, to the dancing snowman; dust-covered picture frames, fake flowers, piles of paper in all colors; unused folders, empty plastic bottles, even a row of diet coke cans neatly lined on top of the cabinets as if they were shiny golf trophies. The wall behind the desk sported a pin board with overlapping layers of memos and photos. A child had gone from newborn to riding his bike; bright yellow sticky notes had gradually faded in color, and the words printed on them had been smeared by the occasional spatter of coffee. Maria Ramirez was so attached to everything she refused to depart even from Huxley's request form, although she was nice enough to make me a copy.

"Did you ever get back to her with an appointment?"

"Dr. Tarantino agreed to meet with her in four months, but Ms. Huxley told me it was too far away. I never heard back from her."

CHAPTER 15

Tuesday, October 14

Ms. Claire Lester crossed the room with an impatient gait, her red pumps tapping arrogantly on the floor. A thick trail of expensive perfume lingered behind her like the wake of an airplane. In her early fifties, Lester sugarcoated her vitriol with hypocorisms and hid her impending menopause behind a thick layer of makeup, fake eyelashes, and three concentric rows of pearls. A woman of little time, I gathered, a few exes, and a disowned child if she happened to have given birth at some point in her ovulating years. The kind of lady who could use more sex in her life but is too sour to find anybody to fill the position. *Literally.*

She dropped a leather briefcase on her client's

mahogany desk, plucked out a few papers, then transferred her conspicuous ass in one of the upholstered armchairs. Coloring her words with a Texan inflection, she gave us her introductory speech on why she'd recommended Chromo CEO Richard Medford not to talk to us until she could preside over the meeting. As she spoke, her client smiled placidly, a cherubic face framed by silver waves of hair.

Medford's hand felt disturbingly soft when I introduced myself. His breath smelled of cocoa butter, and, contrary to his lawyer, his voice was deep and placated, his mannerism conciliatory. "Robert has been a great asset to our company for the past seventeen years," he said. Satish and I took a seat in his sizable office and listened. Beloved by all his coworkers and clients, Robert was devoted to his job, passionate about his field, and undertook every new task like a new endeavor. A faithful of this new-age religion called Stakhanovism, in other words.

"Whoever did this, hurt all of us at Chromo," Medford concluded with a sigh.

I studied the man. He lavished on refined details: gold tack holding a lavender silk tie, expensive man cologne, a Rolex sliding down his wrist as he laced his hands around his crossed knees.

"Any idea why anybody would want to hurt you or your company, Mr. Medford?" Satish asked.

Medford waited for Lester's approving glance before replying, "There's a lot of insane people out there, Detective."

The comment made me scratch my head. "What exactly do you mean, Mr. Medford?"

"Isn't it obvious?" Lester interjected. "My client is talking about religious and ideological fanaticism. Chromo has been doing genetic research for over a decade, always at the forefront of scientific progress: gene therapy, stem cell research, genotyping. And while these highly motivated scientists strive to find a cure for genetic diseases, there are nuts out there who accuse them of playing God or violating the sanctity of life."

Anticipating my question, Satish asked, "Did anyone here at Chromo receive specific threats in the past?"

Lester inhaled, straightened her back, and sent a supercilious glance to her client. "Tell them, Richard," she said, with pompous affectation.

Medford slid a hand to his pocket and produced a stick of lip balm, which he profusely applied to his dark lips. "Robert mentioned being approached by a woman on his way out from work one day. She stopped him in the parking lot and confronted him over some gene therapy experiments he had supervised a few years earlier."

"A woman? Did Dr. Tarantino know her?"

Medford shook his head. "I don't think so. He would have told me. Look, it happened a while ago and Robert mentioned it only once, on our way to a meeting. At the time I shrugged it off as irrelevant, but now…" His voice broke. He brought a hand to his tie, adjusted an already perfect knot, and then cleared his throat. "I don't know what to make of what happened to Rob and Tammy. It just doesn't make sense." Medford frowned, tuned his voice back down a notch, then pointed the lip balm stick at us. "Detectives, a company like ours is always on the forefront of new research, always in the spotlight. We need the praise of the media. At the same time, we attract the attention of a lot of lunatics out there. Their accusations are based on sick ideologies, like this absurdity of violating the sanctity of life Claire just mentioned. In fact, what we're doing here is cherishing the beauty of life, making sure every child can thrive in a disease-free world."

A young assistant in high heels knocked on the door and

delivered a tray with four ceramic cups and a freshly brewed pot of coffee.

"How long have you been with Chromo, Mr. Medford?" I asked.

He flashed me a paternal smile. "Twenty-two years. It wasn't named Chromo, back when I took over."

"Was it your idea to hire Professor Conrad in 1996?"

The smile dissolved. "Conrad was a genius. He fully embraced Chromo's philosophy and ideals."

The lawyer dutifully checked her watched and tapped one shoe. We had exhausted all twenty minutes she'd generously granted us.

"Ideals or ideologies?" I wondered, once we left Medford's office.

"Clever question, Track," Satish said. "When it comes to things like genetics, is there a difference between the two?"

We took the elevator one floor down to Tarantino's office, a luminous room with a view on Culver City Park. A tall ficus plant sat in a corner by the window, its leaves cast under a film of dust. The bookcases were bare of knickknacks, photo frames, or any other decoration. Heavy with volumes of scientific journals and reference books, they exuded a sense of austerity and hard working intellect. The only embellishment Tarantino had allowed in his office was an antique world map hanging behind the desk, and a small picture of his smiling wife and daughter, next to the computer screen.

Diane was already there, dusting Tarantino's keyboard, while our Electronics guy ran his forensic hocus-pocus on the hard-drive. The fan at the back of the desktop was huffing like a plane about to take off.

"Jeez," I said. "Is that thing about to explode?"

"It's the FDC device," the computer tech reassured me. "It's creating a disk image of all volumes and data storage devices connected to this machine."

I nodded, pretending to understand, and didn't bother asking what the heck FDC stood for.

"How did the chat with Medford go?" Diane asked, sealing the last box of evidence.

"Cryptic," I replied. "Why?"

"He seemed uh—interesting."

I raised a brow. "You talked to him?"

"Briefly. This was in the recycling bin." She held an open envelope with Tarantino's work address printed in a neat calligraphy. It was postmarked October 2.

"What did you and Medford talk about?" I asked, donning a new pair of gloves.

"Oh, just this place in Palm Springs where he goes on vacation with his wife. Jim and I go there too, from time to time."

I slid a finger inside the envelope and pulled out the photo of a smiling child in ponytails. "Gaya Nicole White," the print at the bottom of the picture read. "October 19, 1999—January 3, 2008."

I stared at Diane. "Do you know who this was?"

She nodded. "Jerry White's daughter. That's why I'm showing it to you. Do you want me to ship it to Latent Prints?"

The envelope bore no sender. I brought it to my nose and inhaled. Perfume, feminine, by now very familiar. "Yes," I said. "And I can tell you exactly where to find matching fingerprints."

Dear Dr. Tarantino:
I have come across several of Chromo's "Proteus" kids in our leukemia study at the Esperanza. Let's talk.
Sincerely,

Jennifer Huxley, Lab Tech II
Esperanza Medical Center

I mulled over the expression "Proteus kids." I left the letter on the table, grabbed a Corona from the fridge, and shuffled outside in the backyard. Will followed me and crawled around my legs as soon I slumped on the chaise, nose on my lap and eyes set on adoring mode. A few seconds later the pet door clicked and The King joined us. He hopped on the table and gave us his usual disapproving glare.

"You're just jealous," I said.

His Majesty ignored me.

The air was cool, the stars were out, and Venus shimmered above the fringed treetops. The solitary trill of a cricket emerged over the monotonous hum of the Two. It was on nights like this that I cherished where I lived and forgot how much I loathed the traffic jams at the junction between the One-Ten and the Five. When my mother passed, I spent three months renovating the house. A realtor friend of mine told me its value had risen to seven figures, and after years of renting crappy one-bedrooms I was eager to buy my own place. The "For Sale" sign my friend left me was still somewhere in the garage—I never put it out. I thought I'd never get used to all the ghosts of the past, yet we ended up getting along just fine, the ghosts and I.

Proteus kids. I took a long swig of beer and pondered. Will licked my hand, I stroked him behind the ears. The leaves of the eucalyptus rustled in the breeze, their fragrance wavering in the air like fluttering moths. I put down the bottle of Corona, snapped open my cell phone, and dialed through Parker Center.

"Luke went home," a never-heard-before Officer Knudsen told me with a strong New York accent. Right. It was already eight thirty p.m. "What d'you need, Detective?"

"Get to a terminal and search under the words 'Proteus' and 'children' and call me back if you find anything interesting."

"What's your definition of interesting?"

What do they teach these days at the Academy, philosophical reasoning? "How 'bout anything striking you as worth killing for?"

"Yes, sir."

The New York accent hung up, and I dialed Diane's number.

"Too late to ask me out, Track," she mocked.

I drew in air and almost choked in it. "Who's looking at Tarantino's hard disk?" I said, pretending I hadn't heard her. My voice didn't pretend too well.

"We left everything at Piper Tech, with a guy named Banjaree."

The Piper Technology building, on Ramirez Street, housed our Electronics Unit. I'd worked with Amit Banjaree on other cases before. I made a mental note to call him and tell him to search any document with the name Proteus in it. And the word children.

I drained the Corona staring at the black sky above me. Twinkling dots billions of light-years and lifetimes away. I should've thought about life, death, the universe, and what the hell my ephemeral existence was supposed to mean in this overwhelming vastness. But I was in no mood to get sentimental. All I could think of was the "Hey, hon" Diane had so casually blurted on her phone when Mr. Boyfriend called her. And how it stung even though it shouldn't have. So why did I not call her back and ask her out?

What are those, Ma?

The stars, honey.

No, I mean — what are the stars? What are they made of?

She rested a hand on my head and rubbed my scalp with the

pads of her fingers.

They are the eyes of the dead, looking down on us. Protecting us.

I thought of Lily's eyes.

I wondered if they were up there, too.

I failed to protect Lily's eyes.

And now they will be fourteen forever.

I stirred out of the plastic chaise, tossed the empty bottle in the recycling bin, and trudged back inside.

Damn it. I did get sentimental after all.

CHAPTER 16

Wednesday, October 15

Two women laughed out loud, their chortles stifled by the hisses of the milk steamer. A tanned man in a black shirt paced impatiently while waiting for his macchiato, his pompous gait slicing the space around him like Moses sliced the Red Sea. The woman in front of me swayed her long dreadlocks and pointed to a blueberry muffin, her undeodorized body odor covering for a moment the aroma of brewed coffee.

"One latte and one espresso, Detectives."

I took my small cup and downed it in three long sips. "An elm tree?" I said.

Satish shook his second bag of sugar, tore one corner off, and emptied it on the foamy surface of his latte. "*The* elm tree."

"How was the espresso, Detective?" the barista asked me.

"Next to perfection, Mike." Where perfection of course was the one I brewed at home. Mike grinned and showed me his thumb.

The first time I'd ordered an espresso he handed me some washed down concoction in a paper cup. I scowled, walked around the counter and showed him how to make an espresso. I told him if he were ever to serve it to me in a paper cup again I'd take him in. The next day he made it as the coffee deities command, watched me sip it, and then asked, "You were kidding, weren't you? When you said you'd take me in?"

I sniffed the air. "About the coffee, yes. The joint though, I might still change my mind." As far as I can tell, he never smoked a joint on the job again.

A smoky downtown swallowed us as Satish and I shouldered out of the Starbucks doors. The gripping noise of a jackhammer blasted off for a full minute, then died, making the everyday sounds tramping down the block sprout back to life: high heels clacking on cement, a black suit and tie jabbering in a mobile, a screaming child in an impatient stroller. The street trees along the sidewalk rustled their leaves, their nutty scent choked by the exhaust of a DASH bus idling at the red light.

I said, "We were talking about Chromo."

"Yes, we were," Satish agreed. At the light, we crossed First Street.

"So then, what the hell does this elm tree have to do with Chromo?"

"No, Track, you got confused. Not with Chromo. With my old man teaching me how to climb trees."

I snorted. "Sat. I thought we were talking about

Medford and individuals who don't talk to us unless their lawyers are present."

Satish sipped his latte and nodded. "Exactly. Tarantino was a dedicated, hard-working soul. If he's done anything wrong, though, Medford wouldn't know. He's the number one at Chromo, and yet if somebody under his wings screws up, he's got nothing to do with it, and his lawyer is right by his side to prove it."

The Glass House loomed before us, three skinny palm trees doubled on its shiny façade. By the water fountain, three granite slabs held the names of our men fallen on the line of duty. Satish said, "Medford calling up his lawyer reminds me of my elm tree."

"I figured," I said in full resignation. My cell went off, Gomez's name flashing on the display. "I'm down on Los Angeles Street," I told him.

"Don't bother coming up. We got a hit on Huxley's car."

Satish slid behind the wheel and asked, "Where are we heading?"

"San Vicente Mountain Park. The son of a bitch ditched the car along the unpaved stretch of Mulholland Drive."

He jammed the key into the engine. "Give the man some credit, Track. The spot is beautiful."

As Satish whipped through the busy lanes of the One-Oh-One, I made a few calls to the coroner's office to notify them of the dead body found in Huxley's car and arranged for a tow truck to come pick up the vehicle and transport it to one of our garages. I closed the phone and stared blankly at the billboards promising me luxurious cars, excellent medical care, and instant gratification.

"Huxley's dead," I mumbled.

Satish raised a brow. "Correction. Huxley's missing, and

her car just turned up with a stiff inside."

"Huxley's body."

Satish exhaled through his nose. He hummed for a little, then out of the blue said, "I loved my elm tree. I loved the way it smelled, and the sound its leaves made when the breeze ran through its branches. But my favorite part, Track, was to climb it. I was small, light, and so nimble I could get all the way up to the highest boughs. Until the day my mom caught me and freaked out."

"Why?"

"She said back in India children died falling from trees. She said their heads cracked open like coconuts. I was grounded for climbing the elm tree. My siblings went to bed and got a good night kiss. I had to stay up in a corner and wait for my old man. *You wait and see what he'll do to you!* Mom said. So I waited. Eyes heavy with sleepiness, I waited.

"My old man finally comes home, dirty and tired. Mom walks to the door and talks to him. She yells, most likely, but I don't remember a word. I remember her black braid swaying angrily down her shoulders, and her thin waist wrapped by the apron strings. Pa listens quietly. He's exhausted. He mumbles something to mom, then goes and takes a shower. When he's back, he sits at the table without even looking at me. He starts eating and asks, *What'd you do?*

"*Nothin'*, I screech. *I done nothin', Pa!*

"Pa raises a hand. *Sat. What did you do?* And this time he speaks each word slowly.

"I sigh. *I climbed the elm tree.*

"My old man eats his dinner. When he's done, he wipes his mouth and drains his beer. *Go to bed, Satish. Tomorrow you wake up with me.*

"The next morning he gets me out of bed at dawn. We have breakfast together while the sun rises. Then he takes me outside. *Show me how you climb, Satish.*

"My eyes go wide. *Mom's sleeping.*

"*We won't tell*, he promises. I clutch one of the lower branches and pull myself up. My old man watches. Every now and then he says, *No*, and stops me. *You put the foot in the wrong spot*, he says. Or he corrects the way I hold on to the branch to support my weight. He shows me how to do it properly, how to be safe.

"*There*, he says when I get back down. *Now you know how to do it the right away. Don't get caught again.*"

Satish fell silent. He changed lanes and passed a red pick-up truck hauling a boat. I waited. He was still silent.

"And the moral, Sat?"

"Ah, Track, you and your morals. There ain't no moral this time, okay?" I grunted and slouched back in the seat. "I mean," Satish resumed all of a sudden. "If you're a good employer, you can't wash your hands of what happens in your company. You take responsibility. You either tell your people no, you can't climb the dangerous tree, or you check that when they climb, they do it the right way and don't fall off and get caught."

"You're assuming something went wrong at Chromo."

Satish shook his head sideways. "I don't assume nothing, Track. I just told you how I learned to climb trees."

I smiled and stared out the window. Partly disguised by the drooping head of a palm tree, the advertisement for an online degree program read, "Knowledge is power."

Is it really? I wondered.

"What did I tell you?" Satish said, getting out of the car. "This spot is spectacular."

During the Cold War years, San Vicente Mountain Park was one of the Nike Ajax launch sites in L.A. county. Today, the radar tower had become a romantic venue thanks to its stunning views at sunset—provided the Santa Ana winds swept away the dome of pollution lingering on the valley, and the revolting stench of ripe corpse didn't sting the air.

It was a breezy day, with eastbound winds twirling dust in the air and rolling down yarns of tumbleweeds. We left our car at the end of the road, where the trees spread out to yield a glazed view of the Encino Reservoir. Wispy clouds cruised the sky and caressed the haze blanketing the San Fernando Valley. Studded in white and yellow wild flowers, the slopes were populated by the typical chaparral vegetation of sagebrush, *toyon, chamisa,* and scrub oaks. Black fingers of past fires scarred the slopes of the Santa Monica Mountains, stabbed here and there by the skeletons of burnt trees.

We had Huxley's car moved away from the shrubs and all doors, including the trunk, popped opened. Insects spilled out in swarms and funneled in our ears and nostrils. My skin crawled at the sweet stench of decomposition. One of the West Valley officers turned green. He excused himself, ambled a few yards away, and barfed behind a bush, the sound of his retching adding yet another layer of pleasure to the whole experience.

Three men climbed out of the coroner's white van and pulled a tarp-lined stretcher out of the back. I emptied Huxley's glove compartment, set everything on the hood of our vehicle, and sifted through all the papers: car manual, registration, insurance documents, car repair receipts. "Damn it," I mumbled. Holding the lapel of his jacket to his face, eyes watery from the repressed bouts of nausea, Satish came to tell me that no ID had been found on the body either. "How long can you hold your breath?" he asked.

"Still testing," I replied.

"Fill your lungs and come check the trunk."

The removal crew heaved the body out of the car. At the

other end of the vehicle, Satish and I stared dumbfounded at the pool of dried blood and decomposition fluid at the bottom of the trunk. I read on my partner's face the same questions running through my mind: a second victim? And if so, where was the body?

"A-ha! The trunk is where it happened."

The voice made me jump. Blinded by the overwhelming reek of putrefaction, I hadn't sensed the new presence behind me. "Vic's been shot in the trunk and then moved afterward. Dr. Russ Cohen, pleased to meet you, Detectives." The man stretched out a gloved hand. He had a noticeable nose, red and crinkled like an old sponge. Shreds of yellow hair randomly covered his head. "Come on over. Let me show you what I mean."

"Dr. Ellis told us they had a new man on the team," Satish said, as we walked to the gurney.

"Just moved from Maryland," Cohen replied. He bent over the stretcher and stripped the gray tape from the corpse's mouth. A maroon tongue poked out of purple lips. The face had swollen beyond recognition. Dark eye globes popped out of their sockets. Covered in blisters, the skin had taken green and gray hues, the flesh frayed by blackened vessels. There were moths crawling through the hair and maggots chewing off the flesh. The only sign of humanity left on the corpse was a cross hanging from a chain around the neck, an eerie oxymoron of gold over putrefaction.

Hideously humming in our ears, a black cloud of flies faithfully followed every movement we made. We talked while swaying our hands in all directions, looking like dancers in a clumsily choreographed ballet. We were comical and pathetic at the same time.

"My mother-in-law called yesterday," Cohen said, his wrinkly forehead rolling up and down like a swag. "They're having eighty-eight percent humidity right now, over there. I'm not moving back *ever*." He severed the ropes around Huxley's wrists and ankles and passed them over for us to examine. They were made of thick cord, rough to the touch.

"This is hemp," Satish noted, pulling the two ends to test its sturdiness. "The kind they use for sailing is tarred though, and this one doesn't seem to be. Maybe rock climbing?"

"Those are made of nylon and they come with an exterior sheath," I replied. "Too bad they don't sell cadaver-binding cords at hardware stores. Our job would be a hell lot easier."

Cohen produced a shrill laugh with a feminine pitch. "Ah. I like you guys. You have a sense of humor. Must be the nice weather and all. Back east—"

"Tell us about the vic, Doc," I interjected. I already knew more than a hundred reasons to live in Southern California and nowhere else in the world. My only problem has always been how widespread such opinions seem to be.

"Female, I would say maximum thirty years of age." Cohen handed the knife to one of his assistants and got a pair of tweezers in return. The assistant had a meaty face that glistened with perspiration, his cheeks so large they looked like they'd sucked his nose in. In such circumstances, it wasn't a bad idea.

"I understand the owner of the car disappeared?" Cohen asked. He plucked a couple insects for every species he spotted and collected them in small glass containers.

"Eight days ago," Satish confirmed.

"And apparently she just showed up."

Satish gave me a dirty look.

"Interesting," Cohen said. "It would certainly fit the bill." He raised the cadaver's arm and let it drop against the stretcher. Flakes of papery skin clung to his glove and then fell off, pirouetting in the air like plumage. "The body is limp, past *rigor mortis*. The type of insects, marbelization of the skin, bloated abdomen—everything tells me she's been dead several days already."

Cohen brushed a finger along Huxley's left arm. "She was coiled on her side when she died. There's *livor mortis* along the left leg as well. The blood pooled everywhere but in her joints. Her limbs were bent, see these clearer stripes? Right behind the knee, indicating she was in a fetal position when she died."

I followed Cohen's gloved hands until my eyes shifted somewhere else. There was a jade earring dangling from her left lobe. I stepped around the gurney and checked the other ear. No jade there. *She lost one. Or maybe she didn't quite lose it...* An idea crossed my mind. It was just a fleeting thought, and then it was gone.

"She died on her side but we found her lying on her back," Satish was saying.

"Correct. All the blood and fluids from the first hours *post mortis* are in the trunk, and the *livor mortis* is along her left side, not the back."

"Shot in the trunk and then moved," Satish agreed.

"Not right away. From the level of decomposition fluid in the trunk I believe she was left for several hours in there. *Rigor mortis* takes around seventy hours to completely wane."

"Does it mean she was killed at least three days ago?"

Cohen nodded. "Three or four, I'd say on a first guess. It depends on how long the car was left out in the sun. Heat accelerates the process."

Five days earlier Huxley's car had driven into the Tarantinos' property.

"Three shots," Cohen went on, pointing to the holes gaping from the swollen body, two across the chest and one on the right shoulder. "And bruises, from bumping against the sides of the trunk. She took a ride before being killed. And the wrists—she probably fought before she was killed. I'll be looking for defensive wounds and tissue scraps under the nails. See these?" He pointed to the swollen joints. "Micro bruises around her wrists and ankles—they're called *petechiae*. Small injuries from struggling against the binds."

The image of the woman, alive, bound, and locked in what ended up being her coffin, made me seethe. I stepped away and walked around the vehicle. Two men from the SID Field Unit were working on the trunk, one taking photos, and the second vacuuming the inner lining for fibers. *Three shots, of which only two had been deadly.* It had taken one shot each to kill Tarantino and his wife. What were the chances the killer had been the same person?

"Any slugs or casings?" I asked the criminologists searching the vehicle.

"No, sir," one of the guys replied from behind a white facemask.

"How about a lost earring?"

Same answer. My head started toying with ideas, mere possibilities, mismatched pieces of a puzzle. Four victims, one link: Chromo. How many killers, though? I inhaled, calibrating. Re-adjusting my nose to account for a noisy background. And once I felt ready, I poked my head inside the vehicle and sniffed.

Smells have layers, like sounds have frequencies. Disentangling them is like trying to follow a song in a room full of loud people—you have to learn to tune out all other noises.

I grasped a faint feminine smell and tried to cling to it. Too elusive, it kept slipping away. I focused on the man's scent, coming from the driver's seat instead. Sweat, sour, not from exercising but from stress, all around the wheel, left by nervous and slippery hands. A bit of burnt spice in it, cilantro, maybe. It had been covered by the artificial fragrance of antibacterial sprays, the same kind lingering everywhere in Huxley's condo. I crouched on the driver's seat, pushed away the reek of putrefaction, and noticed something else. A tiny blob smeared on the edge of the seat.

"Hey!" I called, to nobody in particular. "There's semen in here!"

"What? We didn't—" One of the Field Unit people emerged from behind the hood and scowled at me. In her hands was the roll of tape she'd been using to lift fibers and soil residue from the front bumper. She came around to the front door, had me step aside, and took a skeptical peek inside.

"I don't see a thing," she said.

"What d'you mean, you don't see a thing? It's right there—"

"Let me get the Orion-Lite."

Damn it. Of course she doesn't see it. She wobbled back brandishing the luminol-based flashlight and a ream of black sheets. With the help of the rest of the Field Unit team, we draped Huxley's Ford to block the light from the outside. The SID woman pointed the Orion-Lite and finally saw it: a little pear-shaped ghost floating under the fluorescence of the forensic light.

"Could be bleach," she said.

"Lift it and bag it," I growled.

I took a few steps away from the vehicle to breathe. The air was harshly dry and dusty, and yet refreshing, compared to the acrid odor of death. Satish and Cohen stood by the medical vehicle, staring at the two assistants as they bagged the victim's hands and feet, and then wrapped the body in tarp, both men wearing a turban of stubborn flies around their heads. The forensic photographer walked to the SDI van, retrieved his bag from the front seat, and swapped the focal lenses of his camera. At the back of the van, the other two Field people carefully packaged the bed comforter found on the corpse.

"Comforter goes to Trace Unit," I told them. "They need to scan for fibers and fluid traces." The two men nodded.

"I hope they had a good lunch," one said. "This is going to ruin their appetite."

"Yeah," the other replied. "Definitely worth a pay raise."

The clearly feminine print of the cover caught my attention. Lavender flowers, just like the prevailing scent in Huxley's house, and the decorative theme in her bathroom. *Of course.*

"Satish!" I called. "We've got to go to Huxley's place. The killer went to her apartment. He obviously has her keys, and—"

"Track."

"*And* we've got to get her computer at work. The woman was onto something. It's what—"

"Track, will you listen for a minute?"

"What?"

"This is *not* Jennifer Huxley. Until we know otherwise, this is Jane Doe."

"What? What the hell are you talking about? If she's not a cadaver, she's the owner of a vehicle with a cadaver inside!"

Satish bobbed his head. "The D.A. office will never sign the warrants without a death certificate. Dr. Cohen has already sent in the request to Huxley's dentist."

"What about fingerprints? If they match the ones on file with the DMV—"

"For a corpse this old, we'd need to re-hydrate the tissue first," Cohen said, handing the paperwork to one of his assistants. "Dental will be faster. I can have one of my guys

X-ray her as soon as she's delivered to the morgue."

"We need to know her identity as soon as possible," I said. "*And* we need it to keep it away from the press for as long as possible."

Satish agreed. "Somebody killed her in the trunk and somebody brought her here for us to find. The longer their wait, the likelier they are to make a false step."

Cohen gave us his word, then dismissed himself with a brisk handshake and shuffled off to his car. I couldn't get my head off Huxley's computer. *She mentioned additional data she was about to obtain*, her boss, Julia Cox, had told me. *Data she wanted but wasn't supposed to have*. I thought of Cox's calculated answers, the fierce defense of her work, and how she'd been vague about the leukemia study.

"We've got to get her computer," I reiterated.

"Track," Satish said in his unfazed, annoyingly reassuring tone. "Cohen has our numbers. He'll call us as soon as he can confirm the identity. Let's go write those damn warrants, and by early morning tomorrow we can get this computer of hers."

"It's going to be too fucking late."

We both stared at the Ford, the open trunk still gaping at us. The Field Unit team packed their tools and gatherings back into the van. By the dirt road, a uniformed officer unrolled the yellow tape to let the tow truck into the cleared area.

I felt as useless as a sprinkler going off during a spring storm.

Satish scratched an old scar on his arm and tilted his head. "You know what this reminds me of, Track?" he said.

"I don't give a damn, Satish!" I snapped. I was tired from standing in the sun, hungry, and mostly pissed off because I knew the right thing to do yet I couldn't do it. I was hardly the ideal listener.

Not the least offended, Satish put up a perplexed face. "What? It reminds me it's been five years since I last washed my car."

"Good thing you didn't kill anyone in these past five years," I retorted. "Gimme the car keys. I'm driving this time."

"Oh, but you know I get even more loquacious when I'm not behind the wheel."

"Don't worry," I said ambling back to his Taurus. "It won't be a long drive. You get a beautiful view of the reservoir, while I ponder over what size burger to order at Johnny Rockets."

He chuckled and slid onto the passenger's seat. "The world is a can of sardines, Track. You either fit in the can or you don't. If you fit, you get eaten. If you don't, you need to learn to swim on your own."

I lowered the windows, cranked up the AC, and made the lousiest U-turn in cop history. "I hate sardines," I growled. "They stink."

A lonely crow cawed its farewell, and after that we vanished in a white cloud of dust.

The killer wasn't the only one possessing a set of keys to Huxley's apartment. I did, too. My guy had been there recently, probably in a hurry, which increased his chances of making a mistake. Maybe he left a muddy footprint this time. Maybe he had to use the john and took his gloves off, leaving a few prints in the bathroom. I don't need a search warrant to inhale.

I waited until evening to go back. I left my Dodge by the curbside, turned the engine off, and took in the neighborhood. It was almost dusk, the sky marred by yellow smears of clouds that quickly bled into twilight. A jogger passed, dragged on a leash by a black spaniel eager for a faster gait. An illuminated bay window displayed a happy family gathered around the table, their healthy smiles straight out of a whitening toothpaste commercial. Two doors down, the muted images of a TV blinked through sheer curtains.

The air was stiff in Huxley's place, all fragrances gone stale since my last visit. I didn't turn the lights on. I stepped inside, inhaled, and immediately knew. *The son of a bitch has been here.* I flew my gun hand to the holster and released the strap.

The living room had been turned into shambles. Straight slashes marred the couch cushions and armrests. The rug was upturned, and the CD column lay flat on one side, disks strewn all over the floor. Books had been pulled from the shelves. A wilted plant had been snatched out of its pot and the dirt shoved on the ground. The desk drawers were scattered on the floor and their contents spilled everywhere. I winced. *The desk.* Something was missing. *Damn it, the laptop!* I whirled my head around, searching. What else had been taken? The kitchen looked untouched—I took a quick glimpse and moved to the bedroom.

It was just a sigh, imperceptible, though clear enough to make me startle. It could've been the breeze, and yet all windows were shut and the air was still. Or a garment left precariously dangling on a hanger and finally coming to terms with gravity. My muscles tensed. I widened my nostrils and sniffed. *His* smell. Strong. No, not in the past. Here, and now. *Damn it.*

I slid the Glock out of the holster and flattened against the wall. Suddenly aware of his presence, I felt the assassin's eyes on me, watching. I inched forward, gun low and ready.

I edged towards the bedroom door and peeked in. Again, that sound, imperceptible to human ears but not to mine. Metal over metal, oil to muffle the friction, slowly rotating. A doorknob. I saw the shadow, quick, flash in front of me. "Freeze!" I yelled, sprang after him to the bathroom and fired. No time to think, just pure instincts running wild. *Get the asshole.* I heard water running, bolted to the shower, and yanked off the curtains. And while I stared dumbfounded at Huxley's laptop happily soaking at the bottom of the shower, the guy sneaked behind me and ran off.

Not contented with my great performance, I wasted another precious two seconds stepping into the shower, getting the laptop, and tossing it on the bed before running after the fugitive. By the time I got out, all I saw was the blur of a car furiously accelerating and disappearing around the street. Not a chance to get a make, let alone a glimpse at the plate number. So there I was: standing in the middle of the road, smoking gun in my hand, breathing in exhaust gas and burnt tire, and looking like an idiot who'd just showered fully clothed.

Shit.

At least I saved the laptop. *Wrong.* I later found out it would've actually been better to leave the computer soaking in the water. The minute I got it out, the damned thing started drying out and oxidizing. By the time we could officially seize the laptop the next day, rust had completed the damage.

Sprinklers going off in the middle of a spring storm are not only useless.

They're wasteful.

CHAPTER 17

Wednesday, October 15

Rhesus's phone chimes. Trickles of sweat drip down his unshaved jaw and shirt. He looks in the rearview mirror. Nobody's following. That was close, he thinks. The phone keeps ringing. Damn it. He pulls to the curb, heaves a deep breath, and picks up.

"Hey honey," *a voice greets him.* "Are you working?"

"I was jogging," *he replies, his breath still short.* "I'm going back to work after dinner." *The silence at the other end of the line is laden with disappointment.* "Look, baby —"

"I know. It's only for a few more months." *She sighs.* "I had a really tiring day."

He coaxes her, smooches a little, and then hangs up and dials another number. Another woman, another voice.

"I couldn't find a damn thing," he blurts.

"Did you get the computer?"

He thinks before replying. Should he tell her about the incident? He decides not to. *"I dropped it in the shower."*

"What? Are you stupid?"

"It's gone. The computer's gone, get it?"

She doesn't reply.

"What are you doing tonight?" he asks, his tone different.

"I haven't decided yet."

Rhesus frowns. *"Is something wrong?"*

"I don't know what I'm doing tonight and something has to be wrong?"

"Relax, I'm just asking. I thought we could — you know."

"You thought wrong, Rhes. I'm not in the mood."

A sudden notion crosses his mind. Childish, yet he can't help but voice it out loud. *"You're not seeing somebody, are you?"*

A guffaw follows, loud and mocking. Offensive.

"Stop it," he warns, but she doesn't listen.

"Oh, Rhesus," she finally says. *"And what is it to you if I'm seeing somebody?"*

Stupid! he thinks hanging up. He swerves back into the street and drives off. He can't concentrate, though. He's pissed at the way she laughed at him. He pulls over again, grabs the cell phone and dials a new number. *"Hey, guess what? My deadline got postponed. I don't have to go back to work tonight."*

"I can't wait to see you," she says, a smile tingling in her voice.

CHAPTER 18

Wednesday, October 15

"Can you see it?" She had pulled the curtains and turned all lights off. She raised her arms, collected her hair, and tilted her head to expose her throat and shoulder. A tattooed butterfly with curly tails spread its wings across her collarbone. "Can you really see it, even in the dark?"

"Hmm," I replied, distracted by her nakedness. Sparse tufts of red hair softened her armpits and sprouted below the smiling bay of her lower abdomen. Everything else was pearly white, like a Galatea awakened to life.

"You like it? I designed it myself."

Hortensia's breasts smelled of cherry blossoms, and her nipples tasted sandy and salty, like seashells washed to the shore. After what had happened at Huxley's condo, I was so damn pissed at myself I needed a distraction. I spent an hour explaining to the responding officers what had happened. A guy from forensics looked pitifully at the soaked laptop, then sealed the scene and told me nothing could be done until the next day. I went home, showered and shaved, had a bite, and then appeared at Hortensia's door with a bottle of wine. Hortensia never asks a question unless it concerns her personally, mostly because she's too focused on herself to wonder what's going on in other people's lives. It works for me, and it's all I care. Tonight, she opened her door, took the wine from my hands and kissed me.

Later in bed, she fussed over her new tattoo to the point of irritation. I reluctantly let go of her nipple and pressed my thumb over her lips. "I can see the damn butterfly, Hort. I can see everything in pitch dark, okay?"

She giggled and moved my hand away from her face. "I can only see your eyes. They glow, like vampires' eyes. I think your doctor's wrong, Track. You're not a chimera. You're a vampire."

She tilted her head backwards and laughed.

"He didn't say I'm a chimera," I said, brushing my tongue down her cleavage and squeezing her nipple between my lips. "He said he needed to find out more about me."

She pulled me closer, bit my earlobe and whispered, "Then be a vampire. Just for me, just for tonight."

"Bullshit." I sunk my face in her navel and slid my hands up her thighs. She moaned, closed her eyes, and so did I.

```
Thursday, October 16
```

It was one a.m. when I got home. I hit the bed and felt

restless. I couldn't stop thinking of how close I'd come to catching Huxley's killer and how foolishly I'd let him escape. The guy wasn't just a suspect. He was the link between the murders: the reason why Huxley had disappeared and turned up dead in her own car, why Robert Tarantino had been shot while making love to his wife, and why Jerry White had ended Conrad's life. Without that link, too many pieces of the puzzle were still missing. Huxley requested an appointment with Tarantino, to which he replied, "Sure, see you in four months." But then he ended up on her couch sipping wine, if not the same night she disappeared, the previous one. Maybe she had some compelling argument to make him change his mind. Or perhaps some compelling curves, and the official business thing was an excuse for secret encounters. Could *Proteus kids* be some secret code the two had concocted for their rendezvous? It didn't fit the picture of the workaholic woman I'd gathered, though. Somebody who worked like Huxley had no time for a lover. No, Huxley wanted to talk to Tarantino for different reasons. *She was going to obtain additional data.* Huxley wanted data from Robert Tarantino — data so crucial it cost three lives, maybe four.

The religious note left by Tamara Tarantino's body bugged me. Huxley wore a golden cross and had a prayer framed in her foyer. Was it really her who drove to the Tarantinos' home that night? To deliver a religious message? Or was she already dead by then?

The killers kept eluding me. A man and a woman were at the Tarantino residence when the homeowners had been executed, and a man and a woman were in Huxley's car. Was it the same man and woman? Her smell was elusive, and every time I tried to capture it I felt like I was running after a concept I couldn't quite grasp. His smell, instead, I finally had, now clearly impressed in my head: musty, sweaty, tangy like burnt cilantro, and yet not completely foreign. It had a hint of familiarity, a component I felt I'd encountered before, though in this new mixture, I failed to recognize it.

I tossed and turned for most of the night, going round in loops, thinking of one hypothesis, excluding it, and then reconsidering and starting all over again. When at five fifty-five the phone rang, I felt like I'd just closed my eyes.

"We have an identity on the body."

"Fuck off, Satish. I had an identity yesterday, too."

"Good morning to you too, Track. You no longer sound eager to go get a hold of Huxley's computer."

Of course I was. I told him to come get me in twenty minutes—the time I needed to brew two Mokas' worth of coffee. We made an additional stop to pick up the computer forensics guy, and by the time we hit the Ten, the sun was just about to rise. A rim of red outlined the San Gabriel Mountains, broken by the fringed skyline of palm fronds and eucalyptus trees lining the freeway. The last stars twinkled and then vanished. Behind red brick walls draped in crawling ivies, a sea of shingle roofs marked neighborhoods of middle-income homes, their propane grills and manicured lawns setting the tone of suburban life.

We arrived at the Esperanza Medical Center—Huxley's workplace—around seven thirty. A security guard accompanied us to the Lerville building and let us in. We followed his master key like the mice followed the magic flute. Except this time no magic was needed: Huxley's office door was already open.

As soon as he saw us, Fabian Payanukis sprang to his feet, his hands frozen on the keyboard. The lab tech I'd met on my first visit to the Esperanza looked tired, pale, and quite shocked to see us. My eyes widened. "What do you think you're doing, tampering with that computer?"

Payanukis winced. "Tampering? No—what—"

Satish squeezed my arm and took over. "Please step away from the computer, sir," he said, as protocol dictated. "We're executing a search warrant on all electronic files in this office."

Payanukis stared at us as if we were wearing our pants inside out. "Does Dr. Cox know about this?"

"She's been notified," the guard confirmed. Our computer tech set his toolbox on the desk and took over Huxley's keyboard, shoving a still stammering Payanukis to the side.

"Why are you doing this? What happened to Jen?" The thick lenses of his glasses enlarged the puffiness beneath his eyes. He reeked of morning breath, of a sleepless night spent in front of a terminal, and consequent need of a shower. Satish and the security guard talked him into stepping out of the office, while I grabbed a chair and sat next to our technician.

"Tell me what the punk was doing logged onto this machine."

The tech furrowed his eyebrows at the screen. He was wearing a nicotine drenched T-shirt sporting the formula $E=mc^2$ on the front, and Einstein's 1951 photo at the back, the one where he's sticking out his tongue at the camera. That morning, it felt as if Albert were staring right at me, saying, *I'm the genius, and you're the dumbass.*

"Hmm." Einstein Shirt typed a few lines of incomprehensible jargon, at which the machine responded with a loud whir. Rows of arcane lingo dribbled down the black screen, the very last the only one I could comprehend: "ACCESS DENIED."

"What the hell is that supposed to mean?"

He exhaled and dropped his hands off the keyboard. "The answer to your question, Detective. The punk was encrypting the hard disk."

"Am I under arrest?"

"No, Doctor," Satish replied, his voice like hot cocoa after a snow fight. "We just need to have a chat, and it would be best if you could come with us to the station. You were one of the last people to talk to her."

Julia Cox drew in a sharp breath and ran a nervous hand through her hair. "How did she die?"

"We can't disclose anything yet."

She knew Huxley was dead. I paced across the hospital conference room while studying her face and perspiration, the fine line drawn by her eyebrows, and the slight tremor of her hands. *She's scared.* For the first time since I'd met her, Cox looked unnerved and fragile. Underneath the white coat, her scrubs were wrinkled and smelled of operating room. She crossed her legs and wedged a hand between her thighs, the plastic of her shoe covers rustling against the linoleum tiles. I winced. *Blue* shoe covers made of Tyvec, like all hospital protective clothing.

"Will I need a lawyer?" Cox asked, her voice tainted with a note of anxiety.

Satish stiffened. The minute a suspect asks for a lawyer our hands are tied. I pulled up a chair and sat across from her. Payanukis had told us earlier the order to encrypt Huxley's hard drive had come from her. The only hope we had to retrieve Huxley's data was to coax the decryption key out of her pretty lips.

"Are you hiding something from us, Doctor?" I asked.

She squinted and a hint of color returned to her cheeks. "Course not," she replied, her voice as bold as a Colombian brew.

"Then you've got nothing to worry about."

Her nostrils widened and her eyes glared. "Better be quick," she said, getting up. "I have patients waiting."

In the hallway she eyed a trash bin and stopped to remove her shoe covers. As she precariously balanced on one foot, I grasped her arm and held out a hand. "Here, let me take that for you."

Cox flinched, taken aback by my sudden gallantry. Her skepticism resurfaced almost immediately. She pursed her lips, slid off the shoe cover, and shoved it in my hand. "Suit yourself," she snarled, removed the second one as well, and then wriggled away from my grasp. I silenced Satish's interrogative stare with a blank face, both shoe covers secured in the pocket of my jacket.

Satish held the backdoor of our vehicle open for her and seemed not to notice the lack of a thank you as she quietly slid inside. Through the side mirror, I watched her lean her elbow against the window and drop her head in her hand.

"Tired?" Satish asked, turning the engine on.

"I was in the OR most of the night."

"In that case, I suggest a cup of our famous LAPD brew," Satish quipped. "It tastes so bad it keeps bears from hibernating."

During the drive back to the Glass House, Cox kept callously staring out the window. She didn't bite on any of Satish's numerous attempts to engage her in a casual conversation, and by the time we escorted her to one of the cubicles at the back of our squad room, she looked distressed, flustered, and eager to leave.

Out in the hallway, Satish clicked his tongue in frustration. "She's been up all night. We can't ask her to take a polygraph," he said, filling a Styrofoam cup from the water fountain, the only drink Cox had agreed to. Apparently, she had taken Satish's comments on the quality of our coffee quite literally.

"And what do you expect to milk out of a poly?" I replied. "It'll tell you she's hiding something, which we already know."

Lies come in all shapes and colors. Some lie open-mouthed, others through their teeth; some with a defiant look on their faces, others as if they'd just stepped on dog shit and needed to wipe it off their shoes. Some lie out of habit because their lives are too damned boring and need the extra kick; others lie through a mist of soap-opera delusion. Some lie earnestly, some because they're entitled to, and some to cover their asses. All a polygraph tells you is a yes, no, maybe. It doesn't tell you what, when, or why. As the old saying goes, the devil's in the details.

Satish's approach was to avoid any direct confrontation with Julia Cox. He asked generic questions about the leukemia study and her relationship with Huxley. Throughout the interview, Cox was as detached as a Greek Caryatid. I rapped my fingers on the table, until I finally lost my temper and bristled. "Dr. Cox, you had one of your lab technicians encrypt Huxley's hard disk the very same day we learned she was dead."

Cox flashed a miffed look. "You're doing your job, and I'm doing mine," she said sharply. "Jennifer was an exceptional asset for my group, and as much as this tragedy strikes me personally, it affects my job, too. The data on that computer has been obtained through my grant and is therefore my intellectual property. I'm entitled to keep it hidden until I'm ready to publish it. There's a privacy act granting me the right to do so, Detective. I suggest you look it up."

I could tell where her rage came from. It wasn't just at me. It was at the gender class I represented. Over the years, she'd seen her career stepped over by men, whether they came in a uniform or in a white lab coat, whether they looked down on her or all over her, acknowledging her looks rather than her work. Her belligerence had become a form of survival: step over before you're stepped on, blurring the lines of what's admissible and what's not. Which is why I felt no empathy. "Quit snowing me with all this privacy crap, Dr. Cox. How long do you think it took me to find out that Gaya White was one of your patients?"

She drew a hand to her chest, searching for the stethoscope she'd left at the hospital. When she didn't find it, she fiddled with the lapels of her lab coat, the back of her hand flowered with light freckles. "I stand by the rules, Detective. It's my job. And frankly, I don't see how knowing Gaya was one of my patients can help find Jennifer's killer."

I raised a brow. "Not even if I told you Huxley found out why Gaya died?"

My bluff had the effect I'd been looking for. Cox's face drained of all color. By my side, Satish tensed. I knew what he was thinking and I didn't care.

"Gaya died of leukemia," she said, her voice low. "We did all we could possibly—"

"Her father doesn't think so," I interjected. "And I have reason to believe Huxley didn't either. Have you ever heard of the expression *Proteus kids*?"

Cox's eyes hardened. She wrapped her fingers around the empty Styrofoam cup, twirled it, then crushed it. "This interview is over," she said coolly. "I won't say another word until I talk to a lawyer."

"Absolutely brilliant, Track," Satish griped.

"You weren't going anywhere either, okay?"

I was downright angry. Angry at the idiot who locked Huxley's computer, angry at the bitch of a doctor for telling him to do so, and angry at the system because I should've gotten that computer days ago, when I started investigating the woman's disappearance. Unscathed by any of my woes, Satish watched Cox climb onto the cruiser taking her back to the Esperanza while happily whistling Charlie Chaplin's tune "Smile"—Nat King Cole's version, for the record, because he's that kind of a classy guy.

"What the hell is wrong with you, Sat?" I snapped.

"With me? What the hell is wrong with me? You're the one who's all revved up."

"I have a thousand reasons for being mad. How are we supposed to find out why Huxley got killed without the data she was working on?"

"We've got smart people down at Electronics. They'll figure out a way to get to those files."

"It'll take months. You should've listened to me yesterday. You knew as well as I did the stiff was Huxley."

"Track, you're a smart guy and yet you still fall for these things. They're legal traps. Had we gotten the computer yesterday, before the medical examiner signed the death certificate with the right name on it, whatever we would've milked out of the hard disk would've been inadmissible. And you know it."

"Shit," I mumbled, shuffling back to the elevator lobby. Satish pressed the call button and then chuckled.

"What's so funny?"

"I just thought of somethin' my old man used to say."

"Amuse me too. I need it right now."

The elevator chimed and the doors slid open. We stepped inside, I pressed the button to the third floor and stared at Satish. Waiting. He shook his head, sighed, and laughed in contentment. "My first day in middle school. I felt all grown up. I wasn't a boy anymore—I was a big kid. So my old man comes over, pats me on the shoulder, and tells me, *Remember one thing, Satish. They're all out there to fuck you.*"

"Your old man said that?"

Satish raised a hand. "Hold on. Not finished yet. *They're all out there to fuck you,* he said, *and the only difference is that some use more Vaseline than others. Stick with the Vaseline son, it's pretty much all you can do.*"

I brought a hand to my head, squeezed the bridge of my nose, and smiled. By the time we got back to the squad room, I was laughing out loud.

"Track, what we did today was provide ourselves with a little more Vaseline. And believe me, when you get fucked a lot, a little bit more can go a long way." He walked to his desk, retrieved his jacket, and slid it on. I watched him step out of the squad room thinking, *Satish Cooper. A man of few words, and always the right ones.*

To the naked eye, the shoe cover I had cleverly — or so I believed — acquired from Cox was the exact same blue as the fibers I'd found on the Tarantino crime scene. I grasped the two ends and pulled. *Tear free,* Diane had said. I'd used enough of these to know it was true. I turned it inside out and concluded it was one oval piece of Tyvek with an elastic band sewn around the edge. The piece had clearly been cut with a blade before the elastic band had been sewn, and little filaments stuck out at the seam of the inner hem. I plucked a couple, pulled, and the trick was done: I was holding a clump of tear-free Tyvek fibers.

I drove to Cal State to drop them off. It was lunch hour and the Trace Unit lab was deserted, save for a beefy face with no neck doubled over a microscope. The face didn't seem too happy to unglue from the optical piece to address my concerns, but I pretended not to notice.

"I need to know if this stuff is Tyvek and if DuPont is

the brand," I said, holding Cox's shoe covers up for him to see. He stared at it with no interest whatsoever. The muzzle of a sheep grazing in a bucolic field of grass came to mind.

"They're all made by DuPont," he said, unsentimentally.

"Flash-spun, not woven?"

The guy nodded. He must've been a genius to see all those things with his naked eye.

"How common are they?"

He shrugged. "I got a lot of fifty boxes right here. Wanna buy some?"

"Fuck off, Einstein." I shoved the shoe covers back into my pocket and stepped out.

Latent Prints was a bit more crowded but equally disappointing. I was eager to find out whether or not fingerprints had been lifted from the funeral card found in Robert Tarantino's recycling bin.

"Novak left and we're backed up," an Indian woman told me, wearing a shimmering red sari underneath a white lab coat. An Indian woman in a shimmering red sari and a white lab coat on top is like Italian wine in a chipboard box. I thanked her and went my way.

Diane was out. I dropped a note on her desk and left the Hertzberg-Davis building feeling as impersonal and dull as a drive-through order delivered through an intercom. *A number four combo, a side of tots, and a large Hi-C.* How anybody can translate that kind of jargon into food is beyond me.

Back at the squad room, I found a printout on my desk, left by Knudsen, the New York officer turned into philosopher who'd searched the wondrous world of the Internet under my request. I stuck a paperclip in my mouth, scanned the first paragraph, and thought, *What a sucker.* It read, "Proteus, one of the early gods of the sea. His children: Eidothea, Polygonos and Telegonos, the latter two both killed by Heracles." *What's this, an essay on Greek mythology?* "Other uses of the word Proteus: a search engine, a bacteria, a syndrome, a synonym for alchemy."

I crumpled the piece of paper, tossed it in the trash, and then called Electronics. Still nothing on Tarantino's hard disk. I tried another number and asked about DNA evidence on Huxley's body or vehicle. Nothing there either — everything was backed up. Mighty frustrating. I was entangled in a jumble of partial facts, suppositions, and pieces of information cluttering my brain with no apparent order. It made me feel like Maria Ramirez's pin board, the collector of everything who worked at the Chromo human resources department.

The data on that computer has been obtained through my grant and is therefore my intellectual property. I grabbed another paperclip and stuck it between my teeth. *Her data, her grant, her fucking intellectual property.* I sprang to my feet, walked to one of our terminals and logged onto the network. After browsing for fifteen minutes, I grinned, as my intuition had been right: dear Dr. Cox could claim whatever privacy on her data. NIH grants, though, were far from private. The National Institute of Health had budgeted for the 2010 fiscal year close to thirty billion in grant money. Of the two million, Julia Cox had received over the past two years, one had bought the Illumina Beadstation, the machine I had admired at the Esperanza lab. It didn't take me too long to figure out where the rest of the money had gone: computers, technicians' salaries, travel expenses, lab equipment. When I folded it all in, what had originally struck me as a conspicuous sum appeared meager. *Where did she get the rest of the money?* On the Esperanza website I found a whole section dedicated to Julia Cox and her team, research, mission statement, publications. A number of philanthropists and private institutions were listed in the acknowledgments for providing additional support to Cox's battle against leukemia. Finally the numbers were adding up. And as I scanned down the list of patrons, one name jumped to my eyes: Richard F. Medford, Chromo Inc. My hand froze over the mouse. The Chromo CEO turned out to be one of Cox's most generous donors.

No wonder the minute I mentioned the Proteus kids you lawyered up, Julia.

Two detectives from Homicide stepped into the squad room triumphantly announcing they had finally handcuffed their suspect after an investigation that had languished for over a year. "Did you get a confession?" another detective asked.

Keegan, an older dick with a Charles Bronson kind of mustache, grinned. He ambled to his desk, slumped in his chair, and propped both feet on his desk. "All I got from the asshole is, *I'll give you a hell of a time in court, you bastard. You've been after me just because I'm a Jew and you Irish dumbasses hate Jews.*" Keegan flew a hand to his breast pocket and produced a cigar case. "You know what I told the asshole? I said, *I don't know about the other Irishmen, but this Irish dick right here*" — he tapped on his breastbone — "*loves you, man. I've been after you for so long, I'd be out of a job without you!*"

I joined the burst of laughter spreading across the squad room. As I swiveled back to the computer screen something new roused my nostrils. A second before I recognized it, my pulse quickened. *Danger.* I inhaled, longer this time, giving my brain time to process the information.

Somebody I know just stepped out of the elevator. Somebody I hate.

I sprang to my feet and darted out of the room, the trail of the new scent leading the way. A foul smell, sour sweat and burnt cilantro, a tang I'd met before.

Huxley's assassin.

I can't be wrong, I know his smell now.

There was no way I could mistake it, the man in Huxley's car, the same individual who rampaged her place, his smell was right there, on the third floor of the Glass House. How the f—

"Good afternoon, Track. I got your message. I'm parked on Los Angeles Street. Are you ready to go?"

I screeched to a halt, flabbergasted. Diane. The assassin's smell. On Diane. I gaped, looking like a total idiot.

"What?" She touched her head. "Do I have toothpaste on my hair?"

I shook my head, still gaping. It didn't make any sense. I didn't want it to make any sense. Diane lost it and scoffed. "Track, what's freaking wrong with you?"

"Nothing," I lied. "Let me go get my jacket."

Diane, I thought, as I left her waiting in the elevator lobby. The Roman name for Artemis, the Greek hunting goddess. Beautiful and wild, a seducer and a killer, as, according to some legends, she slew her lover and companion Orion.

Would Eve have been drawn to the Tree of Knowledge, had she not known its fruits were forbidden?

CHAPTER 19

Thursday, October 16

Diane pulled to the curb, turned the engine off, and stared at the gates. "Are you sure this is the place?"

"Do you expect a cemetery to look any different?"

"No."

Green Lake Memorial Park was a citadel of the dead surrounded by white walls, the bronze statue of a genderless angel guarding its entrance. A row of palm trees emerged behind the enclosure, their skinny trunks lining the blue outline of the mountains.

"Let's move," I said, stepping out of the car and slamming the door. "They're probably at the burial site by now."

I was mad and on the verge of losing it. I felt the beast in me fighting to get out. *What'd you do last night?* I asked Diane on our way here. *Who'd you see, where'd you go?* As I pressed her, she became more and more defensive. *Who'd you sleep with?*

Fuck off, Track! Is this how you hit on girls?

I wasn't hitting on her. I had a hit on her scent.

I'd ridden in her car with the window rolled all the way down. It was all over her — in her hair and on her clothes — somebody else's smell, the same faceless person I had confronted the night before in Huxley's apartment. My eyes saw Diane and my nostrils perceived a ruthless killer. The odor enraged me, more so given the events of the night before. Whoever he was, he'd defeated me and I hated him. How could *he* be all over Diane? Was she a pawn, an accomplice, or just a by-stander?

Maybe you're wrong, Ulysses. Maybe it's not him you're smelling.

I'm never *wrong.*

Then follow her. Stalk her. She's the key to the assassin.

Smells are elusive, though. And so are people.

Diane locked the car and we hurriedly hiked up the incline to the gates. "It's not my fault we left late," she protested.

"Zone F, Detective," a uniformed officer stationed at the entrance told us after checking our identifications.

"Busy?" I asked him.

He shrugged. "Not much. Small, private service. A couple of news crews showed up at the beginning. They took pictures, did their gig right here in front of the gate, and when I informed them they weren't allowed inside, they left."

"There's a better celeb monopolizing the headlines these days," I said, thinking of movie director turned assassin, Jerry White.

We followed the road slithering through the various zones of the cemetery, its edges marked by purple heather and white petunias. Between two rows of poplars, a grid of ground markers was embedded in a field of freshly mowed grass. The sun framed the silhouette of a woman kneeling by one of the stones, while an unconcerned child played her own version of hopscotch between the graves. A smile surfaced on Diane's lips as she silently watched the scene. A warm breeze brushed the tree crowns and then came down to ruffle her hair. *The smell is finally gone,* I noted with relief. My mood instantly changed.

"My mother used to bring me to the cemetery once a month when I was growing up," Diane said.

Me too, I thought. "Grandparents?"

"No. All the children she miscarried until they finally told her she couldn't have any. My parents buried them one by one and made sure they always had fresh flowers." I puzzled over her words, unsure how to take them. "I was adopted," she explained softly.

We left the road and followed a sign pointing to Zone F. In the distance, voices intoned a sad tune, the notes mingling with the rustling of the leaves and the trickling of an artificial creek.

"It's like being haunted by ghosts," Diane continued. "The siblings I never had."

"At least they never stole your lunch box or beat you up in school." It was a stupid comment, yet I couldn't come up with anything better to say. It made her smile. She brought a hand to her face to cover a snort and, in spite of myself, I found it damn cute.

Two black hearses were parked next to the one another under the drooping boughs of a willow. The chant came to an end right as we joined the gathering.

"Keep your eyes open," I told Diane. "There's a good

chance our killer's right here."

She knew her assailant. Somebody so close she didn't mind to let him in at a vulnerable time.

We split, Diane to the left and I to the right. I spotted familiar faces interviewed at Chromo the day before, including a distraught Ms. Hennessy, the receptionist, who kept sniffing and bringing a tissue to her nose. I pictured her the next day, spending hours on the phone describing hats, shoes and faces she had studied and appraised during the ceremony. Including mine.

The priest gave the final blessing and aspersed the two caskets.

Cordelia, the Tarantinos' daughter, stood closest to the burial site. The pallbearers lowered the first casket, and when it reached the bottom Cordelia tossed a pink carnation over it.

Among the forest of dark suits, the hems of a teal blue scarf billowed, soon restrained by a white gloved hand—a smear of color in a sea of black. A matching bow sat on a wide hat, below which blond locks draped the narrow shoulders of a navy blue dress. Sexy pantyhose, with a vertical line drawn over perfectly shaped calves, blended into black high heels. Next to her was Richard Medford, easily recognizable by the mop of white hair crowning his head. Hands clasped behind his back, the Chromo CEO stood like a general at an official ceremony.

Medford's eyes darted, wandering among the bowed heads around him. Something caught his attention, making him shift and crane his head. At the other end of the congregation, Diane met his stare, blushed, and immediately looked away. Medford smiled, licked his lower lip, and then slid a hand around his wife's waist, drawing her closer and making her sway on her precariously high heels. Diane's face slid away, and a different lady caught my attention, standing farther away by a mortuary pillar, her face concealed behind large butterfly sunglasses. Painted in bright lipstick, her lips stood out like a drop of blood on a white wall.

A sudden murmur welcomed the end of the celebration. Feet shifted, heads bowed, arms reached out in muted hugs. The sudden liveliness of the congregation momentarily distracted me, and when I looked back, the mysterious lady had vanished. Like leaves blown by the breeze, the crowd dispersed in random order. Some ringed around Cordelia to offer their sympathy. I had expected Tarantino's sister to stand by her niece's side. Instead, she shuffled away with her husband, her frail figure leaning against him. Cordelia startled when a hand rested on her shoulder. Richard Medford stepped closer and kissed her pale cheek. I searched for the wife in high heels and spotted the teal scarf farther away, her white gloves flirtatiously stroking the expensive jacket of a friend.

"I'm doing okay now, thank you, Dan," she muttered in a low voice.

"Call us if you need anything." He had ash-blonde curls, an important nose, and a square chin charmed by a dimple. Despite wearing shades and a black felt hat, his distinctive features gave him away. I watched him bid his party goodbye and then crossed his path.

"Mr. Horowitz? Detective Presius, LAPD," I said, holding up my badge.

Dan Horowitz narrowed his eyes. "I'm in a hurry, Detective. My wife will have a fit if I don't show up in time for our daughter's ballet performance."

"Won't take too much of your time. I understand the Tarantinos were at your house the night they got murdered."

"Like about a hundred other people," he scoffed.

Peevish guy, I noted. Naturally suspicious, fond of his grounded certainties, and not well inclined towards crowds where it wasn't his ego to shine the brightest. Nothing like the happy Californian he depicted himself to be on TV.

"I'm just curious, Mr. Horowitz. How did you happen to know the victims?"

"Friends of mutual friends," he replied with a shrug. "If that's all—"

"Would those mutual friends include Mrs. Medford?"

The showman froze for a second, looked away, and then smirked. "Detective, everybody *knows* Elizabeth Medford."

"What about her husband?"

The smirk widened and became a grin. He looked over his shoulder, stepped closer, and whispered, "He loves it." His breath infiltrated my nostrils: a greasy lunch wolfed in a hurry and washed down with some herbal tisane his wife—certainly not him—made him therapeutically ingest on a daily basis.

"What do you mean?"

A sneer was all the answer I got. He brought a hand to his forehead to mock a military salute and left.

"You look funny, Track."

"Do I?"

Diane let the wind blow a lock in her face before brushing it away. Around us, voices turned into murmurs and tapered off. Withered strands of grass lay where the congregation had previously stood. "I spoke with Mrs. Medford," she said on our way back to the car. "Turns out, she's not only good friends with the Horowitzes, but knows Jerry White as well, together with a whole bunch of Hollywood people."

"How did that come up?"

"She asked me if we were also investigating Conrad's murder. *Poor Jerry*, as she called him, has been under a lot of stress after his daughter's death, but is basically a saint and wouldn't harm a fly."

I snorted. "And how does she suppose his gun ended up at the crime scene?"

"She claims somebody led him to it."

"How come she's smitten with all these celebs?"

"Exactly what I asked her. She gave me this." Diane handed me a colorful pamphlet with the word CHROMO printed on the first page, then unlocked her car and sat behind the wheel. I slouched on the passenger's seat and flipped through the booklet while my nostrils, with a mind of their own, widened and tested the air for possible unfriendly odors.

Gone. The wind carried it away. Or maybe you were wrong, Ulysses.

Impossible.

"Genetic screening?" I asked, reading off the pamphlet. "What for?"

The engine of Diane's old VW coughed, whined, and finally barked to life. She screeched out of the parking lot and whipped into the street, letting the first gear roar in anguish before switching to the second and third. *Get an automatic for God's sake*, my inner voice screamed. But I learned a long time ago not to ever comment on a woman's driving. It always backfires.

"It's very popular among the rich and famous, apparently," Diane replied, ignoring the afflictions of her engine. "Together with a healthy diet, mindful use of caffeine and alcohol, abstinence from nicotine, and supplemental folic acid, when a couple considers having a child nowadays they're recommended genetic screening. Elizabeth Medford even promised me a special price should I think about it some day."

I smiled. "Did you tell her you're neither rich nor

famous?"

Diane frowned. "How rude of you, Track! What do you know? I could still join the crowds of high society. I could always marry a rich litigation lawyer or a fancy plastic surgeon."

She smiled, but somehow I was no longer amused.

It was a lady's shoulder bag with a leather strap, zipped across the top. And it was sitting on a chair next to my desk. I inhaled. *Still away.* The long hand on the wall clock hit the number twelve and the short one aligned with the number four. A couple of murder books snapped closed with a loud click. Chairs were dragged on the floor and jackets were slipped back on.

"You workin' late, Track?" a detective asked, his lips hugging the butt of an unlit cigarette.

"Gotta hit the trail when it's hot," I replied.

"Nail the dumb director," he said, squeezing my shoulder. "And make us proud."

I stared at the empty desks. A phone rang but I didn't get up to answer. Up on the ceiling, the fan swooshed. My eyes strayed back to the purse. If Diane truly was my key to Huxley's assassin, nothing was going to stop me from finding out. I inhaled again. How long can a lady be gone powdering her nose? Her scent was nowhere close. The smell of bleach and floor detergent coming from the hallway told me the restrooms on our floor had been closed for evening cleaning, which bought me another couple of minutes. I snatched the purse, unzipped it, and went straight for the wallet. Credit cards, no cash, a UCLA alumni card, and finally the one item I sought: the driver's license. I barely had the time to peek at the address, when her scent gently wafted into range. By the time her heels clacked back into the squad room, the shoulder purse lay untouched on the chair, and my hands where in the evidence box on my desk. It contained all the papers and documents we had seized from Huxley's office.

"Where do you want me to sit?" Diane asked, the furrow between her eyebrows addressing the degenerate state of my working place. Damn, she smelled good.

I heaved the ream of papers out of the box and scattered them across Satish's clean desk. "Right here," I said, pulling out the chair for her.

She didn't move. The furrow didn't move either.

"What?"

"You want me to read *all* of those? It's more than fifty papers, and I don't even know I have enough background—"

"You a scientist, ain't you?"

Her nostrils widened for a second. She walked around Satish's desk and dropped on the chair. "I'm a *forensic* scientist," she corrected.

"And DNA specialist. This stuff's about DNA and cancer. Start with the ones authored by Huxley, Cox, or both. That should get us somewhere. Wave if the name Proteus comes up." I got up from my desk and walked to one of the terminals across the room.

"What are *you* doing?"

"Educating myself on a couple of things." I had a few trails to sniff out.

Dan Horowitz's words rung in my ears: *Everybody knows Elizabeth Medford, Detective*, he'd said. *Her husband loves it.* What the heck did he mean? It wasn't just what he'd said, it was *the way* he'd said it. Sneering. Maybe I was reading too much into it. It reminded me of something, though. I browsed the LAPD archives for about twenty minutes until I found what I was looking for. *Amedeus Ilke, age 38, convicted on May 17, 2006 with three counts of trespassing and four of stalking, currently serving a three-year sentence in the California Medical Facility state prison. Officer assigned to the case: Oscar Guerra. Psychiatric evaluation: Adam Washburn, M.D.*

I looked over my shoulder toward the back row of desks. Guerra's was as clean and empty as the streets of downtown on a sultry Fourth of July. I made a mental note to leave him a message and moved on to the next item on my agenda. I had a phone number, quickly memorized while peeking at Diane's cell phone, a first name—Jim—and now the database informed me, a last name: Kowalski. *James* Kowalski. Was it *his* smell I picked on Diane that morning? And if so, what linked him to Jennifer Huxley? I ran him for guns but nothing came up. I ran his rap sheet. Nada, not even a speeding ticket. I tapped on the keyboard. Diane shifted in her chair and the wall clock ticked. She flopped a paper back in the box and picked up a new one. With every movement, she radiated new particles in the air, like drops of black ink on a wet napkin. They drop, stain, spread.

I stared back at the screen. The hell with DMV, NCIC, NLETS, and all police databases. I went back to my old friend Google and typed "James Kowalski." A countless list of Facebook and LinkedIn enthusiasts popped up begging me to befriend them. The hell with them too, I don't cavort with people I can't smell. On the Google bar I added the word "gunfire." Nyet. *Back, back, back,* the clicks of the mouse spelling out my frustration. Kowalski and pistol. *Send.* Rotating glass hour. This time Google was taking its time thinking. And then the light. Not the one hundred watt kind, just feeble candlelight, but promising. I clicked.

SPRINGFIELD, Mass. (July 14, 2008) — Smith & Wesson Corporation announced today that Team Smith & Wesson earned two national titles and posted high scores in each of the eight divisions during the 2008 International Defensive Pistol

Association (IDPA) National Championship held at the Palm Springs Shooting Range in Palm Springs, California.

I skimmed down the document.

... Concluding division wins by Team Smith & Wesson was team member James S. Kowalski. Competing with a model 6904 9mm, Kowalski fired best times in 15 of the total 17 stages to easily take the national title 13 seconds ahead of second place.

I blinked at the screen. *He may not own a gun — officially, at least — but the guy knows how to handle the puppies.* There was nothing else my friend Google could unearth about the man. I shrugged it off and looked up Medford. A few leads came up, and I chose the least obvious because somehow the direction was promising. One click at a time, I surfed my way in the twisted maze called Internet, made of hidden servers and bottomless databases, until I stumbled upon a name: Lizzy Trujillo. As I scrolled down the tabloids, I traveled back in time and plunged into the past, when Lizzy was a seventeen-year-old girl and ran away from home to come to live in the city. All she had was one change of clothes and fifty bucks in her pocket. Not hard to imagine what she did for a living those first few months. She had ambitions, though, and beauty on her side. Her parents filed a missing child report (still in the police records), and nothing happened for a few years over which I lost track of her. Until I found her again married to a young L.A. lawyer, financially well off, and supposedly happily in love. Except something happened.

Imagine yourself a Bel Air mansion, one of those ten thousand square-foot castles with tennis court, ballroom, media room, and a couple of dozen bedrooms. By the swimming pool, leisurely voices lace with live jazz tunes. A loose needlework of wavering lights reflects off the turquoise surface of the water. Waiters in tuxedos scuttle around balancing silver trays with hors d'oeuvres and a forest of champagne flutes. Suffuse garden lights wind around flowerbeds and marble stairs. Couples in all fashions, colors, and shapes stare, judge, and let themselves be stared at and be judged. It's the sort of event one has to absolutely attend if they're very rich or intend to become so some day.

A pretty girl in her mid-twenties emerges from the crowd in a salmon pink gown. She shyly looks around, most faces extraneous to her, yet her eyes sparkle with anticipation. She's looking for somebody, a lover, perhaps, or a patron, or maybe just a friend. Maybe she doesn't know herself. Her beauty doesn't go unnoticed. She attracts the attention of a man, who, at least ten years older than her, is quite skilled in the art of flirting. In no time he's conquered the young woman's heart. Like butterflies coming out of the magician's hat, the girl watches her dreams flutter around her head, tickle her cheeks, and brighten up her future.

Unfortunately, the girl hasn't come to the party alone. Another man claims her as his wife, and the altercation begins. The two shout at one another and soon become physical. The party is ruined, and the rumors spill out in a few tabloids the next day, which is how, about a decade later, I find out about the incident. Together with a familiar name: Richard F. Medford.

It was four thirty. Diane had waded through one quarter of Huxley's papers. I picked up one of the laptops, brought it to my desk, and opened it. *Incident Report,* I wrote. *My unsuccessful search in Huxley's apartment.* I sighed. *Okay, seriously now.* I hit the delete key like a kid would hit the shoot button at an arcade game, and started over with the easy stuff: date, place, circumstances *(Investigation of disappearance of subject named Jennifer Huxley)*, reporting officer (*Det. Ulysses M. Presius*), witnesses (this one was sticky, *None*), and offenders (*Unknown*). I then came to the narrative and got stuck. What the hell was I doing there? In most cases, the officer is responding to a radio broadcast. Me, I was responding to an olfactory trace, which told me the killer had gone back to the victim's residence. I sighed in frustration, wrote the words "gut feeling," stared at blinking cursor, erased them and started over. I tried the word "intuition" instead, but didn't find it appealing either. I grunted, looked away from the screen, and let my eyes wander, searching for an anchor to linger on. I found myself staring at Diane. Her perfectly arched brows, slightly frowning over the paper she was reading. The tip of the pen touching her lips. The damned report in front of me, still blank and waiting to be written.

"Hi, Satish," I said, without turning, a fraction of a second before he entered the squad room. Diane's head shot up. I heard him walk towards us and still didn't turn. "Are you wearing your brown polka dot tie, Sat? You know I hate your brown polka dot tie."

Satish chuckled and slid off his jacket. "Hello, Ms. Kyle," he said, dragging over a chair. "Your presence in the squad room makes a noticeable improvement to the place."

Diane smiled. "Hello, Satish. How are you?" She then knitted her brows together and sent me a sideways scowl. "Now that's the way to treat a lady. Why don't you take notes, Track?"

I cowardly kept my eyes on the laptop. Satish sat next to me with a broad smile painted on his face and his hands laced over his stomach. His cheeks were cleanly shaven, his wavy hair sleek and swept back. He was wearing a charcoal pinstripe suit, a lime green shirt underneath, and of course the brown polka dot tie. Which I already knew because when he does, he also wears a more expensive brand of cologne.

"What got you all groomed up?"

"Just rehearsing for our meeting with Hannah Kelson tomorrow," he replied with feigned indifference. One of the over two thousand stars in the Hollywood Walk of Fame, Hannah Kelson, Jerry White's ex-wife, had always been one of Satish's favorite actresses. And now, at forty-six, when most of her colleagues got lifted, pumped, and tucked so they could stay in the business, Hannah had retired from the big screen and was writing a book about her child's lost fight against leukemia.

"And, I needed to get the squalid smell of morgue off my skin," Satish added, flopping a manila folder on the desk.

I placed the laptop back on my desk and picked up the document. "Huxley's autopsy report," I noted, opening the folder. Something I'd been waiting for.

Diane closed the paper she'd been reading and craned her head. "What does it say?"

Satish summarized it for us. The official cause of death was multiple gunshot wounds to the chest. The slugs—consistent with a nine millimeter semi-jacketed hollow point—had perforated both the right and left cardiac ventricles. The body presented bruises on the arms and legs, and skin lacerations from the ropes at her wrists and ankles. The victim had been restrained first and then sedated with a substance called benzodiazepine. Traces of the drug had been found in the flesh-eating bugs collected from the corpse.

"It's a psychoactive drug," Diane noted, recognizing the name. "It's not OTC, though. You need a prescription."

"Any luck on a TOD?" I asked.

"No earlier than Thursday and no later than Sunday. Cohen couldn't do any better than that," Satish said.

"It doesn't tell us whether or not she was dead by the time the Tarantinos got murdered. We've got to have her fingerprints compared to those found on the first commandment note. Did they collect her nail trimmings?"

"Yes—no traces of DNA, though."

"I'm not thinking DNA." I turned to Diane. "You should take a look at those trimmings and compare them to the fragment from the Tarantinos' home."

Satish clicked his tongue. "Cohen's report states Huxley's brain tissue was *unremarkable*. If traces of anticonvulsants had been found, it would be on the report."

I leaned back in the chair and groaned. "What's new then?" None of these findings answered any of my conundrums.

"Perlite," Satish replied.

"Perlite? Is it something from your childhood the autopsy report reminds you of?"

He laughed. "No, perlite is what's *new* in the autopsy report. Cohen found microscopic, subcutaneous glass shards on the inside of the victim's hands. Further analyses unveiled traces of perlite on the crystals. It's a volcanic mineral."

"What's it used for?"

"Mostly construction material, as an insulator. Interestingly enough, the rope used to bind her—"

"Hemp cord?"

Satish nodded. "Also of common use at construction sites."

"It's a natural fiber, very sturdy," Diane interjected. She sighed, pulled away from the desk, and got to her feet. The small hand on the clock's face had reached the number five. "I couldn't find anything even vaguely close to the word Proteus, Track. Huxley's manuscript is exactly what Cox had told you it was: a genetic study on leukemia cases, all under twelve years of age. When Huxley says 'kids,' she's as generic as she could be. All subjects in the study are children."

"So you basically found nothing?"

"Well, there's one possibility—"

"Shoot." I could tell Diane was being cautious not to jump to conclusions. On the other hand, I was desperate for anything, even far-fetched suppositions.

"These cases of leukemia are treated through bone marrow transplant. Before surgery patients undergo aggressive chemo and radiotherapy treatments in order to get rid of all cancerous cells in the blood. In her manuscript, Huxley describes a subgroup of children whose cancers were so resilient they did not respond to therapy." Diane brought a hand to her mouth and nibbled her thumb. "They died before they could get the transplant."

"How many are we talking about?"

She leafed through the paper. "Twelve."

"You think those could be the Proteus kids Huxley referred to in her letter?"

"I don't know. As I said, the name Proteus is never mentioned in the paper. Mine's a supposition, based on the fact that this subgroup of patients stands out."

Diane's hypothesis made perfect sense. But then the next question was: what linked those kids to Chromo? And more importantly: how were we to bypass all HIPAA and PPA bullshit in order to find out who these kids were?

"I'm off," Diane said, retrieving her purse. "I'll stop by Computer Forensics tomorrow to check on the status of Tarantino's and Huxley's hard drives. Good night, guys."

My nose held onto Diane's trail as it disappeared down the hallway and vanished into the elevator. So damn different from just a few hours earlier.

Satish grinned. "You seem distracted, Track."

I grunted. "Distracted by what?"

"Oh, I don't know. Ladies' charms, maybe?"

Scowling, I retrieved the computer and propped it back on my lap. "Look who's talking, Sat. You and your ugly polka dot tie. Don't tell me you're going to wear it tomorrow to show off in front of Kelson."

Satish slid the tie between his fingers. "What's wrong with my polka dot tie?"

"Did you find out how Kelson and Conrad met?"

"I did a little research."

"Allow me a wild guess, then. They met at Chromo."

Satish's eyes shifted from his tie to my face. "Good job, Track. I see your psychic abilities go beyond guessing a person's attire."

"I can do better than that. White and Kelson went to Chromo in the early 'nineties for genetic counseling. They wanted a child, and Chromo convinced them a good DNA check-up was in line with painting the nursery and buying diapers."

Satish nodded silently, brows curled together in a deep thinking frown. "They wanted to do everything by the book," he said. "White and Kelson. They went to see doctors, counselors, and geneticists. Everything had to be perfect for the baby they were going to have. What a peculiar concept."

"I bet it reminds you of something." I opened the laptop and touched the keyboard. The blank page of my unwritten report came back to life and scowled at me. Outside, the sun had lowered on the horizon, and a sickly pink washed on the walls through the Venetian blinds.

Satish looked at the ceiling. For a moment I thought I'd caught him off guard, that he didn't have a story to share this time. I was wrong. "It does. It reminds me of calendars."

"Calendars," I repeated, typing a few random words on the screen just to make it look less blank.

"Wall calendars, specifically. The ones you use to note doctor's appointments and things like that. Did you have one in high school, Track?"

"No. There were too many things I preferred not to remember."

"Ah, but you see, you weren't playing the clarinet like I did back then." Satish folded his arms across his chest and gazed at the ceiling.

I typed another sentence. "I didn't know you used to play the clarinet."

"I was quite good at it, too. So good in my junior year I decided I was finally ready for the Annual Jazz Competition. Kids from all over the county could sign up for auditions. It was a highly competitive event, because if you made it to the finals, you'd go to the statewide competition. The final prize was a full music scholarship."

Half of my brain was typing the report and the other half listening to Satish. "Did you want to become a musician?"

"My destiny was to become a jazz player. So I signed up and dutifully noted the day and time of the auditions on my wall calendar—my *sports car* calendar. It had the best models: Jaguar XK-E, Porsche 911S, Corvettes... And guess what the month of July was?"

"No idea." I wrote, *I drew my weapon upon realizing the suspect was still within the residence and advanced towards his hiding spot.*

"A 1978 Alfa Romeo Spider. Do you remember those, Track?"

I nodded without paying attention, searching for ways to explain in the report how I ran for Huxley's laptop instead of the suspect.

"I practiced the clarinet six, sometimes eight hours a day, and by the end of the summer I could play my song perfectly. I was proud of myself. I had carefully nursed every single note of my piece. The breathing time, the rhythm—everything was absolutely impeccable. At last, the big day came. The night before I polished my clarinet and my mother ironed my best *kurta*."

I typed the final remarks on the report. I had to justify my choice of course of action without looking stupid. That by itself required some brainwork, which I had already demonstrated the lack of. No wonder the expression "catch 22" was invented in the army.

"The big day I got to the auditorium and it was closed."

"Closed? Why?"

"Shut and locked. And completely deserted. There was a little piece of paper taped to the door with the names of the people who had passed the auditions."

"What?"

Satish chuckled. "You see, I loved the Spider so much I didn't want to turn the page on my calendar. I was dead sure I had the right day and time in my head."

"You didn't even check it?"

"Uh-uh. I checked my clarinet. My mother checked my clothes. My old man checked the alarm clock to make sure I got up in time. I did not check the calendar."

"Man, Satish. That's too bad."

He sighed and got to his feet. "Not to mention stupid. It was a good lesson."

I saved the report, closed the laptop and dropped it on my desk over a pile of old files. "I bet you didn't see it that way back then." I got my jacket and followed Satish to the elevator. We rode the car down in silence, and only when the chime announced our arrival to the ground level, Satish offered one last thought on the matter. "You see, Track, sometimes it's the most obvious things one tends to neglect. Just because they're right under your nose, you fail to see them. Ingraining is the best deceit."

I smiled, bade him goodnight, and watched his car drive away before looking around for my Dodge. "SHIT! Satish!" I called. Too late, he was gone already. Fucking right as always, this partner of mine. It's the obvious things one tends to neglect. My Charger was happily parked in my driveway. Satish had picked me up from home that morning.

Between going back to the third floor, getting the car logs, signing out the unmarked cruiser, and justifying why it needed to go for a ride, I wasted another half hour. Fortunately, by the time I left downtown, traffic had dwindled to a snake of headlights all cruising at the same speed. I could get home in fifty minutes instead of the ninety it took during peak hours. *Un*fortunately, by the time I left I was ravenous, tired, and irritated. It had been a long day, with an ominous beginning and a plain ending. As I went over the events of the day, I concluded that, besides letting my blood pressure enjoy various roller coaster rides, the report I finally managed to put together was the only thing I could actually pin down as accomplished.

I continued to beat myself up as I took the Two northbound, passed the junction with the One-Thirty-Four, missed my exit, and kept heading north. It was the car, really. It drove all the way to the end of the Two, merged into the Two-Ten southbound, swerved into the Lincoln exit ramp, and kept going northbound toward Loma Alta. As for me, being behind the wheel, I had no choice but follow.

Yellow streetlights and tall neon signs sped by the side of the road — some flashing famous store names, others only half-lit and making me feel dyslexic. Soon dark trees replaced the stores buried in wide parking lots. The car made another turn and entered a residential area in Altadena. Ah. *This is where you wanted to go.* Front porch lights washed down middle class doors, the friendliness of the white picket fence revoked by the threatening ARMED RESPONSE sign stuck on the ground by the doorstep.

I slowed, turned the headlights off, and peeked at the door numbers until the car decided it was time to pull to the curb. Across the street, a row of colonial style townhouses loomed over a welcome mat of lawn so uniformly green it looked like it had been spray-painted. The façade of each unit was identical to the next, and seen from the side, they had the disorienting effect of double mirrors reflecting off one another. The first floor of the unit I was staring at was lit, and the bay windows framed a couple eating dinner while a TV yawned the evening news.

I turned the engine off and watched. Something in my head told me what I was doing was wrong. Something in my head told me to shut up and do it anyways. Something in my head switched to automatic, went its merry own way, and pretended not to be there.

The man whispered something to the woman sitting next to him, kissed her, and got up. She picked at her dinner with little interest, while the TV pooled flashes of blue light on her face. The man reappeared a few minutes later, a cell phone pressed to his ear. He paced, listened, frowned. He blabbered something into the phone, then snapped it closed.

Whatever the call was about, it made her mad. She got up and cleared her plate, seething. For the next few minutes, man and woman came in and out of sight, the tone and meaning of their words coded in their body language. He swayed a hand past his head, the phrase spat with the gesture clearly readable on his lips. He snatched his jacket from a chair, grabbed the beer he left on the coffee table, walked to the door, and slammed it behind. The slam I heard.

Now alone, the woman slumped on the couch and dropped her face in her hands. I left her there and followed the man. He drained what was left of the beer can on the doorstep, crushed the can, and tossed it in the trash bin against the sidewall of the building. What an environmentally conscious guy.

I watched him shuffle to the sidewalk, where a black Lexus blinked to life. The engine roared, the tires screeched, the exhaust exhaled poisonous gases. Thirty seconds later everything was back to normal: the street was dark again, the air still and silent. A cricket resumed its interrupted song. The bay windows were dark—the show was over. A faint light was on up on the second floor, behind a cream-colored curtain.

And there I went.

No, yelled a voice in my head. *It's illegal, stop*! I ignored the voice, stepped on the lawn of a private residence without having a search warrant and went straight to the trashcan.

Ulysses, you son of a bitch, stop and leave NOW!

I lifted the lid, took a handkerchief out of my pocket, and, careful not to wipe off fingerprints or saliva smudges, I retrieved the beer can. I stared at it, then brought it to my nose. Malt, alcohol, and sweat. *His*. And a bit of Diane mixed in.

Ha, ha, the voice laughed. *And what are you hoping to obtain with that? Whatever you milk out of the can, it will be inadmissible evidence.*

If that happens, I replied, jogging back to my car and dropping the can into an evidence bag, *I'll tell them a voice in my head made me do it*. The voice shut up and, with my newly retrieved piece of evidence, I drove back home.

CHAPTER 20

Friday, October 17

José Salazar beams his flashlight, a silent blade sweeping the darkness around him. The sky is a sheet of tar, broken only by the shy grin of a crescent moon and the yellow halo blanketing downtown. The jets of the fountain have quieted, and the water is still in the shallow pool. The building looms tall against the night sky, its glistening façade a waterfall of shimmering black.

Salazar adjusts the belt to his waist and checks his gun holster. The familiarity of what he sees reassures him: everything looks in order. He walks to the side entrance, his steps producing a ghostly sound in the stillness around him. He lifts the call box lid and punches in the six-digit number he has memorized at the beginning of the month. Every month a new number. A soft click from the lock grants him access to the building. Ah. I'm the king of the world now, *he thinks, as his military boots echo in the open hall.* He takes the elevator down to the basement, where halogen lights hum tacitly, and AC vents whisper in unison. Nothing else breaks the quiet of the place. Eerie, anybody else would deem it. Not Salazar, though. He loves the intimacy the night offers. In a few hours, the place will be bustling with life. Voices will holler down the corridors, conference rooms will witness brainstorming ideas, equations will be scribbled over white dry boards. Orders will be delivered and rants vented. Computers will sweat line after line of code, centrifuges will spin vials of blood, refrigerators will freeze jars of samples. All of that will happen after sunrise. Right now, everything holds still and waits. It's what makes Salazar love his job so much: his kingdom, the solitude of an empty building, for him to guard, secure, and keep safe until dawn.

The bang, sudden and unexpected, echoes across the walls, so surreal he wonders if he just imagined it. A second bang follows, the sound of metal crushing. Salazar draws his weapon. *The labs,* he thinks, darting down the corridor. Some scatterbrain lab tech must have forgotten to lock a cage, *he reasons* — the most plausible hypothesis. Salazar slams the fire doors open and crosses the basement in its full length. He flicks on the switches. The lab greets him with the smell of hypochlorite and the impersonal sheen of stainless steel surfaces.

A cart lies on its side. Blue trays of vials are strewn on the floor. Salazar steps closer, boots crunching on glass shards. *Who did this?* A clonk this time, then metal dragged on the floor, coming from the wall to the right. A high-pitched scream makes the hair on his back stand up. *The macaques!*

Salazar punches the passcode to the animal lab but his sweaty fingers slip on the pad. *Damn it!* He re-enters the passcode, and when he finally hears the beep and click he shoulders through the door into the bedlam behind it. The reek of urine embraces him, intense. Feces are sprawled on the floor and smeared on the walls. A wreck of open cages and metal bars, spilled feeders and steel trays. The corpse of one of the animals withers in a corner, its skull squashed under a heavy dishpan. Panicked, one of the macaques swings from an AC pipe on the ceiling and squeals intermittently. A second animal shivers in a corner, coiled in a pool of its own excrement. The ones still trapped in their pens clutch to the bars and bang their heads, voicing their distress in shrieks.

The screech makes Salazar jump. A row of white teeth flashes before him, Salazar raises his gun and fires. The monkey collapses on the ground, its face blown off in a star of splintered bones. Frightened by the blast, the other animals cry out. A few run back to their cages, others leap to the door seeking a way out. Straying his eyes across the room, Salazar notices something that doesn't belong: an unlaced sandal, lying on the floor behind a pile of metal rods. And then a shaking foot, legs, the hem of a lab coat. Salazar crouches, clasps one of the wrecked cages and shoves it out of the way, uncovering a sight so gruesome he feels cold chills sweep down his back. He draws in a sharp breath, mesmerized for a moment, before he regains lucidity and finally dials the emergency code on his radio.

CHAPTER 21

Friday, October 17

"*Macaca mulatta*, an Indian species, commonly known as rhesus macaque," a bearded guy in a white coat told me, jotting down notes on a clipboard. "Sixteen of them. Two were already dead, and two we had to put down. The rest we drugged up for a long sleep."

Blue, baby-sized shrouds had been lined up against the wall, each one with a white tag wrapped around it. I scowled, disgusted by the stench. "Monkeys? I get a four a.m. callout and all there's to see is a bunch of dead monkeys?"

The guy raised his eyes from the clipboard. His receding hairline drew an M across the top of his head, and his Freudian beard was gray with rust-colored streaks at the corners of the mouth. He had no lips and no eyelashes, and he stared at me as if the Pope had just strolled in front of us and I'd failed to recognize him. "No, sir. The monkeys are *my* job," he said, tapping the pen on his chest. "*Your* job" — pen pointed at me — "is the DOA who just got to the hospital forty minutes ago." DOA, dead on arrival.

"This proves what I suspected all along, Track," Satish told me as soon as I joined him in the basement of the Chromo building.

"Which is?"

"There's some monkey business going on here at Chromo." His eyes sparkled mischievously.

"Hats off to your brilliant intuition," I said, bitterly. We crossed the corridor, the stench of urine and excrement getting stronger with every step.

"Cheer up, Track. You've been a cop long enough to know that shit happens. Besides, monkey shit is a good omen in some parts of India."

"I hope you're joking."

"Not at all. In some villages they even consider it—"

"Holy shit!" I hollered stepping into the wrecked lab.

"Exactly," Satish replied. "I guess you don't wanna hear what they do with cow shit."

"They lick it to show repentance." Diane emerged from the metal wreckage of lab cages, the animal stench so strong I could hardly smell her. Behind her, Peter — the SID photographer — faithfully documented every smudge speckling the linoleum floors.

Satish stared at her with admiration for her knowledge of Indian trivia, and I with disgust. Diane ignored both and delved right into work talk. "These monkeys were part of Chromo's genetic experiments. The victim was a lab technician. He'd come to bleed the animals."

"Instead he had a change of heart and decided to free

the little critters? And maybe take them for a ride down to skid row and buy them a drink?"

"He wasn't the one who freed them, Track."

"They have a surveillance camera at the main gate," Satish said. "The lab guy came in at his usual time. Then a second figure followed, at two-fifteen a.m."

"How did he get in?"

"He punched in the passcode."

"How many know the passcode?"

"Security and a few others. Mostly lab people working night shifts."

I started pacing. Sticky with urine and organic residue, the floor made annoying popping sounds underneath my shoes. One wall of the room was organized in Formica countertops, locked cabinets, and a couple of sinks. A computer monitor lay shattered on the ground. The stainless steel cages were on the opposite side of the room, grouped in two racks of eight pens each. The top row of the first rack had collapsed in a jumble of broken feeders, dented climbing poles, and overturned dishpans, their foul contents spilled all over the floor. Some of the wire mesh doors had come off their hinges and were sprawled several feet away.

"Any chance they got out by themselves?" I asked.

"No," Diane replied. "The cell doors are locked with a spring bolt. These monkeys wouldn't be strong enough to open them."

"Is this where the guy was found?" Satish said, pointing at the area between two consecutive racks of cages, clearly marked in yellow tape on the floor. All around, different patterns of shoe soles and skid marks overlapped, a bi-dimensional projection of the frenzied rescue the EMTs had performed on the victim.

Diane nodded.

"There's no blood," Satish commented. "What did he die

of?"

"We don't know. When our unit got here, the ambulance was already on its way to the hospital. One of the responding officers told us they put the guy on an Ambu bag because he was hardly breathing."

"You think he walked in on the intruder and there was a fight?" I asked.

"Hard to tell in this mess. We recovered one of the victim's sandals—"

"Let me see it."

It was one of those German sandals with a thick rubber sole. Pretty ordinary, in fact. The sole smelled of monkey urine. I studied the room. There were two doors: the one Satish and I had come from, which gave out into the hallway, and a second one at the back.

"Where does the back door lead to?" I asked.

"Another lab. For bench work, no animals in there," Diane replied.

Satish walked to the back to check it out. I followed, sniffing. The second rack of cages was still hinged to the wall. I could smell the monkeys jumping from pen to pen, the scene forming in my head as their odors mingled and reached my nostrils. Panicky monkeys crying out, banging the cage doors. The smell of blood, one of their own. They're scared. A new scent, an intruder. I stopped, went back, retraced it. The smell inside the sandal gave me the victim. I sensed his presence from the first door up to where he'd been found. Stop. For some reason he never made it beyond that point. But somebody else did. Somebody ran to the door at the back and—

"Track, Diane. Come over here." Satish was crouching by the last cage on the bottom row, the closest to the back door. "This is not fingerprint powder, is it?" he asked, pointing to a fine cloud of white particles flouring one of the steel rods. I brushed it with the tip of my pinky and brought it to my nose.

"Track, we're supposed to lift—"

"It's talc," I said. The cage, then the wall next to it. *The suspect tripped, the floor slippery with urine. He fell and slammed against the cage, then laid a hand on the wall to steady himself.*

"Talc?"

"It makes sense, actually," Diane interjected. "The stainless steel of these cages should have shown human fingerprints. Instead, all we could find were baby-sized ones, from the monkeys. No human prints. Both the lab guy and the intruder were wearing gloves. Lab gloves, most likely."

"You're thinking glove talc?" Satish asked.

"It would make sense, wouldn't it? The guy touches the rod and some talc spills out."

"No." I stood up, hooked both hands on my belt, and stared at the cage racks, all doors dangling with their spring bolts unlocked. "No, it makes no sense."

Diane sprang to her feet and frowned. "Why not?" she challenged.

Proud lady. Her zeal came onto me in a deliciously zesty whiff, which momentarily covered the tangs surrounding us.

I showed her with my gloved hand. "Talc would've come out had he raised his arm, like this. But look." I slid a finger inside the wrist of my glove. I hadn't used talc and had to leave that bit to her imagination. "Whatever comes out when you raise your hand goes straight into shirt cuffs or arm. If you *lower* your hand instead, as he would've to touch the rod down there, no talc comes out. It stays in the glove."

"Then maybe the talc was on him, from when he'd donned the gloves, and then he brushed his arm against the cage door."

"The pattern would be different, as in a smear. That one's a sprinkle. It couldn't come from a glove."

"Still—"

"Okay, you two." Satish jumped in. "I think we ought to find out why the hell a man died in here."

My brain was on a different frequency. I clung onto the intruder's smell and followed it. *He ran out through the back door.* I left Satish and Diane discussing the philosophical differences between sprinkles and smears, and stepped into the adjacent lab. All surfaces were neat and shiny. Rows of glassware and identical tools filed like soldiers on the overhead shelves. Everything was as sterile and impersonal as a funeral home stripped out of flowers. The only exception, a metal cart sprawled on the floor: the intruder ran out in a hurry, knocked off the cart, then fled through a side door. I brought my pinky to my nose again, the tip still stained with a dab of talc. Vaguely perfumed, not a fragrance, soap rather. *Could the intruder be a woman?*

I perused the room looking for a new trace. I found something else instead. Six white tanks crammed on the bottom shelf of a metal rack, their handles sticking out at the top like protruding ears. A blue label to the side of each container read, "Cryo-Cil, Nitrogen refrigerated unit." A memory, five years earlier, in Watanabe's lab. *Cryogenic tanks*, I realized, stepping closer to take a better look. Small size, most likely used for transportation, their contents shielded within an internal core, in a bubble of vacuum and *insulating* material. Sturdy, I considered, yet not immune to a semi-jacketed hollow point.

"Diane!" I darted back into the animal lab. "I want the recordings from the surveillance camera at the gate," I said. "All the way back to October 6."

Diane winced. "October 6? That far back?"

"Yes. That far back."

I got home shortly after dawn. There was a moment along the freeway when the sky ripened, and a palette of burning reds and carmines seeped over the outline of the mountains. It lasted only a few ephemeral minutes, then the colors dissolved and a new day was born.

Once at home I showered and shaved. The bathroom mirror insisted on portraying a tired me with dark circles underneath my eyes.

I hate mirrors. They tend to have a mind of their own.

I ground two cups of coffee beans and got the Bialetti Moka out. For wine and coffee you gotta leave the Italians alone. I filled the bottom of the Bialetti with water—up to the valve, strictly, not above and not below—filled the filter, then placed it on the stove.

I keep a watchful eye on that baby as it brews my coffee. The gas must be turned off when the scent of coffee is just ripe, right in the middle of its aromatic gargles. A little too early, and not all the water has come out. A little too late and it gets a burnt aftertaste. It's one of those things where perfection lies right between timing and precision. The point is not to get distracted.

I slouched on the recliner and watched the morning light draw long shades on the walls. A jay screeched outside, until the trash truck turned onto the street and the rattling and clonking of trash bins sent the jay away. I thought of coffee and dawn and how everything in life reaches an exact peak of perfection and then it's gone. The Greeks had a name for it, but I couldn't think of it. My thoughts seemed to follow the same pattern: they came and went in waves, and by the time I felt I had the right intuition, it was gone and I couldn't get it back. At least dawns had existed for a few million years now, and as for coffee, I could always brew a new Moka.

There were six cryogenic tanks in the Chromo lab. Jennifer Huxley wanted new data. Jennifer Huxley is dead. How long has she been dead? Did she ever go to the Tarantino home that night or was it someone else driving her car? The religious note. It smelled foul.

And on that last thought, I leaped out of the recliner and reached for the phone.

"Latent Prints," I blurted with the scratchy voice of somebody who'd just come out of bed. I had to give my name and business. As if anybody other than a frustrated cop had an interest in calling Latent Prints at eight o'clock in the morning. Really.

"Hold on, please."

I held on. Latent Prints picked up in the form of a Hispanic accent asking again for my name and business.

"Presius. I've got a job request sitting somewhere on your dusty shelves." The accent didn't like that I called her shelves dusty. I didn't care.

"Hold on, please."

I held on. Back in the kitchen the Bialetti started singing. I held on to that, too.

"Hello?" Low, baritone voice this time, as scratchy and annoyed as mine—somebody who probably wanted to use the phone and instead found it already in use.

"Presius—"

"Is somebody helping you out?"

"Not really."

"Hold on."

I held on for the third time. I was so damn pissed I forgot about the Bialetti and got there one second too late. I could smell the burnt coffee. "Fuck."

"Ah, no, this is Lorenzo, sir."

"Who?"

"Lorenzo Agavi. I believe I've been assigned your request."

I gave him the case ID again. Just because he believed it, it didn't mean *I* believed it.

"Yes, sir." I heard him flip over papers. "I've got uh— A note found on the crime scene and an envelope, both filed under the name Tarantino. Correct?" I nodded but didn't utter a word. "Well, I just got it, sir. They're both on my desk as we speak."

"You mean you didn't fume it yet, did you?" There was silence on the other end of the line. "The note from the crime scene. Did you fume it, yes or no?"

"No, sir, but as I said—"

"Great. There's something I need you to look at before you fume it. Do you understand? And then you fume it and play all your cool tricks with it. Understood?"

There was another pause. "Yes, sir. What is it you want me to look at? I'm listening."

I told him. Lorenzo Agavi understood before I could even complete the sentence. I liked this guy. Burnt coffee happens. It's a side effect of life. But this guy—this guy I liked.

Detective Oscar Guerra left a note on my desk. "Lunch Monday?" it read. Laconic, as always, even in the written word. I jotted him down on my calendar: "Oscar—lunch—talk about Ilke case." I tapped the pen against the paper. Strange little animal, the Hollywood business. Movie director Jerry White, showman Dan Horowitz, and all the beautiful, the rich, and the forever young. What did people like Medford and Tarantino have to do cavorting with them? And then there was Medford's wife. *Everybody knows*

Elizabeth, Detective, Horowitz had said.

Nelson's high-pitched giggles from the room next door distracted me. I got up and went looking for the detective-wannabe who was supposed to help me with the Tarantino investigation. She was sitting on Luke's desk, happily chatting her way through tabloids, blockbusters, and TV shows.

"You're kidding!" I heard her shrill. "Did you watch the sequel too? It was to die for!"

"Did you die for those papers I asked you to sort through, Nelson?"

She startled. Luke straightened up in his chair. "Hey Track," he said.

Nelson sulked. "Nothing whatsoever came out of the Tarantinos' phone logs—"

"I'm not talking about that."

She rolled her eyes, hopped off Luke's desk and mumbled a weary, "I'll see you later, Luke."

I followed her to one of the common rooms, where she pointed to an open cardboard box sitting on a large metal table. Next to the box was an unrolled map of L.A. county, with a few areas between North Hollywood and Westwood marked in bright yellow. "It took me the whole day to sort through all phone logs, financial records, bank statements and what have you."

I reached for the coffee pot sitting on a file cabinet next to a snake of Styrofoam cups and helped myself to a lukewarm brew. I hate lukewarm American coffee. It's even worse than American coffee. "And?" I prodded, inhaling the awakening wafts of caffeine.

"Nothing."

A mouthful of coffee went the wrong way down my throat. "What d'you mean nothing? You spent the whole day and got nothing out of it? What d'you get paid for?"

Nelson's pretty lips twitched into a pout. She came so close to my face I smelled Luke's aftershave on her skin. "You know, Track," she hissed, "I used to like you a lot better before you got your D-2 promotion. Still an asshole, but at least you were fun to hang out with on Friday nights." A disgusted look clinging to her dark eyes, she snagged my tie and tugged it. "Look at you now. All dressed up and plastered behind the I-no-longer-have-time-for-you-people shitty attitude."

A doorknob from across the hallway squeaked and a Rape Special lieutenant came out of one of the offices and walked straight to our room. Nelson let go of my tie and took a step back. "Sorry to disappoint you, Detective," she said, her voice tuned back to mellow. "All payments Jennifer Huxley received were from her paychecks. You're welcome to double-check yourself, if you want. In the meantime, I'll go ahead and bring these back to the evidence room." She hurdled the large cardboard box, walked out of the door, and disappeared in the meanders of our cubicle-filled floor. I coughed, readjusted the knot of my tie and nodded a brisk salute to the LT.

Lieutenant Aberdeen was hefty and bilious and wheezed like ten overworked bellows. He drank, smoked, and had drunk and smoked his entire life. You wouldn't have given him a day longer to live and yet he was more resilient than a nest of cockroaches. "How's coffee today?" he asked, going for the pot.

"Lukewarm," I replied, staring at the map Nelson had left open on the desk. She had color-coded a few spots by date and source, and noted the key on a separate piece of paper. Behind me, I heard Aberdeen rip open two bags of sugar, empty them in his cup, and stir for a good thirty seconds.

"The Tarantino case, I suppose?" he asked, craning his

head and staring at the map.

"Huxley, actually. I had Nelson uh— help out."

"Good call. She's indicated a desire to move up in her career." He sent a supercilious glare my way, as if wondering if I had anything to say on the matter. I tried not to and forced my eyes back to the map. There was a green dot marked along San Vicente Boulevard, about four miles away from the Esperanza Medical Center. On Nelson's key I read, "ATM withdrawal in the amount of $500, October 6, eight fifteen p.m." *Curious*, I thought. I had spotted plenty of ATM machines at the Esperanza, and even if Huxley forgot to stop at any of those, why drive four miles away from North Hollywood, where she lived, when she could've found another one on her way home?

"Nelson's okay," I finally told Aberdeen as he sloppily drank his coffee. "She does as told. If only she'd go one step further and connect the dots in between, she'd be a hell of a copper."

Aberdeen slurped down the remainder of his drink, tossed the cup in the trashcan, and then nodded. "I like people who do as they're told," he said. "They're my kind of people."

"They just hired a new guy at Latent Prints," I told Satish as we crossed the parking lot and walked to the entrance of the Hertzberg-Davis Center.

"What happened to Scar Novak?"

"He quit."

Novak, the previous specialist, wore gloves and facemask everywhere, not just at crime scenes. Besides the usual tools of the trade, his workstation sported a Brita pitcher, individually wrapped Styrofoam cups, a couple of bottles of Lysol, and an antibacterial gel dispenser. He cruised the hallways of Parkway—back when the SID was at the glass house—bundled up like a terrorist, gathering the concerned looks of unaware visitors. Rumors spread that the reason for constantly hiding his lower face was a deformed jaw, from which he was dubbed "Scar" Novak. Nobody knew his real first name.

"Maybe he found a job where he didn't have to wear a facemask all day long."

"Yeah. On a deserted island." I held the door to the Fingerprint Analysis and Comparison lab. "Or maybe he conveniently left before the Maldonado tornado hit him too."

Maria Maldonado was a hospital technician wrongfully accused of burglary based on fingerprint evidence signed off by three of our Latent Print technicians. The Unit was under fire and the media pounded with the lingering question of how many other wrongful accusations had yet to be brought to light. Even after the advent of automated databases such as IAFIS—the FBI fingerprint database system where all prints were routinely sent for possible matches—fingerprint evidence was still analyzed by a set of human eyes and a magnifying glass.

I let the door close behind us and added, "I have great faith in the new hire."

Bent over his workstation, one hand on the shaft where a Nikon camera was hinged and the other clutching a magnifying glass, Lorenzo Agavi's most noticeable feature was his mop of black curls. He had small, green eyes, hidden behind oversized glass frames. His ears looked like they wanted to stick out of the sides of his head except there was too much hair to make it that far out. A white coat hung loose over his narrow shoulders, its billows leaving a trail of iodine fumes and ninhydrin.

"Welcome, Detectives," he said over a lengthy

handshake. "I've got some really cool stuff to show you." We followed him to a different workstation where I spotted the first commandment note and the letter Diane had found in Tarantino's paper bin, both sealed in transparent evidence bags. Next to them were the fingerprint cards.

"I just uploaded these guys to the system." Lorenzo logged onto the terminal on his workstation, and the photos of two enlarged fingerprints popped up on the screen. In one, the ridges and loops were well delineated, whereas the second one was blurred on one side and overlapped with a smudged partial.

Agavi bathed me in a caffeine-laden smile. "First commandment note on the left—the only print I found on the piece of paper. The envelope instead had plenty of overlapping prints. The photo on the right is the best shot I got." He pointed to the screen. "They're beautiful, aren't they?"

"I'm mesmerized."

Satish snorted. "What's running through your overworked brains, Track?"

"For one thing, the two are a match."

By my side, Agavi beamed. Buried in the overgrown Afro-mop, his face hung in reverence. I like young people: they're so easy to impress. "You have a sharp eye, sir. My thesis advisor also has a sharp eye."

"Sharp eyes still get in trouble in court," Satish rebuked.

Agavi winked. "That's why we have mathematical tools."

"Wait," I said. "The procedure—"

"Oh, I know." He held up the magnifying glass next to his keyboard—one of those shaped like an upside down wine glass. "I already checked all loops and ridges by eye. But I'm sure you'll appreciate the fact that the computer agrees with my conclusions. Same software that runs underneath IAFIS."

I looked at Satish and beamed. "Told you I liked him."

Lorenzo double clicked on the prints taken from the envelope. "I applied a fast Fourier transform software to separate the overlapping prints and clear out the background signal—plastic surgery for fingerprints." At the click of his fingers, the images on the screen underwent the promised beautification.

"Beautiful. Go on."

"I used three different algorithms to compare the topography in the two sets of prints. The first one uses harmonic functions to renormalize the distortion caused by the different touches." Agavi was so enthralled he spoke of the software like a kid ranting over his brand new Nintendo. "The next two algorithms compare the minutiae across the two images and find all possible matches. I ran both to minimize FAR and FRR. Type I and type II errors," he added as a magnanimous explanation. An eye-opener, this guy.

"Conclusion?" I impatiently chimed.

"Sixteen matching points." Little white boxes numbered one through sixteen made their appearance on the screen, each pointing to the location of the match on the two images.

"So you were right," Satish admitted. "The person who left the note at the Tarantino crime scene had mailed the letter with Gaya White's funeral note inside."

"That person was Jennifer Huxley," I said.

"Well, that seems obvious, at this point. Can we prove it, though?"

"Of course we can." Agavi beamed. "After your call this morning, I pulled up her prints from the autopsy and ran the same algorithm. It's a match."

"How about the other task I asked you?"

Agavi got up from the computer station, walked to his desk and came back with a detailed printout.

"What's that?" Satish asked.

"A gas chromatography-mass spectrometry analysis," Agavi elucidated. "Ran on a sliver of paper from the first commandment note."

I skimmed through the technicalities of the report he handed me and jumped down to the very bottom. "Traces of sodium hydroxide, sodium sulfide—"

"Those are from the chemical pulping. All paper has that kind of stuff," Agavi interrupted. "Go to the next line."

I read on. "Hydrogen sulfide, carbon dioxide, methane, cadaverine, ammonia. And perlite."

Agavi nodded. "And those have nothing to do with chemical pulping of paper."

"I know," I said. "They have to do with cadavers." No wonder the first commandment note smelled foul to my nose.

CHAPTER 22

Friday, October 17

"So Huxley was dead when she left her fingerprints on the first commandment note."

We were back in the car, northbound on the One-Oh-One.

"Correct. Which means, somebody else drove her car to Benedict Canyon last Saturday night and killed the Tarantinos."

"And wanted us to think Huxley did it."

"Once you have a stiff you might as well use it."

Satish cocked his head to the side. "I don't know, Track. I'm old fashioned. If I had a stiff, I'd dump it into a river with a stone tied to its foot. Far west style."

"There are no rivers in this part of the state," I reminded

him. "We dried them up so we could have green lawns and ten-thousand-gallon swimming pools."

Satish shook his head. "To think I have neither. I feel so incomplete."

The day was hazy and traffic steady, all vehicles flowing at exactly five miles over the speed limit, save a few thugs who used aggressive driving as an indicator of high-testosterone levels. We got off the freeway on Santa Monica and entered the tree-lined streets of a Hollywood residential neighborhood. Hemmed in by green strips of lawn, the sidewalks displayed blissful people jogging, walking their groomed dogs, or riding their bikes. Tall palm trees and hedges trimmed to perfection disguised white houses with red shingle roofs.

No wonder Southern Californians are so happy. Where else would you wanna live?

"Still no news on the DNA from Huxley's car," I said. I'd inquired about it on our way out of the Forensic Center, when I sneaked into the Serology lab to dump the beer can I had acquired the night before. The beer can made me feel deceitful and baffled at the same time, as if I'd just found Pandora's box and left it in the lab for somebody else to open.

Diane didn't smell weird this morning at Chromo. Or did she?

Satish shrugged. "You know how slow these things are." He made a right on a private driveway, a narrow street shaded by large oaks. It wound uphill and ended into a wide parking lot overlooking Laurel Canyon Park. Haze shrouded the valley with overlapping layers of azure and periwinkle. Satish carelessly parked his modest Ford between a Jaguar and a Mercedes SLK, unimpressed by either beauty at our sides. Across from the parking lot, banana trees and birds-of-paradise flowers followed the perimeter of a wide one-story building, its tall windows draped by green awnings. The canopy above the entrance read, "Hollywood Golden Racket Tennis Club."

I climbed out of the car and slid on my sunglasses, dazed by the glare of the shiny red Jaguar.

Satish said, "The lab technician's death brought Chromo back in the headlines. Our Chief is going to have to sit down with Gomez and Mirkovic and have a long chat. I'm sure things will speed up with all the pressure mounting."

I sighed. "So now what?"

Satish smiled, dropped his chin, and slid his brown polka dot tie through his fingers. "Now we go meet Hannah."

"Do you have a membership, gentlemen?"

"No, just a shiny tin from the LAPD. You like it?" I replied, flashing the badge right before his nose.

"Oh, absolutely, sir."

"It was a rhetorical question."

Satish elbowed me and took over, not trusting my diplomatic gift. "We're here to meet Ms. Hannah Kelson," he said. The information didn't stir a single muscle on the lad's face. Black suit, spearmint-smelling breath, sleek swept-back hair, and distinguished affectation, the man bobbed his head. "She's outside in the lounge. I will take you gentlemen right over."

It either takes money or an LAPD tin to be called *gentleman*.

The place—one of L.A.'s most exclusive tennis clubs—exuded luxury from every corner. Waxed wood panels covered the walls of the hall of fame, from where the club's most famous visitors beamed down on us, framed in forever-young smiles. Hushed laughs and ice clinking in fancy glasses welcomed us in the lounge, together with expensive perfumes and high society perspiration—which smells just like any other kind of perspiration, it's only disguised better. A bald barman brandished a cocktail shaker, while a husky client barfed a list of tennis competitions he'd won in his leaner years. A mellow jazz tune played in the background. The lights were dim and washed over the display of rum and liquor bottles.

We followed our escort through glass sliding doors. Garden screens covered in creeping bougainvillea embraced the outside patio. Tall hedges hid the view of the tennis courts, their presence given away by the occasional shout, a burst of laughter, the thumps of the rackets hitting the ball. Our chaperone pointed to one of the tables outside, shaded by a blue umbrella.

Disguised by a white sunhat and large sunglasses, Hannah Kelson—Jerry White's ex wife—sat frozen in an ethereal pose, as if she deemed anything around her frivolous and inconsequential. Elbow propped on the table, chin softly rested on the heel of her hand, she sucked on a Virginia Slim nestled between her index and middle fingers. She took a nervous puff, then turned away and blew it all out in one long billow.

I don't generally like women who smoke, yet for a moment I found myself dangling from her red lips like that white cigarette, kissed by a puckered ring of lipstick.

She startled when she saw us approach her table. Even with our pancake holsters hidden away in our waistbands, as we sauntered around the bistro tables in our dark suits and polished dress shoes, we were as distinctive as an Elton John posing in a crowd of Japanese tourists.

Kelson abruptly crushed the Virginia Slim on a blue ashtray. "I'm sorry," she muttered as Satish introduced us. "I quit years ago, after we decided to have a child. When I lost her, though—" Her creamy complexion blushed and her voice trailed off mid-sentence. "How do you do?" she said, letting us shake her limp hand. My eyes wandered over the artificially red lips, the straight nose with small and round nostrils, and the butterfly glasses I had already seen the day before, half hidden behind a pillar.

"Did you know the Tarantinos well?" I asked, pulling a chair over. "You were at their funeral yesterday, Ms. Kelson."

Her smooth forehead creased. She brought a white hand to her face and took off her sunglasses. Her eyes were sharp blue, intense yet clouded. They grazed my face like blind fingers searching for a familiar feature to grasp. She took her time taking in the details of my appearance, her gaze fumbling with the lapels of my jacket, creeping into the hem of my shirt. And I breathed in her scent, extremely pleasant, I confess, despite the slight aftertaste of nicotine. It was delicate, not exuberant, and yet persistent.

I knew from the reports I'd read that Kelson was now in her late forties, yet the woman in front of me looked no older than thirty-two.

"Jerry and I met Dr. Tarantino in 1996," she said. "We stayed in touch, exchanged holiday cards over Christmas." Her accent was American, yet her British origins surfaced in little details: her quiet voice, polite yet chilly, always retreating to an invisible barrier saying, "Private. Do not enter."

"Especially after Gaya's birth?" Satish asked.

I hadn't expected the smile that followed. She brushed a finger along the condensation on her glass, her eyes dreamingly looking away, chasing memories. "Especially after Gaya's birth. We wanted to do everything right, Detective. I grew up taking care of my younger sister affected by Down syndrome. Jerry's aunt has cystic fibrosis, a recessive genetic disease, and then the new case came out—you remember the parents who sued for malpractice claiming a flu shot had caused their child to develop autism?"

"Gregory and Melissa Garrison," Satish confirmed.

"That's right. Greg is Jerry's brother. Jerry took his mother's maiden name when he started directing. We really wanted a child, but between my age and the risk of both autism and cystic fibrosis in Jerry's family, we were scared."

We wanted to do everything right. What is the meaning of "right" when it comes to human life?

Hannah let out a sigh. "So we did the genetic testing, and from the results we were told that both Jerry and I carried the gene for cystic fibrosis. It's a recessive gene, so neither of us is affected, but if we had a child, there was a one-in-four chance that she was going to have it. It's a horrible disease, affects the lungs, skin, everything."

"And Chromo helped?" I asked. "How?"

"Genetic counseling. Our Gaya was conceived *in vitro*."

An overdressed waiter with an attitude materialized by our side ready to fulfill our requests even if we didn't have any. I ordered a double shot espresso and wondered if it came with a price tag that could be reasonably filed under "incidentals" in our expense report.

Gaya Nicole was an exceptionally brilliant child. Kelson laid it out plainly, without a note of pride. To her, it was a fact. "Two grades ahead of her age, she played the violin and excelled in any activity she undertook. Even after the leukemia was diagnosed, she still proved herself extraordinary. I can't tell you how many times Jerry and I felt overwhelmed by the doctors' visits, the chemo and radiation therapies, the nausea, the sense of death creeping into our lives." Kelson sighed and averted her eyes. Her fingers went looking for something, a cigarette, most likely, then changed their mind and rested again on the glass in front of her.

"Throughout her ordeal, Gaya was the bravest of us three. Completely bald, she felt like a tiny sparrow in my arms. And yet, she'd hug me tight and say, *It'll be ok, Mum. Even if I have to go to heaven, it'll be ok.*" A tear rolled down her face. "My baby is in heaven, now," she whispered, dabbing her cheek with the tip of her finger.

Satish and I exchanged uncomfortable glances. Two killer cops, both armed, heavily trained, and look at us. Melting down like marshmallows on a stick. Satish murmured a barely audible "I'm sorry, Ms. Kelson," while drumming his fingers on the table. I tipped my head looking for my million-dollar espresso.

"Did your relationship with Mr. White worsen during those months?" Satish asked.

Kelson shook her head, gently, and just as gently her perfume escaped and found its way to my nostrils. "No. It brought us back together. *Definitely* brought us together. Not as husband and wife. As parents of a dying child."

The overdressed waiter came back with our orders, walking as if he had a broomstick stuck down his throat. By the time it touched the table my espresso was cold. I downed it in one gulp, then loosened the knot of my tie and took the chance to change the topic of the conversation. "How did your friendship with Professor Conrad start, Ms. Kelson?"

Her index finger froze along the rim of the glass. "Michael?" she said. "Michael was a child." She smiled, her eyes sad in a different way this time. "He'd take me out to dinner, tell me how beautiful I was, and then monopolize the conversation with his ideas."

"Ideas you agreed with?" Satish asked.

Kelson's voice changed. "Did I agree with Michael's claims on selective breeding? No, Detective. I didn't. Do I blame him for making such claims? Same answer: no. Doctors and professors used to be revered. Nowadays, they're nerds. TV, tabloids, reality shows, all imposing new role models: college drop-outs, wannabes, self-declared geniuses, and other failures seeking cheap and short-lasting fame. Next generation's heroes. When you look around, Detective, and you see this kind of rubbish, how can you not agree with Conrad?"

I shifted in my chair. A tennis ball smacked in the distance. A blonde and tanned couple emerged from the tennis courts as if they'd just stepped out of a sport gear catalog.

Kelson shook her head. "Poor Michael. So smart, and yet so dumb."

Satish and I winced at the remark. "Dumb, Ms. Kelson?"

She turned to me, a proud glare glimmering in her blue eyes. "Short-sighted," she corrected. And then bit her lower lip until it became white. She was done with us. I read it in the impatience with which her pink fingernails tapped against the glass. I wasn't, though. I had one more question.

"Have you ever heard of the name Proteus, Ms. Kelson? Anything that comes to mind, from conversations with Conrad, or back when you consulted Chromo the first time, or maybe at the Esperanza—"

"Proteus, you said?"

I nodded.

"I'm sorry, it doesn't ring a bell," her lips said. Not her eyes though. *I'm lying, Detective*, her eyes told me. Or did I just imagine it?

I leaned forward. "Hannah. Your ex-husband is a successful man with a brilliant career. Why would he ruin it all and kill a family friend on the whim of a moment?" Again, those blue irises sparkling in an eerie way, talking to me. *Don't go there.* Alarmed, as if afraid to slip away.

I have to. It's my job.

"He didn't do it," she said firmly.

"You really believe that?"

She didn't reply. Satish sighed. "Ms. Kelson. If there's anything we should know about what happened, anything that could help Mr. White—"

"No," she cut him short. "Jerry didn't do it. There's nothing more to say on the matter." She gazed at us, her lashes tingling on my skin. "Not all crimes are punishable, Detectives. Our world is very much imperfect. Justice, when and *if* it happens, is the exception, not the rule."

I sank back in my chair, her statement as unexpected as a lazy eye in a pretty face. What was it supposed to mean? That whatever White was, a killer or a victim, she didn't care? What about Conrad, did she care he'd died? Kelson unfolded the glasses she had left on the table, slid them back on, and then waved at the waiter. The show was over.

The air was cool when I stepped out of the Glass House. Dusk came quickly. The earlier haze melted away and thick clouds cluttered the sky. Up on the foothills, crickets smelled rain in the air and quieted down. Shadows grew longer and blurred into the landscape.

The best time to go hunting.

I merged into the ramp to the One-Oh-One wondering if Nelson and the others would be at Abbey's already, getting intoxicated over the first round of schooners. One mile later I merged onto the One-Ten west (because it was Friday), then detoured on the Four-Oh-Five north (because I didn't want it to be Friday), and finally exited on San Vicente (because the name was stuck in my head). I entered an anonymous parking lot crossed by a row of sickly shrubs— the illusion of a shadow to fight for on a hot summer day.

It should be around here...

As if answering my question, the streetlights flicked to life and a well of light bathed the walk-up ATM machine at the far corner of the lot, the name of the bank wavering in red and blue at the top of the stand. October 6, eight fifteen p.m.: Jennifer Huxley parks her Ford and walks to the ATM. She has little time, working one job during the daytime, and secretly fiddling with another project at night. *Some additional data she was going to obtain.* When? From whom? Yet that night she finds the time to come here and withdraw five hundred dollars in cash. She doesn't go back to work, and it's not until eleven p.m. that a neighbor hears her car pull into the garage.

Where did you go from here, Jen?

The sound of bells chiming made me startle. *It's a recording*, I realized, scanning the modern design of the building across the lot and noticing it lacked a bell tower. The building was circular, with high walls sliced by stained windows, and skylights peeking through a conical roof. At the very top, a cross stood against wine spattered clouds.

Two ladies came out of a side door and crossed the parking lot.

"Father Jonathan looked tired tonight, don't you think Linda?" one said.

"All Souls' is coming up," the other replied. "I bet Father was up late listening to the confessions of a lot of widowers I happen to know."

"Oh, Linda!" The ladies giggled and then shuffled away arm in arm. I walked to the entrance and stared at the glass door, a new thought slowly forming in my head. I raised a hand as to touch the handle but before I could reach it the door swung open.

"I'm sorry," a distinctive man in an old fashioned suit mumbled. He stepped back, held the door open for me, and then disappeared outside.

My steps echoed in the wide hall. The silence was deep yet warm, lulled by the last rays of light filtering through the skylights. Wax, incense, and pinewood—my mother's smell, the day she came to see me in juvie.

Rows of concentric pews departed like rays from the altar. Two philodendrons flanked the tabernaculum, their lobed leaves drooping down like asking hands. The scent of incense and votive candles unearthed long lost memories.

"Can I help you?" The smile was welcoming, chiseled in a surprisingly young face. "It's okay," he added softly as my answer failed to come. "We all falter before God." He walked past me, a breeze of fresh smells swooshing behind—Marseille soap, laundry detergent, beeswax, incense, Luke's favorite aftershave. He clambered up to the altar and blew out the candles. The pungent zest of burnt wax and paraffin coiled into little curls of smoke that took their time before wafting to my nose.

"Father Jonathan?"

"Yes?" Kind, watery eyes hidden behind round lenses.

How old are you, thirty, maybe thirty-two?

"When was the last time you saw Jennifer Huxley?"

CHAPTER 23

Friday, October 17

The key clicks into the lock and the door opens. Inside, the air smells stale and warm: the comforting familiarity of her own place. Diane Kyle steps inside, turns the dead bolt, and slides the security chain. She drops the keys into the woven basket on the console, kicks her shoes off, and heads to the kitchen, flipping on the light switches as she goes. It's dark, it's late, and she's tired. She turns the radio on and pop music fills the air. The living room is scented with the fragrance from the air freshener plugged in a corner. It gives her a sense of home, and it makes it easier to pretend she doesn't feel lonely at night.

Darn it, the fridge is empty. *She opens the freezer.* It'll have to be pizza. *She retrieves the box, takes out the frozen pizza and tosses it in a pan. Oven on at 400 °F, she climbs the stairs* while unbuttoning her shirt. Her thoughts drift to the long day and the weekend ahead.

If only Jim didn't work so much.

She gets to the top of the stairs and sighs. If only.

The thought makes her uneasy. Ex-boyfriends, wasted relationships, too many regrets. At her age, she should be married with a couple of kids in preschool. Her therapist laid it out in one sentence. You need to break the loop chain of abusive relationships, Diane.

A sound, sharp and unfamiliar, makes her freeze.

"Is anybody there?" *she says, her voice shaking. The wind blows and a curtain rustles. Diane exhales.* Silly me. *She latches the bedroom window with slippery hands.* It was just the draft, *she realizes, heart throbbing.* The job is stressing me out. *She turns on the lights in the bathroom and starts the shower. The water pours out and billows of steam warm up the air. Humming softly, Diane slides her shirt off and unzips her pants. The door to the closet is ajar.*

Down to her underwear, she suddenly gasps. Did she just imagine that sound? Or was it really there, a sigh, or a groan maybe, barely audible, and yet unmistakably human. *She bolts out of the bedroom and looks down the stairs.*

"Hello?" *she calls.* "Jim, is it you?" *Maybe his meeting got canceled and he decided to surprise her.* "Jim?" *she calls once more.* "It's not funny, you know?" *The question falls unanswered. She shakes her head and returns to the bedroom.*

Damn it, *Rhesus thinks. He got too excited, craned his head to see better and hit a hanger. A belt fell with a soft clink. Crouched behind a long dress and concealed by the box of a voluminous comforter, he spies through the slit of the closet door. He enjoys the sight of Diane's breasts wobbling like firm jell-o in her black bra. And when she removes her lingerie, Rhesus caresses the weapon in his holster and smiles.* One more minute, *he thinks. He wants to see more. Diane steps into the bathroom and under the shower.* Now she will no longer hear. *The water jetting out of the faucet* and her loud off-key singing muffles all noises. Rhesus slides out of his hiding spot, the steam from the hot water disguising him. He can take her by surprise, and she won't feel a thing. This is not how he wants to do it, though. He stares at her breasts rocking gently while she lathers the shampoo on her head, and at her hips, round and inviting, trickles of water bending around them and caressing her curves.

He clutches the pistol. Cool, comforting. So easy to take her now. Would she still be beautiful frozen in the stupor of death, a trail of blood spilling on her white breasts? Would she scream or would she go peacefully, almost grateful for the quick end? He could take her then, like that. And then he'd steal a lock of her hair. Auburn has always been his favorite hair color.

Next time, *Rhesus thinks. And then leaves.*

Half an hour later, wrapped in a pink bathrobe, Diane opens the oven and whispers little ow's of discomfort as she pulls out the scalding pan with potholders too thin for the job. She tosses away the potholders, cuts out a slice, and drops it onto a plate. The shower calmed her down. Singing to herself, she walks to the couch with the plate in one hand and a glass of white chardonnay in the other. Her eyes fall on the door, making her tilt her head and frown. *It's weird, she thinks.* I thought I left the security chain inserted. *She puts the plate and glass down on the coffee table and walks to the door. A quick rush of adrenaline makes her heart jump. The chain she couldn't swear, but the bolt — the bolt should have been turned. She* always *locks the door.*

CHAPTER 24

Friday, October 17

The tea bag plunged and then floated up again as hot water poured into the cup. Billows of steam rose from the surface, carrying the aroma of bergamot. The place was small: a single guy's dwelling, only tidier. The only decorations displayed on the white walls were a crucifix above the door and a wall calendar hanging next to the fridge. The mismatched furniture fulfilled the sole purpose of functionality. On the table, a checkered tablecloth was spattered with old coffee stains. A *pothos* plant crept down from the top of a cupboard and brushed its leaves against the window fixtures. Like an alien from a different time, a desktop whirred on a small corner desk while unfolding geometric shapes on its screen — solitary witness of the current times in an unusually anachronistic space.

"Honey?"

"Sugar is fine, thank you."

Father Jonathan pushed the sugar bowl towards me and then dipped his spoon into the honey jar. He had feminine hands that showed cleanness and attention to detail. Somebody who dusted frequently and confessed regularly, whose attentive eyes could pick a devout follower from a repentant soul, and tell a liberal from a conservative just by looking at their body posture.

"Do you believe in God, Detective?"

"No."

He raised a brow. "Do you ever worry about the afterlife?"

"No. I'll be dead by then."

He stared at his tea and twirled the spoon. The clinking faded. "Well, I do. I worry about all my brothers' and sisters' afterlife. Including yours."

I thought of the blonde, blue-eyed Christs handed to me on the street over the years, together with cheap propaganda pamphlets and one-day-only sale advertisements. Some people beg for money, some for listening ears, some for new adepts to share their afterlife with. "You said Jennifer came to see you the day before she disappeared?"

He nodded. "Yes. Last time I saw her was last Monday. She came here after work."

"Why did she come to see you?" I fished the tea bag out of the cup.

"The same as most of my parishioners: confession."

Crap. Confession is to a priest as HIPAA is to an MD.

"Jennifer was a brave woman. Up against evil."

I tinkled the spoon against the saucer. "An evil called Chromo?"

He squinted. His head wanted to nod but somewhere in between changed its mind and ended up cocking to the side. A shaving rash flared on his neck and stood out against the blackness of his shirt neckband. He slid an index finger along the inside of his clerical collar, easing for a moment the stiffness of the uniform. When he wrapped his hand around the cup again, the tip of his finger was floured in white. A soap-scented white.

Interesting.

"Those are nice looking sneakers you're wearing, Father."

"Very comfortable," he agreed. "They improve posture, and with all the hours I have to spend standing—"

"I bet they came in handy last night when you had to run away from a crowd of screaming monkeys."

"Wha—I—"

"You know what we found in one of the cages you opened, Father? This fine powder called talc." I stared at him, my nostrils instantly detecting the rush of adrenaline that flushed his face. His left brow twitched. He brought the cup to his mouth with shaking hands, and a few drops of tea spilled and dripped on the tablecloth. "My colleague kept saying it was glove talc, but you see, I happen to have a different theory. I think it was the type of talc used by the clergy, men like you, to ease the discomfort of the starched collar your uniform imposes. I bet we can match what we found at the scene with—"

"Stop." His eyes flared. *Do not mess with my God. My justice*, I read in them. "You're looking in the wrong place, Detective. The evil you're after isn't here. My conscience is clean."

I smiled. "Father, the standing of your conscience is something between you and your God. Me, unfortunately, I care about human law. Right now, you're looking at trespassing and felony vandalism, and I'm not even counting the fellow who ended up on the coroner's table because of this—"

"I had nothing to do with that!" He banged a hand on the table, making the silverware rattle.

I waited for his pulse to come down a notch, then said, "I don't doubt your good intentions, Father. Whatever happened last night, you had your reasons. Here's where I start to get edgy, though. Because you see, if you happen to know important information that could help me bring justice to Huxley's death and you don't disclose it, that's what I find really immoral, whether in front of God or man."

He held my glare. "They're playing God over there. With human life. Jennifer found out. They ruin young, innocent lives."

"How?"

"I don't know. Those monkeys, they inject them with stuff for their experiments."

"Who gave you the passcode to enter the property?"

He sighed and shook his head. "I can't—"

"We could be having this chat in downtown."

"You only have human power…"

"Whatever I have, I'll use it."

"Jennifer gave me the passcode."

"How did she get it?"

He flattened his hands on the table. They were no longer shaking. "I don't know. She was scared. She gave me the passcode and said if something was ever to happen to her, I had to try to stop them from carrying on with those experiments."

The statement, flat-out, made my blood boil. I raised my voice. "Something *did* happen, Father! And all you could come up with was to free a bunch of monkeys? How about come talk to us?"

He stared at me as if I'd completely missed the obvious. "I just found out about her passing. Her mother called me a couple of hours ago to arrange the funeral. Until then, all I could do was pray. Jennifer told me everything under the secrecy of confession. What else could I do without violating the sanctity of reconciliation?"

"It sounds to me you did a little more than praying, Father."

CHAPTER 25

Sunday, October 23, 2005

Rhesus leans over his woman's naked breasts and inhales. They smell good. He watches the wave of goose bumps sweep her skin as air blows out of his nostrils. He kisses a nipple. She clutches his hand and moves it down her navel.

Her eyes are soft now, inviting. Yet they can be so harsh sometimes.

Rhesus yanks his hand away.

"What?"

The thought of those same eyes, a few hours ago. "You were supposed to get rid of her," she had yelled. "Why didn't you do it? Are you still in love with her?"

The question offended him.

He shifts away from her, the resentment still burning in his chest. Seated in a corner, the other man comes forward, his face emerging from the shade cast by a small table lamp. "What's wrong with you?" he asks.

"I want to be paid more."

The woman sits up on the bed. "What? Are you insane?"

"Not any more than you two." Rhesus picks up his pants from the floor.

"Go to hell." The woman flops back on the bed and pulls the sheets over her naked breasts.

The man raises a brow. He licks his lower lip, pondering. "How much more?"

One leg half through his pants, Rhesus freezes. And then he beams. He likes it when he gets things his way.

Monday, October 24, 2005

It's almost dawn and the air is chilly. Rhesus parks his car and then walks away, briskly, despite not having a destination. Sex has helped some. They still want their final kill, though.

"You need to get rid of her," the man told him, slowly counting the bills out of his wallet. The wad was thicker this time – his price tag heavier.

"Why?" Rhesus asked.

"She's too close. She'll find out."

Who am I fooling? *Killing the first time had not been easy. It has become so. He thrived on the adrenaline rush. A killer has the power of life and death. It's an orgasm. You become one with the victim, you force yourself in, the barrel of a gun instead of a phallus, a bullet instead of semen. And then you watch her wilt. The body you have taken is now yours: you have prevailed and deflowered. And the feeling is inebriating, addictive. Again and again you want take your victim's life.*

So then why, Rhesus wonders, why could he not deliver the kill this time?

CHAPTER 26

Monday, October 20

"Still blurry," I said.

"Have faith, Track. Always have faith." Faith wasn't a word I agreed with this morning, after spending the weekend mulling over Father Jonathan's words.

Electronics guru Amit Banjaree let his fingers dance on the keyboard for a few minutes, conferring in an arcane lingo with a DOS window. His thick and wavy hair glistened with gel. Framing his dark lips, his black goatee smelled of curry, coconut, and lentils from the *appam* he had for breakfast. "There, take a look now." He hit the return key. Thin lines dribbled down the screenshot I had originally deemed blurry, the image slowly coming together. I pulled my chair closer and gingerly leaned forward. Amit had a naturally loud voice, especially when he talked about the things he knew best: computers and baseball. Here in his kingdom—a windowless warehouse with a high ceiling poked by large air vent pipes—Amit could easily get enthralled over networks, encryptions, performance, and information retrieval. And when he did, his high-pitched voice rang in my ears with unnecessary decibels. I tried to keep a cautionary distance, and yet the inquiries for which I required his expertise often saw both of us crammed in front of a computer monitor.

"It's coming," he assured me, sensing my impatience in front of the lines painfully dripping down the screen. Around us, a cemetery of laptops, printers, and hard drives sat like antique relics on dusty metal shelving.

"Bingo," I said when I finally made out Huxley's license plate. On October 7, at five fifty-one in the morning, a Ford Focus pulled through the Chromo gate and gained access to the property after securing the correct passcode on the call box. Who gave her the secret number and why, still a blank in a poorly written screenplay.

"Here's what I need you to do now," I told Amit, glimpsing the sparkle of anticipation in his eyes. "I want two freeze-frames side by side: incoming vehicle and outgoing vehicle, close up of the windshield."

"Right away, sir." The keyboard clacked under his fingers. The reflection from the streetlight reduced the features of the driver in either frame to a blur of sparkles. I moved closer to the screen.

"The two patterns are different," I noted.

"The streetlight hits the windshield at two different angles in the two frames."

"Yeah, but look at this twinkle, right here. Can you measure how far it is from the wheel?"

"Given the position of the steering wheel, it comes at

about neck height."

"A pendant. The golden cross—she was still wearing it when we found the body. Given its size, wouldn't it still be visible in the other frame too?"

"If she were at the wheel, yes, especially considering that the vehicle pulled out of the Chromo property at six twenty-one, when the sun was starting to rise."

"But it's no longer visible when the car pulls out of the garage."

I ran both hands through my hair and left them there, mulling over the two frames on the monitor, the grainy consistency of the images tricking the eyes into the illusion of a subtle motion. "Huxley drives her car into the Chromo campus at five fifty-one and somebody else drives her car out at six twenty-one," I concluded.

I smelled him a minute before he stepped into the room. "Chromo seems to be the crime scene of choice lately," Satish said, rapping his knuckles at the doorjamb.

"Hey Sat. Guess where one can find glass with traces of perlite on it?"

"Besides the hands of a cadaver?"

"Besides that. It turns out you can find it in cryogenic tanks. And here's the best part: Chromo has lots of such tanks stored in its labs."

"What are you getting at, Track?"

"Somebody lured Huxley onto the Chromo premises on the empty promise of some specimens. She withdrew five hundred bucks the night before she disappeared. The amount is ridiculous, but I'm guessing she wouldn't have been able to afford more. Whomever she spoke to, they wanted to make sure she agreed to the deal."

"She was *buying* specimens from Chromo?"

I nodded. "Specimens she needed for the leukemia study. Whether they really existed or not, they had to be delivered in a cryogenic tank. She was attacked, the tank broke—probably shattered by a bullet—hence the glass shards and perlite."

"What kind of specimens can be stored in a cryogenic tank?"

"My question precisely, Sat."

"We can brood on our way to the morgue."

I groaned. Something I was *not* looking forward to. I dropped my hand on Amit's shoulder. "Thanks, man."

"What do you want me to do with all those e-mails?" Amit asked.

"Print them. All of them, and have them delivered to our squad room."

"Will do."

"What e-mails?" Satish asked.

"Huxley's. The only thing Cox didn't think of encrypting. Amit's decrypting software is still running on the machine, trying about one million keys per minute. Turns out, even at that rate infinitely many possibilities is an awful lot to cover."

"Well, you certainly don't see something like this every day." Garbed in blue surgical mask, protective glasses, surgical scrubs, and nitrile gloves, medical examiner Dr. Ellis stared at the corpse in front of him. Nathan Kim—age twenty-six, laboratory technician II, found dead on the Chromo premises among a bunch of raving monkeys—lay naked and completely deprived of dignity on the autopsy table. A medical assistant—anonymous eyes framed by the lower rim of the cap and the upper one of the facemask—held a surgical gown for me to don. I grimaced, the reek of formalin closing a knot around my stomach.

"Would you rather bring a souvenir of the vic home,

graciously pinned to your tie?" Satish quipped. I inserted my arms through the sleeves, let the assistant tie the gown behind my back, and then watched him repeat the procedure with Satish.

The smell of fresh blood is enticing. It's life, warmth, excitement. The morgue, though, smells of *old* blood, of cold flesh stored in refrigerated chambers. It smells of death. AC vents blow down from the high ceiling onto the autopsy tables, yet they never wash off the reek that saturates the air. The walls are lined with stainless steel countertops, sinks, and dimly lit view-boxes, black and white X-rays of dented bones clipped to the glass.

Nathan Kim was not a pleasant sight. Round, blood-filled boils covered his face and body, the largest of which sat precariously at the right corner of his mouth. His lips and eyelids were swollen, and his hands looked like blown-up gloves. I pulled up the facemask, secured it behind my ears, and surrendered to the morbidity of the procedure.

"Hemorrhagic cutaneous abscesses present all over the subject, most numerous on the face, arms, and chest," Ellis noted, as the assistant held a recorder close to his face. The medical examiner poked the boil on the mouth, bled it on a small pad, and then stored the sample in a plastic bag, which he tossed on a cart with all other evidence collected from the body: swabs, hair, nail trimmings—all souvenirs to be later delivered to the lab. Ellis then focused on the one and only wound found on the corpse: two symmetrical arches marked Kim's left shoulder, the lines slightly jagged, and the tips darker, where sharp incisors had sunk deeper into the flesh.

"Circular erythema, four-point-two centimeters in diameter, surrounds the bite wound and the contusion area on the subject's left upper arm," he dictated to the recorder. "This over here," he then translated for our benefit, circling his finger over the ring-shaped rash around the bite marks, "indicates a subsequent infection."

"Is it common after a monkey bite?" Satish asked.

Ellis looked at the body in front of him. "The subject shows clear signs of angioedema—see how his face and hands are swollen? The scenario described by the paramedics performing the CPR is consistent with vasodilation of arterioles and constriction of bronchioles. Of course, it doesn't mean much until we cut him open and take a peek inside, but everything we have so far seems to indicate our subject died of anaphylactic shock."

"An allergic reaction to the monkey bite."

"One would certainly think so, Track. Except, here's the puzzle: according to the records we have from Chromo, all employees having contact with the animals are tested for possible allergies. Kim was not allergic to macaques' fur or saliva, or else he couldn't have held the position he had."

Ellis rolled the corpse so we could take a better look at his shoulder. "What puzzles me when I look at this trauma, is the spread and redness of the rash around the bite: it would be more consistent with an infection rather than anaphylaxis."

"Would an infection explain the boils, then?" I asked.

The M.E. sighed—a cue he didn't have an answer. He turned to the stainless steel tray by the table and let his fingers waver over the neatly arranged scalpels and dissecting knives. "You'll have my report by tonight," he said, placing the blade of choice below the corpse's right clavicle. "My guess right now? Whichever monkey bit this young fellow passed him a deadly disease."

I turned on the faucet and splashed chilled water in my face. It did not wash off the butcher warehouse smell stuck to my palate, or the gripping sound of the Stryker saw. When I returned to the autopsy room, red froth had collected between the corpse's legs and trickled down the drain at the bottom of the table. A bloody heart had been casually flopped on the scale and its weight and color recorded on the log. One by one, Kim's organs took a turn on the scale. At the end of the carousel we had a verdict on Kim's death: "The right and left lungs, 550 and 580 grams respectively, show sign of massive edema in the bronchial mucosa resulting in bronchoconstriction. Swelling with diffuse *petechiae* hemorrhage is noted in the brain."

Ellis placed sections of the victim's lungs and pharynges on a metal tray. "I'm sending these to Histology: I want them to test for IgE antibodies and mast cells. My money so far goes on anaphylactic shock. As for what caused it—" He handed the tray to the assistant. "—you guys will have to wait for the tox results."

Everything else in Nathan Kim's body was *unremarkable*. A weird concept, which seems to imply that only strange and out of the ordinary things are worth medical attention. Health is dull. But red boils, golf-ball sized tumors, or a face as green as a British lawn will have the meds jumping up and down in excitement.

"A healthy young man," Ellis noted, wrapping up his examination. "His colon is as shiny and smooth as a baby's."

"I'm sure his mom will be thrilled to hear it," Satish said.

"Somebody should mention it over the eulogy," I added.

Neither of us smiled.

The biting monkey had been identified through the dental marks left on Kim's shoulder, and the necropsy scheduled for the afternoon.

Gray skies and a fine drizzle welcomed us outside, casting the usual views of downtown under a drape of gloom. It shadowed the intertwining highway ramps and the rows of skinny palm trees whose frazzled tops drew sinuous lines in the sky. It blanketed the plain-looking buildings and the colorful strips of murals, the parking lots where bums pushed their junk-filled carts, and the sidewalks where teenagers with pants barely hanging to their butts showed off their monkey walk. Tiny drops of humidity clung to my face and hair as we walked back to our car.

Satish checked his watch. "Twelve-thirty. An hour most of the world associates with lunch."

I unlocked my Dodge. "I'm in a different time zone today."

Satish nodded and slid inside the vehicle. Autopsies are unkind to the toughest stomachs. My phone rang as I jammed the key into the ignition.

"Track. Where the hell are you? I've been waiting here at Annie's since noon."

"Oscar!" I'd completely forgotten about my lunch meeting with Detective Oscar Guerra. "Damn it, don't move. I'll be right over," I tossed the phone onto Satish's lap and swerved into the street.

Satish groaned. "Thank you, Track. I already felt like puking, I didn't need the extra help."

"Okay, gringo. Tell me what this is about."

I chuckled. "I'm no gringo, pal. This is home."

Guerra downed a good swig from his schooner, which he had ordered with a wink and a heartfelt "Hell, it's not like I'm going back to work after lunch," and laughed. "Uh-uh, bro. We were here first. You"—he pointed at me as a representative of a whole class of American invaders—"are gringo."

Oscar Guerra—a sun-burnt face with shrewd eyes and a

broad grin—was as American as I was but never forgot his Mexican origins. A face on which time had chiseled the furrows that come from embracing life in full: ten years in the military, thirteen as a cop, a couple of narrowly escaped shootouts, and hours of horseback riding at his family ranch in Oaxaca. He had a few exes and three or four children probably all with different spouses, something he had once commented with a rowdy, "What the hell, I'm fifty-eight!"

I'd dropped Satish off at the Glass House and then joined Oscar at his favorite place, a dungeon kind of bar that smelled of stale beer, sweaty armpits, and acid reflux. Apparently, the fact that such place was called "Annie's" added to the charm.

I insisted on eating outside. The morgue had me maxed out on foul smells for the day. We sat in the shade of a wooden pergola, the knotty branches of a climbing vine bathing us in a fragrant, twinkling light. Wafts of teriyaki chicken and Philly steak tickled my nostrils and resuscitated my appetite. At a nearby table, a guy in a white shirt, black tie, and spiky hair enjoyed his meal while flirting on the mobile with his girlfriend—the beauty of living in a wireless era. By the salad bar, two ladies in jogging slacks and overdone make-up compared notes on caloric intake and hairdresser bills.

The waiter took our orders while ruminating a wad of pink chewing gum. She scribbled on her notepad and then scuttled off, a whiff of kitchen smells trailing behind her.

"I thought you liked your steak rare," Oscar said, bringing the schooner to his mouth.

"Not today. I spent the morning at the morgue."

He almost choked on his beer.

"It's not funny. Listen, I was wondering if you could refresh me on the Ilke case."

"Ilke? Peeping Tom?"

"Exactly the guy. I believe I read the term *voyeur* in the report, though." I grinned.

Oscar had a hearty laugh that didn't care if it made a few heads turn. "Yeah, that was Washburn. He said it's an actual disease—no, wait, *mental disorder*, that's what he called it. Forget Washburn. Everybody else at the Homicide table knew him by Peeping Tom. Why are you interested in the piece of scum?"

"What did he do?"

"He stalked women, preferably with an active sexual life. He'd study their schedule, patterns, routes, and most importantly, he'd find a way into their homes."

"How to break in?"

"Uh-uh. The guy was sleek and methodic. He'd find a loose window, figure out where they hid the spare key, or snatch the key bunch from their office desk at work. He'd make a copy, and then return it to its exact place. The victims were completely unaware the perv had access to their places."

"He never touched them though, did he?"

"No. He'd have been one hell of a serial rapist if he had. He just watched. Maybe leave a little souvenir on the side. Not so good at cleaning up after himself—that's how we caught him."

"Watched what?"

"You know. The lady taking a shower or using the restroom or having sex. Anything intimate. He'd find a hiding spot and sit there, sometimes for hours, as long as he could get a good peek. We even found a photo album in his place, with names and dates. To Washburn, this behavior made perfect sense. He said it's a form of repressed homosexuality, where the man identifies with the woman's pleasure by watching her."

We interrupted the conversation in honor of the two

juicy steaks the waiter brought to our table. Ravenous appetite and dining etiquette are mutually exclusive.

"Was Ilke ever violent?" I asked, half way through our meal.

"Are you kidding?" Oscar didn't mind speaking with his mouth full. "He was completely innocuous. He broke into tears when we picked him up. Said he couldn't help himself."

"How did he choose the victims?"

"He'd pick a random face in the street or on Amtrak. Anywhere, in fact."

"Random people?"

"Yes. Never met them before, never even approached them personally. Apparently, he felt too shy to talk to them."

I snorted. "Too shy to talk to them but not to watch them slide off their panties?"

Oscar dropped the fork and carefully wiped his mouth. "Look, Track. If you're really interested in this case, you should talk to Washburn. He wrote a detailed report on the guy. *Fascinating,* he called him. *A textbook case.*"

I smiled while sipping my wine. "Yeah, well. Nutcase to nutcase."

"Come on, Track," Oscar insisted with an emphatic sway of his hand. "Give the doc a break. I mean, mentals are his thing. He talks about them like Banjaree talks about computers, or Fraser about firearms. We all have our thing."

"Yeah, right. Oscar, mentals do not qualify as 'a thing,' okay? Anyway, I'm not talking to the shrink. I had my share after the last shootout. All I'd like to know is what Ilke got out of it. Watching, I mean."

"Control."

"Control?"

He smiled and scratched a brow. "Washburn said

voyeurism is a form of control over the sexual partner. Apparently, these people are control freaks."

"But the guy wouldn't even approach his victims."

"Exactly. He remained emotionally detached. As long as he watched he felt in control, not overwhelmed by emotions. In other words, he could *unplug* as he willed. No pun intended."

I had to laugh. "There was *no* plugging."

Oscar shrugged. "Maybe in his mind there was."

I tapped the fork on the table. *It makes no sense.* "What if he did know the victim? What if in fact he made her do it so he could watch? Would it still be a way of keeping things under control?"

Oscar drained his schooner and dropped it back on the table with a loud clonk. "Hell, Track, what do I know? I'm a cop and Ilke was the only voyeurism case I came across. If you want the expert—"

"Then go talk to Washburn. Yes, Oscar, got it. Thank you."

Oscar smiled. "Actually, I was going to suggest you talk to the sleaze himself."

"Ilke?"

"Yeah. As far as I remember, he's booked for another year at least in Vacaville."

Outside, the roar of the nearby boulevard hit me with its usual concert of engines, honks, and the throbbing speakers of a shiny black Carrera. I retreated to my Dodge and closed the door. As soon as I started the engine, Ravel greeted me with the opening notes of *Water Games*. Ah, oxygen for my ears. Except for the nagging voice popping into my head: *Why won't you talk to Washburn, Ulysses?*

Because. I don't like the guy.

Come on, he's just another guy. With a little more education than you, but you've never been intimidated by education, have you?

I don't like the way he stares at me.

I know you, Ulysses, his eyes tell me while his mouth says, "The pattern and depth of the stab wounds indicate this perpetrator has killed before."

I know the animal lurking inside you.

I know the excitement you feel after every kill, the anticipation when you inhale the prey's blood — luring, inebriating.

I know how many times you kept going back to the house, looking for her, or so you thought. Until something snapped and suddenly you weren't the victim anymore. You'd become the predator.

"You went back to the house?"

I nodded. "More than once. I'd jimmy one of the back windows and slide inside. It was empty. The for-sale sign stood slanted on the front lawn. The paint was new, but the stories were old. Nobody wanted to buy that house."

Watanabe's office was in complete darkness, save the neighborhood lights glimmering through the window and a small table lamp carving a cone of light over his desk. It made the circles beneath his eyes look ghastly. "What do you remember?"

What do I remember.

I sank in the chair and looked away. August 1986. I mostly recalled smells, as vivid as a hot, summer day. The fresh paint on the walls, the acrylic coating of the new carpets, the reek of emptiness and abandonment... her fear, still there, in untouched corners, like the closet door under the stairs, or the baseboard in the bathroom.

They found her body sprawled at the base of the stairs, a

pair of pink stockings tightly wrapped around her throat—the only piece of clothing still on her.

She was fourteen.

I'd crawl inside the house and scavenge the traces she'd left, no matter how faint. They frightened me and attracted me at the same time, because wherever I could still smell her, I could smell *him*, too.

"Danny Mendoza, age 19, car mechanic," I said. "He'd made a copy of the house key when Lily's mother left her vehicle at the shop for an oil change. They had nothing on him, absolutely nothing. There was no forced entry. He'd left no prints, no DNA, no nothing. Only a dead body." I swallowed. "Lily's."

"And you tracked down… his smell?"

"He'd drive by the house from time to time. He'd park his red Camaro across the street, pull the window down, and smoke a cig."

"Just that?"

"Just that."

Watanabe's eyes feigned incredulity. "How did you know it was him?"

"I didn't. When I saw him there for the third time, I followed him to the shop. I asked him about his cars. He loved to talk about his cars. And girls. So I asked him about that, too. We became… buddies. Sort of."

Red eyes, waning through thick curls of smoke, the reek of burnt plastic and wet dog, lacing my hands through the sheepskin seat cover as I hear him speak, his words gray and thick like molasses, like the air in the old Camaro. Him, slouched in the driver's seat, a cigarette butt clinging to his greasy hands and a slur pasting his tongue.

You ever had a girl?

No.

I've had many. He laughs. *I make them beg, I do.*

How?

Yellow smiles echoing through the fog of dope.

I'll tell you a secret. Can you keep a secret?

I clutch the penknife in my pocket and nod. And that's when he tells me. How he made a noose out of her stockings, wrapped it around her neck and made her beg. He watched her eyes beg, *Her eyes, man, the way she looked at me, pleading, don't you get it, the more she begged the more exciting it got, I had her, I had to keep her begging me, I made her tell me she wanted more, I made her...*

It was too much to recall. Silence fell. A wall clock ticked somewhere in Watanabe's office. Outside a dog barked at the moon. I squeezed my knees, wading through the murkiness of memories.

Watanabe's flat cheekbones emerged from the cone of light. "Ulysses?"

"Huh?"

"What happened next, Ulysses?"

I shook my head. "I can't—I don't remember." I licked my lips, snatched a bit of time. "They found me a few feet away from the car, my clothes drenched in blood—Mendoza's blood. They uh—they said his throat and eyes had been carved out. They said the stab wounds were compatible with a penknife blade. The one I was holding, precisely."

A veil of clouds covered the moon. The dog stopped barking. Through the window, black silhouettes of palm trees staggered against yellow streetlights.

Watanabe moved away from the table lamp. Darkness swallowed his face. "So the judge denied bail, based on the cruelty of the crime, but revoked the decision one month later," he recalled.

The case had made headlines at the time.

"I told them he'd killed Lily, but they didn't believe me

until they found her clothes inside an old cooler Mendoza kept in his garage. They didn't drop the charges, when they corroborated my story. A jury did, one year later. Acquitted on all counts."

Watanabe's face remained in the dark. His fingers played softly with a pen. "And you can't remember anything of the attack? You must have suffered some wounds too, or else your lawyer couldn't have claimed self-defense…"

I fished a key out of my pocket and dropped it on the desk. We both looked at it. "It was in my personal belongings, when they released me."

"A key?"

"I checked. It was Lily's house key."

Watanabe said nothing.

"From Danny. Don't you get it, Doc?"

I saw his face nod through the shadows. "Your first trophy," he said.

I looked out the window. The clouds had shifted, the moon was out again.

Watanabe tapped his pen. "I found your old medical records, Ulysses."

I raised a brow, unsure how to take the statement.

"Ulysses Moris Presius."

I grimaced. "That's me. Greek grandfather and a longstanding family tradition of obnoxious names."

He bobbed his head, clicked the pen. "Listen. Did your parents ever talk about taking you in for an MRI when you were ten, or maybe twelve? Did they ever mention—" He swallowed, corrugated his forehead. "Do you have any recollection of being at the hospital when you were six?"

"Six?" I shrugged. "Yeah. I think it was one of those childhood diseases. I got it pretty bad and they had to take me in."

"The measles?"

"Must've been, yeah."

"That's all your parents told you? That it was the measles?"

"Look. My parents hated doctors." I scratched my brow, trying to remember. "Mom said when I was little a doctor wanted to drill a hole in my head—her words, not mine. Apparently, the doctor was convinced I wasn't going to live another six months." I laughed. My laughter vaporized under Watanabe's hard stare.

"Nothing personal, Doc. I like you," I joked.

Still, the man wouldn't budge. He rolled the pen between his fingers, his silence as heavy as a next-day hangover.

"You had a brain tumor, Ulysses. When you were five."

He let the words chill out on me, then reached for the brown envelope in his drawer. It looked fatter than last time. He pushed it towards me and let it hang at the edge of the desk. "It's all in there. Two signed referrals from pediatricians, one recommendation for surgery from an oncologist. I made a copy of your CT scan. 'Grade two juvenile astrocytoma'—that was your diagnosis. It's still visible, despite the image being over twenty years old—a mass about half-centimeter in diameter in the left cerebellar hemisphere."

I looked at the image in disbelief. "Oh, come on." I made a face. "Look at me, Doc. I'm thirty-eight and pretty healthy, save a moderate addiction to ethanol and caffeine. Those docs," I waved a hand at the brown envelope. "They *had* to be wrong."

He shook his head.

I forced laughter out of my throat. "Really, Doc. I'd be dead by now."

"Something saved your life. A virus, precisely."

Watanabe pulled a bunch of papers out of the brown envelope. They were photocopies of old documents, some handwritten, some typed on yellowed hospital letterhead. None I recognized. "You changed after that. Your vision, your acute olfactory senses, your—aggressiveness. You weren't born a chimera, you became one."

I narrowed my eyes. "You said—I couldn't be a chimera."

"Not a genetic one, no. You're an *epigenetic* chimera, the most extraordinary kind. The measles killed the brain tumor but turned on ancestral genes that are normally off in most individuals."

Watanabe forked his reading glasses and flipped through the papers. "Visit dates, temperature, BP—ah, here it is. You were hospitalized in April 1976—you'd just turned six. You were running a fever of one-oh-four and having seizures. A doctor named Frank Haynes saw you, one of the two pediatricians who had made the tumor diagnosis six months earlier. He concluded you had contracted encephalitis as a complication from the measles. You were in a coma for about a week. They treated you with anti-inflammatory drugs and analgesic. You had to undergo physical therapy for about three months afterwards." He raised his eyes above the rim of his glasses. "You have no recollection of that?"

It all sounded distant, as if he were telling me somebody else's story, not mine. "Of the hospital? Yes. I hated it. Brain tumors? No. Look. I wasn't the brightest kid in school, okay? And I was ridiculously clumsy in PE—*that* I remember. But I outgrew it."

"Exactly." Watanabe flipped through the papers. "Dr. Haynes actually saw you again—for the last time—one year later. Your symptoms were gone: no more headaches, dizziness, or fainting. He checked your balance, movements, etc. Everything looked normal except—"

"Except?"

"Haynes found your vision and sense of olfaction to be dramatically enhanced: 'Exceptionally fast reflexes, enhanced vision and sense of olfaction. Mild irritability.' He suggested a new CT scan but your parents declined."

I let out a snort. "Of course. By then they realized the brain tumor had never existed, and my mother was right to be pissed."

"And how do you explain the changes after the encephalitis?"

I laced my hands together and leaned forward. "I told you the story a million times, Doc. You still refuse to believe me. We went camping, Dad and I. I got too far from the campground and was attacked by a cougar. I was still in kindergarten." I sank back in my chair. "I never was the same after that."

"How did you survive a cougar attack?"

"I don't know. It roared at me. I screamed and froze. Then it—" I swallowed. I could still see its amber eyes flash before my face. "It barely scratched me with its fangs and left." I shook my head, smiling without meaning to. "My parents didn't believe me either. Said I'd gotten the scratches from tree branches."

Watanabe didn't blink, his face as flat as a board. He stuck a hand inside the brown envelope and fished out one last paper. "Your recent MRI. Take a look." He handed it to me across the desk and pointed to the middle of the skull. "That's your cerebellum. And see the tiny white blob on the right side of the image? You have to know it's there to see it." He stood up, leaned across the desk, and tapped the MRI scan in my hands. "Right there. See?"

I nodded.

"That's the scar your childhood tumor left. A scar,

nothing else. The measles virus destroyed the rest."

I shot up my brows. "You're not saying—the virus—how's that even possible?"

"Viruses kill cells, Ulysses. Tumors are made of cells. There have been quite a few case reports of cancer remission after an unrelated viral infection. In fact, viruses are used in experimental anti-cancer treatments. The measles infection you got in 1976 got to your brain, causing the encephalitis, and it turned out to be a blessing in disguise. It killed the tumor, leaving a tiny scar."

He stared at me.

I set the MRI back on the desk. "Let me get this straight, Doc. A stupid virus I got when I was five saved me from dying of brain cancer but turned me into a monster?"

Watanabe smiled. "Not a monster, Ulysses. A *mezurashii*. A one in a million. The virus turned you into a chimera."

"Don't chimeras have two DNA's?" I asked.

"*Genetic* chimeras have different DNA's in different tissues. But you're not a genetic chimera, Ulysses. You're an *epigenetic* one."

He started blabbering about pseudogenes and that word he liked so much, epigenetics; how genes turn on and off and the environment we are exposed to—diet, diseases, even traumas—can screw that whole "on/off" process. My brain was reeling. I got to my feet and walked to the window. The pale face of the moon filled the sky.

A virus.

A virus turned me into a chimera.

An *epigenetic* chimera—whatever that meant.

"Ulysses? Are you listening to me? Do you understand, now, how the viral infection turned on the ancestral genes that control vision and olfaction?"

I swallowed. "It wasn't the measles."

"What?"

"That doctor—Haynes. He said it was the measles because the stuff was going around at the time. But it wasn't. I—I'd been vaccinated against the measles." I turned away from the window and stared at him, his face carved out of darkness by the yellow table lamp. "The virus was rabies."

CHAPTER 27

Tuesday, October 21

I propped my feet on the desk and stuck a paperclip in my teeth. Roy, a young detective with a square neck and a flat head, tossed a paper airplane in the air and snickered. I caught it midair, crumpled it, and thrust it in the trash bin. They should forbid anybody with a flat head to wear a buzz cut. It's disturbing.

Roy flashed a sheepish grin, which I ignored.

I spit out the paperclip and yawned. The weather was dull, the afternoon was dull, the mood was dull. Until a new spice gently rippled the air. I dropped my feet from the desk.

"Sat."

"Hmm."

"Was there a meeting I forgot about today?"
"No, why?"
"Diane's here."

"Sorry to barge in unannounced," Diane told us, slightly out of breath. I unlocked the door to the captain's office, which we use as a conference room whenever the boss is not around.

Satish pulled a chair and noisily flopped in it. "Track announced you, all right. About three minutes before you stepped into the squad room."

Diane whirled her head and stared at me. "Really?" she asked, a flattered look dancing on her face.

She walked to the captain's chair and slid off her short-sleeve jacket. She was wearing a sleeveless top that held her breasts in the most marvelous way, the balance between what it revealed and what it left to the imagination as poetic as a Shakespearean sonnet.

Something excited her. "I just got back from UCLA and couldn't wait to show you guys."

"UCLA?"

She opened a folder and spread its contents on the table. "I spent the whole day at the Electron Imaging Core, staring into a transmission electron microscope. It's an amazing instrument: it can enlarge objects one thousand times smaller than the section of a human hair."

I sent a sideways glance at Satish. "Imagine Gomez's moles—how beautiful they'd look."

He grinned. "Like the surface of Mars."

Diane glared. "Anyway. I prepared a sample with the blood taken from one of the Chromo monkeys, and this is what I saw." She flipped a picture in front of us. On cue, Satish and I leaned forward and peered at the photo, both feeling as clueless as chipmunks crossing the street.

"What are we staring at?"

"A virus. Nathan Kim's killer."

"I thought the Chromo lab tech died of anaphylactic shock," Satish said.

"He did." Diane tapped on the cluster of circular blobs depicted in the picture. "The virus got into his system through the monkey bite and triggered the massive release of histamine."

I struggled to understand. "Diane, a virus can give you the flu, a cold, or hepatitis. I've never heard of a virus triggering anaphylaxis."

"This was no ordinary virus, Track," she said, flopping back in her chair and retrieving a second sheet of paper. It was a diagram this time. "I analyzed the genome of this particular virus and compared it to a flu strain."

"Hold on," Satish interrupted. "Does this mean the monkeys were sick?"

"Not quite. Look at this: the top diagram represents the genes of the flu virus, the bottom one represents the genes of the virus from the Chromo monkey. I put them together so you can see the similarities."

"Similarities, huh?" I commented, staring at the diagrams. "This is what a color-blinded person feels when staring at a Chagall."

Satish snorted, but Diane wasn't amused. "Guys, you don't understand." She dropped back in her chair, a shade of frustration jagging her brow. "A virus is basically genetic material wrapped in a shell. When the virus attacks a cell, the shell opens up and the genetic material is delivered inside." Diane paused. We remained silent this time. "Now look at these diagrams. This is the gene coding the outer shell of the virus. It's pretty similar across the two species. Now, here"—she tapped to the right of the two diagrams—

"is what each virus will inject inside the infected cell. And this is where the Chromo virus gets strikingly different from the flu strain."

"How?" Satish asked.

"Because these right here are no ordinary genes. They're *human* genes."

The air in the captain's office felt suddenly stale and hot. I rose, walked to the thermostat, and cranked up the AC. The Venetian blinds started tapping against the windowpane.

"How can a virus contain human genes?" Satish asked.

I knew the answer. I knew it too damn well.

We can do it in a lab, Watanabe had told me last night. *We can now make chimeric viruses by mixing pieces of DNA from different organisms.*

"This is not just any virus," Diane explained. "It's been artificially engineered."

"They're called chimeras," I said, in a low voice, the name—chimeras—such a new, intimate detail of my life it almost startled me to hear it coming out of my mouth.

Diane looked surprised. "They are, Track. How did you—"

"No," I interrupted. "The question is *why* was Chromo making these viruses and injecting them into monkeys."

Diane pulled a lock of her hair behind her ear. "I don't know. I need to study these genes better, see what proteins they code. It might be part of some gene therapy experiment. Maybe they wanted to modify genes that cause genetic disorders."

"Are you saying—?" Satish said.

"Exactly what you're thinking: if a virus can be modified in a way that it still retains its ability to enter the cell but deliver the 'right' genes instead of its own, then you've got a way of replacing a defective gene with a healthy one."

"Has it ever been done?"

Diane nodded. "A French group conducted a trial study to cure a defect on the X chromosome. The disease is called SCI, or Severe Combined Immunodeficiency. The study was halted in 2002, though."

I walked back to the table. "Why?"

Diane tilted her head and winced before replying. The implication struck her as the answer came out of her mouth: "Two boys enrolled in the study developed leukemia."

I banged my hand on the table. Hard. "This is what Huxley was onto."

"We have no proof she knew any of this."

"Because we still don't have access to her computer!"

"You said we had her e-mails."

I bit on my knuckles and nodded. I'd flipped through the printouts Amit had delivered to my desk. It was all scientific jargon.

I turned to Diane and flashed her a grin. "Yes. We have her e-mails and we have a scientist."

"Tonight?"

"Yeah. Bedtime reads. Can't be any worse than *War and Peace*, can it?"

Diane gave me a sullen look. "I love *War and Peace*."

"Well, then chances are, you'll love this stuff too."

She stared at the ream of papers piled on my desk and bit the inside of her cheek. I wanted to bite the other side. "You haul it down to my car." She spun around and headed out the door.

Satish sneered and walked to his desk while whistling Frishberg's jazz tune *Peel Me a Grape*. I preferred it when Diana Krall sang it.

On the elevator, Diane gave me a supercilious look. "Just

so you know, those e-mails are not the only thing on my agenda." *Neither on mine*, I thought, basking in her scent. And then shamelessly said nothing. "We need to find out what Chromo was doing with those monkeys. I'll search the literature, see if they published any scientific results in the past few years."

"Medford mentioned gene therapy experiments when we talked to him. And a woman who supposedly confronted Tarantino about them."

"Could've been Huxley."

"It would explain a lot of things, including why she mailed him Gaya White's funeral note. You know what I'm thinking? The pamphlet Elizabeth Medford gave you: what did it say?"

The elevator doors opened, we stepped out, and Diane's scent dispersed. "It was about genetic screening and counseling for perspective parents."

"Yeah, right. Counseling my ass. They did a lot more."

Diane sighed. "Whatever they did, they screwed up."

She clacked her heels through the Glass House doors and across the San Pedro parking lot. I tagged along, nose and all. Mostly nose. Her lime-colored VW was wedged between two cruisers, and her parking would've been perfect had the white lines on the pavement been drawn along the opposite diagonal. She popped the trunk and then stepped aside. I stared at the inside of her car and had a moment of deep cerebral activity.

"Did a macho guy from Trace sell you those?"

She flinched. "Sell me what?"

"The box of Tyvek shoe covers," I replied, dropping the ream of e-mail printouts next to the box I'd just noticed sitting in her trunk. "They're very popular lately. Can be found in hospitals and at crime scenes."

She didn't get the irony. Or maybe she didn't want to.

"Of course they are. They're mandatory for all Field Units. Speaking of which." She opened the passenger's door and retrieved a plastic evidence bag, which she held up to my nose. "Do you know anything about this?"

Ha. Do I know anything about an empty beer can, not-so-legally obtained from a privately owned trash can? I scowled. "What's it doing in your trunk? I left it at the Serology lab."

"I know you did. I'm the DNA specialist, remember? It came across my technician's desk together with the sample from Huxley's car."

"Yes. I wanted a comparative analysis."

She tilted her head. My eyes tripped down her neckline. "Did you make up the log number, Track? It didn't match anything from Huxley's logs." She wasn't scolding. In fact, her voice was mellow, her half smile conspiratorial. I stared, she stared back. And then her lips twitched. Upwards. Darned cute.

"Non-kosher?" she asked.

"Plain view." Still staring. Lips stretching further. "Sort of." Lips sneering. "Hell, D., it's inadmissible, okay? I just need the DNA comparison to prove a hunch of mine." Damn it, they should have women grill suspects in interrogation rooms.

She lowered the plastic bag and stared at the empty can inside. "Budweiser. Funny, it's Jim's favorite." A high-pitched snort forced its way out of my mouth.

The hell of a coincidence.

"I'll tell you what," she said with a sly grin. "You buy me lunch and I'll tag it and log it for you."

She gazed at me, her eyes sparkling. Waiting for me to play along.

"You're letting me corrupt you, forensic scientist Kyle?"

"Only under very particular circumstances."

I was doped. My eyes skimmed over the box of Tyvek

shoe covers in the open trunk of her car, then back to the beer can in her hands. Diane. She smelled heavenly today. Not like last week. Last week was light-years away. Hell, last week could've dwelled in that limbo called imagination. I smiled. She smiled back, my non-kosher piece of evidence secured in her hands.

"Tomorrow," her lips whispered.

"Tomorrow," I replied, watching her slide behind the steering wheel.

You're an asshole, Ulysses.

No, I'm not. Diana Krall's voice hummed in my head. *I saved the fuzz for her pillow.*

"How about this one?"

"It's good."

She groaned and tossed it away. "I hate it."

I shrugged and didn't take it personally.

The place was warm and cozy. Hortensia instead was frenzied and jittery. She was going through her studio like a caged animal, picking up, tossing, hurdling, pushing away. A manager in Santa Barbara had approached her for a show in his gallery and requested ten of her paintings. From what she'd told me of the guy, I had an inkling the manager wanted to request her bra and panties too. Given the torpedo mood she was in, I kept the thought to myself. I sat on her sofa, sipped a glass of the Barolo I'd brought along, and nodded on cue whenever she lifted a canvas to prod my judgment. I can be a good puppy when I want.

Her large, rustic worktable was encrusted with dried spatters of paint and cluttered with jars, oil tubes, and diluents. Frazzled paintbrushes of all sizes sprouted from old cans on her shelves, and rolled canvases filled every corner of the room. Worn out aprons covered in a rainbow of stains hung from the wall next to a vintage tub sink. Two painted eyes stood on the easel and stared, begging for a face. The reek of turpentine mingled with the mouthwatering fragrance coming from the kitchen—pork ribs in barbeque sauce, heavenly roasting in the oven.

Given the state she was in, Hortensia would've made me dizzy, had I not kept my mind occupied with other matters. It was finally coming together. Chromo offered genetic counseling to affluent and ambitious perspective parents. It wasn't just a screening. It was an expensive promise.

"Track."

"What?"

"Are you listening?"

"Yeah." I swallowed the rest of my wine. "Something about your hair. I'm starving, any chance those ribs would be ready by now?"

Hortensia hurdled the box of junk she had collected from all her old painting supplies and dropped it at my feet. "Hell, Track. I don't know why I even bothered making you dinner."

"What? Wait—" No use. She'd already run out of the room, pouting. I heaved the box and took it outside to the trashcan. The night was nippy and a few stars were out, dimmed by the grin of a crescent moon. A warm, yellow halo blanketed the jagged horizon of roofs. The streets were quiet, save for the usual droning of the freeway in the distance. A bicycle squeaked its way along the sidewalk; a TV blinked muted pictures from a window next door; a child cried and a parent hushed her.

Random images of ordinary lives.

Why can't you have a normal life, Ulysses?

Because I'm not normal, Ma.

Hortensia crouched by the oven, checking on the ribs. I waited until she dropped the pan on the stove, then brushed her hair to the side and kissed the back of her neck.

"You weren't listening," she scolded, softly this time.

"I've got a lot on my plate these days, Hort."

She passed me her glass. "Intoxicate me, then. I might rant more, but then I won't mind if you're not listening."

I poured the wine, and then helped her set the table. She transferred the ribs onto a serving dish. The aroma of the braised meat made my stomach growl.

"What about sending 'Chimeras' for the show?"

After I told her Watanabe had finally come up with a diagnosis for me—epigentic chimera—she decided to title "Chimeras" the painting she had dedicated to me.

"Only if you change the title," I said.

"Aw... I *love* the title!"

I looked out the window above the sink. It framed a square of pitch black, a well of light scooped out in the middle by an arching streetlight. A jogger slid out of the darkness and looked up. For a fraction of a second our eyes met, then the night swallowed her again, a frame of my life retained on her retinas for a moment longer and soon forgotten. *Not worth remembering... Does my life look normal when gazing from far away?*

Half way through dinner Hortensia pursed her lips, put her fork and knife down, and frowned as if she had completely given up on me. "What kind of nutcases are you dealing with this time?"

"The rich and spoiled."

"Ooh. Spicy."

"Yes, that too," I added, thinking of Dan Horowitz's comments back at the cemetery, and the conversation I had with Oscar Guerra.

"Anybody crazy and handsome enough to model for me? I just fired the last one. I couldn't take the smell of joint on his breath."

"No, another kind of crazy. These people want everything perfect in their life, even when things are supposed to go wrong."

"Supposed to?"

I nodded, absent-mindedly. We call them mistakes, when in fact they're explorations: the search for new paths in the rugged landscape called life. *There is no evolution without change.*

"And why do you consider them crazy? Just because they wanted perfect genes?"

I winced. "You don't think they are?"

Hortensia refilled my glass. "You're funny sometimes, Track. Of all people, shouldn't you understand best? Something switched in your DNA, and your doctor told you the changes are hereditary."

I swished wine in my mouth and then swallowed. "For a few generations only. Because the *actual* genes didn't change, it's not like—"

"So then suppose there was a way to fix your genes. No matter how crazy the cure sounded, wouldn't you want to try it? Wouldn't you want to jump on that one chance to have a *normal* life?"

I stared at the purple-red shade of the wine in my glass, tiny bubbles clinging to the surface. The *normality* I longed for on nights like that one. The ordinary lives I stared at as if looking out from a window, as if separated from me by a screen, shouting at me, *This is what you'll never be, Ulysses.* If given the opportunity, wouldn't I want another chance?

CHAPTER 28

Wednesday, October 22

I checked my cell phone: everything was quiet from the Glass House. Satish was booked all day in court. I decided to take a low-key day and catch up on a few overdue reports. I got out of bed, pulled on a pair of sport shorts, and went jogging. The sun was rising and the air brisk.

I love the chilliness of Southern California mornings. During the day, temperatures in the valley can rise to ninety degrees, and yet mornings are almost always crisp. The strips of lawn by the sidewalks smell of dew. Whiffs of slowly brazing wood logs creep out of the chimneys and waft down the streets. Sycamores, turned yellow overnight, surprise the eye with wavering brightness. The sounds are hushed: a garage door opens, lets a small car whir out, and then closes again. A crow caws from the top of a telephone pole and then stops, as though baffled by its own voice. Announced by a gargling hiss, a sprinkler goes off. The lawn welcomes the moisture releasing a nippy fragrance of wet soil.

My feet bounced along the sidewalk in consecutive thumps. My lungs pumped air in rhythmical whooshes. A dozen kids whose cancers did not respond to therapy, at least one of them linked to Chromo. A couple poured their anxieties for the child they wanted to conceive into a search for perfection. A religious woman accused Chromo of "playing God" and harming innocent lives. The same woman ended up dead, after being lured over the promise of unspecified data.

Damn it. Yes, justice is indeed imperfect, Hannah. Still, you have choices in life, and murder shouldn't be one of them. Jennifer Huxley chose to fight. *I know what you expected to find in the cryogenic tank, Jen. I just have to prove it.*

I stopped to catch my breath, and the phone in my arm pouch buzzed. I flipped it open.

"Did I wake you up?" Diane's voice was scratchy, her words pasted.

"No."

She hesitated for a second, then drew a deep breath. I imagined her fingers as they pulled a strand of hair away from her face, still warm from bed. "I had a rough night. I told Jim I had enough of him."

I pressed the phone against my ear and said nothing. She didn't like it.

"Are you going to say something? It would be nice if I weren't just talking to myself."

I agreed. She sighed again. "What time are you coming? There's something I need to show you."

"Diane, what the hell are you doing?"

She startled. "I'm crossing the street."

I grabbed her arm and pulled her back on the sidewalk. Going fifteen miles over the speed limit, a truck driver swooshed by showing a dexterous use of his middle finger. His honk trailed off, soon covered by the jingling of the wind chimes hanging from a nearby shop.

"Hell, Diane, this is L.A., not Boston! Didn't your parents teach you to look out for cars when you cross the street?"

"No." Diane's voice slipped into high-pitched indignation. "They taught me to look out for pedestrians when I drive."

Nice utopian view of traffic and other related matters in life. "It might work at cattle crossings where you grew up. It doesn't work in L.A." I was still clutching her arm, squeezing in fact. I let go and stared at the packed sidewalk. North Broadway was a colorful patchwork of striped awnings and store signs covered in elegant ideographs. The usual odors of L.A. streets—sweat, urine, gas exhaust—mingled with the wafts of the merchandise in the store windows: fruits and vegetables laid out for everybody to touch and smell; dried fish and birds hanging from the ceilings; ginger, cloves, anise, and fennel, sold in large jute sacks.

"Why Boston?"

"You could buy a house if you ticketed all the jaywalkers in Boston on any given day. Why did we come to Chinatown?"

Diane smiled. "Because I know a place where they serve the best dim sum you'll ever eat."

"As long as there's enough meat. I'm a carnivore."

"Relax. You'll love it."

She was already walking away, her gait confident as she

jostled the eclectic crowds around us. Faces from different worlds emerged through the folds of an urban landscape: a genderless figure, standing still behind a shop window; a feminine oval, as white and flawless as a porcelain mask, peeking through the sheer curtain of a restaurant; young men walking briskly, their spiked hair and puffed chests a bold statement of past puberty, though their cheeks so smooth they had yet to see a razor.

I wasn't relaxed. My hunch had proven wrong. I was irritated. "You're sure you did the analyses correctly?"

"Yes. The answer hasn't changed from five minutes ago: whoever drank from the beer can you handed over for DNA analysis didn't leave his precious stuff in Huxley's car."

"Damn it."

She sent me a sideways glance. "Why are you still thinking about it?"

"I hate to be wrong."

My nose is never wrong. I rely on it. The beer can carried *his* smell.

Diane froze in the middle of the sidewalk and stared at me, her face hung somewhere in between bewilderment and resentment. "And by what chauvinistic and dick-waving principle should you never be wrong, Track? Or is it a woman telling you so that throws off your testosterone levels?"

I winced. A carillon chimed its hypnotic tune from a shop crammed with knickknacks, souvenirs, and a rainbow of wind spinners and cheap plastic gadgets. A hideous face standing by the door grinned at me for no reason. I stared back at Diane and didn't reply. Yes, I could be plain wrong and let it go. Something told me otherwise, though.

Diane ran the analyses, Ulysses. She's hiding something.

If she is, she'll get me the assassin. It's just a matter of time.

She averted her eyes and resumed walking. "Sorry, you

probably meant it as a joke and I overreacted. I had a rough night, I think I told you already."

"Yes, you did."

We turned into a narrow street. "If it's of any consolation, the two DNA strains could be related."

"In what way?"

"Cousins. Maybe even brothers. There's a high chance of them sharing the same father. I only looked at the Y chromosome, so I can't speak for the mother." Without looking at me, she disappeared behind a glass door out of which wafted warm aromas of simmering onions, sesame, and fermented spices. The hall was large and crowded. Waiters circled the tables pushing around carts. A petite woman in a purple Chinese blouse and black slacks came to offer us a wide smile and an incomprehensible welcome. She motioned to a table where a stiff looking waiter was flipping plates as if they were Frisbees. The waiter bowed, the lady bowed, Diane sat down and asked for an iced tea.

At the opposite corner, a fish tank mumbled soothing sounds. All around the walls, white scrolls of paper depicted young women dancing and bathing along a yellow riverbed.

I hung my jacket at the back of the chair, ordered a Corona, and sat down. "Tell me again what you found out about those genes in the Chromo virus." Diane had spent the night at the lab. She blamed it on insomnia. "What do you think they're for?"

She crossed her arms on the table. There was a dark smear of tiredness beneath her eyes. It didn't make the spice in her scent any less enticing. "It's not easy to explain."

"Try me. I can take scientific jargon. I just can't overdose on it."

She didn't smile. Scientists get so serious when they talk science. "As we age our cells' replicative capacity diminishes. In a child, cells undergo from twenty-five to thirty cellular divisions before they die. In a senior, those division cycles get down to three, possibly four. It's how our body ages: there's less turn over in cell population."

"Skin sags, you lose muscle tone and get wrinkles," I said.

"Basically, yes. Have you ever wondered though, what tells the cells they've reached the end of their replicative cycle? How do they know when they're supposed to die?"

I took the napkin and unfolded it on my lap. "I've been losing sleep over that question, Diane."

She served me a scornful look, with a side of condescending tone. The first cart docked at our table and delivered a plate of shrimp toast and sesame boa. We took one each, did some acrobatics with the chopsticks and chewed.

"Each time a cell undergoes a division, the chromosome ends in the DNA shorten a bit. It's a natural phenomenon and it doesn't have consequences because that part of the chromosome is non-coding—it doesn't carry information. When the ends get too short, the cell dies. It's all part of the aging process. Now, the counterpart of that is an enzyme called telomerase. It prevents the chromosome ends from degrading, and it's believed to increase the cell's replicative capacity. The theory behind it is that by preserving the chromosome ends one can allow the cells to replicate more and lengthen the span of human life."

The next cart delivered pot stickers, shrimp shaomai, and rice noodles. "You mean a person would age at a slower rate?" Diane nodded. "So the genes you found in those viruses would make a person stay young?"

"Possibly."

I stabbed a pot sticker with the chopsticks. No wonder Medford and company loved cavorting with Hollywood people. If I were after the Holy Grail of eternal youth, who else would be my best paying clients?

"There's a problem, though. The chromosome ends are *supposed* to shorten. It's the cell's biological clock. When you mess up with it, you risk making the cell replicate an abnormal number of times."

"Abnormal in what way?"

"A cell that never dies is a cancer cell. It becomes a tumor."

I stopped chewing. For a moment, I think I even stopped breathing. The hall fell silent. Or maybe the silence was inside me. My heart thumped and yet my lungs kept quiet and still. *A cell that never dies is a cancer cell.* The Greeks already knew. The myth of Prometheus was their lesson, and yet here we were, thousands of years later, making the same mistakes all over again.

"Why risk it if the process can lead to cancer?"

"They claim they solved the glitch."

"Who's 'they'?"

Diane wiped her mouth, reached for her purse and produced a paper, which she slid across the table. "Them," she said, pressing her index finger on the cover page. "I found it in the Chromo web archives. It never got published in a scientific journal. It's listed under 'drafts.'"

I pushed aside a steaming tray, turned the paper towards me and read the title printed at the top: "Germ line gene therapy, a new approach through viral vectors." Below, were the abstract and authors' names, both familiar: M.J. Conrad and A.S. Troy. "The son of a— He lied to us!"

"Who did?"

"Troy! He said he never worked on genetics with Conrad."

"You know him?"

"Of course. He was one of Conrad's most brilliant

students. The two worked together for a number of years, but, from what he told us, never on genetics."

Satish and I had interviewed him right after Conrad's murder. He'd told us how only later in his career the professor had switched to genetics.

Diane stared at her watch. "We have an appointment with him at four o'clock. There are quite a few things I mean to ask him."

Our drinks materialized at our table and a pensive Diane swirled the straw into her glass, making the ice clink. "Do you think White and Kelson knew what they were doing when they entrusted Chromo with the conception of their child?"

I shook my head, my eyes skimming the paper in front of me. "They overdid it."

"Yeah, but can you blame them? This was going to be their only child, and Chromo deceived them with the delusion of a genetically perfect daughter. I was an only child too, and not particularly healthy growing up. My parents never talked about my birth mother, but I bet I was a crack baby: always small, sickly and fragile. Every time I landed at the hospital—the usual breathing complications over the flu, or a febrile seizure, or an ear infection—my parents went through hell. They had gone through so much to have a daughter, and fate kept threatening them to take me away. In the end they got lucky. I made it. Kelson and White didn't get lucky."

Only child and adopted, I pondered. Hard to imagine her small and fragile. Her shirt curved around her chest sinking and rising like the cantabile of a Vivaldi concerto. A row of tiny buttons descended from her bosom down to her stomach, and I found myself wondering what it would be like to undo them one by one.

Say something Ulysses, damn it!

"Where did you grow up?"

"In Ohio. By the railroad."

Unusual answer, it made me smile. "*Bytherailroad*, Ohio? Never heard of that town!"

She laughed. "I grew up in the country. Our house was surrounded by corn and sunflower fields. The railroad bordered our property."

Sunflowers—that's what she smelled of. I could see it in her scent. The hours spent in the fields outside, basking in the sun, chasing a dog maybe, or pedaling over a rusty bike. Her mother would come out, hang the sheets to dry, and she'd run back and forth below the line with her arms spread open, inhaling the sun and the wind the fabric had captured in its billows.

The ice in Diane's drink clinked, the straw swirled. "I know it seems funny, but the sound of the railroad is still soothing to me, even after all these years. The train would pass every two hours, day and night. I loved the rhythm—you know, the *boo-boom, boo-boom* of the wheels when they hit the expansion joints." She made the sound with a deep voice and then laughed, tipping her head. Her scent drifted to my nose and carried the image of a blonde child running along the railroad, chasing the train with her dreams and waving at the strangers peeking through the car windows.

"You know, I couldn't sleep my first night away from home, back in college. My roommate was so quiet she didn't even snore. Everything was dead silent, and I missed the *boo-boom, boo-boom* of the train. Can you believe it? I had to get used to falling asleep surrounded by complete silence, when for most people it's the other way around."

"Dorms are hardly ever quiet places, though."

"I know. It was the first week: classes hadn't started yet. Believe me, it was a completely different story when the campus filled up. Besides, after that I've always had a boyfriend to sleep with."

I almost choked on my drink. The way she said it, bluntly. Always. A boyfriend. To sleep with. Come on, Ulysses, what's wrong with you? Isn't that what we all go to college for? Seriously, like you had your B.S. in mind that first year as a freshman! Still. Diane. With a boyfriend. Always. Even now, the ghost of a man lingering on her clothes. And suddenly the image of her with *him* popped into my mind. I shoved it away, but it came back. Jim Kowalski, inhaling her scent. Kowalski again, relishing her skin. Had she really kicked him out of her life or was it one of those relationships destined to swing back and forth?

Two more steaming trays of shrimp dumplings landed on our table, providing a diversion, or so I hoped. For a few minutes I focused on the scents and flavors of the meal. Until Kowalski came back to tickle my imagination. His hands cupping her breasts. His fingers brushing her inner thigh. And all this when she was right there, across the table from me.

Start a conversation, Ulysses. Any conversation.

How frequently do you have sex? Weekly? Monthly?

"What about you?" she asked, fishing me out of the trap my own thoughts were closing on me.

"What *about* me?"

She sucked up a noodle. "Any significant lady in your life?"

I smiled. "I don't discuss my personal life while on duty."

"We're on our lunch break. You're buying me lunch. It's almost a date."

I cleaned up the very last shrimp, placed the chopsticks on top of the bowl, wiped my mouth, and folded back the napkin. "I'm a lone hunter. Solitary, territorial, and reclusive." I was quoting from the Wikipedia page on cougars, my favorite kind of predators. She didn't seem to mind. She tilted her head, looked at me with a hint of interest, and swirled her straw.

"You seem fairly well adapted." There was a devious smile on her lips.

I laughed. "Yeah. Friends seem to cope well with me."

"I thought you said you were solitary."

"I guess I just contradicted myself, then."

The smile on her lips hung on. She exhaled, leaned back, and flattened her palms on the table. "What an ingenious way to skate over a question, Track. Oh, look. Fortune cookies." The child-faced waiter set a little plate in front of us. "I'll pick yours." She handed me the one of her choice. "Go ahead. Open it."

Her eyes sparkled as she watched me crack the cookie open and pull out the little strip of paper. "What does it say?"

I read it aloud: "Your quest will soon find an answer."

Diane grinned. "How exciting! Let's see what mine says."

I forgot what hers said, perhaps because I stopped listening. I fiddled with the fake oracle, my mind drifting over all the unanswered quests stacked over the years of my life. *It's just a stupid strip of paper*, I thought, *with no more insight than a grandmother's weather forecast.*

Nonetheless, fortune cookies ought to be outlawed. It should be illegal to toy with one's hopes like that.

CHAPTER 29

Wednesday, October 22

The first impression was to be stepping into a four-fifty-nine scene—burglary. It took me a few seconds to realize that the tumultuous state of Professor Anthony Troy's office was not the result of a violent break-in but rather the accumulation of years of sloppiness: unread mail, overdue assignments, buried papers, unwashed *maté* gourds, spills of *yerba maté* leaves, and notebook after notebook of thoughts hastily scribbled between lectures. The once white walls had taken a gray-yellowish hue, checkered by the ghosts of past posters, memos, and conference announcements regularly peeled off and replaced. Overcrowded bookshelves sagged under the weight of knowledge, disorderly populated by volumes whose titles had faded and whose corners had been chewed off by the wear of time. A round table and two chairs lay buried under jagged piles of papers and scientific journals. A dry erase board displayed scribbles and symbols written in all possible directions.

"We're just about done, Detectives!" Troy called, as he glimpsed us at the door. Sitting across the desk, a disgruntled student tapped his pencil against the red B-marked on the paper in front of him—the object of contention.

"Forensic scientist," Diane corrected, her remark too low to be caught by Troy.

I smiled. "Technically, you're substituting for Satish."

"Where is he?"

"In court, testifying. Why are you smirking?"

"Because you're still talking to me."

"Ah. Well, it depends. If you keep saying I'm wrong I might reconsider." During the car ride we had once again gone over the traces of saliva retrieved from the beer can and her DNA analyses.

A smile escaped her lips. *Touché. You can tell me whatever you want now.*

The student finally gave up, loudly pushed back his chair, and shuffled out of the office without bothering to proffer any form of salutation.

"These new generations," Troy said, walking around his desk to come shake our hands. "They're slackers. They do everything superficially and still expect top-notch grades." He sighed, gestured to the sofa in front of him, and then slumped into a chair, crossing his arms over his protruding stomach. "What can I do for you?"

I stared at the seating accommodation he'd just offered: sagging cushions, worn fabric covered in dog hair, and a shapeless pillow that stank of sweat and bad night breath.

The sofa was the silent witness of endless nights of brainstorming at the board, and the ultimate refuge when exhaustion finally prevailed at the break of dawn.

"Diane Kyle, we spoke earlier on the phone, Professor," Diane said, shaking hands with Troy and then sitting on the sofa.

Merry the human nose and its shortsightedness.

"Right. You wanted to know about the germline paper."

"And why you conveniently forgot to mention it when we met the first time," I added, joining Diane on the couch. I scooched closer so her scent would cover all other smells. She didn't seem to mind, and neither did I.

Troy gave me a long, condescending stare. "The scientific community ignored us, Detective." He heaved a big breath and scratched his bald forehead until it was red. "Do you think the Manhattan Project would've been part of our history if it weren't for the Nazi's threat? See, this is how peevish humanity is: you need to scare people in order to make room for progress. 'The world isn't ready for this,' they kept telling us. Nobody wanted to publish our study. Cowards. It takes bravery to embrace new, bold ideas."

"Bold indeed, Professor," Diane snapped. "What you're suggesting in that paper has long-term consequences. We're still struggling to understand when somatic gene therapy can deliver an effective cure. And yet here you are, suggesting a completely new way of changing not only an individual's DNA, but that of his or her descendants. You're basically genetically engineering human beings. Of course people are uneasy. They should be."

On our way to Tate University, Diane had explained to me the implications of the paper she had dug out of the Chromo archives. The "immortality" experiments were only the tip of an iceberg whose roots went back to the early 'nineties, when Conrad joined Chromo. In the paper, Troy and he claimed to have perfected gene therapy. They could cure individuals from genetic diseases *and* ensure that their progeny would no longer carry the defective genes.

Troy's round face flushed. "In the paper, Ms. Kyle, we propose more experiments. We had a vision, a fifty-year long plan to bring us closer to the goal. We looked beyond curing individuals: we were healing humanity as a whole. A new generation free of genetic diseases. Our ideas were revolutionary. Think about it: when we wrote the paper, the Human Genome Project was still in its infancy." He glared, his narrow eyes belittling us. "Evidently we were ahead of our times."

A shade of disdain clouded Diane's eyes and spiced her scent. "And you were surprised by that kind of reaction? I can't believe you didn't even think of the consequences if something went wrong."

Troy raised his chin and looked down on Diane. "Where did you get your degree, Ms. Kyle? Some community college where they fed you canned answers and multiple choice tests?"

Spite narrowed Diane's eyes. "I went to UCLA, *Professor—*"

"It's like vaccines, isn't it?" Troy cut her short. "Things do go wrong from time to time, but would you rule them out based on a few incidents? The benefits outnumber the casualties. Stick your nose out of that can they shoved your brains in and think about it: Fermi, Oppenheimer, Feynman—all those brilliant scientists would've never obtained the means and money to produce nuclear fission if people didn't fear the Nazis would get to it first." He leaned forward and growled, "Mark my words: one day some Asian or Arab zealot will start designing super-intelligent humans, so superior they'll wipe the rest of us off the surface of the Earth. People will remember then about

Conrad and Troy's ideas. 'Ah, if only we had listened then,' they'll say."

I could smell Diane's rage. She sent me a sideways glance as if wondering whether I heard the same words as she did. I glared at the man, so puffy in his oversized ego. A visionary and a nutcase. His eloquence had fooled me the first time I met him. I'd pictured him captivating an audience of geeky students, all the valedictorians who at age eighteen have outsmarted the rest of their graduation class and enter the Ivy League crowds dreaming of fame and success. I could see how the same eloquence had fooled people like Kelson, White, and who knows how many others.

I know a little bit of everything, which often translates into knowing nothing at all, he'd told me the first time we'd met. Bullshit. "You know, Professor, for somebody who knows nothing at all, you seem pretty opinionated to me. In case you haven't noticed, some zealot of the kind you mention has already attempted something of the sort. And it's happened right here, in our free and civilized America."

Troy winced, as if dazed by my words. "That was Medford. That man, he doesn't understand a thing about science, but he sure has a knack for business. He saw the potential. 'Rich people spend a fortune in plastic surgery and all sorts of delusional remedies,' he said. 'Imagine how much they'll pay to have the perfect genes. And not only for themselves—"

"For their children too." And this time it was Diane, with her jaw dropped, who finished the sentence. "Too bad you forgot that experimenting with human embryos is against the law, Professor Troy."

He winced, his eyes betraying some kind of bewilderment. "What? We never experimented with human embryos. Our paper is purely theoretical."

The candor on his face made me want to slap him. "Yeah, right, Professor. Chromo has been making money selling your ideas to rich people who could afford them. And now you're telling us you know nothing about experiments done on humans?"

He shook his head, jowls wobbling over his fat neck. "I swear," he said, in a shrill voice. "The germinal paper was never experimented on humans. This conversation is over. Get out."

I got to my feet and spat to his face. "We'll be back. This conversation is far from over."

"Did you hear him? 'Canned answers and multiple choice tests?' Who the hell does he think he is?"

I shrugged. "A scientist."

Diane glared. "I take offense over that, Track."

I grinned. "I'm jokin', D. He's a nutcase and a windbag. Too much brainpower made his fuses blow."

"Do you believe him? About the experiments?"

I shrugged. "If Chromo pushed it as far as to modify embryos based on Conrad and Troy's paper they are in for a lot of trouble."

The evening air was apathetic and the sky pale, tinged with the eerie pink of a setting sun. A nearby cafeteria bathed us with the dull smells of campus catering. The bike racks around the building were jammed.

"You'd think scientists would be humble and open to question things," Diane said, in a bitter voice. "Instead, some get so blinded by the fact that 'they proved it' they refuse to see anything else. It ends up no different than religion."

Shrewd comment. Like in politics, opposite ideologies end up meeting at the other end of the spectrum. "Tell me again how this thing works."

Diane heaved a deep breath to calm herself. "There are two types of cells in the body: the somatic cells and the germline ones. When you change the DNA in a somatic cell, you affect the single individual. You may cure the disease, but the defective gene may still be present in the germline cells, which are the cells responsible for the production of gametocytes. In women, gametocytes give rise to oocytes and in men to spermcytes. If the defective gene is still present in the germline cells, it will be passed on to the individual's progeny. It's only when you modify the germline cells that the change you've introduced—"

"Will be carried on to the next generation. I see it now. They eliminate the genetic disease at the source."

Diane nodded. "They eradicate the trait."

As we crossed the campus, I had to pull Diane aside a couple of times to save her from a collision with the occasional reckless cyclist. Apparently her philosophy that it should be the driver to mind for pedestrians held for four- and two-wheelers alike.

"These are students, Diane. They have midterms and sex in their heads. They don't watch where they're going."

Diane's thoughts were sailing in different seas. "Do you really think White and Kelson let Chromo experiment with their only child? Offer her up as guinea pig?"

"Kelson only mentioned that Gaya was conceived in vitro. Maybe they weren't aware of what was going on."

Diane sighed. "We need to find out if they received gene therapy from Chromo. The therapy would've modified their germline cells, yielding genetically modified embryos." She shook her head. "I can't believe anyone would risk their child's life like that. And for Chromo, to offer something this experimental—it's craziness on top of craziness."

"Diane, you're naïve. People exploit *anything* in order to

make money."

"I *am* naïve. One thing being a scientist has taught me is that there are no certainties, only theories. And theories can be proven wrong."

We climbed a set of stairs guarded by the leafy crown of a magnolia tree, and came to the courtyard in front of the library building, flanked on both sides by a monastery style portico. Bunches of white carnations and yellow roses lay by the pillar where Conrad's dead body had been found, and a handwritten sign loosely taped above read, "WE WILL NEVER FORGET YOU. THE STUDENTS AND FACULTY."

"What are you thinking?" Diane asked.

"I'm trying to convince myself we have enough to put Medford in jail with twelve counts of murder—the twelve kids from Huxley's study who died of leukemia. If I can convince myself, then I might have a chance tomorrow with Udall, the deputy D.A."

Diane's heels tapped on the tiles of the portico and echoed against the vaulted ceiling. "I doubt it. Gene therapy is in its experimental phase, there are virtually no laws regulating it. Even if there were... That nicotine smoking was linked to lung cancer came out in the mid 'fifties, and yet until the mid 'nineties the tobacco industry managed to convince everybody that they weren't forcing people to smoke. They have the right to sell your death sentence one packet a day, it's up to you to take it or not. 'Contributory negligence' they called it."

"What if Huxley proved the connection between gene therapy and leukemia? Then, even if they claimed whatever happened was 'contributory negligence,' it wouldn't hold anymore." I clicked the car key button and by the curbside my Dodge's headlights flickered to life.

Diane grabbed the handle to the passenger's door. "We don't have Huxley's data, Track."

"We'll get it." I slumped behind the wheel. "I'll talk to Udall tomorrow. Damn it, I swear we'll get it. I want Udall, White and his big lawyer—all of them down at the homicide table. If we need to cut the guy a deal, we'll cut him a deal, but I want him to talk. Chromo screwed up. The only one who can tell us the whole story is White, and I want to hear it from beginning to end."

"But what do you expect him to tell you?"

"That Chromo sold him hocus pocus. Listen, you don't kill based on a hunch. White shot Conrad because he understood what the man did to his daughter. If he talks, he can give us probable cause for a warrant. More than one, in fact. I want to canvass not just the company, but Medford's house and cars, too."

"You think Medford did it?"

"The guy's too smart to dirty his own hands. But he's the one with the most at stake. Huxley's discovery was going to bring down the whole corporation. Even if all he did to shut her mouth was a phone call, I'm gonna turn his house inside out until I can prove it."

We fell silent. The Five was a garland of red and white lights, each carrying its own end-of-the-day frustrations, tiredness, what-shall-I-have-for-dinner thoughts, and a few new-age smart commuters who plugged in an audio book and let the mellow voice of a narrator wash away their traffic anxieties.

"It's late. I'll take you home," I said as we passed the sign announcing the junction to the One-Thirty-Four. It made no sense to go back to downtown.

Diane hesitated. "My car's at Cal State."

"I'll pick you up in the morning."

I'm tired. And after I drop her off I can go home.

Yeah, right.

Diane watched the street while nibbling her thumb,

pools of yellow streetlight flashing on and off her profile. I couldn't get the conversation with Troy out of my head. I knew she couldn't, either. Five miles into the Two-Ten, I swerved into the Lincoln exit ramp. The car knew the way. I just followed.

At the next turn Diane stirred. "What did you just do?"

"What? Nothing, I'm driving."

"How did you know the way?"

Man. "I just guessed."

"You looked me up!"

"I didn't."

"Fine." She slouched back against the headrest. "No more directions. Keep guessing."

"You never gave me directions!"

"You should've asked."

Women. Mother Nature played a trick on men when she decided to make them so damn attractive. To dope us from all the extra talking they do. I had two choices: stick to my guns and take a random tour of Altadena, or take her home. I took her home, pulled on the driveway and turned the engine off.

"Why did you look me up?"

"I didn't. It's illegal to look up a fellow LAPD." That's why I peeked at her driver's license instead.

She stared at me, in defiance at first, and then her eyes softened. Her lips twitched upwards. *Damn it, Ulysses, just grab her and kiss her.* She wouldn't have pulled away. I know. Her scent told me. *The top button of her shirt, right below her throat…*

Call it destiny in reverse: my cell phone rang, at which Diane bade me goodnight and stepped out of the car. I watched her walk to the door, insert the key, and then vanish inside, while the mobile screeched in my ears, *Pick me up, you dork*. Hell, I wanted to pick *her* up. One should have the guts to smash those wireless devices. They have a tendency to ruin your life.

I looked at the number and rolled my eyes. Great timing.

"'T's up, Hort?" I drawled.

"I think Gary wants to sleep with me."

Surprise! Had I told her the night before, she would've turned me into stone like Medusa. Gary was the manager who owned a gallery in Santa Barbara, a yacht in Venice, and who knows what other luxurious wonders that his lucrative business entitled him to. As the saying goes, "Art for art's sake."

"Do you think I should sleep with him?" Hortensia sounded as casual as though she'd just asked what I had for dinner.

I groaned. "I think you're old enough to decide for yourself."

I could see her thin, golden brows pinched together in a furrow. "Track, you're not helping."

"What the hell do you want me to say?"

"Uh, let's see. Considering you're the guy I'm currently sleeping with, I would've imagined a somehow stronger opinion on the matter, one way or the other."

As hard as I tried, I couldn't find the flaw in her argument. The rest of the conversation didn't go too well. I was tired and not in a mood to put up with her. Hortensia treated me to a complementary "fuck off" and hung up. I closed the phone, tossed it on the passenger's seat, and started the car again. The headlights flickered one more time on the façade of Diane's condo. *Dark and silent.* I backed out of the driveway and left.

I have to call Udall to set up a meeting with White and his lawyer. Once the man talks, I want the signed search warrant on my desk in two hours. The key point is to get White to talk, shed some light onto this murky business of getting genetically engineered children. Shed some light...

I slammed on the brakes. *Shit, the lights!* I made a reckless U-turn and gunned the vehicle back where I'd come from. The reek of burnt tire stung my nose. There were no streetlights along the road, only private garden lights playing peek-a-boo between the dark silhouettes of the trees. I clenched the wheel, flattened the gas pedal, and cursed. *Three minutes — three fucking minutes I've been parked on her driveway listening to Hortensia's nonsensical rants, without ever noticing how wrong things were.* I pulled onto the driveway, drew my gun, and sprung out. *Dark. Not the fleck of a light in any of the windows.*

I surveyed Diane's property while dialing her number. I could hear her phone ring from inside her home, yet after four rings the answering machine went off. I walked all around the building. Not a single window had lit up. Parked on the street a few yards away was a van with a professional seal on the sides, something about carpet cleaning.

Was it there when I dropped her off?

She was inside — I could smell her from the door. I stood behind the doorjamb and tried the doorknob. It yielded.

She would've locked it.

I pushed it all the way and inhaled.

The place was in complete darkness. I smelled her first: sour. *She's terrified.* I widened my nostrils and inhaled more. Blood, hers, and gun oil, no gunpowder though. *Not yet.* The smell of the intruder came next, harsh, and extraneous. *Not Huxley's assassin.* A man, smoker, sweating profusely. I clasped the grip of my Glock and edged inside, back flattened against the wall.

Hidden in the tall grass, the prey feels safe. It holds still, its head down, a few twigs tickling its muzzle. It can smell the predator. In a split of a second it has to make a decision: stay hidden or run. The enemy is too close to break loose. It will pounce, and once it does, the end will come fast. The prey decides to stay. The winds blow against, carrying its smell away from the predator. To remain hidden is the best strategy.

The predator advances. Low on its belly, nostrils wide open, and all senses wide alert. The flick of a sprig, the whiff of a new scent. It can detect everything. Nimble toe pads go unheard on soft turf. The prey can only hope the winds won't change direction. Because once they do, it will no longer be able to tell where the predator is.

The living room was orderly, only a mug on the coffee table, and a few sprawled magazines. No ransacking, no open drawers, no slashed cushions. I froze.

The kitchen.

I could smell them, two distinctive scents coming from the same spot. I heard their uneven breathing. Diane's small intakes of air, one after the other, frenetic and difficult. *He's half choking her.* He couldn't see me. Human eyes are imperfect. And he couldn't hear me coming, either. Surprise is a feline's deadliest weapon.

The shades of the window above the sink were open, and the iridescence from outside bathed the countertops in a milky light. I followed their scents until I saw them. He was crouched behind the kitchen island, holding Diane down, thrusting the barrel of a gun to the side of her neck. He pressed a filthy hand to her mouth, yanking her head back and making it difficult for her to breathe. *He's waiting for me. Once I step into the well of light he'll shoot.*

I held the Glock in position. "Drop the gun and let her go," I said, making him jump. Blinded by darkness, he didn't expect me this close.

He squeezed Diane closer and retreated farther back. "Come out, you son of a bitch, or I'll kill her!" he yelled. Coarse voice, ragged from years of nicotine and alcohol.

I weighed my options. "Okay. Don't shoot."

He hesitated. "Your gun. Make it slide on the floor towards me."

He can't be that stupid. I lowered the gun on the floor where he could see it but didn't let go. "I *will* kill her if you don't do as I say," he snarled. He slid his unarmed hand down and squeezed Diane's left breast, so hard she whimpered. The gesture, coupled by her outcry of pain, sent blood pulsing to my head.

I kicked the Glock toward him while drawing my backup from the ankle holster—an S&W 340PD with full-on .357 Mag loads.

Try and fool me, asshole.

He grabbed Diane by the waist and pulled her back towards the glass doors to the kitchen balcony. Diane wriggled away and tried to sink her elbow in his stomach. In the fraction of a second his upper torso became visible, I held the revolver on target, thumbed off the safety, and fired. The blast kicked both of them backwards. The glass doors shattered into pieces and shards flew everywhere.

I smelled blood and I couldn't tell whether it was Diane's or her attacker's. His gun clonked to the floor, shiny with blood. His eyes were red shots of rage. He shoved Diane against me and threw himself through the French doors and down the balcony.

"You okay?" I shouted to Diane.

I glimpsed her give a shaky nod and bolted after the fugitive. I'd almost blasted his arm off with my revolver, and yet the asshole was so high on adrenaline he charged through broken glass and jumped six feet down the balcony. *Adrenaline, and maybe a little help of PCP.* I leaped after him and chased him through the shrubs down the arroyo, his path flashing with the trail of blood.

The prey panics and runs. Once the predator pounces, its only hope is to outrun it. The chase will last only a few seconds, maybe minutes, and only one will prevail. The predator's claws come closer to its hind legs. The prey feels the jaws draw nearer, breathing on its back. One final pounce and it's over. Sharp claws delve on its back and dig into the flesh. Next come the incisors, deep, clenching the throat: they fasten around the windpipe and crush it. The prey's lungs wilt, longing for air. Blood oozes into the predator's mouth as it tightens its jaws, its sweetness making it growl in anticipation. It feels the prey's muscles tense under the siege and then finally relent. The last frantic spasms of death.

The hunt is over.

CHAPTER 30

Wednesday, October 22

I was covered in glass shards, dirt, and blood—how much was mine and how much the attacker's I could not tell. Rage blinded me. My head throbbed.

What the hell happened there?

I was clutching something in my fist. A watch, not mine.

"Track!"

All windows in Diane's house were lit now, and two light posts illuminated the backyard. She saw me emerge from the shrubs delimiting her property and came running towards me. I slid the watch in my pocket. I should've tossed it, but I didn't. I couldn't.

The ghastly look in my eyes made her stop. "Track?"

Is it really you?

I no longer know.

She was shaking. "I called the dispatcher. Where—where is he?"

"Dead."

"What?"

"I said he's dead!"

Diane stepped closer and raised a hand to touch me, maybe reassure me. I startled and jumped back. "STAY AWAY!"

She winced and retreated. A window from the adjacent condo opened, and an apathetic face leaned out. "I called the police!" she hollered.

"WE *ARE* THE POLICE!" I yelled back.

"Let's wait inside," Diane mumbled.

I slumped on the couch and dropped my head in my hands. "Who the hell was that?" I demanded.

Diane looked bewildered, but by now I could no longer tell if it was because of the attacker, or me, or a combination of both. She went to the sink and filled two glasses of water, propped one on the counter—most likely intended for me—drained the other and filled it a second time. "I don't know the man. He grabbed me from behind when I stepped into the house."

"How did he get in?"

"I don't know."

"What did he want?"

"Hell, Track. I said I don't know!"

The responding officers found us yelling at one another. The K-9 unit followed. Their tracking dogs cut loose through Diane's backyard into the arroyo behind her property. They found the body in a matter of minutes, covered in blood, dirt, and dead leaves.

"Do you have a place where you can spend the rest of the night, Ms. Kyle?" one of the officers asked. The balcony glass doors were completely destroyed. Diane turned to look at me. For a few seconds she held my gaze. I stared back blankly. Such an idiot I am at times.

"Yes," she finally said, her eyes on me. And then she turned, reached for the phone, and dialed. "You better show those cuts to the paramedics," she told me while waiting for the call to be picked up.

CHAPTER 31

Thursday, October 23

Diane Kyle steps into the elevator and looks in the mirror. Her reflection stares back, frazzled and distraught. The sleeping drugs had finally kicked in last night, though it must have been three a.m. when exhaustion prevailed. It had bought her only a few hours of obliviousness, after which her eyes sprang open again, the anxiety still there, relentless.

Somebody was in my house. A stranger tried to kill me. Why?

The thought was terrifying: the unknown threat, the violation of her home and shelter, her nest, her safe haven from long days spent either at a gruesome crime scene nitpicking evidence from a dead body, or at the lab, centrifuging vial after vial of blood. I need a refuge I can coil in and forget the wake of violence I see every day.

Where else can I go at night?

She'd taken the sleeping drugs hoping for a dreamless rest. It didn't happen. Like a scratched disk, her brain stumbled over and over again on the same image: her own body collapsed on the kitchen floor, auburn hair matted with dry blood, and a red slash gaping across her throat. She knows it's herself she's staring at, and yet she feels detached. It's just another body. She stares at the wound, her thoughts reeling over the usual technicalities: blade-inflicted, straight incision across the tracheal rings, quick death by suffocation, as the victim inhales her own blood and chokes. And that's when she realizes she can't breathe.

The elevator chime startles her.

Not my floor, *she thinks, grateful for the diversion. A man steps inside. She grimaces, the tension in her jaw unyielding, making her unable to reciprocate his smile. A few minutes later, her heels drum nervously on the linoleum of the third floor. Her eyes dart around, searching for a familiar face – one face.*

"Ms. Kyle?"

She startles. "Sorry, I'm uh – a little tense."

"Detective Presius said the meeting won't be for another half hour," *the officer tells her.*

Diane winces. "What meeting?"

"The one with the deputy D.A. You can wait in the evidence room if you wish."

"Where – Where's Track?"

"Closed meeting in the lieutenant's office."

Is he in trouble? Should she say something? He rescued me last night. "Can I wait at his desk?"

The officer shrugs. "This way."

"How did he – I didn't tell him I was coming."

"He told me you were coming from the west wing elevators one minute before you showed up. He does weird things like that all the time. Are you sure this is where you want to sit?" *she asks, staring at the deranged status of the desk they have come to.*

Diane nods.

CHAPTER 32

Thursday, October 23

Gomez drummed his fingers on the desk, his eyes fixed on the OIS report—Officer Involved Shooting—in front of him. Wide, flat phalanges, with nails clipped so close to the flesh a rim of dried blood decorated his thumb. I tried to follow his stare, guessing which line his eyes where at. Not that it mattered. Half of it was circular nonsense, vain attempts to justify the events of the night before. All I could remember was rage. Throbbing inside, blinding me. Screams reverberated in my ears, it could have been my own voice though, I couldn't tell. Something splintered, a tree branch, or maybe a bone. I remember the distinct sound of a crack, followed by the smell of blood. A metallic tang on my nose and palate, foul, and disgusting. Seeping all over me. Like tar it stuck to my skin. Stained me. *What the hell happened?*

They had taken me to the station, seized my revolver, and had me sitting at a gray desk where two officers from FID—Force Investigation Division—stared at me with dull, icy-cold eyes. One of the two—a hefty cop with a crooked nose and a boxer's jaw—I had the pleasure to meet over the Carmelo OIS investigation. He wasn't wearing deodorant, and the raw scent of his skin hit me like a first violin going out of tune in a Vivaldi concerto. He stood in front of me with his hands dipped in his pants pockets and his cock leveled at my face. "What happened this time, cowboy? Did your finger slip on the trigger?"

"I'd like to slip a fist on your fat mouth," I replied to his cock.

The two officers kept asking the same questions and I kept giving the same answers. They hated my guts for making them work through the night, I hated theirs for exactly the same reason. By four a.m. the coffee tasted like lukewarm water, and the ticking of the wall clock felt like nails hammered in the head. I sat through the turnaround between the graveyard and morning shifts, through the arrogant steps of those coming in, freshly showered and deodorized, and the shuffling away of the tired ones, with droopy eyes and yawning jaws. Until finally somebody came to tell me I could go home to shower and shave. I would've argued it was the FID officers stinking up the place, but I figured the privilege I'd just been given might be revoked. So I got up and left, only to come back a few hours later and be summoned into the LT's office.

Gomez never turned to page two of the report. He pushed it aside and produced a computer printout—the con's rap sheet. "Burglary, twice, street dealing, three times, and innumerous counts of robbery."

"Somebody paid him to break into Kyle's apartment," I

said.

The LT sighed, swiveled away from his desk and got up. He shoved both hands in his pockets and started pacing. "I just got off the phone with the M.E." He looked out the window, refusing me the privilege of eye contact. "I understand you disarmed the man in the victim's house, is this correct?"

"Yes, sir."

"Then he fled outside and you chased him."

"Yes, sir."

"I told the M.E. to bump up the priority on this one. The con's on his table as we speak."

I shifted in my chair. "Why?"

Gomez spun around, his breath exuding billows of frustration. "You ask me why, Track? He told me about his findings on the scene: broken ribs, numerous contusions, *and* a bullet hole at the back of his skull."

I chilled. "A bullet—where?"

"He was whacked in the head, Track. A disarmed man, one you'd already shot in the arm with a weapon which— you'd been warned before—you're not even supposed to carry!" He stared at me for a few seconds longer, his eyes bulging and his brows clamped together in one long eave across his forehead. "You're getting a suspension for carrying a non approved weapon, and if it turns out that weapon killed the—"

I swallowed and held his gaze. "I fired inside the house because he was armed and dangerous. I chased him after that. I didn't kill him."

I'd shot the man in the shoulder, not in the head. There was no way he'd jump off the balcony with a hollow point in his skull. I thought he'd died from shock, from the gunshot wound. What the Lieutenant had just told me changed everything.

I had *not* killed the loon.

Somebody had been waiting in the bushes and acted quick, as soon as the fugitive reached the bottom of the arroyo, those two seconds before I reached him...

Gomez resumed his post behind the desk and opened my package. He read aloud: "James A. Phillis, age 26, shot three times, two to the chest and one to the head." His eyes surfaced above the rim of his reading glasses.

I swallowed. "Armed robbery, solo foot pursuit. Clean shooting."

Eyes back on the file. "Karl T. Yates, age 54, one shot through the forehead."

The other one was a miss. "Domestic call. Suspect opened fire from the window. Clean, again."

"John K. Carmelo, age 32, six rounds, one to the head and five to the chest." I didn't reply this time, and Gomez flipped the page. "Danny Mendoza, age 19, slit throat and numerous stab wounds, two to the chest, two—"

I slammed my hand on the desk. "Self defense," I hissed through clenched teeth.

Gomez's partner was one of the responding officers at the time and he never believed my story. At the bail hearing he testified the crime was unusually cruel. I served one month of preterm jail, rotting in one of the most violent juvies in the US because I wasn't granted bail. I was beaten up, locked down, drugged, and ridiculed. I learned to thrive on discipline. It taught me to control my instincts, to channel my drive.

I learned to hate killers and chase them down.

I learned to hate myself because I'm a killer.

Gomez slid off his reading glasses and closed the folder. "I'm sure you had your reasons to put your boots to the sleaze last night, Track. All I wanna see on the fucking M.E. report is that it wasn't you who killed him. He was disarmed, do you understand that? You're going down this time, and you're going on your own." He stared at me one more minute and then gestured to the door. I got to my feet, but by the time I touched the doorknob he called me back. "I'd hate to take your badge, Track," he said. I nodded and left.

I felt the glares. Conversations hushed as I walked by. I glimpsed the smirks on the young officers who sought my job. A badge like mine, only with their name on it.

"Deputy D.A. Udall's here, Track," Satish said poking his head into the break room. "And—"

"Diane, I know."

I looked at the Styrofoam cup in my hand. Black coffee, Colombia roast. Bitter.

Satish bobbed his head, then stepped inside and flashed me one of his ecstatic stares. "Do you know the best part of hitting rock bottom, Track?"

I replied with a heartfelt no. He smiled. "You've hit it. And all there's left to do is pick up your sore ass and get going again." He snatched the half empty cup from my hand and tossed it in the trashcan. "Come on. We've got work to do."

"Not true," I replied, my hands still cupped around the no-longer-there Styrofoam cup.

"What?"

"What you just said. Get going again is *not* all there's left to do. Occasionally, rock bottom may turn out to be awfully comfortable. So comfortable, one may consider spending some time down there."

He chuckled. "Good answer, Track. You're starting to become more and more like me."

I shook out of my daze. *Gee. Did I hit it that hard?*

Deputy D.A. Enrique Udall was smirking as Diane showed him the Conrad Troy paper and explained the implications of the study. He didn't do it on purpose. The man *always* smirked, his jaws stuck in an airy dolphin smile. Even when his eyes frowned, his lips twitched upwards. Ironically, it worked to his advantage in the courtroom: he smiled through opening arguments, motions to dismiss, and objections; through the bantering of the opposition and the closing arguments. In the meantime, the opposing lawyers wasted energy wondering what the hell he was sneering about and felt the pressure.

Diane raised her head as we stepped into the room, and for a moment our eyes met.

I don't know what happened, Diane. Don't ask me.

"I understand Ms. Kyle will unveil the mysteries of gene therapy for us, won't she?" Satish said, taking a seat.

"Not just that. I'll tell you how Chromo screwed up." She was looking straight at me. "I found Huxley's data, Track."

She passed me a printout and I read it as she walked to the dry erase board. It was an e-mail to Jennifer Huxley from a Jodi Thistlerthorn. It read:

Hey Jen, I apologize for the delay — I got swamped with a lot of work and couldn't get to your data until yesterday.

I ran a paired t-test and came up with a highly significant p-value. Even if you drop the standard assumption and use a Wilcoxon, the p-value is still less than 10^{-4}. Attached is the spreadsheet with the details. I hope this helps!

Jodi.

I read it twice, then turned the paper over. "And where's the data?" I asked.

"It was attached to the email. I called Amit and he

retrieved it for me."

I brought a hand to my forehead, the first sign of a migraine gnawing its way through the bridge of my nose. "Are you telling me we've had the data all along?" I thought of the decryption code still running in Amit's warehouse. *We had it all along.*

Satish chortled, always ahead of me on these things. "It helps to know what to look for."

"That's right, Satish." Diane's voice was a crescendo of sourness. "I had no idea what we were looking for until I found Troy's manuscript. Jodi Thistlerthorn is a statistician at USC. I called her this morning. She met Huxley at a workshop, and the two became friends. It wasn't unusual for Jennifer to email her with a particular stat question. When I asked her specifically about this data set, though, Jodi admitted that sending unpublished data to a non-collaborator was out of line."

Udall took the e-mail I passed him and then stared at Diane over his round lenses. "Even though I don't understand the technical language, she seems to have answered Huxley's question."

Diane nodded. "Exactly. Jodi told me Jennifer pleaded with her, stressing the importance of these particular data and how she couldn't have the analyses run by her own collaborators at the Esperanza Medical Center."

"Did she say why?" Satish asked.

I snorted. "Because she had a lovely, nosy boss. Can you translate the answer for us?"

Diane uncapped a marker, drew the schematic outline of a chromosome and circled one leg. "This is a non-coding region of chromosome eleven. People believe it has no biological function. When the Human Genome Project was completed five years ago, one of the major findings was that the vast majority of our DNA does *not* serve any purpose.

They call it 'junk DNA.' This is the region Huxley was looking at, and this is why I think Cox disapproved of it. Cox wanted to look at specific genes that were linked to leukemia, whereas Huxley was wasting time and resources looking at a portion of DNA that doesn't get transcribed."

I inhaled. "So then why *did* Huxley even bother looking at it?"

Diane turned to the board. "Because in this region she found this, this, and this." As if stabbing the chromosome she'd drawn, Diane inflicted little marks along the circled leg. "Remember those twelve patients in Huxley's manuscript? They all had these three mutations. The other children didn't have them. I searched the literature and found nothing about these mutations: they've never been observed before."

We all stared at Diane. I wondered what she thought of us, of our wrinkled foreheads and furrowed brows, trying to look at least half as smart as her, while grappling the concepts she was throwing at us.

"Why would those mutations matter if they all occur outside the genes?"

"I don't know, Track. And Huxley didn't either. But when she handed the data to her friend Jodi, the numbers spoke for themselves: whatever effect they have, it's there, and it's deadly."

"Meaning they caused the leukemia?" Satish's turn to look smart. Udall instead sat back and smirked. His dolphin smile did the work for him.

"Yes. That's the meaning of Jodi's email."

"So where did those mutations come from?"

Diane sighed. "Well. Suppose those twelve kids in Huxley's paper *are* the Proteus kids. And suppose Huxley believed that Proteus kids was a code name Chromo used. Hence these kids, just like Gaya White, came out of

Chromo's magic hat. Given Conrad and Troy's statements in the paper I showed you, we can reasonably assume that the magic hat involved meddling through gene therapy. Are you guys with me?"

Satish and I nodded. Udall smiled placidly. Diane turned to the blackboard and drew two circles, one small, one big, then tapped the small one. "Imagine this is the virus that's been modified so it carries human genetic material. You would expect it to attach to the cell—the big circle—and deliver its genes."

"And that's not the case?"

"Not always, Satish. Because what the virus often does is a little reshuffling. Mother Nature's way to ensure genetic variation. Conrad and Troy claim they have a way to keep the reshuffling under control by modifying further the viral proteins. They do, in fact. But they have completely overlooked regions outside the genes. The so-called 'junk DNA.' Their mistake was to believe that because those regions are non-coding and are lost after the DNA splicing, they would be harmless. Huxley's data proves otherwise. Twelve kids developed an aggressive form of leukemia because of these mutations."

Non-coding DNA. Pseudogenes.

The non-coding genes Watanabe talked about.

"They may very well call it junk," I said, "but if that region gets activated and those mutations are deadly, then it's the end."

Diane nodded.

I stared at the board and heaved a big breath. Jennifer needed proof. More data, and it had to come from Chromo. *Tarantino's smell on Huxley's couch.* Did a friendly conversation take place that night, or was it threatening? And if so, who threatened whom? Diane's voice became a soothing background as I drifted off, and my mind reeled back to the meeting I now knew had taken place the night before Huxley disappeared. I could finally see what happened that evening.

Her hands shake as she pours the glass of wine. Liquid sloshes out of the bottle and stains her pristine counter. "Shoot," she mutters, the spill fogging her brain like the static of a bad reception. She puts the glass down and reaches for a cloth to wipe it off.

"Sorry to keep you waiting," she says to her unexpected guest as she brings him the wine. He takes the glass from her, smiles, and then sits on the couch. His eyes are kind, she finds. Maybe it's all those years of Sunday preaching, or maybe the same yearning that compels her to clean the house and organize the closets, which now prompts her to fix his wrongdoings. Whatever the reason, she believes she can trust this man. She wants to redeem him, wipe every red stain off his speckled conscience and make it as immaculate as her floors and windows. She tells him what she's discovered. "What you did is bad in the eyes of God," she says. Are those the right words? "Innocent lives. Imagine what those children went through. Imagine the parents."

Robert Tarantino listens while sipping his wine. What is he thinking? Is he seeing what she's saying?

"What do you want me to do, Jennifer? I want to make things right. I want another chance." His eyes look truthful. "Tomorrow morning," he tells her. And then he leaves her a note with a passcode.

"I want a search warrant for Medford's office and home," I said.

Udall raised a knotty hand in the air. "Hold your horses, Track. I haven't heard of any crime so far."

"What else do you need?"

Diane heaved a deep breath and joined us at the table. "He's right, Track. There's no crime. When you dig out Chromo's records you will find that each one of these parents were handed a ream of consent forms to sign in order to get the services they requested—and note the choice of verb here, *requested*. All Chromo did is perfectly kosher: they provided a service, and the recipients were at all times informed of the risks and caveats."

Udall flashed his wisdom in the form of his peaceful smile. "In the eyes of the law they did nothing wrong."

I swallowed the bitter aftertaste in my mouth. My head was throbbing. "What about the three murders?"

"It's the only way to go. Indict for murder, if we can."

"Medford owns a gun," Satish said. "Though it doesn't match the caliber of the bullets found in the victims' bodies."

"On the other hand he had plenty of motive," I said, raising my voice.

"Given what you guys just told me, any religious fanatic out there had plenty of motive too," Udall insisted.

"Then why did Huxley also end up dead? Think about it. What's more likely: a lunatic entering the Tarantino home and whacking them both based on some who-knows-what biblical reason, or Tarantino turning into the weak link and needing to be rid of?"

"What about the first commandment note, then?"

"To set us on the wrong track," I said. "Ideologies are out there to cover somebody's ass. Whether they believe in them or exploit those who do."

Udall exhaled through his nose. He drummed his fingers on the table and then slammed his palm flat on the surface. "Let's see what Jerry White has to say on the matter. If he can give us a possible motive for the murders, we may be able to justify the warrants. But if we find nothing linking Medford with either the Tarantinos' or the Huxley murders, then I'm afraid there's very little we can do for those children."

Hannah Kelson's words rang in my ears: *Justice is the*

exception, not the rule.

"If his lawyer will let him talk to us." I pushed my chair back, got up and left the room. My future as a cop was in the hands and knife of a county coroner, while the people I wanted in jail for the rest of their lives were as immaculate as a baby in the eyes of the law. I needed a substantial dose of painkiller if I wanted to be at least half functional by the time White and his lawyer showed up.

CHAPTER 33

Thursday, October 23

Cleanly shaven and beautifully packaged in an Armani suit and tie, movie director Jerry White's appearance had quite improved since the first time I'd seen him down in Felony. Swept back, his longish hair showed the first signs of thinning around the temples. The earring shining from his right lobe enhanced a handsome profile, drawn by sharp, harmonious lines. Seated next to him, his lawyer scribbled a few words of slanted handwriting on a piece of paper, shoved it back into his briefcase, and let his booming voice hush the usual preliminary exchanges between Udall, Satish, and me.

"Let's spare everybody's time here," he started. "My client's keeping his mouth shut until we hear what's on the table."

I had the pleasure to meet Ray Epstein in the courtroom: husky, with a square face mottled by moles, and small eyes crowned by bushy brows. A man with an imposing voice and a passion for the spotlight. In court, a squint of his gray eyes could shrink you down to the size of a mosquito. Renowned for berating witnesses and demanding straight answers to convoluted questions, he had firm principles and pliable ethics. As for me, I could smell his acid reflux within four feet, which is why I still preferred to deal with him from behind the witness stand than in a small room, sitting at the same table.

"We're out for the big fish, Mr. Epstein," Satish said. "It would benefit your client to help us out."

"You've got nothing whatsoever on my client," Epstein barked.

"*Au contraire*," I said. "We've got the victim's blood in Mr. White's car and his weapon on the scene."

Epstein regarded me with the same interest granted to the cuticles of his pinky fingers. He jacked up one of his overgrown brows and smirked. "It's all circumstantial."

A ghost in his black suit, Jerry White seemed oblivious to the conversation. He stared at his polished fingernails for a few minutes, then at the cobwebs clinging on the ceiling. He scanned Udall's striped tie, Epstein's briefcase, Satish's dark hands brushing the table. His gaze lingered on the yellow walls and on the linoleum floors. Under long lashes, White's blue eyes leapt restlessly from one point to the next without ever crossing any of the stares woven around them.

How much do you miss her, Jerry? Does the silence ever scare you, the space around you voided of her laughter, of her hurried steps to the door to come greet you at the end of the day? Did you really think shooting Michael Conrad was going to drive all those ghosts away? You pulled the trigger on him, Jerry, because you never found the guts to pull it on yourself. The stupid mistakes you made throughout your life: the novelist career you wanted to pursue and never got to, the high school crush you let slip out of your fingers and never married, soon replaced by one relationship after the other, none too lousy to give you grief, and none too significant to cling to your life for the long haul.

And then Gaya happened. Beautiful, innocent Gaya. An undeserved gift, or maybe you didn't see her as such, maybe to you she felt like another Oscar night where you get the standing ovation for all the hard work. Don't all artists think of their creations as their children? Did you think of Gaya as your best masterpiece, for which you had to do a little extra, and pay a little extra, but wasn't she worth every bit? Fate took her away from you, though. Not even fate — human mistake. Who did you hate the most, the ones who fooled you, or yourself for letting them fool you? Tell me, Jerry: if you really had the guts, would you still point the gun at Conrad, or would you rather press it against your temple? To put an end to all those mornings when you open your eyes and it's right there in front of you, your shame, your foolishness, your regrets... Your inability to go back and start over, do things the right way, this time.

"Mr. White," I called.

He winced, his thoughts fluttering off his head like flakes of dandruff.

"It wasn't only Gaya," I said. I spoke slowly and kept my voice low, until the jabbering lawyers quieted down. "Twelve kids, Mr. White. Twelve lives cut short. Maybe more — others who haven't developed the disease yet. All based on an empty promise. What did they promise you? Academic brilliance? Longevity? Perfect beauty?"

Epstein shifted in his chair. "Detective —"

"I just want the truth," I prodded.

Jerry White kept his lips pursed. I said, "Conrad was a visionary, but his murder won't avenge your daughter. It's the fools who gave him the money to do what he did I want to get my hands on. Not just for Gaya. For the other eleven kids who died like her."

For a moment, the silence around me was deep, lulled by the AC vent above our heads. Epstein scratched his opinionated brow. "Don't say anything, Jerry."

"Do you think your lawyer has Gaya's interest at heart?" I challenged.

"Detective—"

"I don't blame you for gunning a man who deceived you, Mr. White—"

"Enough, Detective!" Epstein spat. Both Udall and Satish tried to say something at the same time, and it all overlapped in a rattle of different pitches clashing together. Satish slid across the table Huxley's letter to Tarantino. "Have you ever heard the expression 'Proteus kids,' Mr. White? The woman who wrote this letter lost her life because she believed it's what killed your daughter."

I leaned forward and pressed a finger on the piece of paper. "This woman was about to prove that when Chromo promised you the perfect child, they also sealed her death sentence. These are the people who ruined your life. They should pay for what they did."

It was the winning stroke. I saw it in the man's eyes, as they rose from the letter and stared at me. They were clouded with hurt. He tightened his jaw and a vein pulsed across his temple. "They never promised—"

"Jerry, be careful—"

White bristled. "Shut up, Ray. What the hell do you know about what Gaya went through? What do you know what it was like to watch them stick a needle into her arm and tell her, 'Don't worry, it's going to be over soon?' And she believed it. She smiled, the little angel. She smiled and nodded, and it never *was* over, the shivering, the vomiting, her teeth rattling in the middle of the night. Her bones crackling as I picked her up."

His voice broke. Nobody interrupted this time. He hid his face in one hand and sobbed. "She was the joy of my life, that little girl of mine."

Udall shifted in his chair and exhaled. Sadness overrode the dolphin smile. Epstein pulled down the outer corners of his brows. He propped a hand on White's shoulder and shook his head. "My client spent nine months by his dying daughter's side. You can take your circumstantial evidence and ditch it in a landfill. No jury is going to indict when they hear what the child had to go through."

"I can think of three different motions to prevent any testimony pertaining Gaya White from entering the courtroom, Ray," Udall said.

"I want to tell them, Ray."

Finally what I wanted to hear.

"What?" Epstein's jaw twitched with a hint of irritation.

"You heard me. I want to tell them what those bloody bastards did to us. They ruined us. And you are wrong, Detective," he added, pointing a finger at me. "They're *not* going to pay, no matter what *you* do." His eyes were red and spiteful. "Do you know what would be fair pay, Detective? To make them go through what I went through and watch their own child die the way mine did."

He widened his nostrils and banged a hand on the table. "Except it wouldn't be true justice, either. Because there would be another innocent life wasted away just like my Gaya's. No child should ever endure any of that."

Epstein shot to his feet. "This meeting is over. My client and I need to confer—"

"Shut up, Ray. One more word and you're fired."

The lawyer dropped back in his chair.

"Did they promise you the perfect child, Mr. White?" I asked. "Is that why Gaya had to be conceived in vitro?"

White frowned, taken aback. "What? No, that was—that was to avoid the cystic fibrosis gene." His lips stretched upwards and he gave out to a long, bitter laugh. "No, no. It's a lot subtler than that, Detective. You'll have a ball proving this one."

I sank back in my chair, failing to understand.

"Conrad," White said. The name came out of his mouth like a spit of venom. "*Professor* Conrad. Hannah was enthused by him. 'He's so smart,' she'd say. 'He really understands the stuff.' He wanted to play his game, prove he was a genius. Oh, yeah. I shot him good. In the face, I did."

Epstein jumped out of his chair looking as if an ant had just bitten his ass. "Jerry, as your lawyer, I advise you not to—"

"I shot him, Ray," White spat. "He deserved it. The son of a bitch screwed up. 'You're done playing almighty creator,' I told him. 'Start over with your own life, instead of playing with others.'"

Epstein scratched his wide forehead. His mouth opened as if about to say something, and then shut again, following his very own advice.

I asked, "If it wasn't the perfect child, what did Conrad promise you? Why did you blame him for Gaya's death?"

Jerry White inhaled. He drank from the glass in front of him, clonked it back on the table, then stared at it as if his whole life had been written in it. "It was the cool thing to do back in the late 'nineties—Chromo's one-million-dollar idea. Scientifically proven to work thanks to that Conrad genius. That's what all those parties at the Horowitz's were about— to sell us out on Chromo's fountain of youth deal."

Satish let out a whistle. "Did you say fountain of youth?"

White nodded. "One hundred percent safe gene therapy,

guaranteed to keep you looking twenty-five well into your sixties. The price my child had to pay." He raised his eyes to me and they were sad eyes. "I can't prove it, Detective, but I know"—he beat his chest with a closed fist—"I know it in my heart that's what killed my Gaya. The stupid gene therapy that made us look twenty years younger stole my Gaya's life. Proteus was the code name for the gene therapy treatment." He snorted. "Proteus was some immortal god, wasn't he?"

The genes Diane found in the monkey virus.

It finally came together. Even in her death hour, Tamara Tarantino looked way younger than her forty-eight years of age. Same with Kelson, and Medford's wife, too. They all looked younger thanks to the Proteus therapy—the gene therapy Diane had discovered when looking at the virus in the dead monkey.

Satish rapped his fingers. "Let me get this straight. You and your wife received the youth treatment, not Gaya, correct? Yet you claim that's what caused your child to die of leukemia?"

"Don't you see? It screwed up our genes. They gave us shots, one million a pop. That was in 1998, for about six months. Then we decided we were going to have a child, so we stopped. The in vitro thing—it wasn't just the cystic fibrosis we feared. Hannah was afraid the therapy might've messed up some genes. So she went back to her friend Conrad. He reassured her everything was fine. 'Just do in vitro fertilization and everything will be fine.' My ass."

Chilled silence fell in the room. Epstein's knee rattled impatiently under the table.

So much for wanting to do everything right, Hannah.

I swallowed. "Does Chromo have more of your embryos?" I asked.

He nodded.

"Then we may be able to prove it, Mr. White."

Embryos. Huxley's data, to be delivered in the cryogenic tank Tarantino had promised her. It shattered in her own hands, scattering glass shards and perlite all over her, probably as she dodged a bullet from her attacker.

It was empty, Jennifer. They fooled you.

"How many others received the treatment?" Udall asked. "Any chance Chromo would have other embryos besides yours?"

"I know we weren't the only ones. A lot of people signed up during those parties, and a lot were convinced to do in vitro fertilization if they decided to have a child." That bitter laugh, again. "Would you say no if somebody offered you eternal youth?"

His eyes met mine.

Your child will never see her youth.

I passed him pen and paper. "Write down the ones you know."

White took the pen and started scribbling. I glimpsed a few familiar names: a plastic surgeon, a few lawyers, more names from the showbiz industry, including Horowitz's.

Epstein straightened up and slammed a stocky hand on the table. "You got what you wanted, gentlemen. Manslaughter, two years of probation, no jail time."

"Come on, Ray," Udall said. "We're talking murder!"

"Before you guys start dancing on your haggling toes," I interjected. "Mr. Udall, I want your signature on a search warrant to turn the Chromo lab inside out. No matter how many embryos they have in there, I want to pluck them out one by one."

"You'll have it by tomorrow."

"Will you testify it in court, Mr. White?" Satish asked.

Jerry White jotted down the last name, put away the pen, and pushed the notepad towards me. "It won't bring my Gaya back. And it will never do justice to her, to the other kids, or the woman you mentioned who lost her life. And yet it's still better than rotting in jail and watching the bastards get away with everything."

I drew the curtains and closed the door. I sat on the floor, my back against the wall, and an empty bottle of Corona next to me. And I stared. A penknife, an empty shell, a leather wallet, a house key. Carmelo's silver case. And now a watch. Fake leather and plastic—a cheapie. And it wasn't even *my* trophy—a bullet to the head killed the piece of scum, not the round I'd blasted into his shoulder.

Will finished his dinner and came rasping at the door.

I rolled the watch in my hands and ignored him.

Gomez had called me minutes after I'd gotten home. The SID field unit canvassing the arroyo behind Diane's property had found a slug—a rimless .40 Smith and Wesson. If the M.E. fished a 10mm caliber bullet out of the ex-con's skull tomorrow I was out of the woods: I had .357 Mags in my revolver and my Glock hadn't fired a single round last night. Of course, Gomez didn't put it so nicely.

Somebody wanted Diane dead. They paid an ex-con and when the ex-con failed they drilled a bullet in his skull to make sure he kept quiet. A 10mm caliber, I thought. *Same as the bullet drilled into Tarantino's head.*

I picked myself up, put everything back in the tin, and the tin underneath a wood plank in the closet. Not the watch, though. The watch I brought to the garage, smashed it with a hammer, and tossed the pieces in the garbage.

I went to the fridge and grabbed another Corona. The evening breeze made the blinds in the living room flutter. It carried a new spice in the air.

The King hopped down his windowsill and fled through

the pet door.

Get the door...

I didn't.

The doorbell rang. I didn't move. And then I did.

"You haven't talked to me all day," Diane's opening line. Flustered, tired, and heavenly smelling.

I stood at the door and winced. "What do you call what we did at the meeting?"

"Work." She glared, my words stinging. "Aren't you going to let me in?"

Her scent was pungent and enticing, sweet and spicy like an Indian *chai* tea, the sweetness drawing me in, and the spicy burning my tongue.

Watch it, Ulysses, said a voice in my head.

Will shoved himself between Diane's legs and licked her all over.

"Aw, isn't he a sweetie?" Diane cooed. "*Unlike* his human," she added, sending me a sideways glare.

"Don't blame him. He's tried very hard to train me. Beer?" I offered, lacking anything better to say. She shook her head and paced inside, her eyes darting around my place, my one-man refuge, my cave. I should've worried about the molehills of crumbs scattered on the rug, or the coffee table ringed by espresso cups like a puddle under the rain. Details I never cared about jumped at me: empty beer bottles lined on the floor by the recliner, a gun holster carelessly left on the mantel, old stains on the couch cushions, a black sock dangling off a bookshelf from the last time I'd been desperate for a bookmark. CDs sprawled next to an old player, a few issues of Game & Fish piled on top of it. Did my armpits smell, did my feet stink, did my breath— Diane turned abruptly, her face blank, unimpressed. Without praise or blame.

I handed her the Corona she'd refused. "Here, it'll make

you feel better." She took it, her eyes clinging on me like cobwebs. She walked to the couch, dropped on it, and brushed her hand along the spot where Will had slouched a minute earlier. Her fingers raked a clump of tawny colored hair. "You have a cat? I love cats."

I sat on the recliner. "No, uh—It's more of a cousin."

Diane frowned. "A cousin with fur?"

I tittered and for a moment she joined in. Not for long, though. "Glad to see you haven't lost your sense of humor." She wiped the smile off her face.

It wasn't a joke.

She took a swig of Corona, my eyes drawn by the smooth line of her neck. She lowered the bottle and swallowed slowly, her thumb drawing circles along the wet glass. "So. Troy didn't lie to us. They weren't experimenting with human embryos."

I shrugged. "They experimented with humans, though."

She bobbed her head, gravely. "Then the humans had children, and the children paid the price for their parents' vanity."

"Udall is working on the search warrants for Chromo's labs. Once we get a hold of all the embryos, do you think you can prove the gene therapy caused the leukemia mutations in the children's DNA?"

Diane stroked the beer bottle with her thumb. "Yes, if we can show the therapy messed up the germline cells. If the embryos have the same mutations Huxley found, we can confirm her findings."

Diane took another swig then set the bottle on the coffee table. "Did you hear about the slug?"

I nodded, she swallowed. "I can't believe it. There must've been two of them, and one… killed the other."

"Can you blame him?"

Hurt stung her eyes. "It's not funny, Track!" She ran a

hand through her hair and shook her head. "I'm—I'm so stressed out. I still can't figure out how he got into my apartment. And why—what did he want from me? Rape me? Kill me?"

"Both."

Diane scowled. "What?"

"I said both."

"God, Track, that really, really helps." She clonked the beer bottle on the coffee table, got to her feet and walked away.

Should I stop her? Or should I let her go?

I darted behind her. "I meant—"

She never got to the door. She spun on her feet and glared. "Do you at least wonder why I wanted to talk to you today or do you not give a shit?"

Funny how Gomez had yelled to my face the exact same way that morning and yet I had unflinchingly held back his gaze and pretended his breath smelled like rose petals.

Diane's flushed skin was ambrosial, and the more upset she got, the spicier her scent became. I would've stopped breathing if I could. But I couldn't. It was everywhere: on her skin, on her clothes, in her hair. The ancestral call of pheromones reeling me in, like the Sirens calling out to the sailors who dared cross their sea… I stepped back. *Last night I would've taken her with my eyes closed. Last night I hadn't killed an unarmed man for no other reason than revenge…*

"I wanted to thank you," she whispered. Softly, suddenly drained of all animosity. "For last night, Track, for risking your life for me. You kept avoiding me instead. Why? Do I disgust you?"

"No." I swallowed. "Definitely not."

She came closer and this time I didn't move. All the *what-if* castles I kept building in my head eroded away, and all there was left to stare at and take in was *her*. Diane. The beast in me purred in contentment. Tamed.

"Do I scare you?"

"Scare me? No. I'm scared of me, Diane. Of what I might do to you."

Was she intrigued when she tilted her head, stepped so close I felt the warmth of her breath on my mouth, and asked, "What *might* you do to me?"

My hands sought her, found fabric instead. I knew *exactly* what I'd do to her. "I might peel these clothes off you," I whispered. *Make my skin touch yours. I'd want to inhale you, let our scents mingle, let myself be part of you —*

"Like this?" Her fingers snapped the top button of her shirt and my hand followed, tracing her skin as she went along freeing it. The sight of her cleavage made blood pulse in my head. I slid my hands down her shoulders, kissed her neck and then her lips. They were good lips to kiss — soft and embracing. Searching. Her shirt fell to the floor. I picked her up, brought her to my bed, licked the base of her throat and continued my way down. And then I froze. It was right there, on her bra. *The* smell, the bloody assassin's scent. On her bra, damn it, of all places.

"What?"

I read desire in her eyes. The spicy zest of her skin, the pheromones, calling me in.

It's not. Can't be. Not the same person. The DNA didn't match.

You're wrong about the scent, Track. Wrong.

I unfastened her bra, tossed it away, and removed it from my thoughts. After that I drowned in her scent, sweet and sticky like honey.

"You feel good, Track," she whispered in my ear. "You feel good."

I couldn't find the words to tell her how good *she* felt. I just purred. I rocked her and purred.

CHAPTER 34

Friday, October 24

Diane was sleeping. I couldn't. I had to check the bra again. And when I did, the surge of loath I felt scared me. I could kill because of that. I had already.

At three a.m. I banged on Hortensia's door. "What happened?" She showed up in a white T-shirt and nothing else, neither over nor under. I stepped inside and slouched on her couch, even though she hadn't invited me in.

"My place is taken." I scanned with no interest the clutter of paint jars, brushes and canvases populating her studio.

"By whom?"

"It doesn't matter. I'll just lounge on your couch for the time being. Will be gone by morning, promise." Or so I hoped.

She shrugged and turned the bolt. "Whatever. You smell different, though." She shuffled back to her bedroom and slammed the door closed.

Smells, I thought. *What the hell does* she *know about smells?*

The first thing I inhaled when I woke up was turpentine and oil paints. The sun had just risen. It poked through the slats of the blinds and blinked in my eyes. I was cranky and exhausted.

"Gary was a doll yesterday," Hortensia chirped half an hour later as I dragged myself into her kitchen.

"Hmm."

She gaped at me. "What the hell happened to you?"

I must've looked pretty bad for her to notice. "Diane Kyle showed up."

Hortensia clonked the coffee grinder on the counter. "Oh. Who?"

I retrieved two mugs from the cupboard, sat at the kitchen island, and waved a hand. "She's..." I pinched the bridge of my nose. "We're investigating this case together."

"Ooh." She clicked her tongue. "No wonder you smelled different. How closely have you two been investigating?"

I glared but said nothing. Hortensia went back on the attack. "Did you kiss her?"

"Worse. I slept with her."

This time she pulled her lips together and sucked in air. "Oh my!" And then she laughed and nudged me on the shoulder. "Are you going to make me jealous, my Ulysses lost at sea?"

I *was* lost at sea. Ulysses—Homer's one—had tied himself to the mast of his boat not to fall prey to the Sirens' chants. What was I to tie myself to?

Hortensia's laughter faded pretty quickly. She filled the coffee filter and asked, "So, what are you doing here?"

I stared at her hair. It draped her shoulders in a fan of red and golden threads, wavering back and forth as if they possessed a mind of their own. As if each sway were a chorus of— "You're disappointing, Track."

Hortensia's question fell unanswered. "Gee, Track. I didn't know you were so typical."

I clutched one of the mugs and squeezed it. "Typical?"

"She came to your house?"

I squeezed harder and nodded.

"And she made a move on you?"

Damn it, I wasn't going to share that much. "Hort—"

She left the coffee maker and leaned across the kitchen island. "You're such a typical representative of your gender, Mr. Presius. A lady comes onto you and you feel your masculinity suddenly threatened because she made the move instead of you. So, what do you do? You leave. Congratulations, Track. Turns out, you're just like everybody else."

"That's not why I left."

She turned the coffee maker on and opened the fridge. "Why'd you leave, then?"

I twirled the coffee mug.

"Track?"

"Hell, Hort. Her bra smelled like the killer I'm after, okay? Do you wanna know what size it was, now?"

The half a gallon of milk in her right hand froze in mid-air. "Are you serious?"

I nodded. From the bottom of the mug, a distorted reflection of my right eye looked back at me and scowled. Hortensia propped the milk carton in front of me. "How did this happen, Track? How did you let her fool you like this?"

I bristled. "So now I'm a fool. A *typical* fool, right, Hort?"

I slammed the mug on the countertop so hard the handle came off.

Hortensia was relentless. "Well, yeah! She came to your house and seduced you."

"It's not her!" I shouted. "It's her damn boyfriend!" Hortensia gave me one of her looks. I hunched over the kitchen island and squeezed my temples between the heels of my hands. "Or a sibling of her boyfriend's, or some other fucking bastard who needs to rot in jail," I growled.

Kowalski has no siblings, Ulysses. You've looked into it.

"Whose smell was on the woman you slept with?"

And who ran the DNA analyses.

What was I supposed to say? It didn't make any sense, and yet there was no way I could stay away from the woman. In fact, I was already regretting leaving her in the middle of the night. I wanted to run back to her. *Maybe she hasn't awakened yet, maybe it's not too late...*

"A man tried to kill her two nights ago," I blurted out in the mist of my denial.

"He didn't though, did he? I bet the idea was to ambush and kill *you*," Hortensia replied. It was the final stab to my already wounded ego. She shook her head. "That's what happens when you get personally involved in these things. You lose lucidity."

I could no longer listen to her. I slammed my hand on the table, got up and left.

"I hope she won't kill you," she called after me. "It's hard to say 'I told you so' when you're dead."

Could I really be such an idiot? Fall for a woman on the trail of a scent, like a bug flying right into the honey jar and drowning. *Sweet death*, I thought, Diane's inebriating scent still clinging to my skin. *Sweet death.*

By the third cup I started feeling the caffeine jitter. I hated drip coffee. And I hated it even more when it came in a Styrofoam cup. It was like getting drunk with malt beer in a Chianti cellar. I crushed the cup, tossed it in the trash, then opened the blue murder book on my desk. My eyes glazed over.

Diane's exposed throat, a pearly offering to my searching mouth. Diane's navel, arching under my touch. The more I tried to run away from them, the more those images came back, haunting me. A movie in slow motion gradually accelerating and finally screeching to a halt. Diane, in my bed, a stroke of light from the window brushing her hair. How long until she realizes I'm not there? Until she calls my name and she understands no answer will come? She gets out of bed, her fragrance trailing behind her. If I were still there, I'd cherish the warmth of her body on my sheets. I chose to leave, instead. How much longer until she feels betrayed? Abandoned, maybe. Or maybe just used.

Wasn't that the plan, Ulysses? To use her to get to the killer?
Turns out, she used you, instead.

Udall dropped by around ten. He shuffled to my desk and sat on Satish's chair, the knot of his tie slightly skewed, and the black briefcase with the tattered corners swinging by his side. He laced his fingers across his stomach and stared at me smirking. Always smirking.

"Aren't you going to ask me how I did yesterday, Track?"

"You always do well, Mr. Udall."

He crossed his legs and flashed a blue sock at me. It nicely matched his tie. "Jerry White got away with one count of voluntary manslaughter—five years on paper. He'll do one if we're lucky." This time the smirk seemed out of place. Picture a dolphin crying.

I gulped down the lukewarm remains of my third coffee. "Between you and me, Mr. Udall: can you blame him for what he's done?"

"Track, I've been doing this for quite some years now. I've learned to look at the one action and put it in its context. I can't afford likes or dislikes towards the victim. All victims have equal right to justice. And murder is always murder."

I shook my head. "Except this particular story doesn't have one victim only, Mr. Udall. Gaya White was a victim, too. And the other children, whose parents were fool enough to believe in eternal youth."

Udall exhaled. "Their parents made a stupid choice. They played with their own lives. Too bad it was the kids who ended up paying the price."

I tapped the empty cup on the table and sighed. A little Satish-like wisdom came to me. "Some people have a hard time growing up. If you tell a five-year-old, 'Give me your piggy bank, and I'll give you the most gigantic lollipop on the face of the Earth,' is he going to say no?"

"Naïveté is White's crime, then?"

I shrugged. "Or too much faith. Some people believe in God, others believe in science."

Udall nodded, the chain of his glasses bobbing in unison with his jowls. He slapped a hand on his knee, crouched to retrieve his briefcase, and then rose to his feet. "I'm glad you do your job and I do mine, Track." So was I. He took a few steps and then turned around. "I almost forgot. Chromo does have more embryos. White and Kelson weren't the only parents who opted for in vitro fertilization after the rejuvenating gene therapy. However, if you want those embryos, you better get a written consent from each one of the rightful owners."

I raised a brow.

"The parents, Track. Or donors, or whatever you want to

call them. When you go to Chromo, you must get a log with the info on what belongs to whom. You can seize the evidence, but you can't look at the embryos' genes without destroying them, and you can't destroy them without the parents' consents."

"Every one of them? It's crazy."

"You know what's crazy in this case? Think about it: who are the *real* parents?"

I watched him trot away, his briefcase swinging and his question ringing in my ears. It beat any of Satish's best riddles.

CHAPTER 35

Friday, October 24

"Where did you hide it?"

He frowns, startled by her sudden rage. "Where did I hide what?"

"The gun," she hisses. She no longer cares to hide her feelings. She feels the danger, like claws drawing near and closing around her throat. She wakes up in the middle of the night unable to breathe. Her medications no longer work to quiet the erratic firing of her neurons. Everything is falling apart. The woman she dreaded, her rival, is still alive. She followed her car the night before. If the loser won't do it, I will, *she thought. Headlights off, she pulled behind her parked vehicle and waited. Nothing happened, though. The woman she was after never came out of the house. The bitch. She considered snatching the gun and walking*

in there. Recklessly. What the hell, everything is going to the dogs, anyways. *At least the satisfaction of seeing her heart ripped open. But the glove compartment was empty. The weapon she'd left inside was gone.*

Her husband stands in front of the dresser mirror and completes the half-Windsor knot of his necktie. He thrives on little details like this. She watches the nimble movements of his fingers as if hypnotized. Intimacy no longer means anything to her, and yet this part of his routine — the knotting of his necktie in the morning, as he checks that the dimple sits right at the center of the knot — feels like a private snippet of his life. Something she can still steal away from him. And make it hers.

"Where's the gun?" she demands.

He turns, his eyes blankly staring past her. Oh, she hates him for belittling her in such subtle ways. *You're nothing to me*, his eyes say. *Nothing.*

"You're getting too emotional about this," he replies coldly. "I don't think a weapon in your hands would be a good idea right now." He picks up his briefcase and walks down the stairs.

How can you do this to me? After all these years. She throws her arms around his back, shrieking. He clutches the banister and jerks backwards, sending her slamming against the wall. She hits her head and wilts on the carpeted stairs. A photo tumbles down from the wall.

"Don't you ever do that again!"

"Madam?" *a voice calls from downstairs.*

"Everything is okay, Lucia, go back to work," he says, adjusting his jacket.

He walks away. She hears the door downstairs close behind him, the garage open, the car pull out and vanish.

Tears run down her cheeks. Not pain. Humiliation.

How can he belittle me like this?

Cluttered by tears, her eyes rest on the fallen photo frame. Through the jagged line of a wounded glass, a girl beams in her glittery leotard. Azure, her favorite color, although you cannot tell *from the black and white picture. Her arms are stretched out, her posture calculated and yet natural, perfectly at ease on the balance beam. She's just completed her exercise and now she smiles confidently at the camera. Proud of herself.*

What happened to you? she cries staring at the photo. *What happened to your dreams?*

CHAPTER 36

Friday, October 24

Traffic spread apart and then reunited along the intricate three-dimensional network of ramps and junctions of L.A.'s cemented arteries. A uniform, relentless flow. Green signs and overpasses glided above us, while intersecting lives swept by our side: a hand pressing the mobile to the ear; a cigarette clinging to manicured fingers; the bobbing head of a teenager wrapped in his own world of deafening drums and screeching electric guitars.

I stared out the window, the vehicles sailing by a parody of human life. Individuals trapped in their own box, shielded from the outside noise and pollution. They all had their destination, their plans, their solitudes masked by busy schedules and frantic work hours—the few social interactions filtered through small mirrors bearing the warning "Objects may be closer than they appear."

You better keep your distance if you don't want your little world to be crushed.

"It's almost Halloween."

"Hm-mmm."

"I miss patrolling on Halloween night."

"Hmm."

"Kinda fun with all the kids running by the cruiser, yelling, 'Trick-or-treat, smell-my-feet,' and guffawing at my face as I pretend to be scared."

Hands on the steering wheel, Satish turned to look at me. My eyes remained glued to the window.

"Did you call her?"

"No." And I wasn't going to attach any justification to it. We passed a pick-up truck with a rattling fridge strapped to the deck, the blanket wrapped around it flapping angrily in the wind.

"We should make sure she got it."

I heaved a sigh of frustration, reached for the phone, and dialed. *She'll never pick up.* Every unanswered ring hit my eardrums like nails on a blackboard.

Hang up, Ulysses. She'll never pick up.

I heard the click followed by silence. *Hurt, voiced by a million unspoken words.*

I inhaled. "Hey, listen—Did you get the tank?"

Seconds hammered by. "It's here." Glacial.

"Did you take a peek inside?"

"No."

I turned to Satish, placidly driving along. "We're under a little pressure," I said.

"Pressure?" Diane replied, raising her voice. *It's going to come down now.* "Get yourself here, Track," she hissed, "and explain yourself to my face. Let's see if that puts a little pressure on you. And don't you tell me you got a callout because I already checked."

The dropped line beeped into my ear. "Okay," I mumbled for Satish's sake before closing the phone. I hoped he hadn't deciphered any of the metallic squeaks coming out of the wireless gadget.

"She'll look into it," I added, hoping it would finally close the matter. Satish nodded, drove silently for a few more miles, and then asked, "Still scratching your ass on that rocky bottom and finding it comfortable, Track?"

I forced a laugh out of my mouth, though it sounded more like a squeak. "Actually, I think I took the elevator to paradise but the ride turned out to be too fast."

Satish smiled. I tapped the cell phone against the window and groaned. "I belong in hell, Sat. Not heaven."

"Don't we all, Track?" he replied. "Don't we all."

In Greek mythology the power of life and death was in the hands of the three Fates. The existence of every mortal being was a thread: Clotho spun it, Lachesis decided what length it should get to, and Atropos cut it when the time came.

I saw them that day, in Chris Hopf's hospital room, one of Cox's leukemia patients. By the windowsill, the three monsters played with the boy's thread of life, pulling and tugging and teasing it with the blades of their scissors. The strand wasn't made of fibers. It was composed of two coils held together by four molecules. Some of the molecules were feebly connected, and whenever Atropos' scissors lingered in their proximity, they trembled as if about to lose their grip. They reminded me of pearls strung on a worn out thread: soon the time comes when they finally break free and spill on the floor, bouncing off in all directions like children at the end of a school day.

Joseph and Melissa Hopf had already lost their first child to leukemia. Two months after burying the nine-year-old girl, six-year-old Christopher, their second child, fell ill with the same disease. Wrapped in white hospital sheets, blue eyes sparkling from underneath hairless brows, Chris stared at the mobile of paper airplanes hanging from the ceiling while his mother read Sendak's *Where the Wild Things Are*. More books lay on the bed next to him: a children's space encyclopedia, a book about the planets, another about astronauts. A family of teddy bears sat on the night stand, each one holding a get-well card. All around, flashy wallpaper with red-nosed clowns broke the dullness of the gray linoleum floors. A vain attempt to make the room look child-friendly when in fact it lacked the essence: a child's smile.

"Hi, Chris," Satish said, drumming his knuckles against the door. "How are you feeling today?"

The boy stared from above a hospital facemask and squeezed his mother's hand. I read awareness in his expression, a young man trapped in a child's body. He knew what lay ahead. He'd seen it in his sister.

I don't believe in destiny. I believe we have choices in life. And yet, looking into the boy's eyes, sparkling with youth though sunken into a scrawny little face, no bangs brushing down his forehead, I couldn't help but feel a profound surge of loathing. *Somebody sealed your fate, Chris, before it had even been written. They yanked your thread off the Fates' hands and meddled with it, snatching your dreams away.*

Mrs. Hopf closed the book and sent an interrogative glance to her husband, standing by the window. Mr. Hopf had a long face with sharp edges, and flat cheeks studded by old acne scars.

"Is this a bad time?" I asked, showing the LAPD badge.

Chris's eyes bulged at the sight. "Can I see it?" he asked, stretching out a hand and exposing small flowery bruises on the inside of his arm.

"I want to be an astronaut when I grow up," Chris's voice came from behind his blue mask. His fingers traced the reliefs on Satish's badge. "Detective would be pretty cool, too."

Seated at the edge of the bed, Satish smiled. "When I was your age, I dreamt of becoming a plumber."

The boy's eyes widened. "A plumber?"

Satish chortled and his voice trailed off in one of his stories.

Outside the door, the usual coming and going of visitors, nurses, and medical staff populated the corridors; trays of IVs and medications traveled from one wing to the other; white coats carelessly discussed dinner plans over histology results and patient charts; an old lady in a fluffy pink robe stared at us for a few minutes before resuming her random cruising of the hallway, faithfully followed by a rattling IV pole.

Across from the nurses' station, sitting nervously at the edge of a blue chair, Mrs. Hopf whimpered and covered her mouth with one hand. By her side, her husband clasped his head and growled like a wounded animal. He sprang to his feet, paced furiously back and forth for half a minute, and then slammed both fists against one of the windows, resting his forehead on the glass pane.

Hopf held still, hands and forehead glued to the window. "So it's all my fault," he muttered. "All my children went through, all my goddamned fault."

I shifted uncomfortably. "No, sir. But I do need your

help to ensure the ones to blame get the punishment they deserve."

"But you said it's for a murder investigation. Not for deceiving us."

"Correct. It's a caveat—"

Hopf turned away from the window and glared at the ceiling, at the gods dwelling in the skies, cruel fates who gave him the power to know and to choose.

Just one bite from the tree of knowledge and you will die.

"I wanted the very best for them. I wanted their life to be a dream. They got a nightmare instead." He shook his head and looked at his wife. She opened her mouth as if about to say something, but never did, her parted lips hanging in an open question mark. "Do you know what it is like to spend days, weeks, months, by your child's side in a hospital, Detective? Time no longer exists. The life you used to have, dictated by morning commute, work, meetings, lunch hour—it's all gone. A deception. A mirage of what it used to be before you realized how futile it all was." He sighed, his voice cracked with pain.

What he said next came out of his mouth in a low drone, the eulogy of a mourning father. "When an emergency breaks, time spins out of control. You feel the hours irreversibly slipping out of your fingers, like a handful of sand you want to hang onto and yet the more you squeeze, the more it falls through. And when you finally open your fist, there's only a few grains left on your palm.

"There are moments when time flows as viscous as glass, and even though you know it's moving, you can't really see it. Time mocks you, Detective. It makes you simmer in pain, with its stubborn unwillingness to progress forward when you want it to, and its swirling out of control when instead you want to hold it back. The joy you felt at some point has vanished, like a fluttering butterfly setting on your finger. It shows you her beauty, and for a moment you think, it's here, right here, I have it, it's mine. And one second later it's gone and it will never come back. You had it, but the one moment was elusive, so ephemeral you can't stop but wonder, was it real? Or did I just dream of it?"

He pressed hard the knuckles of one hand against his lips and spoke no more.

His wife sighed. "Where do we sign, Detective?"

CHAPTER 37

Friday, October 24

Lucia Hortega hears the sudden rumble and gasps. Dios mio, el terremoto! she thinks. By her feet, a bucket of water jerks and sloshes all over the floor. Angry thumps follow, as of objects hurdled against the wall. From upstairs, she realizes. Another crisis. Mira que disastro, Lucia groans, looking at the puddle sprawled on the floor she has just cleaned. Should she say something? Or should she just pretend she didn't hear? Ni modo, she's going to yell either way.

Lucia tiptoes upstairs and pokes her head into the master bedroom. The dresser lies on its side. The bottom drawers have been yanked away and upturned on the bed. The top ones hang open like jaws dropped in astonishment. Humps of crumpled clothes are scattered across the room. A nightstand lamp has crushed on the floor. The bed sheets have been pulled off and the mattress exposed.

"Madam – " Lucia whimpers.

"GET OUT!"

Puta, *Lucia mutters, running away.* Puta sucia. Guess who'll have to clean up all the mess.

Crouched by the bed the woman is finally exultant. Her pulse quickens as she brushes the barrel with the tip of her fingers, a shiver of anticipation sweeping down her spine. I found you, my darling. He thought he could fool me. Keep you away from me. *She smiles, brings the weapon to her cheek, and savors its scent: metal, gunpowder, oil.* I'm ready, now, *she thinks.* I'm ready.

CHAPTER 38

Friday, October 24

"Kids shouldn't be allowed to get sick," Satish said over a plate of *moussaka*.

I sunk my teeth into the gyro sandwich I had ravenously ordered, and then wiped my mouth. "And how do you plan on going about fixing the problem?"

"People like Julia Cox are doing their part."

I refrained from uttering a nasty comment just because my mouth was full. Satish put down his fork. "Track. One needs money to do things, and money doesn't always come from the cleanest sources. What are you going to do? Either you stall, or you keep going and make the best out of it." He squeezed the fork and shrugged. "Call it cynical. Not all patriotic people love their country. In fact, most of them don't."

"Another metaphor I don't understand."

"You don't need to understand my metaphors to appreciate them."

"And you don't need to break the law to be a dishonest person. Look. Maybe Cox didn't do anything wrong in the eyes of the law, but she knew what she was doing when she hampered Huxley's efforts. She selfishly put her career first. Assuming she had nothing to do with the gene therapy thing, which I haven't completely excluded."

"I don't know, Track. Had she gone along with Huxley and tried to implicate Chromo, she probably would've ended up dead, resulting in one more homicide and one fewer doctor to fight for these children."

"Man, Satish. What's wrong with you today? She accepted money from Chromo—that alone tells you she was involved, whether or not she knew about the Proteus therapy." I shook my head. "Sometimes I don't know where you stand, Sat. Do we even have a reason to do our job, or should we all go home and accept the world for the fucking bitch it is?"

Satish sank his fork in the last bit of *moussaka* left in his plate, and then brought it to his mouth. He chewed slowly and thoughtfully. He swallowed, then wiped his mouth. And while he did that, I chomped down and gulped the rest of my sandwich in three bites.

"Christopher Hopf does," he finally said.

"Does what?"

"Accept the world for the fucking bitch it is."

"He's a dying kid, he doesn't have a choice."

"Maybe this is our problem, Track."

I didn't know what he meant and didn't have time to mull it over, either. "It's getting late. We've got to get back to work." I waved for the check. Satish propped his elbows on the table and let his eyes wander off, a peaceful, daydreaming stare painted on his face.

I signed the check, grabbed my jacket from the back of the chair, and adjusted the holster hooked on my belt. Even though with time you get used to having this constant ballast embracing the small of your back, there's always a time of the day—after lunch, or after sitting for too long—when it uncomfortably reminds you of its presence. We walked out of the café—Satish by my side still wearing his airy smile—and by the time we got back to the vehicle I gave up.

"Fine, Sat. What the hell does this whole story remind you of?"

Satish inserted the key into the ignition and beamed. "Why, Track. I thought you'd never ask." I groaned. "It reminds me of my sister Rhani's new bicycle."

"A bicycle."

"A brand new bicycle," Satish repeated, pulling out of the parking lot. "Rhani was seven when Santa Claus finally got her one, after pleading and pouting for two years. She was so thrilled she hopped on and rode in the backyard for hours. *Watch me go with one hand*, she'd yell. *Watch me go with no hands.* And in all the excitement, she forgot to look ahead, slammed against the porch railing, and hit her head. My brother and I guffawed, while my mother came running out of the house yelling, *What was that?* And then everything went silent.

"Rhani lies still on the ground, the handle of the bike jammed against her chest, and the front wheel spinning.

"Ma screeches. *Rhani!* Eyes wide open, Rhani stares at the sky and weeps. My brother and I sneer and go back to play. My old man picks up his daughter, dusts her off, and then puts her back to her feet. *Walk*, he says, and she walks. *Raise your arms*, he says, and she raises both arms. *Jump*, and she jumps. *Talk,* and nothing comes out of her mouth. *Talk, Rhani.* Nothing. *Say papa.* Nyet. *Say mama.* Nada. Ma wails, pulls her hair, and squeals, *It's a concussion! We need to take her in.* And at those words, Rhani's eyes bulge. Pa takes her inside and sets her on the couch with an ice bag on her head. Then they scuttle off, Ma to call the hospital, my old man to get the insurance papers.

"*What if they keep her?* Ma shouts. *Let me get some extra clothes, just in case.*

"Rhani starts sobbing. She goes to her bedroom, gets her canvas tote, throws in her colored pencils, her journal, a pen, and her favorite doll. She takes her piggy bank and an old car I once gave her. While Ma frets around the house—now she prepares snacks, just in case the waiting at the ER gets to be long—Rhani comes to the backyard and hands me the old toy car and the piggy bank.

"*The piggy bank is empty,* she says. *But from now on you can use it for your savings.*"

"Wait a minute... I thought she couldn't talk!" I interjected.

"Of course she could talk. She was just fine."

"Then why didn't she say so?"

"I don't know, and she didn't know either. She was seven. I bet she was too afraid to say anything because she thought they were going to yell at her."

"Instead they took her to the ER?"

"Yeah, though she didn't know that's where they were taking her."

"Where did she think they were taking her?"

Satish chuckled. "She gave me her most valuable things, and to my younger brother she left a rock—but it was her favorite rock—and then hugged us both.

"*Let's go, Rhani,* Ma calls while Pa pulls the car out of the driveway.

"*What's wrong with her?* I ask my brother as I watch her shuffle away and get in the car with her head down and her shoulders drooping. My brother lifts his head from the dirt hole he's been digging in the backyard. *Dunno*, he drawls and resumes digging."

"We're almost there, Satish, and I'm still missing the point," I pressed, as our vehicle merged into the right lane and took the next exit.

"The point, my very impatient Track, is: my sister confused the word concussion with adoption, which was confirmed by Ma's erratic behavior, taking her clothes, preparing her food, and shoving her into the car. She thought they were taking her some place where they'd give her up to strangers who would then become her new parents."

"Concussion for adoption?"

"She was seven. And she'd never heard either word before. She had a friend in school who'd been adopted and who told her parents give up their daughters when they no longer have money to feed them. And Rhani thought Ma and Pa were so mad at her for ruining the brand new bike they were going to give her up."

Satish parked the vehicle and smiled. "You had to see Rhani's eyes when she came back home. She'd left thinking she was never going to come back."

That was the story for the day. No moral, although I could see it for myself this time, a lesson of wisdom learned from the most unexpected of teachers—a seven-year-old. Some things you have no control over. They make you feel powerless. The only way is to go along with it. Accept and endure. Satish was right, I'd read it in Chris Hopf's eyes. And what was I going to do with my life? Was I going to let the currents carry me along or was I going to oppose it? And if I did, to what use?

"Nelson got five consent forms, Gregov another six. Looks like we're almost there." I closed the phone. We were two forms short before we could look at all the embryos we had seized from the Chromo labs.

"Good," Satish said, staring at the mansion in front of us. "Because this is where it's going to hit hard."

Surrounded by impeccable lawns and lush palm trees, we were standing in the driveway of a Mission style home gone overboard, with red Italian shingles, white adobe, and two circular sections flanking the main entrance. Creeping bougainvillea decorated the three-bay garage with clusters of purple flowers. Arching glass doors carved the ground floor and showcased spiral staircases and crystal chandeliers. A sundeck sprawled over what looked like a ballroom and continued towards the back of the house, where the smell of chlorine gave away the presence of a swimming pool.

Satish walked under a two-story high gable and pressed the doorbell. It chimed with the opening notes of Amazing Grace—nice touch, given the setting. The mahogany door boasted stained glass panes laced with wrought iron swirls. A housekeeper with small, mousy eyes and pink, mousy hands opened it. She squeaked a few apologetic words before surrendering to our LAPD tins and letting us in. As soon as we stepped inside, Dan Horowitz came darting down the stairs. He stopped halfway down to point an index finger that wanted badly to be a middle finger. "Just so we're clear. I know what you guys are after and I'm *not* cooperating."

I looked up at him and squinted. "What exactly do you presume we're after, Mr. Horowitz?"

He clutched the banister, his face as colorful as red

grapes. *Sour* red grapes. "You have slandered my friend and colleague Jerry White. And now you're trying to throw dirt on Chromo and its scientific accomplishments. This is a private home, Detectives. I'm under no obligation to welcome you inside."

Satish bobbed his head. "Oh, we never expect to be welcomed when we talk to people—"

"Out."

"Calm down, Dan. I answered the gate and let them through." Mrs. Horowitz emerged from the loft in a black jogging outfit, which clung to her skin in a constrictive way, as if her naked body wanted to burst out of it. Her teats held taut and high, yielding the slightest nod as she walked down the stairs, her unflinching nipples staring down on us through her shirt. "Nice to meet you, Detectives," she said in a mellow, flirtatious voice. She spoke like a Japanese cartoon character, with no other muscle on her face moving but her lips. Her cleavage was glistening with a film of perspiration, and her hand—as I shook it—felt warm and slippery, as if she had just stepped down from a treadmill. Her sweat smelled just as expensive as her clothes.

Horowitz watched his wife greet us with fuming eyes, then hobbled down the second half of the stairs. "Don't get too friendly, Jenna." His pursed lips promised belligerence at us, at the maid who'd let us in, and at the spouse who'd opened the forbidden gate.

"Mr. Horowitz, we have information about your daughter's health," Satish explained. "Her life may be in danger."

Six-year-old Vanessa Horowitz was one of the few Proteus kids who was still in good health. The news we brought did not upset either one of the parents. Horowitz stuck to his part as the tough, resilient guy who wanted nothing to do with law enforcement, and his wife played along as the weak link willing to put in a good word, a few batting of fake eyelashes, and nothing more. The conversation moved over to one of the numerous living rooms in the mansion, and at times assumed louder and more colorful tones. Even when presented with the number of kids who'd fallen sick and died, the Horowitzes didn't budge. Somehow, paying one and a half million for a few embryos was easier than jotting down their signature on a piece of paper.

The greed with which they clung to their frozen gene pool baffled me. "We haven't decided what to do with the embryos," Horowitz said. "And until we do, those embryos are ours and we want to keep them."

Ours. What a peculiar concept. *My* genes, *my* DNA. What's *ours* when it comes to what we are?

Pulsing lights reflected off the surface of the swimming pool outside and blinked through the arching glass doors. A Picasso-like lady with a giraffe neck and abnormally large eyes gaped from above the stone fireplace. A bronze cupid played in a corner, and an alabaster dancer on the side table defied gravity in the most graceful way. I almost wanted to jump and catch her in midair. Above us, the ceilings soared; below us, the Italian tiles floored us. It was all part of the Horowitzes' *ours*: imported rugs, granites, marbles, and natural stones. The pale face of a child, her head leaning against the doorframe at the back, her naked feet propped one over the other, and clear blue eyes lost in a world too big for her. Yes, sometimes money can buy that, too.

Jenna Horowitz followed my eyes and whirled her head to find her daughter peeking at us from the open door. "What are you doing here, Vanessa?"

A pudgy nanny emerged behind the child. "I'm sorry, Mrs. Horowitz. She really wanted to see you. Her knees hurt."

Vanessa's legs were as white and thin as the alabaster dancer's. She ran towards us and sunk her face in her mother's lap. A mesh of purple capillaries netted the inside of her knees, and small, round bruises bloomed all over her arms. I scowled, my LE training quickly surmising child abuse.

Jenna Horowitz gently pushed the child back to the nanny. "It's too cold for shorts, honey," she said, her voice as motherly as a GPS recalculating the route. "Dorothy, please bring her upstairs to change."

Dorothy came to grab Vanessa's hand. I asked, "Where exactly does it hurt, Vanessa?"

The girl turned and stared at me, the faintest brows hanging above her blue eyes. "Here," she said, pointing to her right knee. "And here. And here. And here." When there were no more joints to point at, she wrapped her small fingers around the glimmering heart hanging from her neck and said, "Do you like it? Aunt Gracie gave it to me for my birthday."

Jenna Horowitz shot to her feet, closed her hands around her child's shoulders, and turned her to the nanny. "We took her to the doctor last week, Detective. Vanessa is perfectly fine. These are just growing pains."

"Did you have the doctor check those bruises?" I prodded.

"My wife told you already." Dan Horowitz got up from his seat. "Dorothy, take the child upstairs. And you two get out of my house. We're through talking."

CHAPTER 39

Friday, October 24

She lies on the ground with her eyes closed. Her cheek is pressed against a hard surface, scratchy, cement, most likely, pebbles painfully poking her skin. She tries to stir. Each fiber in her body throbs. Get up. *She opens her eyes. Everything is blurry. Her head feels heavy, her tongue pasted and sore. She tastes blood.*

It happened again.

Slowly things come back into focus. A lawn, a few feet away from her, three steps, a door. Unfamiliar. Where am I? *And then she remembers. She raises her head, the movement too brusque, it makes her nauseated. The sun is pounding on her, and the cement underneath scalds her knees and hands. And yet she's shivering cold.*

She sits up, at last, and stares at the house in front of her. The doorbell. Nobody was there. I rang and rang and nobody ever came. Nobody. *She feels threatened, scared, defeated.*

She remembers walking up those three steps and pressing the doorbell, lightheartedly at first, assuming somebody would come to the door. Nothing happened. The curtains remained drawn, the place held still and silent. Her plan fell apart. She recalls the smell of camphor invading her nostrils, the odor of her grandmother's clothes at every turn of the season. Her fingers started to tingle, as numbness oozed up her arms and legs, and her mouth filled up, thin threads of saliva drooling down her chin. And then came the familiar taste of bitter almonds flooding her palate, the memory flashing before her eyes. She's a child again. She climbs up the almond tree and plucks off the green nuts, when they are still fresh and tender. She breaks them open and eats the inside, soft and crispy at the same time. She suddenly feels deceived, as the one she just popped into her mouth is horribly bitter. She grimaces and spits it, staring incredulously at the broken shell in her hand.

"What happened, Lizzy?" her brothers call from a tree nearby. "Did the ogre come eat your bum?" They laugh.

Horrified, she gazes at the little worm crawling out of the cracked nut in her palm. "I just ate a worm," she squeals over her brothers' guffaws. The more she screeches, the more they sneer.

That memory never left her, nor the bitterness. It had become the ill omen of her disease, the premonition of the storm to come. She recalls feeling the surge, quickly gnawing at her. Who knows how much time I've been here, *she thinks, staring at the driveway. Familiar blotches of maroon decorate the spot where she's been lying. She touches her head, prodding, feeling the tenderness where she hit falling down. Her hair is hot, heated by an unmerciful sun, and her hands and arms are scraped, from the thrashing. Her tongue is swollen and sore, the taste of blood fresh in her mouth.*

She looks around, dazed. A crumpled piece of paper and her open cell phone strewn a few feet away. Crawling, she collects them both. I've called the number, *she realizes, staring at the display. She'd brought with her the scribbled address and phone number and then called, one last resort when nobody answered the door.*

Oh my God, she gasps, touching her pocket. And then she exhales a sigh of relief. Still there. Safe, in her pocket. The storm has passed, the damage has been contained. Time to pick herself up and call a cab. Plan B, she thinks, staggering back to the street, her hand caressing the gun in her pocket. Plan B.

CHAPTER 40

Friday, October 24

The tank stood on the counter. A display attached to its side monitored the internal temperature. Perched on a stool next to it, Diane nibbled the tip of her thumb and glared. A centrifuge hummed in the background. The rest of the lab was deserted, the weekend anticipated in the list of unfinished jobs hanging from the pin board.

I set the papers on the counter next to the cryogenic tank. "These are the logs with the IDs," I said. "We can take out all the embryos but the Horowitzes'."

I waited for a reaction but none came. Her eyes were as beautiful and stony as a Helmeted Athena's. Silence clung to her lips like a drip to a faucet. Any second and it'd break loose.

"Can we discuss stuff later?" I offered.

"You trashed me." The drip broke loose.

"I did not."

"Then why did you leave? You could've left a note. You could've called to say, 'hey.' To say something, *anything*."

Right. I could've said, *What the hell's the assassin's smell doing on your bra?* But I was greedy. I wanted her in my bed and the killer in handcuffs.

She's the key to him.

"There are things you don't know about me, Diane."

And things I don't know about you.

"You're right," she replied, her voice creamy and sour like yogurt. "I believed you were different. Instead, you're just like everybody else. I know what you're going to say. That you're another no-commitment guy who freaks out the morning after."

I banged my fist on the counter and turned away from her, seething. Not at her, at myself.

Diane's eyes were shiny with tears. "I thought you were human, Track."

"I'm less human than you could imagine." It was a paradox. I'm not human and I'm not an animal. I'm both.

And yet it was me as a whole who longed for her.

What kept me away was my human part, exactly the one she didn't recognize as such.

Because the animal couldn't care less. The beast just wanted her. Who feared for her safety to the point of denying himself—*that* was the human side of me. *I'm a killer and a predator. I have no control over my instincts.* How was I ever going to explain any of it to her?

I paced across the lab, while Diane nibbled her little thumb. Until Christopher Hopf's eyes materialized through the anger fogging my mind. *Endurance*, they said. I froze.

Who was I to damn my own existence when there was a child who didn't even know if he was going to blow out one more candle on his birthday cake? I blew so many candles, Christopher. If I could go back, I'd pluck them off all those sugary cakes my mom made and give them all to you. If I could, Chris, I'd duel Clotho with my bare hands, yank my thread off her claws, and knot it to yours. Make yours longer. Make it last through the years of college, through your first kiss, through the scholarship flying you off to space one day, like you dream of when you close your eyes at night. *My own damned existence I would give to you.*

I grabbed Diane, pulled her down from the stool she was stubbornly perched on, and squeezed her, burying my face in her hair. "I saw a terminally ill child today," I said. "We need to stop this insanity. He'll die anyways, but at least we can make it stop."

Diane wrapped her hands around me and said nothing. Only when the catharsis was complete we let go of one another.

"Let's get on with it," I whispered. Diane nodded, her eyes averted.

The price of forgiveness.

She rested a hand on the tank, lifted the lid, and said, "I pick the canister, you pick the straw." Like mermaid's hair wavering in the currents, the vapors of liquid nitrogen billowed out, puffed upwards for a second, and then drooped down on the countertop. Diane pulled up one canister—a long, hollow tube with five sticks poking out at the top. "Pick one, quick," she instructed, and as I complied, she briskly placed the canister back and closed the lid again. I held the straw from one end as if it were some sort of unidentified and suspicious object.

"Hold it in your closed fist."

"What?"

"In your closed fist, Track, like this." She took my hand, placed the straw on my palm, and then closed it. She kept her hands over mine, closed her eyes and counted. I stared at her closed eyelids and thought of how enticing her lips tasted.

"...ten," she whispered, opened my fist, took the straw, and placed it into a glass pan she had previously filled with liquid warmed to body temperature. "It's thawing." She touched the pockets of her lab coat. "Shoot, I forgot—You don't happen to have a paper clip, do you?"

"Of course I have a paperclip." I dug one out of my pocket. "It's a little misshapen, but—"

"I need to stretch it anyways."

She took it and straightened it into a wire. She removed the straw from its little tub, cut the two ends with a pair of scissors, inserted the paperclip through one end, then tilted the straw and transferred all its liquid into a small dish filled with biological solution.

"There," she said, staring at the transparent liquid. "Our first baby, Track," she joked without meaning to be funny. "Just woke up, ready to be killed."

"Diane, please."

She snorted. "You don't think we're killing babies, do you?"

"They're no babies. They're man-made creatures with a death sentence built into their genes."

Diane sighed. "We're all born with a built-in death sentence, aren't we?"

Geez. Between her and Satish I was surrounded by philosophers.

"D.—"

"Defrost the other ones just like we did for this one. I'll prepare the PCR solutions."

I was on my second straw, when Diane said, "There. I

just killed a human being."

"It's a single cell, not a human being," I replied, placing a new straw in its warm bath and lifting the tank lid to retrieve another one.

"How can you be so detached?"

I couldn't tell her why. When you live the mistake, you can't help but wonder: had I been given a choice—live as a monster or succumb to a brain tumor—would I have spared my own life?

Fully aware of the potential monster held within, would I have thrown the miscreation down Mount Taygetos, or would I have graced its life? And if I did let it live, would you have called it a grace or rather a curse?

My phone rang, putting an abrupt end to my digressions. "Detective, I have a Dan Horowitz on the other line," the dispatcher said. "He said he needed to talk to you. Shall I pass him on?"

I pondered. *Horowitz. Quite unexpected.*

"Yes." There was a moment of silence on the other line, too short to hang up, too long not to wonder whether the guy had played a prank on me.

"I'm calling you from the UCLA hospital, Detective," I finally heard. And it was Dan Horowitz's voice. The tone, though, was different. The waterfall had turned into a weeping trickle. "My daughter—" his voice broke. I waited. "The doctor had ordered some blood work at her last visit. The growing pains—they're not what Jenna and I thought they were." Another pause. Silence is the harshest judge. "They called us at home right after you guys left. She's got it. Just like the other kids. And it's advanced already."

I inhaled. The bruises and the joint pain. I thought somebody was beating the crap out of the child. Instead, it was the disease spreading through her blood. *Shit.* I felt like puking. "I'm sorry," was all I could pull out of my dried up mouth.

"Flush those fucking embryos down the toilet, Detective."

"I'll need you to fax me a consent with both your signatures."

"Give me the number."

When I hung up my cell phone kept blinking. *You have one new message*, the display informed me. I dialed the voice box. Crackling static. And then words. Random, shuffled. Not making much more sense than the static itself. A joke, maybe. Or maybe not. I called Luke. It took him one minute to associate a name to the number on my display. It puzzled me at first. And then it clicked into place.

"Diane!" I shouted, making her startle. "Call Julia Cox at the Esperanza Medical Center for me, will you? Beg her, plead with her, do whatever. There's one fundamental piece of information I need. She'll say it's a breach of privacy. You tell her I'll handcuff her if she doesn't surrender it."

"That's not pleading."

"Then use your charms. Tell her somebody's life depends on it. Call me when you find out. I gotta go before it's too late."

She clutched the sleeve of my shirt. "Go where?" Diane stared at me. Beautiful, befuddled, and still very much hurt. *If only I could take it away*. A million words wouldn't describe what I felt. I kissed her and she let me. And then she whispered, "You know I hate you, Track."

"Yeah. You should." And I kissed her again.

CHAPTER 41

The hedges needed pruning, the yucca plants wanted to be trimmed. The lawn was sad and pleaded to be mowed and weeded. Palm trees suffocated in beards of wilting fringes. The stucco had cracks, the awnings had tears, and the gutters sagged under the weight of dead leaves. I'd never seen such decay in an upscale neighborhood before. The door wasn't locked. I touched it and it yielded. Somebody had buzzed it open.

I stepped inside.

Silence, at first, then a harrowing screech, followed by the unmistakable thunder of gunfire. I drew my Glock and ran into the hallway. "POLICE!"

Fingers of red stained the carpeted stairway, coming down like shadows at sunset. I ran up the stairs and crouched over the body. Young, dark eyes stared at me upside down, frozen in stupor. She lay with one hand unnaturally jerked behind the head, and the other clutching her white apron, a gargle of blood oozing from her chest. A maid, I guessed from her uniform. She was still warm, yet her carotid had stopped throbbing. I hissed a four-seventeen code in my radio.

I've come too late.

Elizabeth Medford had called my cell phone and blurted pure nonsense into my answering machine, a random shuffle of words struggling to get through. I recognized it just the same: a plea for help, the aphasic phase preceding an epileptic seizure.

Cox confirmed she was taking anticonvulsants—Diane called me on my way there.

Elizabeth Medford was the mysterious epileptic woman at the Tarantino residence the night of the murder. She had waited downstairs while the hired killer finished the job. Was he now after her? To wrest her silence, once and for all? I'd gunned my Dodge through the freeway rushing to the Medford residence, while my mind considered all possible shootout scenarios. I'd come too late.

The silence following the gunshot unnerved me more than the overwhelming smell of blood. *More, from upstairs.* "Drop the gun!" I yelled, stepping around the body. I inhaled, thirsty for *his* smell, the assassin's.

There was a long and dark corridor at the end of the stairway, the walls plastered with oak wood panels. I followed the scent of blood and fear, bitter, foul and unmistakable.

Somebody hanging between life and death.

It came from the last door at the end of the hallway. I edged around the corner and peeked inside. The signs of a struggle were everywhere: an overturned nightstand, strewn clothes, a gushed pillow.

A curtain rod hung to the wall from one end only, a white drape heaped on the floor like a kneeling angel. Blood soaked the king bed, where a body lay, eyes to the ceiling and arms above the head in a belated surrender.

A shadow skidded in and out of vision. Taking in the whiff of gun oil and ducking to dodge the bullet came in one swift reflex. I fired back, two rounds, aiming with my nose instead of my eyes. I heard a moan and saw the shooter leap behind an archway that opened to a sitting room. Gun low and ready, I crept into the bedroom.

Medford lay on the bed, two holes weeping steadily from his stomach and soaking his white shirt. He stared at the ceiling with gray, bulging eyes. They were soft and clouded and sad. His hair, white and puffy, drew a halo around the head. *There*, I thought, bending over to feel a pulse. *Medford achieved beatification.* I sniffed the air. The husband was dead and the wife missing. *Where's the asshole—*

"Put the gun down. *Please.*"

I flinched. The feminine scent. I'd overlooked it. I was after the assassin, not her. *She* was supposed to be the victim.

Elizabeth Medford emerged from behind the arch, a Beretta clutched in her right hand. She rested a hazy gaze on me, her pupils two black wells in a circular rim of blue. A red trickle wept down one of her legs—the aftermath of one of the two rounds I'd fired earlier. The left side of her head was matted with dried blood and her pale arms were scraped. *She had the seizure right after she called me.*

"Please put the gun down." She pointed a shaky barrel at me, both hands wrapped around the grip as though it were a lifesaver.

I raised my Glock, slowly, without aiming, just to warn her. "Let's not play this game, Lizzy."

Her head hung to the side and her brows curled. A blue vein across her right temple pulsed. "Who are you?" Her eyes strayed away like the tails of a kite.

Lizzy, the girl who'd run away from home decades earlier to come to the city, the girl who had already found happiness and yet had not recognized it. I'd pieced her story together researching old police records and tabloids, the same day I found out about Kowalski's winning title at the Palm Springs Shooting Range.

Lizzy wanted more and found it one night at a party, when a distinguished man seduced her the old way, challenging her current lover with a rivalry over her beauty. The party went to the dogs, and the girl became famous.

Money and power embraced her, yet happiness never followed. Instead of dreams, she found herself chasing lies, betrayal, corruption, and money.

It had seemed just another story at the time, until I pieced it with Horowitz's malicious sneer, when at the Tarantinos' funeral he'd told me, *Everybody knows Elizabeth Medford, Detective.*

What about her husband? I'd asked.

He loves it.

It had taken me a while to grasp the meaning of the reply. Horowitz's sneer had said it all. Oscar Guerra later confirmed it: voyeurism is a form of control over the sexual partner. Richard Medford sold his wife's body for his own enjoyment and manipulated DNA for revenue. He had it all: control over money, sex, and life.

"Give me the gun, Lizzy." I stretched out my left hand and edged closer. "He threatened you, didn't he?" I pointed to the dead husband. "You shot him because of what he made you do." She quivered but didn't shift the aim of the barrel. "I can fix this for you, Lizzy. You had to kill him, so he would no longer hurt you. Give me your gun and I'll fix it."

I kept my voice low and steady, seeking her trust. I stepped closer.

"Stay away!" she screeched. The sirens of backup wailed from outside, startling her.

I could've shot her then. It would've been quick and risk free. But I needed the name of the killer, the man her husband hired to whack Huxley and the Tarantinos. She was the only way I could get to the man. She was wounded and frightened and I knew I was going to get the damned name out of her mouth.

"What's that?" she yelled.

"The ambulance. They're here to help."

"Tell them to go away! Tell them or—" She bent her arms and pointed the gun at her throat. She pressed so hard the barrel sunk in her white neck.

"Don't shoot." I reached for the radio with my left hand. Slowly, so she could see what I was doing. "I'll tell them to wait. You be good, Lizzy, okay? You've got to be good, now." She nodded, yet her index finger remained hooked around the trigger. I radioed a ten-forty-seven code, armed and dangerous. *Stay ready but let me try and handle this.* A name, damn it. I just needed one name out of her mouth. "They won't be coming, Lizzy. You can relax. It's just you and me, now."

Her hand shook, the mouth of the barrel still glued to her neck. "How do you know my name?" Her voice came from far away, as though searching for its way back.

"I know a lot about you. I know you hated him." I pointed to Medford, on the bed between us. "He made you do stuff you never even dreamt of doing. You shot him to make him stop."

Her eyes jumped from me to her husband, then back to me. Even dead, Medford controlled her. "You needed help,

Lizzy, and you called me."

She frowned. "I called you?"

The reaction enraged me. I had to swallow and inhale. *Don't lose it, Ulysses.* What the hell happened, then? Huxley's killer, the ghost I'd been chasing from the beginning, the gunman Medford had hired so he didn't have to get his hands dirty himself, was still missing. Where was *he*?

"You were in danger, Lizzy, and you called me. You had a seizure. Isn't that how you injured yourself? Why were you scared, Lizzy? Was it your husband? Or was it the other man, the one who killed Tamara and Robert Tarantino?"

"It was you then—" She sucked in short puffs of air. I inhaled her: fear, disgust, rage, confusion. Fear again. Wild, ancestral. "You never opened the door." Her voice was raw, guttural. "You hid her from me. You hid her inside your house. I wanted to shoot her. I wanted to see her die."

I frowned, struggling to understand. Elizabeth Medford—Lizzy—was at my house. Why? "Who was it you wanted to see dead?"

"That woman," she screeched, the weapon dangerously shaking in her hands. "The woman he loves! She came to your house. I followed her and waited, but she never left that night. *You* hid her from me."

I felt the adrenaline shoot down my spine. *Diane* came to my house and never left. She wanted to kill Diane. I swallowed. "Who loved her? Your husband?" Rage polluted my voice. *Don't lose it.*

Lizzy swayed her head backwards. "Why would I care who my husband loved?"

Not her husband. Another man. The assassin. *Il sicario*, the hired killer. *The name. I need his name.* "Who loved her then? Tell me!" I raised my voice, quickly losing control. It was a mistake. She returned the barrel to her throat. I winced. "Put the gun down, Lizzy. Put it down and then tell me the name. Everything will be fixed. Your husband can no longer hurt you."

"Mom used to call me Lizzy... Nobody has called me Lizzy in a long time..."

Her eyes wandered off, hazed by the ghosts of past memories. I took another step towards her and held out a hand. "Give me the gun."

"Stay back. You think you're good just because you guessed my name, huh? You know nothing, you stupid cop, nothing!"

She smelled like a wounded animal. Threatened, desperate, and with nothing left to lose. I was walking on a tight rope, carefully calibrating every movement, every word. *One mistake and I fall in the void. The wrong reaction and the trigger goes off, the bullet fired. After that, everything is irreversible.*

"I do know about you, Lizzy."

A nerve in her temple twitched. My words resonated in her ears like a tape played underwater.

"You'll do great things in life, Lizzy, Mom used to say."

Her dilated pupils jumped from me to other points in the room, as if she were in front of an audience, invisible faces around her nodding and listening.

She smiled from time to time, a mere twitch of her lips. Her speech faltered, switching from snarls of rage to whimpers of self-commiseration, and with each mood swing the barrel of the gun jerked and trembled, sending spikes of adrenaline through my veins.

Active shooter, my body told me, and the instinct in such a situation was to shoot back. Head or chest, whatever is easier, shoot to kill. I resisted the impulse. I didn't want her to take her life. Not before she had told me exactly how things had unfolded. *The killer*, I kept thinking. I just want his name.

When I thought she had calmed down, I prodded again, "What happened to Robert and Tamara Tarantino? Who killed them?"

She jerked her head backwards and started crying. "That Huxley woman kept pestering him, appealing to his conscience and all the church bullshit. And he was falling for it, the stupid fool. They're all wimps, they are."

She inhaled, swallowed, and lowered her voice. "Rob said he had no idea it would come to this. He'd done it for a better humanity, like the professor had said. Instead, the Huxley woman convinced him that all the kids were sick. They were dying. She said, *If you have a conscience you have to turn yourself in.*"

It was coming together. Huxley had spoken to Robert Tarantino, and Robert had faltered. He'd realized the genetic experiments had been a major screw up, that the children they had "created" were all dying. Medford had seen the danger.

If Tarantino spoke out about the experiments and admitted the company's failure, it would have marked the end of the Chromo corporation. There was no other choice but kill him—and Huxley with him.

Lizzy made a dark, guttural sound that rose in pitch and became a scratching laughter. "A conscience, she said. Look at me, cop. Do I look like I still have a conscience? *He* took it from me." She swayed the gun towards Medford's body and then whirled it back to her throat. "I don't have a conscience because of him. He sucked it out of me and made me dirty, so dirty..."

She was getting dangerously close to the point of breakdown.

I opened my left hand and motioned to her gun.

"It's going to be okay now, Lizzy. Everything's going to

be okay. It's over. Richard can't hurt you anymore. Give me the gun. I'll take care of it."

"I fell in love again. He loved me."

"Who loved you?"

She ignored my question. "When he embraced me, I forgot everything else, even the pig of a husband watching us. I wanted him to love me. Only me."

My attention perked up. *Now* she was talking about the killer. Her lover, the man who'd murdered for her.

"The other one—he had to kill her. I wanted her head, his tribute for me." She laughed, and her laughter turned into tears.

I was lost again. There was another woman and I didn't know who she was. But I didn't interrupt her. She was talking, and I couldn't afford breaking the spell. I just had to listen and hope I could make sense out of her rants.

"He didn't do it. He still loved her. The bastard couldn't do it. I couldn't do it, either. You hid her from me." She pressed the gun so hard against her neck it drew a white ring on her skin.

He still loved her. You hid her from me. Diane. Kowalski. The assassin *had* to be Kowalski!

"The name, Lizzy! What's the name of the man you loved?"

"You'll tell them right? When they come, will you tell them he made me do it? I had to, because of what he made me do." She had pronounced the last word in a shrill, a little girl pleading for help.

"Listen to me, Lizzy. Put the gun down and you can tell them yourself. You'll explain everything. You'll tell them what he made you do, and who helped you do it. The man you loved. He killed Huxley and the Tarantinos', didn't he? You have to tell me his name, Lizzy."

I was so close I thought I had it.

"What? No…" She shook her head. "He's not—Richard made him do it!"

"Who killed Huxley, Lizzy?" I pressed, my voice swelling with frustration. "Who shot Tammy and Robert? It wasn't you, was it?"

I'd gotten only a few feet away from her. But I still wanted the fucking name.

"Do you want him to go loose, Lizzy? You pay with your life, you go through all this, and then you let him go free? Who pulled the trigger, Lizzy? Tell me!"

A nerve across her brow twitched. Her chest rose and then lowered. A drop of sweat lingered by her temple and then ran down. Her chest rose as she heaved a deep breath and then froze. "I don't know his real name. He goes by Rhesus. He's the one I love."

The reek of blood and nitrate reached me before the roar of gunfire. I yelled, but it was too late. She'd tricked me. I thought she'd calmed down. It was a matter of minutes and she was going to surrender both gun and name. I dashed to her side, but there was nothing I could do: the bullet had blasted off her windpipe. Air mixed with blood gargled out of the open wound.

Elizabeth Medford stared at me, her eyes suddenly emptied of all emotions: rage, fear, desperation—it was all gone. She was Lizzy again, the Lizzy her mother had once believed was going to do great things, the Lizzy who'd come to the city with a box full of dreams to fulfill.

"What did you do, Lizzy?" I whispered.

She blinked, parted her lips as if about to say something, and then closed her eyes. Behind me, I heard Nelson radio to the backup stationed outside.

"It's okay, Track," Satish mumbled, materializing by my side. "You did good. You couldn't have done more."

"Did you hear everything?" I stood up and holstered the

Glock. I'd clutched it so hard, my fingers were sore.

He nodded. "A couple of times we were ready to break in. I had to keep the men at bay."

"All for nothing. She didn't give us the assassin. Only some fucking nickname—Rhesus."

"Do I radio for CPR?" Nelson asked.

I shook my head. "She's gone."

Nelson spoke into the mike and informed the EMTs to get ready for two more bodies.

Satish examined the gun in Elizabeth Medford's hand. "It's a Beretta."

"I bet it'll match the bullets found in Huxley. Her husband used her," I explained, turning my eyes to Medford, his arms raised in a frozen surrender, and his stare glued at the ceiling.

Too late to be sorry now, you asshole.

"Why people do the things they do, escapes my mind. This guy was a perv. He did it all: he paid to watch his wife get fucked, made money selling genetically modified embryos, and hired an assassin to get rid of whomever came in his way."

"And this assassin you say is still at large?" I nodded. "What do we have on this guy?"

What do we have? I asked myself. A nickname and a smell, refuted by DNA evidence. I brought both hands to my head and paced. My pulse was finally slowing down, yet my frustration still simmered.

Across from the bed was a bookcase filled with trophies and photo frames. I picked up a small picture—a young woman, beautiful, smiling at the camera.

She was still Lizzy back then.

I put it back, and a second photo frame caught my attention, towards the back of the shelf. Somebody had scribbled in one corner, *Palm Springs Shooting Range, July*

2008. Two men stood next to each other, grinning, one holding a rifle, the other a smaller caliber pistol, a Smith & Wesson, maybe—the photo was too small to tell for sure. It wasn't too small for me to recognize the faces of the two men, though.

Shit.

I turned to Satish. *Expectations disguise the obvious,* he'd said days earlier. It *should have* been obvious. To me, at least.

"Where's Diane?" I demanded. We'd talked on the phone briefly as I was driving to the Medford residence. *Cox confirms it, Track. Elizabeth Medford is on anticonvulsants,* she told me. *Where are going you now?*

To meet a murderer.

She'd spoken a few words of silence, and then: *Don't get killed. I want you back.*

Satish winced, taken aback by my sudden alarm. "I thought you saw her last."

"Did she come with the Field Unit team outside?"

"I haven't seen her, but I was up here—Track! You can't leave!"

I stopped at the door and slammed my fist against the wall.

Nelson stared at me wide-eyed. "By now the FID guys have a poster with the word 'WANTED' stamped across your face."

The FID, damn it. I'd fired my gun again, and even though the victim had killed herself with her own pistol, I still had to surrender my weapon and respond to the investigation. I couldn't afford to waste more time. I swallowed my rage and offered a pleading face. Satish echoed it with a grimace of his own—the "What the hell am I going to do with you, Track?" face. "You have your backup?" he asked, stretching out a hand. I slid my gun out of the holster and let him have it.

"I got another Glock," I said. "They kept the revolver. You'll cover for me, won't you?"

"As long as you come out clean. I'm not wiping no ass of yours."

I grinned and left. I heard Nelson mutter, "They're going to add 'Dead or Alive' to the poster with your face on it."

I ran down the hallway and leaped through the stairway. The EMTs had covered the body of the housekeeper, and a swarm of crime investigators and officers had spread throughout the first floor of the house. I glimpsed a few familiar faces outside by the front porch—Carolyn Ling, Peter Hanes—yet Diane was nowhere to be seen. I dropped a hand on Carolyn's shoulder, making her flinch. "Did Diane come with you guys?"

She nodded. "She was here a minute ago."

I whirled my head, inhaled, and scanned the air, seeking the wake of her scent. The driveway was a jam of vehicles, all with the bar lights throbbing. A cacophony of radios barked over different frequencies. The medical stretcher rattled up the doorsteps.

The FID officers are on their way. I wasn't going to let those losers hold me hostage again.

"Detective—"

"I need to get something from my vehicle." I ducked under the yellow tape the officer was unrolling, ran to my car, unlocked it, slumped behind the wheel, and screeched away. My cell phone went off almost immediately. I turned it off and tossed it on the passenger's seat. *They can look for me later.*

CHAPTER 42

Friday, October 24

Diane's phone rings. She stares at the display absent-mindedly, a lock of hair coiled around her finger. She bites her lip. Voices reverberate from the house: officers coming and going, EMTs wheeling out a stretcher, crime scene investigators gathering up their tools of the trade. It's over, she thinks with a sigh of relief. Though her heart won't stop pounding.

She flips open the phone and drawls a tired "Hello" into the receiver.

"Where did you spend the night?" Rhesus jumps at her.

Diane swallows. "At a friend's." His silence frightens her. "Look, I told you already. It's over, okay? You've slipped out of my life. I'm tired. It's over," she repeats, after a pause. And as she says it, she feels lost. What does she have left, now?

Once again, her therapist's voice rings in her ears. *You have to break the cycle, Diane.*

"How about we talk things over?" Rhesus cajoles, his voice strangely mellow. Forgiving.

She lets go of the lock she's been playing with and runs a hand through her hair. *What is there to save?* "You're coaxing me again. I know you won't be there."

"Tonight is different," Rhesus says. "In half an hour, Diane. Be there."

CHAPTER 43

Friday, October 24

Engraving is the best of deceits, Satish had said. *Expectations disguise the obvious.* To me at least, it should've been obvious.

Richard Medford moved in the highest circles of society looking for clients, naïve victims for his company's genetic experiments, and sexual partners for his wife.

A perverse game that gave him power and control.

It was for one of their threesomes that the Medfords hired a thug they met at a VIP shooting range in Palm Springs.

He goes by the name Rhesus.

The hoodlum satisfied both husband and wife and, given his dexterity with firearms, turned out to be a precious find when a glitch threatened the promising future of the Chromo corporation. A glitch named Jennifer Huxley. From paid sex to hired gunman, Rhesus climbed up the job ladder until he stumbled upon the last request. A kill he couldn't fulfill, not even when he hired somebody else to do it. A job he was now determined to finish.

James Kowalski's house was in Encino, in a cul-de-sac at the foot of the Santa Monica Mountains. An old, one-story bungalow, it sat on a strip of lawn sandwiched by barren land, the golden hills behind it speckled with dwarf pine trees and sagebrush. A box hedge circled the house and sided the walkway. The grass could've used more watering but had gotten used to whatever it got. A couple of planters sat below the front windows. They looked like they'd wanted to bloom at some point but nobody encouraged them to.

There was only one building in the immediate vicinity, and it was under construction—a wooden frame draped in plastic sheets.

The next closest property was half a mile down the road: an unkempt house, with old paint peeling off the wood planks and dark windows gaping like black eyes. The landscaping amounted to a parched *agave* plant and a coiled yucca sprouting out of dried and yellow turf. Stuck by the curb, a "For Sale" sign groaned intermittently, like in a Western movie, when the sun is blaring and nothing ever happens except for the squeaking of an old board setting the cadence of boredom.

It looked like Kowalski did not appreciate loud and gaudy neighborhoods.

It was past six thirty when Diane pulled into the driveway. All windows inside the house were dark. From my Dodge, parked on the street a few yards back, I watched her turn off the engine and climb out of the car. She took a quick look around, hunched over the passenger's seat to get her purse, closed the door, and locked the car. She tapped her heels to the doorstep while rummaging through her handbag. I slid the Glock out of the holster and got out of my vehicle.

The sun had set and the colors were fading, blurring into layers of blues and grays. It was the hour when my vision enhanced and my senses sharpened. The hour when predators went out prowling for prey. I inhaled. He wasn't here, *yet*.

Diane jammed the key into the lock, turned it, and then pushed the door open. I slid behind her and held it before she could close it again. Startled, she let out a shriek and staggered against the wall. "What are you—"

"When's Kowalski coming? Did he tell you to come here?"

"What? Yes, I'm supposed to—Where the hell are you going?"

I entered the house and angrily wandered around, thirsty for his scent. His smell enveloped me. Strong and deceiving, as it had always been. Pungent sweat with a spice, burnt cilantro. Everywhere.

"Stop it, Track! What do you think you're doing? You have no right to do that. You don't have a search warrant—Track!"

I was possessed. I touched everything—tables, chairs, drawers—and searched everywhere. The foyer opened up to the living room. There was a small office to the left with a desk, a few chairs and various bookshelves. A desktop and a couple of laptops took over the working space.

The living room was tersely furnished: a couch, a lounge chair, two recliners and a console, all outdated and non-matching. The only modern touch was the forty-two inch flat screen TV. To the back was the kitchen, separated from the dining room by a breakfast nook.

I wasn't interested in the kitchen. I went straight to the master bedroom, yanked open the closet and peeked inside. I rummaged into drawers, upturned rugs, dug into storage boxes.

I pulled the sheets off the mattress, stopped and inhaled. Diane's scent wafted out of the unmade bed and blew on my rage like wind feeding a fire.

Diane whimpered. "Track, you're out of your mind. You scare me."

I *was* scary, and I knew it, and I didn't care. I found it, at last. The man hadn't even worked too hard to conceal it: it was in a wooden box, at the back of a nightstand drawer. Huxley's missing earring, the proof I needed. It was *him*, the man sleeping with the woman I wanted *and* the assassin. Same thing. Fate had played yet another trick on me, deceiving me with my own deception, only subtler. Like me, Rhesus was a chimera. Unlike me, Rhesus *was born* a chimera—a *genetic* chimera.

There are two types of chimerism, Watanabe had explained.

It was indeed Kowalski's DNA on Huxley's car, and Kowalski's DNA, again, on the beer can I had retrieved from Diane's house.

One person with two different DNAs.

A mosaic of two individuals fused into one.

Of all people, I should've known.

I moved to the bathroom, stuck my nose into the dirty laundry basket, pulled the shower curtain, and opened the cabinets. What I saw hit me with a spark of lucidity. I snagged the bottle, clutched Diane's arm and pinned her against the wall. "Whose stuff is this?" I yelled, brandishing the medication inches away from her face.

She swallowed. Her skin exuded a ragged smell of fear. "Mine. I can't sleep when I'm by myself. I need drugs."

"This stuff is yours?" I repeated.

"Yes." She closed her eyes.

"And what the hell did you think when you read in Huxley's autopsy report this stuff had been used to put her out?"

She tried to wriggle away from my grasp. I closed my fist around her arm and held her against the wall. "A lot of people use it!"

"So what?" I yelled, despising her denial. Despising myself, my own denial, the beast of all deceits. "Don't you get it? He's been using you, Diane! The Tyvek covers, the perfect murder scene — he knew it all thanks to you!"

She opened her eyes and stared at me. Did she see it then, the animal lurking inside me?

"What? No, Jim's — Jim's not perfect, but he's not a killer. You're out of your mind, Track, you're—" Her eyes clouded, her voice lowered. "Is that why you bailed out on me? Because you thought I was double game?"

"What?"

"Look at you! So sure of yourself, and yet you have no proof. You're so full of hatred you don't have a speck of heart left to love a stupid woman who's fallen for you."

I let go of her. I saw my reflection in her eyes, the dew of her tears cluttered on her lashes. All the words I'd been wasting, incapable of saying the ones that mattered the most: *I love you*. I *was* full of hatred. I was so enraged I'd shut off my senses. My nostrils didn't detect the change in the air, the new, subtle whiff creeping into the rooms. My ears didn't catch the hushed tweaking of the wood floors, or the rustling of silent fingers along the walls. And my eyes, my *powerful* eyes, have the typical Achilles's heel all feline eyes have: once there's a source of light, they can no longer see in the dark. It becomes the perfect hiding spot.

CHAPTER 44

```
Friday, October 24
```

Rhesus glances at Diane's VW parked in the driveway and smiles. A twinge of anticipation nibs at his fingers. He touches his gun holster. Today his revenge will be complete. He will have Diane, one last time, at gunpoint. He wants to see terror in her eyes. What they had no longer excites him. He needs more. There's a new lady in his life, a dark queen whose heart still escapes him. Tonight Elizabeth Medford will have Diane's head. I'll kill her this time, *he thinks*. And then I'll empty the rest of my magazine down the throat of that pimp husband of yours, Elizabeth. You'll be mine, then. Just mine.

Rhesus walks up the steps to his house fogged with excitement, imagining the scent of Diane's blood and the auburn lock he'll steal from her. The door's not locked, though. And the voice he hears from inside is not Diane's. Somebody's yelling. "He's been using you, Diane!" *the voice says.*

A fucking cop. Rhesus creeps closer, enough to spot the two of them arguing. It's over. The cop knows about him. He touches the gun. His head is reeling. He could risk it all and shoot now. Quite the prize to kill an officer. Diane's lock and the sleuth's police badge.

No. Too risky.

The draft makes the front door click closed. Diane startles. "Did you hear that?" *she says. But when she peeks into the hallway, she finds it deserted.*

CHAPTER 45

Friday, October 24

I ran into the living room. "He was here, damn it!"

"Who? Jim? My God, Track. Please don't—"

Tires screeched outside. I leaped to the window, cursing to the fool I was. I drew my gun and yanked the curtains open, ready to fire on the fleeing car. Rhesus's black Lexus SUV wasn't running away, though. It was gunned towards the house.

My eyes darted to Diane: she had just come out of the bedroom and was heading to the front door.

Outside, the car flattened the box hedge, knocked over the planters, and skidded on the grass.

Accelerating madly, it spun to the side and aimed at the west corner of the house. I grabbed Diane by the waist and hurled her back against the opposite wall. The ground shook. Glass exploded and shattered into pieces. Debris and chunks of masonry rained on us from the ceiling. And when all other sounds ebbed off, the car engine went on roaring. Inside.

"What the hell was that?" Diane cried. "It came from the office!"

"Don't move."

I inched forward and peeked around the corner. The SUV had come full force through the external wall to the office. The black hood jutted across the gaping wall like a stranded orca. Splintered studs and fringed wallboard sprawled over the tinted windshield. A rattling noise came from the vehicle, an intermittent clack followed by muffled thuds. I stepped closer. The SUV gave a jolt. A noise followed, of a door slamming closed and steps running away. *The asshole's making a break.* I spun around, springing for the door, but something stopped me. *A hiss.* Accompanied by a distinctive smell, sulfur, maybe—

"Diane!" I dragged her down as she came towards me. We fell against the foot of the sofa, and on impact, my gun slid out of my hand and skidded across the floor. For a moment, Diane wriggled and bucked. I held her down and buried my face in her hair. There was no time to explain. The blast was thunderous. The house groaned and whined and more rubble rained on us. Diane froze, clasped my hand, and squeezed it. Everything crushed and the inferno enveloped us. I felt the heat wave scorch the skin on my back. Thick, black smoke followed, creeping into my mouth and nostrils.

"Back door," I hissed into Diane's ear. "Cover face—crawl."

"What happened?" she wheezed. I wrapped my arms around her and pulled her from the floor.

"Gas line—hit, exploded. Save breath."

I crawled behind her to the kitchen, our hands groping over glass shards and debris. I reached for my radio but the damned thing only gave me static, the LCD display dying before my eyes. *Fuck.* I must've hit it when I landed on the floor. Behind us, the fire crackled and hissed and leaped forward in consecutive bursts. We got to the back door. I helped Diane to her feet and made sure she got out. "What the hell are you doing?" she yelled when she saw me going back.

"I need my gun. Go, Diane, move!"

I covered my mouth, kept low, and retraced my steps into the inferno. A new explosion shook the house. By now the SUV had turned into a skeleton of wilted metal.

Smoke was everywhere, black and thick. It felt like I had a yarn of steel wool stuck down my throat. *The gun. Get the gun and run.* I crawled behind the sofa, groping over singed carpet and rubble. The house gave a jerk, the ceiling creaked, and flecks of burning debris hissed against my face.

I needed the gun. I held the collar of my shirt against my mouth and nose and crept closer to the flames groping like a madman, my rage smoldering wilder than the fire. I found it at last, stuck underneath an upholstered recliner whose fabric glimmered with swirls of red embers. The grip of the pistol scalded my fingers, yet I clasped it and rolled away. I slammed against something hard, I couldn't tell what. I couldn't keep my eyes open. I coughed, got on my knees, coughed again. *Out. Get. Out.* I crawled until I hit a wall, spun around and hit a second wall.

By then, I knew I was lost. I could no longer tell where the way out was. All I could see was smoke. All I could *breathe* was smoke. The reek blinded me.

Around me, the flames crackled with sadistic gusto. I reached for the radio again, pressed my finger on the TUNE key and exhausted all possible frequencies. The bitch was as mute as a cod.

I felt a spasm and coughed so hard until there was nothing more to cough and my lungs had turned inside out.

I wanted to weep yet my eyes were as dry as sandstone. Spotlights flickered in my vision. They clustered and migrated and formed the image of two yellow eyes.

I coiled onto myself and wailed.

Home. Back. Home.

CHAPTER 46

Casper Wilderness, April 1976

Shhh.

Quiet.

The eyes won't see you if you're quiet.

The eyes are smart, they can see in the dark. They can smell you, too.

Just be quiet, and still, and you'll be safe.

Just be… quiet…

The boy wheezes, sharp breaths whistling through his teeth. He closes his mouth, but his heart's pounding too fast, small lungs starved for oxygen.

He squats under the ferns, the rustling of leaves beneath his body sending shivers down his back. Around him, trees groan and creak. A faint moonlight quivers through the crowns.

Not enough to see.

The eyes can see in the dark.

He touches his pocket, but the flashlight is no longer there. He must've lost it when he fell the first time. Without a flashlight he has little hope to get back to the campfire. And even if he does find the way...

The eyes are so quiet... they can be anywhere now.

His left foot hurts. He tries to move it, and sharp pain shoots up his leg. A whimper escapes his mouth.

Shh! Quiet! If you're quiet you can get out of this.

If you're good the eyes won't see you.

Slowly he slides a hand down to his leg. He feels blood, warm, burning through his skin.

The eyes will smell it. The eyes will smell the blood and find you.

The eyes will kill you.

He has to move. He can't hide for too long. Bare fingers rasp the soil beneath the leaves, trying to mix his smell with that of the earth, searching for cover, and warmth.

Shh!

He bites his lip to keep his teeth from chattering.

A noise, close to his ear, like a breath.

The eyes make no noise.

But the eyes can be warm when they breathe on your back. They prowl silently, moving swiftly in the darkness, until they come close, so close all they need to do is pounce—

The scream thrusts out of his lungs and cuts through his throat.

The eyes don't like screams.

The eyes are angry now.

He can see them hovering, flaring in the dark, white

fangs glistening below.

Run!

He sprints, heart drumming in his throat, and claws pouncing behind him. Branches snap against him, scraping his legs, his wound burning, slowing him down...

Fingers of moonlight flash on his face, making his vision falter, the trees around him like black soldiers blocking his path.

A tree root snaps around his shoe. His feet sway in the air, the ground beneath gone, only to come back full force against his face, leaves and rocks and twigs tumbling around him.

The eyes roar behind him, a long howl of victory over their prey.

Everything's spinning, the trees, the few stars through the treetops, the eyes so close now he can feel warm breath on his face, almost reassuring, until sharp claws pierce through his chest and then all he hears is his own voice breaking through the night.

```
Encino, Friday, October 24, 2008
```

A scream.

No, not a scream. A blast. Loud, deafening.

Walls splintered, hissed, crackled. Glass shattered.

Fangs. Sharp, against my hand.

The cougar.

Move, it said.

You move, asshole.

I didn't want to move. It was hot, so hot I wanted to peel my skin off.

Move.

Cougars don't talk.

I couldn't see, I couldn't breathe, and the thing kept poking me. I touched it and it scalded me.

A fork.

Kitchen… I'm in the kitchen.

A glimpse of light emerged through broken glass.

The window – the kitchen window's in pieces.

The thin thread of oxygen coming through the shattered glass shook me out of my torpor.

A dream. The cougar isn't back. It was a dream.

I tried to move, pain shot through my entire body. I coughed, wheezed and finally crawled, the feeble light my north star. I hit something hard. Smooth surface, cool at the top. I grabbed the rim, and pulled myself up. Through burning eyes I saw the sink, cracks of light simmering through the window above it. I opened the faucet, splashed water on my hands, arms, face, then clambered over the sink and shoved myself full weight through the broken glass.

Falling into void never felt better.

I had a sudden memory of rolling in the grass as a child, the scent of freshly mowed lawn, the coolness of the earth against my skin.

In reality, cool air filling your lungs after you've waded through a burning house stings like hell. I rolled in the grass, rasping like an asthmatic ninety-year-old. Everything inside me stung and throbbed, every breath a sharp blade slicing through my throat. I wheezed and coughed and waited for the pain to subside.

And then I remembered.

Revenge. Rhesus. *Diane!* I sprang to my feet and ran to the front of the house. *Gone.* Diane's car was gone. He'd taken her somewhere, but where? I whirled my head, searching, clinging to a last hope she'd appear from a corner, safe and unharmed. Behind me, the flames were devouring the bungalow, washing the landscape in a pool of red light. Billows of smoke rose high in the sky. The blades of an approaching helicopter swooshed in the distance.

My eyes fell on the construction site on the adjacent lot. The timber frame delineated a two-story home with a gable roof. The walls of the lower level had been covered in house wrap. The upper level was a skeleton of vertical studs. Trusses and sheets of plywood were piled along one end of the lot.

The air was stiff with the acrid odor of burning. The winds had picked up, feeding the fire and drumming against the plastic sheets draping the house under construction on the lot next door.

I inhaled but to no avail. My nose burned, my throat stung.

The lower hem of a sheet of tarp flapped in the wind. A coil of rope lay on the ground where Diane's car had been parked. *Hemp* rope, the same found around Huxley's wrists and ankles. I grabbed it and brought it to my nose. Kowalski's sour sweat hit my nostrils like a punch in the face. *He took more ropes. For Diane this time.*

The helicopter came closer.

Waiting for help was an eternity I couldn't afford.

I bolted to the Dodge across the street. I slid behind the wheel, jammed the key into the engine, and then slammed my fist against the dashboard. Where the hell was I to go? Damned be the City of Angels, so vast each life is but a drop lost in an ocean of humanity. I felt mocked, desperate and defeated. Rhesus, the King of Thrace, the human chimera versus the animal one. I thought of all the Greek mythology that had enthused me growing up. Theseus killed the Minotaur. Hercules slain Nemean lion. Perseus decapitated the Medusa.

The monster always loses, Ulysses. You're the monster. You lose.

No. I'm a killer like him, I can think like him. I can beat him at his own game.

I screeched into the street and floored the gas pedal. A fire engine wailed in the distance. I grabbed the phone I'd left on the passenger's seat and one-handedly dialed the first number in my mind. "Sat!" I yelled when he finally picked up. "Place an all-points bulletin on Diane's car, NOW!"

"Where the hell are *you*?"

"I'm—" The battery died on me. If the Universe has indeed a purpose, that night the whole Olympus had gathered to fuck up my life.

CHAPTER 47

```
Friday, October 24
```

Rhesus feels safe now, soothed by the familiarity of the place. He slows the car, rolls down the window, and breathes in the brisk air of the night. The stars are out and the temperature is chilly.

He thinks of his burning home, the price he had to pay. It will be hard to resist the temptation to go back and scavenge the debris once the fire's out, looking for a shiny LAPD badge. He'll have to be patient and wait before he can collect his prize.

Rhesus smiles. Such damn luck the cop went back for his gun. He couldn't have hoped for a better turn out. He'll claim defective brakes on the car and collect the insurance money on the house. The money will buy him a new life, with Elizabeth by his side.

A moan from the back shakes him out of his reverie. "What is it, my darling? Too much of a bumpy ride for you?" He stares in the rearview mirror and laughs. "You can scream as much as you want, my love. Nobody will hear out here."

The rim of the Santa Monica Mountains is a wavy black line against the deep blue of the night sky. Frazzled tamarisk shrubs whisper in the breeze, as they overlook the illuminated valley. Rhesus parks in his favorite spot and gets out of the car. This is where it all began, where he killed his first prey and collected his first trophy. There's a comforting sense of peace coming from repetition, a liturgy renewed through the same actions. Rhesus looks down on the valley and stares at the geometric quilt of blinking lights.

"We have an audience tonight," he says, sliding his gun out of the holster strapped around his thigh. With a press of his thumb, he releases the empty magazine and inserts a loaded one. His fingers are nimble, his movements dictated by a well-rehearsed ritual.

Rhesus racks the slide to chamber a round before topping off the mag. He smiles, the sound giving him a thrill of excitement.

He brings the pistol to his nose and inhales. Metal, nitrate and gun oil. He walks to the back door and opens it. Diane lies on her back, her eyes fiery with hate. Her mouth is gagged and her hands and legs tied, and yet she looks nothing like defeated. Her glare is a load of spite. Rhesus grins, a wave of desire bulging in his pants. "My precious prize."

He clutches the grip of the gun and slides over her, pressing the barrel against her side. "Be good, now Diane," he croons in her ear, his free hand unbuttoning her shirt and sneaking into her bra. "After all, we've done this many times already."

The bang on the roof almost makes him lose the grip on the gun. He topples over and Diane is quick to slam her bound feet into his stomach. "Bitch!" He smacks her, sinks the barrel into her throat and cranes his head out the window. Darkness.

"Who the fuck's out there?"

The thought that there could be somebody out there unnerves him. He scrambles back behind the steering wheel and turns the engine on. His headlights wash onto ghostly trees surrounded by bushes. "Fuck!" He shifts to first gear and makes a U turn, holding the gun against the steering wheel. The tires skid on gravel, his foot pressed against the gas pedal. Diane wriggles and kicks the back of his seat with her bound feet. Rhesus hits the brakes and swerves. The thrust makes Diane slam against the back of his seat. He turns and smacks the butt of the gun in her face, splitting her cheek open.

"Fucking bitch!" he yells at her.

The right wheels are stuck in the runoff. The more Rhesus gives gas, the more the tires skid, throwing off gravel and dirt. His frustration flushes down the side of his face in heavy drips of sweat. "Damn it!" he bellows, slumping against the back of his seat. He wipes his forehead with the back of his hand and stares through the windshield. "What the —"

CHAPTER 48

Friday, October 24

As soon as the car got stuck, I pulled away from my hiding spot. Lights off, I gunned the Dodge ahead, jerked the steering wheel to make a ninety-degree turn, and blocked the road. I slid out, ducked behind the hood and yelled, "Get out of the car, NOW!" I flew two rounds and put his headlights out.

Silence fell. I couldn't see inside the vehicle and didn't know whether or not Diane was alive. *She wouldn't be in the front seat.* I fired again. The driver's side window shattered into pieces.

"Drop your gun or I'll kill her!" he bellowed. His voice came from the back of the car.

"You squeeze the trigger and you're dead. Either way you'll be dead. You lost, asshole."

Seconds slugged by. I held the gun steady and clenched my teeth.

"OK," he cried. "I give up."

I waited. "Open the back door and toss the gun."

The door opened slowly. Something flew out of it and hit the dirt with a thud. It glimmered like metal, but I couldn't be sure. I held my ground. "Let Diane out," I ordered.

The car gave a few jolts. She emerged, at last. Gagged and bound, she bent backwards in an unnatural way. I flinched and saw it, the gun pointed to her head. Rhesus shielded himself with her body, a hand clutching her waist, and the other wrapped around the grip of the pistol.

Son of a bitch.

"Changed my mind," he said. "I may lose, but you won't have her either." He paused, his dark eyes fringed by Diane's locks. They glimmered slyly. "Last chance to save her and be a hero, dick."

I inhaled. *We meet at last, Rhesus, king of Thrace.* No longer an epic character, a metaphoric inbreeding between what I knew of him and what I'd imagined. This Rhesus was real, and I loathed him. I loathed the gun he held against Diane's head, the way his eyes lingered on her, the smell of his body, how his voice vibrated in my ears.

I smelled the adrenaline in his sweat—a wild excitement enthused by ancestral chemical signals, both sexual and aggressive. When Ulysses came out of the Trojan horse and lowered the gates of Troy to let the Greeks into the city, the soldiers walked through the streets burning, looting, and raping. The drive to kill mixed with the sexual desire—same hormones, an identical ancestral call.

I loathed Rhesus's thirst for blood because in it I

recognized my own. His smell was muddled with Diane's fear. Her eyes were sprang open, her head tilted, exposing the veins pulsing in her neck. There was dried blood on the right side of her face and smeared on her forehead. She was no longer fighting.

Rhesus bristled. "Drop the gun, you fucking cop! You fire, I fire, she's dead. Don't you get it?" A shrill of frustration wavered in his voice. The barrel shook against Diane's temple.

"You're dead," I hissed, my finger itching around the trigger.

"You wouldn't risk her life."

"Try me."

In the low light of a half moon, a drop of sweat glistened against the side of his face. I was no longer looking at him, though.

I was staring at Diane, a multitude of what-ifs fogging my mind with their meaningless existence.

Shoot, her eyes told me.

I could kill you.

Shoot. Now.

The bastard kept his head hidden from me. There was one way only to finish him: shoot him in the head. Any other spot, even if mortal, he would've had the time to pull the trigger and kill Diane.

The strain of holding Diane in that unnatural pose finally paid off. Rhesus shifted backwards, the gun in his hand faltered, and his face came in full view. I fired.

Time mocks you, Detective.

It took an eternity for the bullet to strike. A whole eternity during which I envisioned Diane's blood splattered all over Rhesus's face, her eyes accusing me. Or worse, hating me.

Diane let out a shriek through her gagged mouth. She

fell forward against the car and onto the ground. I smelled blood, but it wasn't hers. Rhesus staggered backwards. The gun dropped from his hand. I leaped over the hood and fired four more rounds, all to his chest. Rhesus collapsed, quivering like fabric caught in the wind. I watched him die and kept on watching long after that. His looks defied the image of him I had concocted in my mind. Even in the grimace of death, Rhesus was surprisingly handsome.

The sharp edges of his face were softened by a goatee, neither sparse nor thick. He had small, gray eyes underneath dark eyebrows, and his black hair—sleek with hair gel—curled loosely on his neck. A small hole wept from the middle of his forehead.

His body stopped jerking and yet his eyes remained open. On me.

Diane gave out a loud moan. My body was numb, my legs heavy with exhaustion. Sirens wailed in the distance, then lights wobbled uphill, towards us. I left the Glock on the ground, crouched by Diane's side, and loosened the knot keeping her mouth gagged. As soon as I freed her, she let out a deep sob, cracked like the edge of a broken glass. I went on working on the ropes on her wrists as she kept making the sound, neither of us speaking a word. Rhesus's blood had sprayed all over her. The headlights of a vehicle washed on us, a second one followed behind, its roof throbbing in red and blue. I heard car doors open and close, voices, radios. Satish ran by my side and helped me free Diane.

"Fucking punctual," I grumbled.

"Thank the FID guys. They had an all-points on your car. We would've never found your location."

We freed Diane, helped her roll over and sit up. Her wrists and ankles were bloody and swollen. She was hyperventilating. "I'll help her to the cruiser," I told Satish.

"Tell the guys to take her to the hospital." Satish nodded and walked over to the officers. They were staring at Rhesus's body and initiating the calls to the station.

As I picked her up, Diane leaned her head over my shoulder and wept. "I didn't want to believe it," she sobbed. "I thought he loved me."

I didn't say anything. I had enough trouble blaming myself. I'd led Diane straight into the lion's mouth, running back for my gun instead of protecting her. And then I pulled the trigger. I could've killed her, yet I pulled the trigger. *You're so full of hatred you don't have a speck of heart left to love a stupid woman who's fallen for you.*

I delivered her to the back seat of the cruiser and brushed the back of my fingers on her wounded face. She was scraped, bruised, exhausted. And beautiful. "I gotta go," I said.

She clutched my shirt and pulled me closer. "Where?" Her voice was coarse and pained.

"I'm in a jam with the FID. They're looking for me."

"Will you come back?"

I knew what she meant. I didn't know the answer, though. "I'm dangerous, Diane. I could've killed you. I—" I didn't have the guts to voice the rest. *I would've killed you. I'm so full of hatred I would've killed you in order to kill him.*

She laid a hand on my face and smiled a sad smile. "I've always liked to play with fire."

I kissed her wondering whether I would ever kiss her again. Every kiss should be like that. Those are the ones that leave a knot in your throat and keep you awake at night. I watched the cruiser back up and roll away, the siren and pulsing lights lingering behind a moment longer.

"The FID are on their way," Satish said, behind me. I nodded, my eyes watching the blinking lights get smaller and smaller. "How'd you know you'd find him here?"

We walked back to where the body was. "This is where he brought Huxley. Predators are methodical with their hunting strategies."

I gave Satish a brief and partly confused account of what happened.

The coroner's retrieval cruise arrived, together with two more cruisers.

Lastly, the two FID detectives made it to the scene. Tires crunched the gravel, and doors opened and slammed closed. I heard the stretcher rattle along the road ruts and a familiar voice ask where the hell I was.

Satish gave me a friendly nudge on the shoulder, before joining the cruise.

I sent one last look to Rhesus's sprawled body, then turned around and walked away. As I went, I slid the badge wallet out of my pocket and tossed it on the ground.

"You lost something, cowboy," the familiar voice said from behind.

I turned to face the FID dick whom I'd met over the Carmelo shooting and who loved my guts so much. He was holding my tin.

"This your car?" I pointed to the silver sedan next to the ambulance. He smiled sheepishly, holding up my badge as if I hadn't realized it was mine. I opened the back door. "Keep it," I said, hopping inside the vehicle. *I no longer deserve it.*

The FID detective mumbled something into his radio. His colleague appeared, holding the gun I'd dropped by Rhesus's body. The two confabulated, their hands pointing to the car to confirm my presence inside. They finally ambled over and started the engine.

"Looks like it's going to be another long night," one of the two mumbled, half serious, half mocking.

Another fucking long night. *Tonight, the monster won over*

the human. I did not gather my trophy, this time. Inhaling his blood was my victory.

I had not chosen my existence. Unlike the Proteus kids, I had nobody to blame for the mistakes encoded within my genes. Unlike Jerry White, I had nobody to take my revenge on but myself.

Life is a constant struggle to understand who we are.

The cruiser wobbled along the dirt road, the million lights of the valley shimmering under a dome of yellow. I stared at L.A., my home and my harshest judge.

Tonight, my victory has the bitter aftertaste of defeat.

~ THE END ~

THE SCIENCE BEHIND THE SCENES
A look into Track's condition

As Watanabe states in CHAPTER 28, Track is an epigenetic chimera. Most people are familiar with genetic chimeras, i.e. two fertilized eggs fused into one morula (the early stages of an embryo), resulting in one individual with two distinct DNA's.

Track's DNA, however, is the same everywhere. That's because he is an epigenetic chimera, not a genetic one: while his DNA is "normal", the types of genes expressed in his cells are different.

For the majority of us, the cells throughout our body carry the same DNA. What distinguishes a brain cell from a skin cell is not the DNA, rather, it is which genes are expressed ("turned on") and which are not ("turned off").

How does the body decide which genes should be turned on and which should be turned off?

DNA is packaged inside the nucleus. You can think of it as a messy ball of yarn wound around little spools called histones. Each gene in the DNA carries information to make proteins. Cells depend on proteins to carry on their functions and communicate with one another. In order to make proteins, the information must be read off the DNA and translated into yet another code, the RNA. However, like I said before, the DNA is tightly packaged in the nucleus, in a structure called chromatin.

When it's time to "make" the proteins, the chromatin reassembles itself. The spools (histones) move around and present some genes while hiding others. The genes that are presented are "expressed" and the information is read and transcribed into RNA[1]. The genes that instead remain hidden are not expressed (hence "turned off").

This is the heart of epigenetics: the mechanisms that ensure what genes are turned off and on in different tissues at different times of our lives. These conformations allow our body to adapt to the environment and, as it has been reported in numerous studies, even though these changes are not encoded in the DNA, they can be inherited for quite a few generations.

Save a few random mutations that accumulate as we age, our DNA stays the same throughout our life. And yet our body has the incredible ability to adapt to the environment: our immune system "learns" to recognize different pathogens. Our brain acquires new skills as needed. On the flip side, immune diseases can arise at some point in our life. We all react differently to the environment because we all have different genomes, different starting points. But the way we, as individuals, adapt as the environment changes around us (i.e. diet, climate, stress, etc.) is orchestrated by epigenetics.

Diet can affect the epigenetic landscape of our body dramatically. For example, a diet high in fat during childhood will prompt the body to create more storage for the fat and make it a lot harder to lose weight as adults. And this can affect future generations, too. Mouse studies have shown that epigenetic changes induced by environmental stress can last up to four generations[2] even though they are not coded in the DNA.

Human DNA is made of three million base pairs, of which only about 20 percent are used to code genes. Up until a few years ago people believed that the remaining 80 percent was useless, to the point that it was dubbed "junk

DNA."

How did we end up with such huge DNA if all we need is 20 percent of it?

Most of the DNA we carry is historical. As the tree of life grew new branches, it kept the old ones. New genes formed and the old ones were silenced. Not erased from the DNA, but silenced: each gene has a "start" and an "end" that signal where to start reading the information and where to stop. By introducing an "early end" the gene is effectively silenced and will no longer be used to code proteins. By holding on to ancestral sequences that at some point in evolution gave rise to different species, Mother Nature ensures that no information is lost. Who knows, maybe the climate will change again bringing us back to the glacial era. So, just in case, somewhere in our DNA there are genes that generations of environmental pressure and selection could turn on again and grant us survival (as a new species) in such harsh environment.

Take the vomeronasal organ for example: it's an olfactory sense organ found in all mammals, yet in humans it lost its function, as evolution replaced the chemical stimuli once detected through the sense of smell with visual ones. We still have the genes that encode the vomeronasal organ, but they are silenced.

Similarly, the genes that allow us to detect sweet flavors are the same across most mammals, yet they are silenced in cats[3].

It turns out that what was originally dubbed as "junk DNA" is far from junk. Not only does it hold our history, but it's filled with markers and signals responsible for epigenetic changes.

So, what happened to Track? Some of the ancestral genes turned "on" as a result of something that happened in his childhood. Which genes? Well, this is where my poetic license comes in, but if you don't allow an author his or her poetic license you'll miss out on the most fantastic premises.

When I started writing *Chimeras*, my driving question was: if we have silenced predator genes in our DNA, what if a sudden life-threatening trauma were to "awaken" them through epigenetic changes? What if those silenced genes were to be expressed again, genes that control our vomeronasal organ, for example?

Chimeras touches many other scientific topics, besides chimerism and epigenetics. Again, I don't want to give away plot spoilers, but you'll find that most of the topics (for example cancer, oncolytic viruses and telomerase) are discussed on my blog under the label "science behind the scenes":

http://chimerasthebooks.blogspot.com/

And if after reading my blog you still have questions, please don't hesitate to drop me a line at **eegiorgi@gmail.com**.

And please consider sharing your thoughts on the book by leaving a review either on Amazon or on Goodreads. Thanks!

REFERENCES

[1] SL Berger. *The complex language of chromatin regulation during transcription*. Nature 447, 407-412 (24 May 2007).

[2] Crews D, Gillette R, Scarpino SV, Manikkam M, Savenkova MI, Skinner MK. *Epigenetic transgenerational inheritance of altered stress responses*. Proc Natl Acad Sci U S A. 2012 Jun 5;109(23):9143-8.

[3] Jiang P, Josue J, Li X, Glaser D, Li W, Brand JG,

Margolskee RF, Reed DR, Beauchamp GK. *Major tuste loss in carnivorous mammals*. Proc Natl Acad Sci U S A. 2012 Mar 27;109(13):4956-61.

ABOUT THE AUTHOR

© E.E. Giorgi 2014

E.E. Giorgi is a scientist, a writer, and a photographer. She spends her days analyzing HIV data, her evenings chasing sunsets, and her nights pretending she's somebody else.

BLOG: chimerasthebooks.blogspot.com/
PHOTOGRAPHY: elenaedi.smugmug.com/
GOODREADS:
goodreads.com/author/show/7954733.Elena_Giorgi

Made in the USA
San Bernardino, CA
12 April 2014